This is madness, Sofi thought wildly. She wanted to defend herself. Get his badge number. Report him to his supervisor. This was unconstitutional, a violation of her civil rights! Illegal? Who was he to call her illegal? But her words came out all jumbled. The officer gave her an annoyed look.

Sofi took a deep breath. "You must be mistaken. I've been living in San Innocente for fourteen years. I am a lawful resident."

"Do you have any paperwork to prove this? A Mexican passport? Maybe an advance parole form that gives you permission to leave the United States? Visa? Anything?"

Sofi stared at him in horror.

"Is this where you live? Maybe your parents can straighten this out. That's if they're *really* legal residents as you claim. . . ."

Also by Malín Alegría

Estrella's Quinceañera

Sofi Mendoza's Guide

to Getting Lost

in
MEXICO

by
Malín Alegría

SIMON PULSE

New York   London   Toronto   Sydney

SIMON PULSE
An imprint of Simon & Schuster Children's Publishing Division
1230 Avenue of the Americas, New York, NY 10020
Copyright © 2007 by 360 Youth, LLC d/b/a Alloy Entertainment and Malín Alegría
All rights reserved, including the right of reproduction in whole or in part in any form.
SIMON PULSE and colophon are registered trademarks of Simon & Schuster, Inc.

Produced by Alloy Entertainment
151 West 26th Street, New York, NY 10001

Also available in a Simon & Schuster
Books for Young Readers hardcover edition.
Designed by Andrea C. Uva
The text of this book was set in Electra.
Manufactured in the United States of America
First Simon Pulse edition July 2008
4 6 8 10 9 7 5 3
The Library of Congress has cataloged the hardcover edition as follows:
Alegría, Malín.
Sofi Mendoza's guide to getting lost in Mexico / Malín Alegría.
p. cm.
Summary: When Southern California high school senior Sofi Mendoza lies
to her parents and crosses the border for a weekend party, she has no idea that she will
get stuck in a Mexican village with family she has never met before, unable to
return to the United States and the easy life she knew.
ISBN-13: 978-0-689-87811-4 (hc)
ISBN-10: 0-689-87811-7 (hc)
[1. Identity—Fiction. 2. Culture conflict—Fiction. 3. Mexico—Fiction.
4. Family—Fiction. 5. Mexican Americans—Fiction.
6. California, Southern—Fiction.] I. Title.
PZ7.A37338Sof 2007
[Fic]—dc22
2006052264
ISBN-13: 978-0-689-87812-1 (pbk)
ISBN-10: 0-689-87812-5 (pbk)

To the amazing women who paved the road I walk on,
Abuelita Olga and Abuelita Guadalupe

A las admirables mujeres que forjaron la vereda que hoy camino.
Mis abuelitas, Olga y Guadalupe

Author's Note

This book was inspired by the real-life story of Martha and Carmelia Luna from Santa Paula, California. They were denied reentry into the United States after visiting TJ for an afternoon. Martha and Carmelia had come to the United States when they were still children and had lived in California for sixteen years with work permits. They were CSU college students and were looking forward to completing their degrees. However, by visiting Mexico that day, they had voluntarily deported themselves without knowing it. Martha and Carmelia's story is not unusual on the border. However, their voices have been ignored, dismissed by mainstream media, and overlooked in the U.S. immigration debate. Unlike the characters in this work of fiction, these girls will not be allowed to petition for reentry for another ten years. My heart goes out to them and their family.

Although my family is from the border, I decided to move to Rosarito, BCN, for the writing of this book. While there, I fell in love with Mexico's contradictions and charm. My dad helped me find a place and hooked me up with the *familia* Tellez, who became my second family while I was in Mexico. Señora Tellez taught me a lot about the border, and about cooking, and knew all the *chisme* around town. I'd like to thank my neighbors Vanessa, Diana, José y Ana, *por compartiendo sus vidas conmigo*. Gracias, Abuelita Olga y Tío Carlos, *por los muebles y sus consejos*. Thank you, Glory, for being a great friend and taking me out on the town. A special thanks to my *tía* Gloria, David, Nana Lupe, and Robert for the shark memories and for letting me shower at your place when the water ran out in

Author's Note

Mexico. Thanks, Barber family, for letting me crash when I passed through. Chuy, it was fun exploring Baja *contigo*. I couldn't have finished the book without all the free coffee refills and long hours of people-watching at the outdoor cafés and bars along Boulevard Benito Juarez. All the people of Rosarito were very warm and friendly, even the cops. Ha! Many thanks to the Madrigal family for sharing their stories and home in Woodland with me. Thank you, Rosemary, for your extra eyes! You saved me from a nervous breakdown. To my friends Charles and Lisa, thanks for your suggestions throughout my countless revisions. And thank you, Mom, Bill, Suni, Kiki, Lucy, and Jelly, for your hugs, creative ideas, and support! Finally, I'd like to thank the amazing Lynn Weingarten for being a fabulous editor and cheerleader. I also owe a great deal of gratitude to Alexandra Cooper for working on this manuscript. Her patience, careful attention to detail, and vision shaped this novel into a real gem. *Gracias*, David Gale, Alloy, and the entire Simon & Schuster family, for your continued support *y buena energía*. Y José L, thank you for being you.

latnbaby7: whats the harm in a little white lie? Sofi Mendoza typed into her desktop computer.

Her best friend Taylor Wilson's response blinked onto the screen a second later. **Yogi_T:** its not like youve never lied before. ☺

Sofi grabbed the hairbrush off her white dresser to scratch her arms. It was the fastest way to relieve the itching caused by the hives. The outbreak was stress-related. She'd postponed the conversation all week, but now, Sofi was out of time. Just thinking about what she would do made her heart race and her arms break out in red bumps. Sofi bit down on her lower lip and started typing again.

latnbaby7: yeah but this is different.

Steve McCanne's Memorial Day bash was sure to be the hottest party of the year. Sofi'd been to a couple of parties before, but she'd always left early because of her strict curfew. As a graduation present, Steve's folks were letting him turn their vacation house near Tijuana, Mexico, into a wanton wonderland. Steve had promised no adults, plenty of booze, and tons of opportunities for unregulated debauchery. The best part was that Nick Hoffman was sure to be there.

Nick Hoffman was Sofi's secret crush. He was a total Abercrombie babe, with the deepest blue eyes, the sexiest shaggy blond hair, the cutest cleft in his chin, and the most irresistible smile. Nick was also the nicest guy in the entire world. Everyone at school adored him. He'd been voted most popular guy in the senior class and drove the coolest Range Rover.

Nick was captain of the wrestling team and would be going to USC in the fall. What more could a girl ask for?

A profile icon appeared on the screen. It was a picture of a girl with golden brown hair, bewitching blue eyes, and popping cleavage. Olivia had logged on.

SxyLivy: sof is it true that u can tan topless in rosarito?

Sofi straightened up like she'd been whacked with a ruler. Ever since they'd been invited, all Olivia and Taylor could talk about was Mexico. Course, Steve's party was going to be the hottest thing since the thong, but Sofi didn't understand why they kept asking *her* questions. Dumb things, like would they catch Montezuma's revenge if they drank the water, or where are the coolest clubs? Sofi released a long breath. She combed back her long black hair with her fingertips and knotted it into a messy bun. Olivia and Taylor were her girls, but sometimes they were a tad maddening. The idea of traveling to Mexico brought up a series of uncomfortable mixed emotions that left her feeling confused. And itchy.

Although Sofi had been born in Mexico, she didn't have a Wikipedia-like knowledge of the place. She'd been three when they left Tijuana. Her mother was from Mexico City, way down in the south of the country. The faded square photographs of her mother's family were totally foreign to her. Olivia and Taylor knew this, but that didn't stop them from asking. It drove Sofi crazy, because her friends had vacationed in Mexico countless times before, while Sofi had never been back. They probably knew more about the country than she did. Their persistent grilling made her uneasy. It made Sofi feel different, and that wasn't cool. Not that they ever said that; but it was implied, which was kind of worse.

latnbaby7: you swear im a wettie ☺

SxyLivy: right. lol

Sofi smirked; then she looked at the photo on her desk. The picture was of Sofi and Goofy at Disneyland when she was ten. It was the one and only family vacation where both of her parents had taken several days off from work. Sofi knew that her parents loved her. They'd sacrificed a lot to make her as comfortable as possible. How could she do this to them? A pang of guilt gripped her as she typed.

latnbaby7: im still not sure if im even going

She leaned back in her padded desk chair, rubbed her socked feet on the carpet, and waited.

SxyLivy: u have 2 be there!!!!!!

Sofi smiled.

Yogi_T: im not going if youre not

SxyLivy: what about operation papi chulo??!!??

Sofi bent forward onto her desk and rested her chin on her palm. Olivia was right. Operation *Papi Chulo* was too important. She couldn't walk away from it now. Not after all the money she'd spent on lucky charms, love spells, and special prayers from a hole-in-the-wall Wicca shop at the pier. The owner of the store, an aging hippie with a sparkly purple headscarf, had told her that the man of her dreams would fall for her and she'd blossom into a real woman. A week after the fortune-teller's prediction, Nick had broken up with pom-pom airhead Sarah Baker. It was the divine thumbs-up she'd been waiting for. Now Nick was free for the taking. He was her destiny. Her *papi chulo*. And she couldn't let him slip away.

"Sofia Esmeralda Mendoza de la Cruz!" her mother yelled from the hallway. Sofi straightened up in her chair and brushed off some loose cookie crumbs that had fallen on her navy blue T-shirt and pink fleece sweatpants. Every time her mother called her by her full name, she knew she was in trouble. Sofi's mother, Evangelina, who insisted that everyone call her Evie because it sounded more *americana*, stood in the doorway with a wet toilet brush in her hand. She was wearing a loose violet dress shirt and a black skirt that hugged her large shapely frame. Her wavy brown hair was cut short above her shoulders. Evie had a lovely face with bright eyes, a prominent round nose, and an infectious smile when she laughed. But when she was mad, like now, her frown could stop Sofi cold in her tracks. "What is this?" She waved the toilet brush over Sofi's head like a sword.

"Oops." Sofi smiled. "I was going to finish right after this last message." She glanced quickly at the computer and decided to sign off. Her mother had a thing about sanitation. She woke up every day at five to scrub the place down. Every room in the house (except for Sofi's) smelled of pine and was decorated with only modern, streamlined Ikea furniture. The windows had a Windex shine, and the tile in the bathroom was Clorox lemony fresh.

"We don't ask you to do much," her mother said in a thick Spanish accent. "Focus on your homework and do some chores."

Some chores! Sofi wanted to scream. All she did were chores. Her parents were always on her back about school or her responsibilities. As much as she tried to please them, it was never enough. They never let her hang out on school nights or date. She had by far the earliest curfew of anyone she knew. "I know, Mamá. I was going to do it."

"So you left the brush there so the toilet could clean itself. Look at this mess," her mother said, pointing at the jumble of freshly laundered sweaters, clean tank tops, dirty skirts, and jeans scattered on the floor. There were stacks of romance novels, Robert Jordan books, issues of *CosmoGIRL!* and *Seventeen*, an English–French dictionary, and a World Civilization textbook by Sofi's nightstand. Her desk was covered with loose papers, miniature figurines she collected from gumball machines, and random junky school supplies like broken pencils, heart-shaped erasers, and inkless glittery colored pens.

Okay, so Sofi didn't have the cleanest room in the world. She had bigger things to worry about, like school, boys, and all the parties she missed out on. Sofi's parents were very caring and wanted her to be happy, but in some ways they were very old-school typical Mexican immigrants. They were plagued by American culture and kept her on a short leash. (Sofi thought they just watched too much TV.) As far as her parents were concerned, school was her top priority, and family always came first. She was expected to work, help around the house, and be the model "good" daughter. Boring. Now, with high school almost over, Sofi had no memorable adventures or crazy nights to look back on. She couldn't let high school end like this!

The tired, hurt look on her mother's face snapped Sofi out of her thoughts. Despite all of their suffocating rules, they were still her loving parents. "What's wrong?"

Evie sat down on Sofi's black metal–framed bed.

"My manager wrote me up."

"You got fired?"

"No, no nothing like that." Evie waved. "This *gringa* came in to return a shirt. But she had no receipt and the shirt had sweat stains. I told her we couldn't accept it because it was used. The lady got mad. She said she couldn't understand my accent and complained loudly. People started to stare. I didn't know what to do. Then the manager came over. He yelled at me. He said something about how important this woman was and that we have to be flexible." Her mother looked down at her small manicured hands.

Sofi hated to see her mother like this. She looked so small and defenseless. "Did you tell him about the stains?"

"Why?"

"Mother," Sofi huffed, getting up. Her room was small but it was ten times better than the cramped one-bedroom apartment next to the 7-Eleven where they'd lived when she was little. "You've got to stand up for yourself. You can't let them talk to you that way. It's not fair."

"But *mija*, we need the money." Her mother was right. The Mendozas were in serious debt, even though they were frugal and clipped coupons. If it hadn't been for the scholarship from her mother's church, college would have been totally out of Sofi's reach.

Sofi looked at her mother with feelings of shame and pity. She couldn't help it. Her parents were fixated on the American dream and talked constantly about how America was the best country in the world. It was the only place where hard work and persistence actually paid off. It was nothing like Mexico, where politicians were crooks, cops abused their power, and if you were poor, there was no way to get ahead. They were so proud to live in America, yet when they interacted with Americans, they grew quiet and nervous. After fourteen years, her parents were still uncomfortable with their accents and lack of formal education. They tiptoed around their white employers, white neighbors, and anyone in an expensive suit as if they were God Almighty. It made Sofi's skin crawl.

Sofi refused to be like them. She was just as American as her friends, and once she went to college, she could stuff her parents' issues in a closet. No one there would care whether she cleaned her room or not! Once she got to the dorms, she would call the shots. Sofi would go out whenever she felt like it. She'd decide *which* parties to go to. She could even take off to spend the weekend with Taylor in Santa Barbara. No problem. Woo! College was going to rock. Then, after she graduated, she'd be sure to make tons of money so she and Nick could hire a maid to clean the beautiful house they would buy together. She couldn't wait. Nick was going to make all her American dreams come true.

There was only one small problem: She'd tried to attract him telepathically, but so far it hadn't worked. Whenever she was around him she got really nervous and said stupid things. Like at that horrible assembly when she sat next to him for a whole hour. She couldn't stop sweating even though the heater in the auditorium was broken and the room was freezing. The worst part was how her stomach grumbled uncontrollably. Nick heard it and offered her a Life Saver to eat before lunch. It was so embarrassing. But now, with the fortune-teller's blessing, Sofi was ready to fulfill her destiny. She had to go to that party!

Sofi's mother was lying back on the bed with her eyes closed in relaxation. Evie worshipped silence as if it were a sign of the family's elevation in status. The noisy roar of a gardener's leaf blower outside made Evie's eyes pop open.

In San Inocente, proximity to a good seashore view established your family's position in the community. Downtown SI was loud because it ran alongside Highway 101. The constant beeping of semi-trucks backing up, mufflerless cars, and the noisy chatter of people stopping for gas used to lull Sofi to sleep as a child. Now her bedroom window faced white mini–Taj Mahals with Roman pillars and modern glass palaces. Those who lived along the coast or at the top of the hill were looked upon with awe. The fact that Sofi's family lived in a town house at the bottom of the hill didn't bother her mother, because it was a private gated community, with a hillside address.

"What happened to your arms?" her mother asked, sitting up. Sofi grabbed her Mat Maids gray pullover from the floor and tugged it on. She hated lying to her parents. Lying to her teachers, boys, and classmates wasn't so bad. But her folks . . .

"I don't know. I just broke out, I guess."

Her mother nodded knowingly. She seemed to have let go of the work incident. "Have you been to the gym?" Sofi crossed her eyes and flopped back into her chair. She hated the gym. Her mother thought exercise was the new wonder drug of the millennium. Got a pimple? Go to the gym. Got a D on your chem midterm? Go to the gym. World hunger? Go to the gym. Evie and her friends Rosalba and Ana Michelle went three times a week. Sofi resented her mother for blaming all of her problems on her lack of gym fanaticism.

"What's for dinner?"

"Your favorite." Her mother rolled her eyes and said, "Mexican," as if it were a silly joke.

"Nice," Sofi said, scrambling down the hall. Evie's mother–daughter moments made Sofi uncomfortable. It was bad enough that her parents never allowed her to live a normal teenage life. They always wanted to know where she was going and with whom. Sofi never felt like she had enough money when she was out with her friends, so she had to work on weekends answering phones at her mother's church to pay for new clothes or to go to the movies. Plus, she was the only girl at San Inocente High without a cell phone. Horrible!

The living room (which they never actually lived in) had two large bay windows and a sliding glass door that opened onto a small patio. Sofi's mother relished this open space, creating a relaxing haven with rows of potted daffodils, hollyhocks, and lush ferns. It was where the family ate, when the weather permitted. Sofi's mother liked it because it was easy to clean. Over the metal banister there were a playground and a square-shaped pool for the Rancho Sueño Estates residents. On the white plastic table were three bags from Taco Bell—Sofi's favorite.

Her dad walked in from the garage with heavy steps. Ed Mendoza carried three sodas in the crook of his right arm and his suitcase in his left. He was a small man with an easy smile, a neat mustache, and soft brown eyes that always seemed deep in reflection, hidden behind wire-rimmed glasses. People said Sofi looked like him, but except for the caramel-colored skin, Sofi didn't see the resemblance. She rushed over to him, planted a big noisy smooch on his always-smooth cheek, and took the warm cans away from him.

"Hi, Dad," she called over her shoulder. She sat down at the table in the kitchen and dug into the Taco Bell bag. Ed stood in the entryway, his starched white shirt stained with underarm sweat, dark shadows looming under his eyes, a soft smile dancing on his lips.

"How are you?" he asked carefully, enunciating each word. Sofi looked up, her cheeks crammed with Taco Supreme and tried to reply, but her words sounded jumbled, like she was underwater. Disapprovingly, her father raised his index finger and waved it back and forth slowly. "No talking with your mouth full." Sofi hated when he did that. Her dad had a rule against everything; even when she was home, she felt like she was in school. Ed Mendoza also had a thing about manners, grace, and style. It drove Sofi nuts, because he was always correcting her. Ed paused to smile at the bronze plaque on the coffee table. He'd earned it after completing his ESL/GED program at the community college. On the bottom was etched, "Yes, you can!" Sometimes, Sofi wished her parents would just be normal. But to them, being normal meant becoming more American.

Sofi nodded and chewed every last bit of hard taco shell and seasoned mystery meat. Her dad carefully put down his suitcase in the hallway closet and hung his suit jacket next to a dingy denim jacket he used on weekends when he worked as a carpet layer. Ed paused to make sure the jacket hung exactly two inches away from the other one. Ever since he'd been promoted at the San Onofre power plant he'd taken to wearing suits, although it was not a requirement.

The sound of Sofi's crunching filled the silence of the neighborhood. He laughed heartily at the faces she made while eating, and tucked his American flag tie into his buttoned-up shirt.

"In youth we learn, in old age we tutor," he said, tucking a paper napkin into his collar. Sofi crossed her eyes in annoyance. A couple of months ago, her father had gone to a Dress for Success fair in Irvine, where he'd picked up a book of achievement-oriented quotes. He studied it feverishly, as if the answers to all of life's mysteries were encoded in the pages.

She stared back at his expectant eyes. "Who said that?" She took the bait. Her dad loved to play the "Who said what?" game. It was his own form of *Jeopardy!* except that he had all the answers.

"Why, I did. Made it up on the drive home."

Thankfully, her mother came down in time to save Sofi from a "What does that school teach you?" speech. Her parents loved to give speeches and, sadly, as their only child, Sofi was forced to be their captive audience. Evie had changed into something more relaxing, a pair of jeans and black pumps. Her worry lines were hidden under a fresh coat of makeup. Sofi's mom always tried to look immaculate, as if she expected company to pop in at any minute.

"Darling, you look scenic," Ed said. Sofi rolled her eyes. Her dad liked to try out new words to improve his vocabulary, but it usually sounded pretty lame.

Her mother smiled, snatching the MexiMelt out of his hand. "I don't know what you mean, but I like it."

"It means that you're as lovely as a beautiful painting." They laughed like a young couple. Sofi leaned back, studying the flirtatious exchange. They seemed to be in a good mood. She wondered if she should just tell them about Steve's party. Honesty was something her dad rattled on and on about. Maybe if they knew that Olivia and Taylor were going . . .

"Speaking of beautiful paintings . . . ," Sofi jumped in. She had to ask. Steve's party was this weekend. Her heart started to pound in her ears. There was a 99.999 percent chance that they would say no. Not just a regular no, but a *hell no!* But Sofi had to go. If there was no Rosarito, then there would surely be no Nick, no prom, no happily-ever-after, and she would have to die all alone with a bunch of cats. Sofi hesitated and decided to test the waters. "Some girls at school are going to TJ."

"Tijuana." Her mother snorted. "Why?"

Sofi looked down at her food, feeling her cheeks burn. "I don't know. I guess because of the beach and stuff."

"That's insane. That city is too dangerous." Her father grunted, taking a long drink from his soda. He glanced at her sideways. "You're not thinking . . . ?" His look made Sofi squirm and shake her head adamantly.

"Oh, no, not me. I would never do something like that. I was just saying . . ."

"I don't understand," Ed continued, "how parents could even think about letting their children go down there. That's the problem with kids in this country. They get to do whatever they want and end up get-ting into drugs. They don't understand the world. It's full of desperate people who'll do anything—rob, rape, or kill—for drugs or money. American teenagers are too reckless and ignorant. All they care about is having fun."

"There's nothing wrong with having fun," Sofi mumbled.

"*Gracias a Dios,*" Evie interrupted, "that our Sofi is not like that." She reached over and squeezed Sofi's hand. "I don't want you hanging out with those kinds of people. Those people will only get you into trouble. Study, *mija,*" her mother pleaded. Sofi nodded slowly. *Those* people were her friends. How could she make her parents understand that there was nothing to worry about?

"And how are your finals going?" Ed motioned to Sofi's hives. "Been to the gym lately?"

Sofi cringed at the word *gym*. "My teachers want us to review everything we've ever learned for the exit exams. They're crazy."

"See that, Evie?" Her dad pointed at Sofi's speckled arms as if they were creepy-crawlers in his glass of water. "That's my point. Sofia needs to focus. No distractions." Sofi studied their faces. Her dad was up to something. Whatever it was, she knew that she wasn't going to like it.

"I don't know," her mother hesitated, wiping her mouth very slowly as if she was choosing her words carefully. "It's what college is all about. Oprah said—"

"That's what I don't want," he interrupted. "Barry from the plant told me about a girl who went to a dorm party and some guy put something in her drink."

"Dad," Sofi interrupted, "they're called roofies. I know about that stuff. Don't worry."

"How do you expect me not to worry? You're my only daughter. You don't know about the world."

"That's exactly why I need to go away to college. I need to experience these things for myself."

His body stiffened and his eyes shot wide in horror. "You want someone to put something in your drink?"

"No, no, I didn't mean that." She waved her arms in alarm. "I meant that . . ." Sofi looked from her mother to her father and sighed. They wouldn't understand. They came from a totally different world. "I'm seventeen years old. I'm almost grown up."

"Ms. All-Grown-Up can't even clean the toilet," her mother cut in. Sofi rolled her eyes and started playing with her silver hoop earring. She didn't like where this was going. "How do you expect to live all by yourself when you can't even do your chores?"

"That's not fair."

"Fair? What does fair have to do with this? You need to focus on your studies. You can't mess up."

Sofi felt her chest tighten.

"And we talked about it. Your mother and I want you to live here next year," her father said, as if she'd won the grand prize on *The Price Is Right.*

No! They couldn't do this. Sofi pressed her lips tightly together. This was the last straw. She knew that she would explode if she allowed the flood of emotions to surface. Not after seventeen years of planning for freedom. Sofi had worked hard for it. Her mother had promised! They'd even gone to look at the dorms on the campus tour. UCLA was supposed to be her big escape from an overprotective hell. Sofi looked at her parents eating quietly before her. They wanted her to stay close to them forever and have no life whatsoever. It was insane. Sofi had to put her foot down. If not now, when?

"This is so not fair!" Sofi shot out of her chair and balled her hands into fists. Her parents stared back, stunned. "I never get to do anything I want. All I'm asking is to live my own life in college. My friends get to go out and have fun now. And I don't complain. They go on vacations together and to parties—"

"You are not like your friends." Her mother cringed and put her food down.

"No, I'm not. I always have to stay home, do chores, and study like a prisoner."

"You're not a prisoner," her mother said.

"Let her vent." Her dad started picking at his food. *"Pa' que se le quite."*

"You think your life is rough." Evie stood up quickly. Her chair made a scratching sound against the patio tiles. "When I was your age we had to walk five miles to school. No car. No bus. No taxi. We"—she pointed at her chest—"had to pay for everything: books, paper, tests, even our desks. My mother worked all the time to feed and clothe us. I left school to help my family. And I'm still helping them. Do you know what it feels like to go to bed hungry?" Sofi shook her head. There was no reasoning with her parents. They always came up with the same frightening starving-children stories, which Sofi swore were total exaggerations.

"Okay, okay, Mom. I get it. I'm sorry, okay?"

"I don't think you do." She walked over to Sofi, either to emphasize her point or to make herself seem bigger than her five-foot-four-inch frame. "You don't understand how lucky you are. Don't you see what big sacrifices we've made to give you all this?" She motioned to the walls of their tan town house with its terra-cotta shingles.

Oh, she's good, Sofi thought. Her mother could guilt-trip a nun into giving up Sunday Mass. There was nothing Sofi could say.

She tuned out her mother's rant. Images of driving down to Rosarito and dancing cheek-to-cheek with Nick floated into her head. Her parents were acting ridiculous. There was nothing to worry about. They were prisoners, caged behind their fears of the unknown. Sofi couldn't allow their insecurities to rule her. She was going to Rosarito. Sure, it was wrong, but Sofi had her own life to live. Her parents would never understand *her* reality. They just didn't get it.

"Fine. Whatever."

"I knew you would come around." Evie smiled as she patted her husband's shoulders in approval.

Sofi took a deep breath and cleared her throat. "The Wilsons invited me to their cabin near Joshua Tree for Memorial Day weekend."

While her mother was the queen of guilt-tripping, Sofi knew how to get on her parents' soft side. They were suckers for keeping up with the Joneses. Because of their immigrant status, her parents did everything in their power to *seem* like the model American family. Things like dressing smartly (which was short for maxing out all the credit cards on nice clothes) and speaking correct English were high priorities. Her dad had like a dozen of those "Follow me to America" English-language tapes and used to listen to them religiously on the way to work. It was really embarrassing, because he used to practice over-enunciated conversations with strangers at the mall like, "How is the landscape of your motherland?" or "Can you tell me where the chaps' lavatory is?" Thank God he stopped doing that!

"Will her parents be there?" her father asked, studying her body language.

"Oh, totally. Yes." Sofi nodded. She pressed her lips tightly together. "We've got finals in three weeks, so we plan to get an early start and spend the time studying, you know." Had she said too much? Her mom and dad looked at each other, weighing the situation. Sofi knew what her parents were thinking. In addition to wanting to look good, her parents also had very big hearts and liked Taylor. Plus Taylor's parents had a grand beach house right on the cliff and threw big soirées for the city's bigwigs. Sofi's mother nodded ever so slightly.

"Well, I guess we could let you stay the weekend," her dad said, "since all you're going to do is study and—"

Sofi jumped into his arms. "Thank you, Dad."

"Now that's more like it." Her mother patted Sofi on the back. "I know you're upset about the dorms, but your father is right on this one. If you want, maybe we can talk about extending your curfew." Her father raised one eyebrow, but Sofi didn't care. College was months away. She would deal with that when the time came. There was only one thing on her mind at the moment. Operation *Papi Chulo*.

2

"Check it out," Olivia cried, pointing ahead. "Me-hee-co!"

"Woo!" Sofi hollered as Taylor's blue 4Runner approached the Mexican border checkpoint. She decided that this Saturday morning would be the first day of the rest of her life. *TJ is huge*, Sofi thought as the emerging gray storm cloud turned into a far-reaching landscape of houses and buildings. All of a sudden she felt very small, dwarfed by the looming mega-city with radio towers reaching up toward the heavens and smokestacks spilling soot into the sky. It had to be ten times bigger than San Inocente—the L.A. of Mexico. A green sign with white lettering announced, FIREARMS ARE ILLEGAL IN MEXICO. It struck Sofi as odd. "I hope you guys left your AK-47s at home," she joked. Then the reality of the situation sank in like a punch to the stomach. She was entering Mexico, the land of her parents, without their knowledge. She was not going to allow herself to freak out.

"Darn." Olivia snapped her fingers. "I got my bazooka in the back." As they inched closer to the border, Sofi held her breath. Her parents had crossed this same border fourteen years ago.

Obstructing the skyline was a huge concrete overpass for people to walk across into Mexico. Underneath were a series of haggard-looking tollbooths. She turned her head to the left. Cars were piled bumper-to-bumper, waiting to cross into the United States. Scary-looking agents with guns strapped to their waists directed traffic. Sofi bit down on her lower lip as they passed a sign that read, LAST U.S. EXIT. This was it.

Her stomach quivered. A Mexican officer sat in a chair facing Tijuana. He watched the cars pass quickly through the Mexican checkpoint. Each lane had a traffic light. Cars that got a green light could go forward. Cars that got a red light had to veer to the right for inspection. It seemed too random, too chaotic, but Sofi wasn't sure how things worked in this country. They got a green light and all three girls breathed out in relief.

"That was it?" Sofi asked, fidgeting with her seat belt. She could hardly see anything from the backseat. "They didn't ask for IDs or nothing."

"I don't think Mexico has an illegal-immigrant problem." Olivia yawned loudly, stretching her solid arms in the air.

Taylor smiled at Sofi in the rearview mirror behind her favorite vintage '80s big circle sunglasses. They looked sophisticated on her freckly heart-shaped face and straight nose. She had her golden blond hair tied back into two thick French braids. She was wearing a cute Banana Republic white-ribbed cotton halter with khaki shorts, chandelier earrings, and white beaded T-strap sandals. Taylor turned the 4Runner west onto the scenic toll route, which ran alongside a long sheet-metal fence decorated with red and black graffiti.

"Where do I go?" Taylor asked, sounding a little frantic. Cars were streaming past her in a chaotic attempt to get through the piling traffic. "There are no lanes."

Olivia pulled Steve's e-mail from the backpack. It took her a minute, because her ankle-wrap platform sandals got caught in the heap of junk lying between her feet—her heavy backpack, random CDs, a red makeup bag, books she knew she wasn't going to read, and a grocery bag loaded with Hot Cheetos, cans of warm soda, and chocolate.

"Today, Olivia," Sofi warned.

"I'm ready, I'm ready," she cried, shaking her wavy honey-brown hair. Olivia Munchmeyer was a Lane Bryant girl with a thick, curvy body, big boobs, and the healthiest attitude. "It says here"—she pointed to the MapQuest map—"to stay on your right." Taylor's shoulders were hunched forward with tension. She pushed her shades up on top of her head and bit down on her chapped lip. The road was bad, full of potholes that made them bounce back and forth.

"These are the craziest directions I've ever seen." Olivia crammed a handful of Hot Cheetos into her mouth.

"Just tell me what it says!"

Olivia gave Taylor an annoyed glance. "It says that we'll pass a graffiti wall with tall light beams." She looked up from the paper. "Holla."

"Is that the border?" Sofi asked, dumbfounded. She was looking at a high metal fence that trailed farther than she could imagine. She never thought the border would look like this. To the south was Tijuana, a city veiled in a sheet of gray smog. A pang of guilt stabbed her as she thought about how green and fertile her neighborhood was in comparison. Out here, everything felt dry and thirsty, as if the United States used up all the water and sprinkled down the leftovers. There was a rough, raw texture to the buildings; highway dividers crumbled down in sections; and limp, sad trees clawed the cracked earth along the fence. The border seemed to do more than just separate two nations. It changed the air, making it heavy and hard to breathe. Even the sun seemed murky and hazy on this side.

"We're definitely not in California anymore," Olivia joked and slapped her thigh.

Taylor's knuckles were white from gripping the steering wheel too tight. "Why did I decide to drive here? We should have just gone with Steve," Taylor moaned.

"Girl, you're doing great." Olivia patted her shoulder. "You're totally kicking ass. You know what they say. If you can drive in Me-hee-co . . . you can—"

"Give it up, Olivia. You can't cheer for crap."

Sofi unbuckled her seat belt and hugged their headrests. "Okay, girls. It's time to go over Operation *Papi Chulo*."

"Yes, *ma'am*." Olivia saluted with a big cheesy grin on her face.

Her dad was a sergeant major at Camp Pendleton. She knew all about covert operations.

"This is what I was thinking. We get there. Dump our stuff and find Nick. Hopefully he'll be at the beach, because I've got on my hot white bikini," Sofi said, snapping the strap from under her pink lacy tank. She'd chosen it because it made her caramel-toned skin glow, and she always got lots of compliments in it—granted, they were mostly from other girls and old-lady types, but they were compliments just the same. "If he's not at the beach, whatever, we'll make do. The main thing is that you two need to help me get some alone time with him. I'm sure that the moment we start talking, things will just, you know, click."

Sofi imagined Nick noticing her from across the sandy beach. He would be stunned by her gorgeous petite figure in her padded white bikini top. (She would be holding her belly in, of course.) And, like a magnet, he would be drawn to her. Nick would be tongue-tied at first, searching for something funny to say. She'd smile encouragingly. Taylor and Olivia would distract the other guys, giving Nick enough time to scrounge up the courage to ask her out. Then Nick would take her to some romantic Mexican restaurant with cloth napkins and mariachis. There, he would realize that he was madly in love with her and ask her to be his girl.

"Okay." Olivia hesitated, looking at Taylor for support. "Now, don't take this the wrong way."

Sofi's face dropped.

"No, it's not the plan. The plan is fine. And Taylor and I are cool with creating a scene so that you can be alone with Nick." Olivia took a deep breath. "My only worry . . . is you."

"Me?"

Taylor scrunched up her nose and nodded.

"Yeah, you," Olivia said. "'Member when Scott sent you that birthday-gram? And you totally freaked?"

"But that was different. Scott was a total nerd."

"He's a nice guy," Olivia insisted. "Not going to win any beauty contests. But kind of cute."

"Are you listening to yourself? Scott's nice, but he's got a snaggle-tooth. So gross." Sofi made a disgusted face.

"But you kind of liked him until he sent you that gram."

"No." Sofi shook her head. "I just felt sorry for him. There's a difference, which he confused, and that's okay."

Olivia huffed, "Well, I just don't want you to go through all this trouble and then find something wrong with Nick, too."

"Don't worry. I won't. Nick's the one."

Sofi crossed her arms defensively and looked out the window. She wanted a boyfriend more than anything in the world. Whenever she saw couples at school making out in the hallways, she felt like such a loser and wondered what those girls had that she didn't. Not that Taylor and Olivia were relationship experts. Taylor was still getting over Ryan, this loser who'd dumped her the day before Valentine's, and Olivia had messed around with half the wrestling team. But they still had more relationship experience than Sofi had, which was none.

"This time it'll be different," Sofi said, sounding more confident than she felt. "It's my destiny. Plus, you guys will be there to give me that kick in the butt I'll need if I start to freak out."

"Kicking ass is my middle name," Olivia said warmly. Sofi smiled, thankful for Olivia's friendship.

Olivia lived down the street from Sofi with her dad and four linebacker-like brothers. She'd had her eye on the new girl in the neighborhood as soon as Sofi's family moved in, even though Sofi hadn't known it at the time. They'd formally met after the second week of high school. Greg Matherly had started picking on Sofi in Spanish class because she couldn't roll her *r*'s. In kindergarten Sofi's parents placed her in English-only classes because she had a lisp. They were concerned that two languages would be too difficult for her to master. Although Sofi grew up hearing Spanish, she never had to speak it until high school. Greg couldn't believe that someone who was born in Mexico was taking intermediate Spanish. His outburst drew lots of snickers in the class. Sofi turned beet red and ran out of the room in tears. Olivia caught up with her in the girls' bathroom. She had her own reasons for wanting to get back at Greg. That afternoon, with the help of Olivia's friend Taylor, they TPed Greg's Ford truck and wrote "STD Matherly" in soap on his windshield. Sofi had been friends with the two girls ever since.

"You two are the greatest," Sofi said.

A banged-up Toyota Camry with a busted headlight was driving dangerously close behind them. It seemed like the driver wanted to run them over. The car raced past them, followed by a brand-new black Escalade with tinted windows, and then a series of throwback cars from the early '80s. Sofi was surprised to see so many jalopy contraptions on the road. There were cars with taped windows and huge dents, graffiti-decorated vans with money signs scribbled onto the back windows, and a dust-coated VW bug with ink-black smoke gushing from the tailpipe.

"So this is where cars go when they die," Sofi joked.

Taylor and Olivia laughed.

"Oh my God," Olivia cried. "Check out that billboard." It was an advertisement for Britney Spears's new perfume. "That stuff stinks." She crossed her eyes and sighed, "Only in Me-hee-co."

"Directions, please," Taylor asked.

"Okay, okay, stay on the right no matter what. There will be signs," Olivia continued, reading from the paper in her hand.

Sofi scooted over to the opposite side of the truck. Laundry was waving in the breeze from clotheslines tied to rooftops. People walked along the sidewalk, alone and in twos and threes. *I was born somewhere in this city*, Sofi thought. What a weird feeling, to be a stranger in her birthplace. Her parents probably walked down these same streets before moving to the Other Side. A pang of guilt stabbed her in the chest. Sometimes her dad talked about his sister, who still lived around here. Luisa was her name.

"You all right back there?" Olivia asked.

Sofi looked up, surprised. "Yeah, I'm cool."

"You're kind of quiet."

"I'm just taking it all in." Sofi took a deep breath and nodded. "I'm fine." A shiver ran down her back even though it was 75 degrees outside. Something had changed when they crossed the border; Sofi couldn't quite put her finger on what it was . . . but she felt different somehow. Disconnected from her friends, maybe?

Suddenly, a young man dashed in front of them despite the high-speed traffic. The girls shrieked as Taylor swerved to avoid hitting him. Was he going to dash to the Other Side? What would make a guy do something as crazy as that?

"Oh my God, did you see him?" Taylor shouted.

"Only in Me-hee-co," Olivia sang out again.

"What is that?" Sofi asked. "Your new catchphrase?" Olivia gave her a toothy grin.

"Look, it says Rosarito right there," Sofi said. Her bangles jangled together as she gestured to a big green sign along the highway. They drove up a steep hill that led to an area called Playas de Tijuana. A brown station wagon was on the side of the road, steam rising from under the opened hood. A gang of kids peered out from the back at passing motorists. The 4Runner crept up the incline behind a rickety old truck carrying propane gas tanks in the back. They left the big crazy city of Tijuana behind them and headed toward the coast.

"Woo!" they hollered when the car emerged from the high mountain pathway and into the bright sunlight overlooking a breathtaking view of the Pacific Ocean.

"I was afraid we were lost for a minute," Taylor said. "TJ is nothing like Cancún, but this I can do." She nodded, looking at the beautiful coast that kept the dismal TJ haze at bay. Beyond the modestly built, brightly colored boxlike homes was the dark blue water. Olivia nodded in approval and stuck in a mix CD she'd burned the night before, as the truck carried them south, past half-finished white mansions with swaying Mexican flags.

Olivia sighed. "Beautiful sun, beautiful shore . . . now all I need is some beautiful men, and I'll be happy." The truck wove up and around the toll road that hugged the curves of dangerously steep cliffs.

Fifteen minutes later, the blue 4Runner drove under a cement arch that said BIENVENIDOS A ROSARITO in red cursive lettering. They all lowered their windows. Sofi stuck her head out to get a better view of the party town she'd heard so much about. A fistful of dust smacked her in the face, making her cough. It had followed them from Tijuana and coated Taylor's truck like a sheer veil. The air was filled with gas fumes from passing cars and trucks that surely did not pass a smog check. Sofi remembered how that morning while she was bringing her bag down, her parents had given her a hug and reminded her to be on her best behavior. It felt wrong to deceive them like this, but it was the only way to make her dreams come true. Sofi sighed, looking out the window. It was sunny outside, not a cloud in the light blue sky. She pushed the uncomfortable thoughts into a small closet in the back of her brain. There was a mission to accomplish, and Sofi was not about to let anything ruin her weekend.

The main drag, Boulevard Benito Juarez, was a four-lane street with young palm trees dividing the two-way traffic. The town was alive with a festive flair. Huge Mexican and American flags were for sale on the street corners, waving in the breeze. The 4Runner was forced to go five miles per hour, because the street was packed bumper to bumper with cars that had California license plates. The sidewalks were jammed with foot traffic. Music bumped from everyone's car. The aromas of sizzling meat and frying chicken fused with car fumes and the scent of the salty sea. There was an excited energy in the air and everyone seemed to be drunk off it.

"Lobster!" Taylor sang out, just before slamming on the brakes. "Yikes! I almost killed that little boy," she said, mystified, as a group of small children jumped in front of them and started juggling colorful balls. The little brown kids dressed in grimy clothes, their hair uncombed, made Sofi's heart break. They looked like her with their sun-baked skin and soulful brown eyes. Where were their mothers? After tossing the balls expertly in the air, three chubby little hands chased the open car windows, begging for change.

"They're so cute," Olivia said, reaching into her jean shorts for some change.

"Here." Sofi passed a couple of dollars into the small hands that appeared in front of her. She wanted to give them more.

"Whoa now, big spender." Olivia waved off a couple more kids who seemed to appear out of nowhere. "Can't start giving out that kind of cash or else we'll have nothing left for beer."

"Oh, c'mon, tightwad," Sofi joked. "I'm sure they need the money more than we do."

Olivia shrugged. "Yeah, sure, but if you keep giving away all your money, they'll all come down on us like seagulls and then we'll *never* get rid of them. I've seen it a hundred times. Poverty is bad everywhere. My dad says that what those kids need is to be in school, not learning how to beg."

"That's not fair," Taylor interrupted, shaking her head. "You say it as if they chose to be poor."

"Hey, my dad knows these things. He's seen it all. Plus, we didn't come down here to feed the children."

"True," Sofi agreed.

"I really don't care who you feed as long as I can get some lobster." Taylor flinched. "Was that bad?"

"Not if you get it with a side order of that," Olivia said, pointing to a tall, beefy *papasito* in cargo shorts and flip-flops. His chocolate biceps glistened with coconut oil. She admired him over her glasses. "Come to *mamá*."

"Check out what's coming at two o'clock." Sofi gestured to a beautiful surfer boy with long hair and jean shorts.

"Breathe, Olivia. Close your mouth and breathe," Taylor said.

"I'm gonna need mouth-to-mouth," Olivia groaned, placing her hand over her heart. Sofi laughed. Olivia was always acting over the top. Her friend lowered the sun visor to check her face in the mirror. "So, this is where all the hot men are." A car full of Latin guys pulled up alongside them and honked. They were all adorable, with gelled-back hairstyles and honey-gold skin. At the stop sign one of the guys jumped out and approached Sofi's window.

"Hey, cutie," he said, checking out Sofi's jean miniskirt and tanned legs. The boy's light brown eyes sparkled, and his Caesar cut and dimples made him look angelic. In his black T-shirt with Aztec designs, sagging olive-colored pants, and brown sandals, he reminded her of the guys who hung downtown. Sofi felt her chest tighten and her pulse start to race. He had the cutest lips that curved up at the corners. She froze.

"You should pass through Club Iggy's tonight," he said with a soft lisp as he handed her a flyer with a picture of three girls wearing nothing but Daisy Dukes.

"Thanks," Sofi mumbled, and raised her window. She could feel her face get hot. The guy did a double take, wondering if maybe he had said something wrong, then shrugged and raced back to catch his ride.

"You did it again," Olivia chastised over her shoulder. "That guy was totally into you. I'm sure he could've got us in for free."

"Pleeease." Sofi waved the announcement in Olivia's face. "No, I didn't. Look at this flyer for booty-shorts night. I ain't no booty girl."

"Like hell you aren't," Olivia said, slapping Sofi's leg playfully. "Hey." Olivia looked back down at the directions and tapped Taylor on the shoulder. "I think we need to turn there."

Steve's parents owned a three-story Spanish Colonial house with huge bay windows overlooking Rosarito Beach. Their custom-built home was identical to every other house in the Linamar secured-housing community five miles outside of town and down the street from the Fox movie studios where the film *Titanic* had been shot. His living room was decorated in a festive Mexican style. Framed paintings of children and flowers hung on the walls and looked over the carved wooden furniture.

"*Buenos días*," Anthony Daly greeted them from behind the black minibar. He was mixing strawberry-colored margaritas in a sleek chrome blender. Green Day blasted from the stereo system behind him. Lauren Filbert and Emily Scots were already in their bikinis, lounging on the couch, drinking from giant margarita glasses. The two brunettes screamed when they saw Taylor, Olivia, and Sofi.

"Oh my God!" the girls cried at the entrance. They dumped their stuff on the terra-cotta floor and ran over to hug their friends.

"Mat Maids in the house!" Olivia cried out, raising her arm in the air.

"Holla!" Lauren responded.

"Who else is here?" Taylor looked around the room and sniffed the air—someone was burning gardenia incense in the house.

Emily stood a head taller than everyone else. She wore her shoulder-length hair in a messy bun held together with chopsticks. "Well, Mary and Joanna are here." She rolled her brown eyes. "I think they said some more cheerleaders are arriving later tonight."

"What about Nick?" Sofi asked. He was the only person she cared about.

"He's out with Steve, riding bikes in the sand dunes."

Sofi frowned.

"C'mon, Sof, don't worry," Olivia said. "Let's check out our new home." The girls ran around like kids in a toy store. Taylor screamed when she saw the hot tub on the outside balcony, and Sofi loved the huge hammock. It would be perfect for snuggling at sunset.

"Guys," Olivia shouted from the top of the stairs. "You got to check this out. I love this place. I don't think I'm ever going to leave." Sofi and Taylor followed the sound of her voice. Olivia was at the end of a long hallway. As Sofi walked, she peeked into the other rooms. Luggage was tossed on top of queen-size beds. There had to be at least four bedrooms on this floor, and there was still a whole other floor yet to be explored. Just then, Sofi slammed into Sarah Baker, Nick's ex.

"Sarah," Sofi yelped. "What are you doing here?" Sofi wanted to kick herself for assuming she wouldn't be here. Everyone who was anyone was at Steve's party. Damn it!

Sarah stood in the bathroom doorway, looking gorgeous as ever in a pink string bikini, jean miniskirt, and sandals. She was tall, with a perfect, curvy body. "Hey, Sofi!" She tossed her wavy blond hair over her shoulder and hugged Sofi as if they were lifelong friends. Taylor stood there, her mouth open wide. "I'm so glad you guys are here. We're going to have fun, fun, fun," Sarah cheered. Sofi's heart flopped. Was she here to win back Nick? How would Sofi ever be able to compete with a girl who did backflips for fun? They watched Sarah walk down the stairs and then hurried into the room at the end of the hall. Olivia was jumping on the bed when they entered. Sofi quickly closed the door behind them.

"This is so not fair," Sofi said, covering her face with her hands.

Taylor sat on one of the beds. "I can't believe she even came."

"What are you guys talking about?" Olivia asked, flopping onto the floral comforter. The bedroom was painted sky blue and had two large beds separated by a wooden coffee table with large cast-iron nails. There were bright yellow flowers decorating the room.

"Sarah," Sofi said, leaning against the door. "She's here."

"No way." Olivia shook her head in disbelief.

"Yes way."

"So what do we do now?" Taylor looked at Sofi with her hazel eyes.

"I don't know. I don't know," Sofi cried out in frustration. She stomped around in a circle. She hadn't expected this.

"Well," Olivia said, walking over to the vanity mirror to check her face, "let's go get some fresh air."

"Yeah," Taylor agreed, putting her hand on Sofi's shoulder.

Olivia was right. Fresh air was the answer. Sofi needed to be distracted, and Boulevard Benito Juárez was full of interesting new sights, sounds, and smells. She pushed thoughts of Sarah Baker out of her head.

Rosarito was a beautiful dream come true, and Sofi wanted nothing and no one to wake her from it. The street was clogged with vendors tempting clients with their wares. "Tacos!" "*Chicle!*" "Very cheap!" Their voices blended together like a song. Women with long dark hair sold silver necklaces, bracelets, and earrings displayed on velvet-covered tables. Kids with sad gazes sold gum, wooden snake toys, or beaded jewelry. Indigenous women with long thick braids and dark shawls pushed vending carts under which babies slept. Tourist shop after tourist shop sold the exact same merchandise: hand-woven hammocks, colorful serapes, corny T-shirts printed with pictures of naked girls or lewd jokes, Aztec artifacts, and even Mexican jumping beans!

All of a sudden Sofi felt herself being watched. She turned to the right; was she getting paranoid, or had the shop clerk at the candy store just checked her out in a not-so-friendly way? Sofi turned to the left and swore she recognized the hat vendor from someplace. Their eyes met. And the woman grilling meat behind the counter of the Rock and Roll Taco Shop directly in front of them? She had the same hurried expression as Sofi's mother. Sofi felt her heart pounding.

The hairs on the back of her neck stood up. She couldn't stop thinking about her aunt and all the other family members who might live around here. Her father wired money to his sister in Rosarito every couple of months. Sofi never asked about her and just assumed that she was poor. Sofi looked down at the woman selling *chicle* on the street corner: Could this be her aunt Luisa? Would she recognize Sofi? Would she tell her parents and get her into trouble? Suddenly, Sofi realized that she was standing all alone. Where had Olivia and Taylor gone? Panic gripped her for a second. Her pulse raced wildly. What would she do alone in a foreign country? She didn't even have Steve's address! But then she saw Taylor wave at her from the end of the block, and she sighed with relief.

"Sorry about that. Hey, where are we going?" Sofi asked when she finally caught up with them.

"We're following them." Olivia pointed to a couple of guys ahead who kept turning back to look at them. The three guys looked like military boys, with their buzz cuts and loud voices: totally Olivia's type. As a big girl, she preferred a big man who could make her feel petite. They took a right at Señor Frog's, a three-leveled disco that looked dead and abandoned in the sunlight, and headed straight for the beach.

The Rosarito shoreline was breathtaking. All three girls paused to soak in the vision before them. Sure, the view was beautiful, but the girls were used to sand. What they couldn't believe was that all the hot clubs were right on the beach! It was totally slamming and reminded Sofi of an MTV spring break show. An old LL Cool J song blasted out of one of the clubs, and couples were dancing in their swimsuits on the sand. People-watchers enjoyed the view from plastic chairs under palm-covered umbrellas. A dozen guys wearing T-shirts emblazoned with their respective club names waited eagerly to take orders. A Latin guy with a shaved head and a Club Zone shirt jogged up to them.

"You ladies wanna drink? We got free shots of tequila."

Taylor looked at Sofi, who looked at Olivia.

"Yeah, sure," Olivia said, not sounding very sure. The guy waved them over to a green canvas umbrella that had the Dos Equis logo printed on it. Olivia shrugged her shoulders. As they walked over, Sofi caught a whiff of horse manure. She fanned herself and noticed that the saddled horses stood in tight formation along the side of the Papas and Beer club for riding tours. She shaded her dark eyes to scan the horizon. There were surfers bobbing with the tides waiting for the perfect wave. Dozens of tents set up for campers dotted the shore, and food vendors were selling fruit salad, shrimp cocktail, and an odd dish called Tasty Locos.

They sat down in the white plastic chairs and watched the waiter hurry off to a makeshift bar twenty feet away. Sofi leaned toward Olivia. "So, what are we doing?

"I don't know," Olivia said, sounding excited and confused.

"You're not eighteen," Taylor reminded Olivia. "That's the drinking age here. I'm not about to get in trouble for you."

"Yeah, but you heard him. He offered free tequila shots."

"I don't know if I want to drink tequila." Sofi hesitated, but she didn't want her friends to think that she was uptight. "Well, not this early in the day. You know?"

"Well, I'm not worried. It's you two who should be—," Taylor began.

"Shut up. Shut up," Olivia whispered quickly. "He's coming." Their waiter was built like a wrestler, with broad shoulders and short legs. He had pretty hazel eyes, but he was definitely a bad boy. The tattoo on his arm said *Vato Loco*.

"Ladies." He placed three thimble-size cups of gold liquid in front of them. "This round is on the house." Olivia looked at Taylor, who was looking at Sofi uneasily. The waiter noticed their hesitation.

"You guys are eighteen, right?"

"Oh, yeah, sure," Olivia said really loudly, picking up her shot and downing it like a pro. Sofi and Taylor followed. The tequila jolted her system, making Sofi gag. Olivia's eyes bugged out and her cheeks turned bright red. "Um . . . can we get a bucket of beer, too?" The waiter smiled and headed back to the bar.

The minute he was out of hearing distance, Sofi squealed. "Oh my God! That was sooo nasty. It tasted like acid."

"I'm sticking to beer," Taylor announced, pushing her sunglasses up her nose. "It's good for artery disease, you know."

"I swore that guy had busted us there for a minute." Olivia breathed out in relief, her chest heaving.

"Busted you," Taylor corrected. Olivia crossed her eyes, to Sofi's amusement.

"I think we're cool," Sofi said, looking around her for the first time. "I bet half the people out here are underage." Each table had a crowd of kids who looked to be around their age, drinking and laughing way too hard. A guy with a thick black ponytail and a faded Sean John T-shirt came over to sell sunglasses and henna tattoos. Sofi ignored him. "Check out all the hot-looking *papis chulos* here." She was eyeing a group of guys across from them. The guys were definitely checking them out and waved flirtatiously.

"Talk about finger-lickin'!" Olivia waved back.

"You're trouble," Taylor joked, leaning back and kicking off her sandals.

"Girrrl." Sofi pulled off her shirt. "I'm all for getting some this weekend."

"Getting some from whom?" Taylor leaned in close.

"Nick, of course." Sofi blushed, then paused, remembering the new twist in the plot. "So what am I going to do about Sarah?"

"Sarah is a joke," Olivia said in a quiet voice. "I can't believe she's even here."

"I don't know." Taylor scratched her neck softly, thinking. "Girls can be territorial. Just because she doesn't want Nick doesn't mean that she wants anyone else to have him."

"So what do I do? What would you do?"

Olivia smiled at Taylor. It was the same look Olivia got when she discovered a new prank. "We're going to have to step up your game plan. T and I will take care of Ms. Sarah Baker." Taylor nodded. "You worry about Nick."

"Excuse me," said a tall skinny guy with wild thick curly hair. "My name's Josh. I don't mean to bother you. But you see, me and my friends have this bet." He pointed to a group of guys ten feet away. "And I was hoping maybe you could settle it for us."

"Bet?" Olivia asked, straightening up in her seat.

Josh turned to Sofi. "Yeah, well, we were wondering what you were?" Sofi gave her friends an annoyed look. Not the "what are you" game. The game that always ended with the person saying, "But you don't look Mexican."

"I think you're Hawaiian and my friend said Brazilian. The loser has to take a shock."

He pointed to an old man standing beside the table with leather skin and thin white hair combed neatly over his head. The man was holding a battery charger connected to two worn-out cords with metal handles. It was an unusual and painful method of entertainment. Olivia laughed and clapped her hands. Sofi rolled her eyes. She hated how people were always trying to figure her out as if she were some strange creature from another planet.

"Well, actually, you're both wrong." Sofi smiled.

"Darn," Josh said, pretending to be upset. "Chris," he called over his shoulder to a guy with a blond crew cut, "we're both wrong!"

"C'mon," Taylor said, grabbing Sofi's hand. "I want to see this." The girls walked over to the other table and watched both guys get shocked. The old man looked bored as he carried out his job. He increased the intensity of the electricity until each boy screamed out, "Enough!"

"Hey, boys," Olivia said, sitting down in an empty seat. "So, where's the party tonight?" Taylor and Sofi stood behind her, feeling wallflowerish, until Josh and Chris offered their seats. Josh grabbed an empty chair and put it next to Sofi. A Daddy Yankee song was playing in the background, and Olivia started dancing in her chair, to all the guys' approval.

"You like this song?" Josh asked. Sofi's heart began to race and her hands were starting to sweat. Josh watched her intensely with his beady brown eyes. He made her nervous.

She nodded.

"So, you never told me what you are."

"I'm American."

He gave her a confused look. "No, I mean, where are your parents from?"

"My parents are Mexican."

"Really?" Josh laughed as if she'd told a joke. "But you don't look Mexican." Sofi rolled her eyes. Could he be any less original? What was a Mexican supposed to look like? Did he expect her to be wearing a big sombrero or an off-the-shoulder peasant blouse?

Two teenage Mexican girls walked up holding booklets and called out, "Braids." Sofi grabbed a booklet and started looking at the different hairstyles as if they were the most interesting thing in the world. She needed to get away from this guy. He gave her the creeps. Sofi flipped through the small photo album with headshots of American tourists with thin braids that lay across their scalp, straight back, to the side, or in zigzag formations.

"Hey, T. Want to get cornrows?" she kidded. "We can post them on MySpace. It'll be hilarious."

Taylor scrunched up her nose in disgust. "That takes forever, and I don't think I have the head for it. But . . . it gives me a great idea." Sofi frowned. She'd wanted an excuse to stop talking to this guy. Josh was still there and following their conversation.

"So," Josh interrupted, getting close enough for her to notice his extra-long nose hairs. "Do you have a boyfriend?" His hairs were gross and waved like tree branches in a hurricane when he breathed. "I love your tan."

"It's not a tan," Sofi said, leaning as far away from him as the chair would allow. She noticed that both of her friends were relaxed and enjoying themselves. Sofi wanted to hang out and be cool, but not with this guy. "Olivia, don't you think we should get going soon?" She motioned with her head. "Ni-co-la is waiting for us."

Olivia leaned over. "Hello? Do you not see all these *papis chulos*?" She dismissed Sofi with a roll of her eyes. Olivia could be so self-centered at times. This was supposed to be *her* weekend. Sofi looked at Josh. He was a total Backstreet reject, with long sideburns and too much jewelry. Sofi checked her watch. It was past three. Nick would be at the beach house by now.

"We really should go now." Sofi got up.

"Yeah, I'm starving," Taylor said to Olivia.

"I know a great place for fish tacos," Josh volunteered.

"Thanks." Sofi patted his hand. "But my boyfriend, Nick, is supposed to be meeting up with us." Josh looked disappointed.

"Nick?" Chris asked. "You talking about Nick Hoffman?"

Sofi stared back in shock. She didn't know what to say. This was *no* fluke. She looked at Taylor. Had she told him? Did he know him? "No, not Nick Hoffman," Sofi laughed nervously. "Nick . . . Nick Roberts. That's my hubbie."

"Oh," Chris said, looking at Taylor. "I just thought since you guys were staying at Steve McCanne's place, I figured . . . Steve and I are old buddies from baseball camp." Sofi wanted to die.

"We should go." Olivia jumped in, saving Sofi. She turned to her new friend and made plans to meet him at Papas and Beer that night. When they were out of hearing distance Olivia grabbed Sofi by the arm. "Oh my God, Sofi. That was close."

Taylor couldn't stop laughing. "Talk about coincidences. I was going to tell you, but you were all into Josh."

"What? Señor Nose Hair? You must be joking. Did you see those things?" Sofi wiggled her fingers under her nose to demonstrate. "I was dying for a weed whacker." Taylor busted up laughing.

"You're totally exaggerating." Olivia smiled, glancing back in the guys' direction.

"Please, a little hair, okay, that's natural, but when you can braid that crap it's just plain nasty."

Olivia took a long breath, getting real serious. "Okay, but that's what you get when you tell people Nick's your boyfriend."

"Do you think I jinxed myself?" Sofi asked, covering her mouth with her hands. Olivia and Taylor both shrugged.

The rivalry between San Inocente's cheerleaders and the Mat Maids had begun three years ago. When Taylor, Olivia, and Sofi didn't make the cheerleading squad, they went off and formed their own crew. The wrestling team was so much hotter anyway, with way better bodies. Traditionally, Mat Maids were just like cheerleaders, with uniforms and pom-poms. They went to all the wrestling games (including away games) and were usually the only people in the stands besides the coach. The best part was that each year they chose a "secret guy pal" and bought him food, water, and special treats for the game. But the SI Mat Maids were unique. They didn't do flips, cheers, or wave pom-poms. SI Mat Maids were known for their virtuous fund-raising for charitable organizations—and as party girls. They were secretly known for their pranks, like TPing rival teams' vans, putting Vaseline under the door handles, and writing messages on their car windows with soap.

"No pushing, ladies," Sofi cried out from the middle of the living room. "I want my hair like that," a girl shouted over the chatter. "Hey, it's my turn," someone else complained. Sofi smiled and took in the scene. That evening, Taylor had gone back to the beach for phase one of Operation *Papi Chulo*. When she'd walked in with the four hair-braiders, all the girls at Steve's house had wanted to have their hair done. The hair-braiders sat quietly on the couch, combing out four cheerleaders' hair. Their small dark hands moved expertly, creating complicated webs of hair.

"You don't think it's too much?" Sarah Baker asked Olivia, who was sitting on the floor waiting her turn.

"Oh, no," Sofi jumped in. "The red beads look great. It's gangster."

"I can't believe you girls did this!" Sarah grabbed Olivia's hand. "It's just so kind of you."

Olivia shrugged, smiling cheerfully. "You know us Mat Maids. We just want to make everyone happy."

"I'm glad we can be friends again. This whole rivalry thing was getting bad. The pranks were not good for school morale. I see that you got over that thing." Sarah lowered her voice. "Mat Maids is such a better place for someone of your size." Olivia sucked in her teeth and forced a smile. Sofi cringed and wished there were something she could do to erase the hurt look from her friend's eyes.

"Hey," Sofi cut in. "How about you get All-American braids. You know, red, white, and blue beads. Wouldn't that be hot? I think I heard Nick saying something about kids at school not being patriotic enough." A sneaky grin danced on Olivia's lips.

"You're kidding, right?" Sarah started to laugh. "He never mentioned anything like that before."

Nick leaped down the stairs two at a time. Sofi's heart started to pound. A clean citrus aroma surrounded him. His hair was still wet and messy as if he'd just towel-dried it. He was wearing a striped polo, navy cargo shorts, and flip-flops. His big blue eyes twinkled with amused curiosity. He was so gorgeous. Sofi was dying to grab him by the collar and give him a big kiss. "I didn't know we were having a slumber party."

"Nick," Sarah squealed, trying to get up. The hair braider held her down by the shoulders. "What do you think?"

Nick looked around, confused. He coughed loudly and mumbled something while turning away.

Taylor pushed Sofi into Nick. Her breath caught. What was she supposed to say?

"Hey," was all she could come up with. Her chest ached as if her lungs were burning.

"Did you guys do this?" Nick looked around at the scene.

"You know us Mat Maids." She smirked. *You dork! Say something cool. Something interesting.*

"How long does it take?" he asked, eyeing Sarah sideways.

Sofi huffed, raising her arm in the air. Her hand narrowly missed his cute nose. "Hours. Two minimum." Nick smiled. He was so perfect in every way. Losing herself in the softness of his sweet lips, she thought about her checklist.

Nick was romantic. She'd seen him give Sarah a dozen tulips for her birthday last year. He dressed in only Abercrombie & Fitch. She knew it for a fact, because she'd followed him several times in the mall. And now he was actually smiling at her. Her dreams were on the brink of coming true!

"Sweet." He nodded. Steve McCanne rushed down the stairs with Anthony and three other guys from the wrestling team. He came up behind Nick and winked at Sofi. It made her cringe. Steve thought he was God's gift to all women because he had a six-pack stomach, had won a couple of skateboard competitions, and was in a magazine. Big whoop-de-do. Sofi thought that his new grunge-style unshaven-goatee look was so not becoming.

"Papas and Beer, ladies," Steve shouted with his arms in the air. Steve and Anthony were both wearing polo shirts and cargo pants. She wondered if they all shopped at the same store.

Nick took Sofi's hand, making her breath catch. Her body relaxed into mush; it was hard for her to follow his words. "I owe you," was all she heard before he took off with his boys out the front door.

"Ahhhhh!" Sofi cried, not caring who heard.

Taylor ran up to her. The excitement in her hazel eyes betrayed her low voice. "You did it. I'm so proud of you."

Olivia jumped in. "I want to know everything."

"It's all going according to plan."

"Hey, guys," Sarah Baker called out from her chair. One-fourth of her hair was plaited in thin, tight braids. "Aren't you going to get your hair done too?"

Olivia looked at Sofi, who turned to Taylor.

"Maybe next time," Olivia said, before taking off upstairs.

According to Steve McCanne, Rosarito was where the freaks came out at night. Each club blasted rump-shake songs, designed to transport everyone into euphoria. New Wave, rock, hip-hop, and rap played all at once, jogging the senses. It was a roller-coaster ride through the FM dial. The air was heavy with desire and the scent of sizzling meat. Gorgeous guys and scantily clad gals strutted down the boulevard while car traffic was at an utter standstill. Motorists hung out of car windows and flirted from behind the wheel.

Sofi pulled at the bottom of her denim miniskirt as she hurried to catch up with her friends down the block. Sofi's mother would die if she saw her dressed like this. Her boobs were practically falling out, and her skirt barely covered her butt. Olivia and Taylor took big, confident strides, stopping every now and then to flirt. Sofi followed behind them in the shadows. She felt like a ball of rattling nerves. All those years of fantasizing, dreaming, and wishing for Nick to notice, and now the moment had finally arrived. But instead of feeling elated, Sofi was even more afraid than ever. Olivia and Taylor motioned for her to hurry, but the black spiked heels that Taylor had lent her were pinching her toes. Why hadn't she worn the cute strappy sandals she'd bought last week?

Olivia and Taylor strutted toward the clubs. Sofi couldn't help but stare wide-eyed all around her. She'd never seen anything like this before and was secretly jealous of Olivia and Taylor's nonchalant attitude. Sure, they were more traveled and experienced than she was. But Sofi refused to let that get to her. Not tonight of all nights. She pushed back her shoulders and raised her head in the air. She was going to strut too, even if she twisted her ankle.

Olivia's boobs, like high beams, attracted all kinds of attention. Cute boys tripped over themselves to invite them for drinks. Sofi stiffened up; her cheeks burned. It was hard for her to accept the compliments, even though she knew she looked good in her turquoise halter top. Taylor kept up easily with Olivia's pace. She was wearing a gold shimmery top cut low in the back and hip-hugging jeans that showed off her new belly piercing. She'd even sprinkled gold shimmer powder on her cheekbones and freckled shoulders. Taylor looked positively divalicious.

"Now remember, ladies," Olivia said, adjusting her cleavage.

"What happens in Rosarito, stays in Rosarito," they all said in unison. It was cheesy, but they loved it. They walked down the block toward the Tahiti-inspired Papas and Beer nightclub on the beach. Sofi could hear her heart thumping loudly and swallowed.

"Whoa, check out that line." Taylor groaned, peering at the crowd that snaked around the block. Rowdy college students drank from plastic cups and joked with one another as they waited to be let in. Obvious out-of-towners in Baja T-shirts and palm-printed shorts huffed in annoyance at having to stand next to so many already-drunk people. Sofi noticed how they were all falling prey to the numerous vendors and children selling gum and plastic roses on the street. Who could resist a little girl in shabby clothes selling *chicle?*

"I don't want to wait in that," Taylor said, pressing her burgundy-colored lips together. Sofi stood in the middle of the street, mesmerized by the sight of all the children out past ten o'clock. Shouldn't they be home and in bed? Sofi couldn't help but wonder if she was the only one who noticed. Her friends seemed much more interested in getting into the club. A taxi honked loudly and Sofi jumped.

"Sof," Olivia called, waving her over to the VIP line. Their names were not on any of the lists. However, Olivia was able to get them past the line by flirting with the bouncer. Sofi reached for her friends' hands before racing down the dark staircase toward the music. This was her first time inside a club. Her brown eyes danced around the place, trying to savor everything, down to the very last detail. The sound of the thumping music bounced off her chest. A gigantic green papier-mâché lizard hung from the balcony above her. Olivia kicked off her heels and ran toward the center dance floor, which was covered with sand. She started to sway to the beat and pointed to the bright stars above — no roof.

"Hey, let's go up there," Taylor said, pointing to the bleachers on the second floor. From up above they were able to see the entire club. Sofi liked it better up here. She wanted to see what other girls did. Bobbing couples were grooving on top of raised platforms and wooden picnic tables.

Olivia stared out quietly over the rail. She had a huge frown on her face.

"What's the matter with you?" Sofi asked. Olivia gestured to a couple of drunken girls who were shrieking in annoying high-pitched voices and dancing like porn stars.

"Hoochies," she sneered.

"Oh, c'mon." Taylor poked Olivia's side. "They're no competition." Olivia was unusually quiet.

"I know," Sofi said. "We're *waaay* too sober. We need to get into the party mood. C'mon," she said, motioning for them to follow her. Alcohol, Sofi thought, was what they needed. Not that she was into drinking, but there was something about P&B that demanded it. Sofi noticed Olivia watching the broad-shouldered hunks staring at the dancing girls. They didn't even glance up as Olivia's boobs walked by.

"I could break that girl with two fingers," Olivia said from her stool, motioning to a waiflike little thing with stringy hair convulsing offbeat to the music as if she were choking on a chicken bone. She had a Papas and Beer bumper sticker covering her tiny breasts.

"Scandalous," Taylor gasped, covering her mouth and pointing. Ten guys were under a lifeguard platform taking pictures. The girls on top moved like they were auditioning for a bump-and-grind rap video and pretended not to care about the guys taking shots of the view up their skirts.

"I hope they're wearing underpants," Sofi said, trying to hide her shock.

"Probably not." Olivia huffed and turned around as if bored. The truth of the matter was that they were *waaay* out of their element. They'd entered some *Girls Gone Wild* alternate universe. Guys were begging for lap dances, to see some breasts, or look up their skirts. The ladies seemed more than happy to oblige.

Sofi and her friends watched the wild burlesque show from a tiki bar with grass skirts lining the counter and bamboo wall paneling. A Mexican woman with a ponytail and a P&B shirt was wiping the counter.

"*¿Qué te puedo ofrecer?*" the bartender asked, assuming Sofi spoke Spanish.

Sofi smiled nervously at Olivia and Taylor, silently begging them for help. They were in the same Spanish class. Sofi really wanted to order a glamorous drink, like a Cosmo or something. But she didn't know how to say *Cosmo* in Spanish. Why hadn't she paid more attention in Mr. Reyes's class? Sofi's parents bragged about her crappy Spanish verb conjugations as if it were a sign of their assimilation. Sofi had just stopped trying after a while, tired of people laughing and making fun of her. "*Cosmo-oh, por favor.*" Sometimes it was just better to sound like a *gringa*.

"*¿Cómo?*" The woman frowned, leaning forward.

"Cos-mo-oh?" Sofi repeated softly.

The bartender shook her head with an irritated look. "*¿Eres mejicana?*"

Sofi's heart started to beat loudly. "Well, yeah, I guess. I was born in Mexico, but—"

"And you no speak Spanish?" the woman asked in disbelief.

Sofi felt her cheeks burn. Why did everyone expect her to speak Spanish? What was the big deal anyway? "T," Sofi said, turning to her friend. "How do you say *Cosmo* in Spanish?" The bartender shook her head.

"Forget that," Olivia interrupted, pushing Sofi aside. "I need something stronger." She looked at the list of exotic specialty drinks scribbled above the bar. "I'll have an Orgasm."

Sofi started to laugh. "You pervert."

"What's that?" Taylor asked curiously.

"You don't know what an Orgasm is?" Olivia cried in disbelief.

"Oh, shut up!" Taylor snapped. "As if you do?" Olivia nodded with enthusiasm. "Just make sure she doesn't put any water in it." Taylor leaned over the counter to watch the bartender mix it. "You know about the water here."

"Don't worry 'bout that. It's got everything but water," the bartender joked. Sofi turned away, upset. Why was she treating Olivia like they were old pals, but glaring at Sofi for not speaking Spanish? It was so not fair.

Three Orgasms later, the girls were ready to party. So what if the place was crawling with hoochies? There were plenty of guys to go around. Sofi was feeling very warm and fuzzy and started swaying in her seat. She was about to get up to use the bathroom when Nick walked through the door.

"All right," Sofi said, making an effort to sit up tall on her stool. "He's here! I need a plan. How about if I just go up to him and start touching myself like this," she said. She started rubbing her hands up and down the sides of her body and grinding her hips in quick little circular motions, her tongue sticking out of her mouth as she licked her lips like a freaky snake. Taylor and Olivia doubled over laughing. "Come on, guys. I'm serious!"

"Why don't you just get a club and hit him over the head." Taylor started to giggle as she held on to the counter, trying not to fall off her stool.

"I think you should just attack him," Olivia slurred, combing her small fingers through her thick hair and eyeing a guy at the end of the bar. "That's what we came here for, right?"

Sofi shrugged her shoulders and turned away. "But I don't want some drunken night of passion." She pushed her long hair back. "What will I tell our kids? I want him to woo me, take me out, shower me with roses. . . ." Sofi stuck her finger into a glass, trying to catch the last few drops.

"Ride up on a white stallion." Taylor giggled, making a galloping gesture with her hands.

Olivia glanced around the club and then grabbed Sofi by the hand. "I got your stallion." She led Sofi through the mob of hot, sweating bodies to the other end of the dance floor, where a girl was riding a brightly lit mechanical bull. The red, blue, and yellow beams of light zigzagged across their faces. "Mount your noble steed, my darlin'. This is the twenty-first century. You need to sweep him off his feet."

"You think?" Sofi asked, getting excited. They watched a girl on the bull. Her hips gyrated in rhythm with the bull's motion. This was a great opportunity to show Nick that she was a total sex goddess. What a fabulous idea! Nick would see her on the bull and think that she was the hottest girl at the club. Then he'd be so smitten, he might just ask her then and there to be his girlfriend. "Where do I sign up?"

"Now, hold on tight," the operator warned as Sofi straddled the bull. Over the sea of onlookers, Sofi saw Nick. Olivia and Taylor went to grab him to make sure he didn't miss Sofi's big debut. A Black Eyed Peas song poured out of the mega-speakers, and the whole crowd screamed in delight. Sofi knew that this was her moment and shook her shoulders in rhythm to the music. Everything felt right.

The bull began to jerk back and forth. Sofi's skirt hiked up her thigh, exposing more than she meant to. Was her underwear showing? She wanted to pull her skirt down, but she had to hold on tight as the animal twirled around. Nick elbowed his way to the front of the crowd and waved at Sofi. Oh my God. *This is it*, she thought as she raised one arm in the air and tried to gyrate her hips as sexily as possible.

"Hi, Nick," she yelled. Then, all of a sudden, the bull jolted way too quickly and Sofi lost her grip. It took one instant for her to realize that something was very wrong. Her head was spinning and she saw flashes of light and fell forward, tumbling off the bull, out and onto the cushioned floor. The crowd cheered and Sofi wondered if maybe she'd accomplished her mission. But then her stomach wrenched violently, and before she could stop herself, she'd hurled her lobster lunch all over the mat.

"Ahhh, gross!" the crowd echoed.

Someone loomed over her, asking if she was all right. Sofi tried to respond, but her stomach did a backflip and she puked again. The audience cheered louder. Sofi leaned her head back on the firm, matted floor. Spittle hung from her lips and her hair was wet with vomit. Her mouth tasted raw and sour. The club and all the faces above her began to swirl. Taylor and Olivia carried her out to a waiting cab.

"Where's Nick?" Sofi asked, trying to calm her throbbing head.

"He's in the bathroom," Taylor said with a hint of a smile playing around her lips, "cleaning the vomit off his shirt."

"You can't stay there all freakin' day," Olivia shouted, pulling down the thick brown comforter.

Sofi tugged the comforter back over her head. "Just watch me!" she called from under the covers, curling herself into a tight ball. She squeezed her eyes shut, wishing that the nightmarish events of Saturday night would disappear.

"Like hell we will," Taylor said, tag-teaming with Olivia and tearing the covers away from Sofi.

Sofi jumped up in the same wrinkled clothes that she'd passed out in. Her throat tasted vinegary. She knew she smelled gross. "What the hell's wrong with you two?" She stomped over to the blanket on the floor, pulled it over her shoulders, and got back in bed. Sofi was not going to leave the room until it was time to go home. Her weekend was ruined.

"You can hide from Nick all you want," Olivia said, checking herself out in the full-length mirror. She applied a layer of clear lip gloss with her index finger and then retied the black sarong around her full hips. Sofi sat straight up, squinting. Bright light burst in through the open curtains. Locks of her hair were tangled like strands of seaweed on the shore. A stiff piece was stuck to her forehead.

"I'm not hiding," Sofi finally said in a small voice.

Taylor looked up from the opposite bed. She was giving her legs a quick run-over with her pink razor. Her hair was pulled back into a ponytail. "I don't get what the big deal is. The boy *did* stop by to check in on you."

"He did?" Sofi perked up. There was still hope. "Where is he? What should I do?"

"The first thing you should do is wash that hair," Olivia said, making a face. She jumped onto Sofi's bed. "And then go check out Sarah's new do. She looks like a Conehead. It's hilarious. Who would have known that under all that fluff there was an alien screaming to come out?"

Sofi sat up, grinning from ear to ear. "Yes!"

Taylor opened the hatchback to take out her sun umbrella. They'd parked on Boulevard Benito Juarez and paid a kid with helmet hair five bucks to watch the car.

"You're not planning to bring that, are you?" Olivia asked, putting on her chunky glasses.

"Of course I am. What, are you crazy? I don't want to get melanoma. We could've stayed at Steve's house, but you"—she pointed at Olivia—"have issues with your new best friend."

"Me?" Olivia said innocently. "I think she blames you for that rash she got."

Taylor shrugged. "Buyer beware."

Sofi laughed. The three of them were kind of hiding from Sarah Baker. Sarah was determined to make them get their hair braided too and had practically forced the girl who braided her hair to stay all night.

"I'm sure they'll have umbrellas," Sofi said, getting out.

Olivia swung her Betty Boop tote bag over her shoulder. "For the right price, I'm sure we can find some cute cabana boys who'll fan us with big palm leaves if we want."

"Yeah, T, it's not like we landed on the cold side of the moon." Sofi adjusted the straw cowboy hat she'd borrowed from Olivia.

"Oh, fine." Taylor shrugged, shoving the umbrella back in and closing the trunk. "Happy?"

Sofi glanced around. For some strange reason, she felt awkward in her short shorts and white sandals. Indecent. The locals, walking around them, were in full dress, long slacks and shirts, as if oblivious to the beach just a few feet away. Four teenage boys with Ricky Martin–style spiked hair stared as they walked past. The girls walking behind them gave her cold glares. Sofi wondered if there was an icky green booger hanging from her nose.

"You guys notice how people stare around here?" Sofi whispered. She glanced down at her black one-piece suit.

"No, I didn't, but now that you mention it," Olivia said, glancing around, "you're right."

"I wonder what they're thinking," Taylor said, adjusting the straps on her white lacy shirt, which fell down her shoulders.

"The girls are probably just checking out our clothes and the guys . . ." Olivia smiled and pointed at her breasts.

"Hey," Sofi cried, "how come everything has to be about your boobs? We small-breasted women get no respect. Maybe they're checking out that hairy mole on your back calf." Olivia glared at her. "Or Taylor's—"

"Long slender legs," Taylor finished.

"Yeah, long slender legs." Sofi nodded. "Is your mind always in the gutter?"

"Always!"

On the way to the beach they passed some puke crusted in the doorway of a club. Sofi felt nauseated and cupped her nose and mouth with her hand. "I'm never going to drink again."

It was past noon and the sun was high overhead. Sweating workers ran back and forth in organized chaos. Tattoo artists and souvenir vendors wove through the tables, looking for customers. Olivia bought a pink sarong to match her bikini. Taylor chose a couple of friendship bracelets for her younger sisters and a pair of red beaded earrings for her mom. Sofi just looked at the merchandise. She couldn't bring back any evidence of her trip. The air was cool and crisp, blowing the foul horse stench away. Seagulls walked in circles, scavenging through the leftover trash.

"This has to be the dirtiest beach I've ever been to." Taylor scrunched up her pierced nose, picking up an instant-camera wrapper that was tossed two feet away from an empty oil drum. She picked up a couple of empty cigarette boxes and a plastic cup and tossed them in the trash. "Don't these people care about where they live?" Olivia and Sofi shrugged. Silently, they made their way down the beach away from the clubs and found several white lounge chairs under a beautiful white canvas umbrella.

"Oh, yes." Sofi kicked off her flip-flops, pulled down her shorts, and stretched out in the black one-piece she'd bought last year to go swimming in at the gym. She wasn't in the mood to look cute and pulled her hair out of its ponytail to scratch her scalp. She'd messed her hair into a fuzzy ball. It felt good. She covered her face with her green hand towel. "Maybe after a quick nap I'll feel better."

"What you need is another beer," Olivia recommended as she raised her arms up to stretch and yawned noisily.

"Don't try to corrupt her," Taylor scolded in a joking manner.

"More beer? You crazy." Sofi peeked out over her towel. Taylor was covering herself in layers of white extra-strength sunblock and Olivia was gazing out at the crashing waves. Except for a few families walking around and the vendors, the beach was relatively empty. "All I want to do is take off my head and bury it in the sand."

"I think you should take it easy tonight," Taylor warned, adjusting her shades. "You don't want to get out of control like those other girls from last night."

"Oh, c'mon," Olivia interrupted, "you only live once. Besides, no one is going to find out." Taylor huffed in annoyance. Sofi thought of her trusting parents waiting for her at home. "Okay," Olivia said, turning to Sofi. "So what's your plan for today?"

"Plan?" Sofi asked. "There's no plan. All I want to do is shrivel up and die in some unmarked grave."

"Please." Olivia rolled over onto her stomach. She was wearing a bright pink string bikini with the Playboy bunny logo stamped all over. It looked very glamorous with the large white bug-eyed shades she'd bought last week at the mall. "Last night was no big deal."

"Yeah, right." Sofi closed her eyes, trying to relax.

"We've all gotten drunk and made asses of ourselves at one point or another. It's a rite of passage."

"Speak for yourself," Taylor interrupted.

Olivia turned over and opened last week's *People* magazine. She sneered at the pencil-thin, airbrushed celebrities. "What you need to do is just go for him. Heck, sneak into his bed. Something. You got to put it out there. Stop waiting for him to come to you. Chivalry is dead. You want him, you take him. That's what I would do." Olivia stopped and Sofi looked up. She was watching someone coming toward them. "Who's thirsty?"

A short husky guy with short messy hair, white khakis, and a faded blue cotton shirt walked over to them. He had Sofi's complexion, thin lips, and a slightly crooked nose, like it had been broken years ago and never set straight. ROSARITO BEACH HOTEL was stitched in yellow cursive over his breast pocket. His loose shirt didn't hide the rolls around his waist.

"Really, darling," Olivia said, waving her magazine at Sofi. "I don't understand why you get your panties in a bunch over Nick, when there are so many Mexican flavors to choose from." The guy stood over them and smirked behind dark shades. He looked like a waiter. "*¿Hola?*" Olivia said, waving her fingertips. She lowered her sunglasses to admire him better. Sofi wondered what her friend was up to. The boy was so not a *papi chulo*. Maybe she was trying to get a free drink?

"Finally." Sofi huffed in annoyance. "I was starting to wonder if there was any decent service around here. We need a bucket of beer? And quick, 'cause my head is banging." The guy continued to stand there with a crooked smile on his face. Sofi looked from Olivia to Taylor, confused. "Did he not hear me?" She raised her voice. "*Cer-ve-za, por fa-vor.*"

"Excuse me," the guy interrupted in crisp, unaccented English, "but are you ladies staying at the hotel?"

"Well, of course we are," Sofi lied. "Do you think we'd be wasting your time if we weren't?"

The guy considered the three girls for a moment. "Well, may I ask to see your hotel wristbands?"

Sofi stood up. "We left them in the hotel room," she stammered, looking to her friends for help.

The guy smiled a big toothy grin. "Then I'm going to have to ask you to leave, because we don't have wristbands here and you are obviously lying." Sofi heard her friends snicker behind her.

"Okay, fine. You caught us, but why can't we stay here? There's no one else using the chairs." Sofi turned to the right and then the left; this part of the beach was deserted.

"These chairs," the guy said, sounding impatient, "belong to the people who pay to stay at this hotel. This whole area is off-limits to the public." He waved his arms in the air as if he owned the place.

"Off-limits?"

Olivia slithered in between. "C'mon, *amigo*, we're just trying to have a good time in your country," she said in a sexy drawl. "We could pay you?"

The guy sneered as if disgusted. "You have to go."

"Why?" Sofi asked. This was ridiculous. He couldn't kick them off the beach. Weren't beaches open to the public?

"Because I said so," he replied. The edges of his lips curved; he was clearly enjoying his power in the moment.

"Let's go," Taylor said, tugging at Sofi's hand. But Sofi wasn't having it. She didn't like to be bullied and wasn't about to let this mere waiter treat them rudely. Sofi thought of her mom's manager and the mean lady from the store.

"And what if we don't?" She crossed her arms defiantly.

"Then I'll have to get security to kick you out." He reached for the walkie-talkie at his waist.

Olivia grabbed Sofi's wrist. "We should go, Sof." But Sofi shook herself free. He couldn't talk to them like this. They were Americans!

"Well, we don't want to stay at your stupid beach anyway," she said, and turned to leave when she got a better idea. Sofi walked right back up to the cabana boy. "Keep your stupid chair!" She kicked it at him. Olivia and Taylor ran back to fetch Sofi and pulled her away before the guy could call the cops.

That afternoon the house was quiet. Lauren and Emily were on their way to a spa for facials, when Olivia, Sofi, and Taylor returned from shopping. They had to keep their voices down because a bunch of guys were sleeping in. Sofi learned from Lauren that Nick, Steve, and Anthony had gone back to the sand dunes. Sarah and a couple of cheerleaders had tagged along uninvited. Sofi would have been crushed, if it weren't for the Post-it Nick left on her door. It now itched in her palm. She reread the note excitedly, engraving every detail of his messy handwriting into her brain.

Hope you feel better.
See you tonight at P&B.

Nick

"Let's go," Sofi called. Olivia came running down the stairs, clutching her gold mesh evening purse to her chest with one hand and blowing on her freshly painted red nails.

"How do I look?" she asked, modeling her gold-colored chiffon camisole and denim skirt. She'd flat-ironed her wavy hair and swept her long bangs to the side, making her look very Hollywood glam.

"Fabulous, darlin'," Sofi said, tossing her loose curls to the side.

"It's not too much?" She motioned to the iced Playboy bunny necklace hanging around her neck.

"On you? Never," Sofi teased. "Let's go, Taylor!"

"Coming," Taylor called out from upstairs. Sofi checked her face again and reapplied a layer of lipstick. Her stomach felt queasy. She prayed that nothing embarrassing would happen tonight and ruin her chances with Nick.

"What did you do to your gym shirt?" Olivia gasped when Taylor emerged at the top of the staircase. Taylor had complained about not having anything to wear, even though she had a duffel bag full of cute tops. So she'd cut up her PE shirt so that it fell off her shoulders, and she'd cut the sides apart and tied them back together with tiny knots. Freckled skin peeked out from between the shredded material.

"Like it?" She twirled around, her ruffled skirt rising.

"Fabulous," Sofi said, wishing that she'd done the same thing. It looked really good in a trailer-park-trashy kind of way. But her mother would have killed her if she'd done that to one of her shirts.

Sofi took a deep breath. "Operation *Papi Chulo*, Take Two. Here we come!" *This is it*, she told herself as they walked out into the night. This was the night all her dreams would come true.

"He's not here," Sofi shouted above the thumping rap song. She grabbed Olivia's hand and pulled her away from the guy she was dancing with—a tall skinny guy with a bad Beatles haircut.

"Relaaax," Olivia said, fixing her skirt. The air was hot and sticky.

Steam rose off the dancing bodies and drifted up into the starlit sky. The end of the weekend seemed to be on everyone's mind.

"I've circled the place four times," Sofi said frantically. "This is our last night here and it's already midnight."

Olivia huffed loudly. The boy glared at Sofi, impatiently waiting for her to finish. "Well . . ." Olivia tried to come up with something inspirational to say. "Don't lose hope?" It sounded lame, but Olivia was never one for deep sentimental thoughts.

Sofi took the hint. She walked around looking for Taylor, who would know what to say. Sofi made the rounds searching for a blonde in a dark blue PE shirt. Blinding lights and hazy smoke swallowed up her steps. When she finally spotted Taylor, she couldn't believe her eyes. Taylor was standing on top of the bar, her arms raised up over her head, dancing her ass off. Someone had stuck a P&B bumper sticker across the back of her skirt. A crew of guys watched from below, cheering. Sofi ran over to rescue her friend, but when Sofi tried to help her down, Taylor waved her hand away. She had a big, alcohol-infused grin on her face. She motioned for Sofi to come on up. Sofi shook her head and dragged her lonesome self to the bar.

This was just great, Sofi thought, feeling way too sober. The same female bartender greeted her with a bored nod. Sofi prepared herself for a long night of drowning her sorrows. "What can I get you?" the bartender asked. Sofi frowned. What a failure of a weekend. Yesterday, she'd made a total fool of herself in front of Nick and now he was nowhere to be found. "A shot of tequila," Sofi said. Why was falling in love so difficult?

Just as she was about to order another shot, loud male voices pierced through the Sean Paul jam. Sofi looked up to see Nick, Steve, and a couple other guys acting obnoxiously loud and drunk. Security had them cornered near the back entrance. By the time Sofi reached them, Olivia was already there trying to calm Steve down. Sarah was nowhere in sight. Sofi looked for Taylor, but she was busy giving a lap dance to some ugly-looking dude. The beefy security guard finally let the guys in after a stiff warning not to cause any trouble inside the club.

"What the hell happened?" she asked when they sat down at a table on the edge of the dance floor.

"Goddamn Mexican cops!" Nick cursed, grabbing Olivia's Corona and chugging it.

"Those pigs put a gun to my head," Steve cried, getting up from his seat and sitting back down. "It was straight out of some movie."

"Whoa, rewind," Olivia said, leaning over the table.

"Come on, Steve." Sofi patted his hand. "Take a deep breath and start at the beginning." He took Olivia's beer from Nick, finished it, and began:

"We were on our way back from the sand dunes when we got pulled over. This cop said I was speeding when I totally wasn't. My dad warned me about that. Anyway, then he said that there was some report on stolen bikes and he wanted to see my registration. Which is stupid, 'cause no one's got papers for motorbikes!"

Olivia shook her head in confusion. "Why didn't you just give the guy a bribe?"

"Huh?" Nick looked ill. He was having a hard time following the conversation. Sofi wondered if he was going to hurl.

"C'mon, guys, don't be so naïve. They pay their cops crap over here; that's why there's so much corruption." Olivia knew what she was talking about. Before moving to San Inocente, her dad had been stationed in Germany and Guam. Olivia knew a thing or two about how things worked in foreign countries.

"Well, damn," Steve finally said. "I'd heard about that, but . . . Damn." He shook his head.

"Did they take the bikes?" Sofi asked.

"Naw." Steve slouched back in his chair, looking totally deflated. Sofi couldn't help but feel sorry for him. Yeah, he could be a punk, but no one deserved to be treated so cruelly, not even him.

Olivia grabbed his hand. "C'mon, Steve-o, let me buy you a drink."

She gave Sofi a wink when she passed. Sofi was finally alone with Nick. A hot jam with East Indian backbeats came on. Nick stared at her from across the table. She felt her anxiety crawling up her legs, then tightening her chest. Sure, Nick was a little tipsy, but weren't people more honest and in touch with their true feelings while inebriated? Sofi took a deep breath. It was now or never.

"Wanna dance?"

"Why, Sofi," Nick said, smiling sleepily. "I thought you'd never ask." He followed her to the dance floor. At first Sofi just stood there, frozen. *Breathe*, she screamed in her head. *Be cool. Don't mess this up!* She tried to sway with the rhythm, but her body felt stiff. Nick studied her curiously. The hairs on the back of her neck stood up. Nick placed his hands on her hips and pulled her close to him. They moved as one. Nick smelled like stale beer. Sofi closed her eyes and tried to lose herself in the moment. *This is it*, she thought. Their first dance would lead to their first kiss and then dating, the prom, marriage, and happily-ever-after. But somehow, being surrounded by a bunch of topless dancers and horny couples chugging beers was not very romantic. She knew what she had to do.

With the jolt of tequila still coursing through her veins, she took Nick by the hand and led him out of the club and onto the beach. The colored lights emanating from the club and the fireworks bursting above created a quasi-romantic backdrop. She shook her sandals off and felt the familiar cold tickle of sand between her toes.

She held her breath and looked intently at Nick. He was her dream guy. Tall, smart, incredibly gorgeous, everything she'd ever wanted. She smiled, feeling a little light-headed. She'd dreamed of this moment countless times in her bedroom, on the way to school, and during study hall. But this time, it wasn't a dream.

Sofi closed her eyes, leaned in, and kissed him softly on the mouth. Nick's lips were nothing like the pillow she practiced on at home.

As their lips parted, her heart fluttered. She'd never kissed a boy she liked before.

"You know, Nick, I have a confession to make." He stood there and stared into her eyes. *Wow!* Sofi thought. *I can't believe how cool he is.* "I've really liked you for a long time."

Nick moaned, pulling her toward him, covering her mouth with his and sucking on her lower and upper lips. He wrapped his arms around her waist and held her close. Sofi flinched at the intensity. His mouth urgently sought out her tongue. She tried to calm her panicking mind by telling herself that this was love. It was hot, fiery, and out of control. She breathed deeply, trying to relax. "Damn, Sofi baby. Someone's gotta write a warning label on you, 'cause you're the bomb," he said between moist kisses up and down her neck.

Yes, she thought, as she arched her back, offering him, her soul mate, more skin to kiss. Nick was breathing very fast through his nose. His hands explored the curves of her body. "You're so hot, baby, your ass is on fire."

"Huh?"

"*Latina caliente*," he whispered in her ear. Those two words broke the spell like a searing hot brand to her brain. Sofi stared at him in shock. "You know you got the hottest ass in school." Nick laughed out loud to himself. "I told Steve I'd tap dat hot Latin ass by Monday."

Sofi rubbed her eyes, not understanding. Was this some torrid fantasy gone wrong? Nick licked his lips and began to gyrate to a Lil John song playing in the club. He was oblivious to her. Had he really said that to Steve? Did he see her as just hot Latin ass? It was too horrid to conceive of. Was this Nick's true jerk-off self radiating in the glow of the crescent moon above? Sofi cried, "No!" and covered her mouth in horror.

Nick smirked wickedly, keeping his fingers clasped behind her waist. "Don't worry, baby, I know what you want." Sofi's eyes began to water. She didn't want this. "And you know I got it. I'm XL."

"Huh?"

Nick leaned close to her ear and said in a breathless voice, "I'm extra-large."

"What?" Sofi cried, pushing him away.

"What's the matter, baby?" Nick held his arms out to her. Sofi's temples started to pound as her chest constricted. Her head told her to run while her heart ached to stay. Nick took a step toward her. She pulled back. "This is what you came out here for, isn't it?"

"Get away from me," she whispered. Tears streamed down her cheeks.

"Sofi, baby, let me just show you. . . ."

"Get the hell away from me!" She ran back into the club barefoot.

"There you are," Olivia shouted over the thumping gangster rhythm. Sofi was sitting in a dark corner, leaning against the wall with her head down and her knees pulled up. "What are you doing out here all by yourself?"

Sofi shuddered. She didn't want to talk to anyone. Didn't want to explain about Nick. She just wanted to disappear.

"Sofi, what's wrong? Talk to me. You're freaking me out." Olivia kneeled down and put her hand on Sofi's head. Sofi jerked away.

"I'm such a fool," she murmured, raising her head. There were people laughing and dancing all around her, but to Sofi they were a million miles away. Nothing existed but the curdled pain pouring from her heart and flowing out through her tears. She wiped her running nose with the back of her hand. "I can't believe what just happened."

Olivia sat next to her on the floor. "What?"

Sofi looked out at the dance floor, replaying the scene in her mind. "It was awful. Nick, he's . . . he's turned into a jerk-off pig like Steve." Olivia was silent. "All he cared about was getting into my panties. I thought that he was different. Special. All the signs pointed to him being the one. You saw the couples' astrological chart I bought." Olivia nodded. "It was horrible, Olivia," Sofi turned to her. "He said all this crap about me being a *Latina caliente* and how he was XL. It made me feel like some desperate, horny hoochie mama looking for a quickie." She became real quiet. "He didn't see me. Doesn't know anything about me. It's just so wrong."

"Nick's an ass," Olivia blurted out, unable to stay quiet a moment longer.

"But he's not supposed to be," Sofi cried into her forearms.

Olivia took a deep breath. "You need to forget him."

"How am I supposed to forget my soul mate? Tell me that, huh? I've spent my entire life preparing for this moment and now it's all gone. Done. Finito. Over."

"Sofi, you're too good for him. You deserve better."

Better! Red-hot anger welled up in her stomach. "What do you know? You don't know anything about love." Olivia jerked back as if slapped. "Nick is great. Everyone likes him. Maybe he's just too drunk? Or afraid of getting hurt? Maybe he needs more time?"

"Maybe he's just a jerk-off!"

Sofi's eyes filled with fresh tears. She hated Olivia's words. They were mean and heartless. They stung.

"If he's so great and noble, how come he's making out with Sarah Baker at the bar right at this very moment?"

"What?" Sofi straightened up and followed Olivia's finger with her gaze. There was Nick, sitting on a bar stool and making out with Sarah Baker. This was too cruel. "I want to go," Sofi said.

Olivia sighed. "Yeah, I know. This club sucks anyway."

"No, I mean I want to go home. My home. San Inocente, California," Sofi said, getting up.

"Girl, you're crazy. It's like two in the morning."

"I don't care. I want to go. Where's T?"

Olivia yawned loudly and scratched her head. "I think she's giving some dude a lap dance upstairs."

By 6 a.m. Monday morning, Sofi was ready to go. Tossing in bed for hours, dissecting the scene in her mind, hadn't helped. She reviewed everything she knew about Nick for clues, warning signs, anything that would help this make sense. No matter how she looked at it, it didn't add up. Nick was supposed to be a nice guy. Everyone liked him. But he hadn't been nice to her. She'd revealed her deepest, most private feelings to him. Nick had treated her like a piece of meat and then gone back to Sarah. They were probably upstairs getting it on right now! Sofi felt empty inside. It was as if someone had cut her open and taken out her heart.

"Oh no!" Taylor cried from the bathroom. Sofi and Olivia jumped out of bed and rushed into the blue-tiled bathroom. Taylor stood in front of the sink, wearing a white tank top and boxers. Fat tears poured down her red cheeks. She was scrubbing roughly at the huge purple hickeys covering her neck like a dalmatian's spots. "This is horrible. The prom is Friday. What am I supposed to do? My mother's going to kill me. That animal."

"You weren't complaining while you were giving him that lap dance."

Taylor turned, horror stricken. "I did not!"

Olivia smiled and grabbed the digital camera from her purse on the dresser. "Ha!" She scrolled back to a photograph of Taylor smiling gleefully next to a guy with gold-capped teeth, horrible acne, and blond cornrows.

"Give me that." Taylor reached out for the camera.

"Don't remember that, do you?" Olivia ran from her and jumped on the bed.

Taylor paced the floor, trying to remember the events from the night before. "I was drunk, okay. Besides, he said he was a rapper."

"Yeah, right. MC Proactiv!" Olivia howled, sticking out her tongue.

The shades were down in the living room. Taylor had gone out to get gas and a couple of last-minute gifts. Sofi had never seen Taylor so embarrassed. When Taylor demanded they leave, Sofi was only too eager to start packing. All she wanted was to slip out without bumping into anyone, especially Nick. This was not how she had imagined her weekend would end.

She tiptoed through the living room. Olivia's shallow breaths were right behind her. She huffed loudly, dragging her heavy bags and souvenirs behind her. Sofi turned and offered to hold the rolled-up *Scarface* poster Olivia bought the day before. She glanced down at the sleeping bodies lying comatose on the living-room floor. *What now?* she wondered. How could she begin to imagine a life without Nick? The man of her dreams. She still loved him. It was painful to imagine them holding hands with the beautiful California sun dipping into the sea in front of them. It was painful to remember the words he'd spoken or him kissing Sarah at the bar. Sofi was having trouble separating her fantasies from reality. It was all so very painful.

Taylor was outside wearing a gray turtleneck with shorts, cuddling a baby Chihuahua in her arms. Sofi sighed. Cute, furry animals were Taylor's weakness. She was always rescuing hurt birds or adopting stray cats. Sofi hated dogs—even the cute, cuddly type. She'd been bitten as a child and still had the scar to prove it. Olivia was about to shriek when Taylor raised a finger to her thin lips and whispered, "She's sleeping. Isn't she adorable? I think I'll call her Chichi."

"You're not planning to bring her across," Sofi said, staying back a good five feet. She gave Taylor an unsure look.

Taylor put Chichi down and covered her with a thin blanket. "The guy told me not to worry. It's done all the time." Taylor smiled reassuringly. "He gave her a sleeping tonic. She shouldn't wake up for a couple of hours. C'mon, Sofi. Don't freak out. I swear she won't bother you."

"I don't get why we have to take off so early. We should at least stay for the barbecue," Olivia complained as she loaded her bags. She wanted to stay and play with the boys.

Sofi put one arm around her. "C'mon, Olivia, it's not just me. T wants to go too."

Taylor helped Sofi load her UCLA duffel. "Yeah, Livy," she said. "We have to beat the traffic. Remember, your dad thinks you're sleeping at my house."

* * * *

Sofi watched as the Rosarito skyline faded away and slowly changed into barren land and housing developments. She rested her head against the window. All she could think about was Nick. This weekend was supposed to be the beginning of something truly amazing between them. After this weekend she was supposed to have one of those fierce, passionate, exciting lives she'd read about in romance novels. A life of excitement and true love, and all of her dreams coming true. Life was so not fair, she thought as the 4Runner headed north toward the United States of America.

"I am so over Mexico."

Traffic at the border was at a definite standstill. It seemed like everyone in Mexico was trying to get out. Smog greeted them like a dingy, unwelcome guest as they approached TJ. Taylor's thigh bounced nervously. She kept checking the rearview mirror, making sure the dog was still asleep. Indigenous women came by with groups of little children, weaving between the cars. The children were juggling balls or begging for change. Men in floppy straw hats came by selling hammocks, Powerpuff Girl shoe racks, T-shirts, and Popsicles. It was hot and the air was thick and sticky. U.S. border agents in dark blue uniforms patrolled between cars with their fierce-looking Labradors sniffing for drugs.

After what seemed like forever, the girls finally reached the border booth. A lean white guy with a military-style buzz cut and dark shades asked them curtly where they were born.

"I was born here, in Tijuana, but I live in San Inocente." Sofi smiled nervously while handing him her green card.

"What were you doing in Mexico?"

"Having a good time," Olivia said, leaning over Taylor.

"What are you bringing back?"

"Nothing much," Taylor stammered, "just some gifts." The guy seemed satisfied, but he held on to Sofi's identification as he slowly traveled around the 4Runner.

"What do you think he's looking for?" Taylor asked between clenched teeth.

"Probably drugs," Sofi answered. What else was there? The officer stopped at the back. He shaded his eyes to see through the darkened glass into the hatchback. Taylor let out a barely audible yelp.

"Miss," he said, motioning for Taylor to come out. "Is this your car?"

"Yes," Taylor said, her face turning ghost white.

"Would you mind opening the back?" That's when they knew they were busted. Even Olivia's breasts could not get them out of this mess. The immigration officer discovered Chichi and sent them over to secondary inspection as though they were a gang of criminals.

Secondary inspection was no joke. A large woman with unruly eyebrows and a hairy mole frisked them, and her slobbery dog sniffed all over their stuff. Cars passed slowly, watching the scene as if it were an episode of *Cops*. Taylor and Olivia looked scared. What were they going to do now? They were sent over to Officer Cohn, a tall, nasally guy with threadlike lips that disappeared into his mouth when he spoke.

"Now, ladies," he said in a serious and utterly terrifying tone, "you know that the illegal trafficking of animals into the United States is a very serious offense punishable by possible prison time."

The girls sat on the opposite side of the room on heavy-duty black vinyl chairs. Officer Cohn shuffled through some papers on his sturdy, chrome-legged black desk. An old computer hummed noisily next to him. Sofi pressed her lips together to keep from crying. She couldn't believe this was really happening. Her stomach was turning somersaults. She looked to the right at a red oak bulletin board. Tacked up to it was a flyer advertising a government-sponsored barbecue, a calendar with a picture of the Grand Canyon gorge, and several office memos. Sofi tried to force herself to take deep breaths. There was no way her parents would understand this. They would definitely never let her live in the dorms now. Heck, she could kiss UCLA good-bye. Olivia's muffled tears distracted Sofi from her thoughts. Olivia feared her dad more than prison. Taylor reached out and squeezed both their hands. Her slender palms were cold and clammy.

"You two are minors," Officer Cohn said in a gruff voice, pointing at Olivia and Sofi. He was holding Taylor and Olivia's ID in one hand and Sofi's green card (which was actually pinkish white, not green) in the other. She had to turn over her card to prove her lawful status. As a resident, Sofi could go to war, work, and live in the United States. She just couldn't vote. It was so embarrassing, because she didn't like to admit that she wasn't really an American. But this was not the time to worry about what her friends would think. "It's illegal for you to be in Mexico without an adult." *Oops*, Sofi thought. They hadn't actually known that. There were no signs indicating that at the border crossing, nor had Steve mentioned that tiny little detail.

A petite female officer with an oversized CIP cap walked into the room. She handed Cohn a computer printout. *We're dead*, Sofi thought. They would call their parents, impound the car, fine them to hell, and possibly ship them off to juvie until they were old enough for—

"Miss Sofia Mendoza." Officer Cohn's voice startled her. He paused a moment to finish reading the paper.

"Yes," Sofi answered in an unfamiliar squeaky voice. Her heart was pounding loudly in her chest. She started to feel faint. Was she having a heart attack?

"How old are you *really*?"

"Seventeen, sir."

Officer Cohn gave her an eerie look. He seemed to be trying to figure something out and reread the paper in his hand.

"And your social security number is . . ."

Sofi recited it.

"According to the number you gave, my computer tells me you're supposed to be four. Do you know why this might be?"

Sofi shook her head, not understanding. This made no sense. There was a pain in her chest, like indigestion but worse. She looked at her friends, who stared back wide-eyed.

"This card is obviously a fake. It's a federal crime to use false papers. Not to mention identity theft to use someone else's number." He waved the card in her face like a blade. "I want to know where you got it. You illegals think you can just fool anyone with any number."

"What?" Sofi cried in shock. This was a mistake. Sofi knew that she was not officially a citizen—not yet, at least. Her dad explained it to her once, about all the paperwork and lawyers' fees, and that they had to prove that they'd been here a number of years before they could even apply. With the new immigration laws, they had to have a U.S. citizen, like a relative or a boss, sponsor them. Sofi's parents were trying to get their employers to sponsor them, but it was a long process with no guarantees. She had lived in San Inocente most of her life. She was a Mat Maid, for God's sake. She couldn't be illegal!

"I don't know what you girls think you're trying to pull." Officer Cohn waved his finger at Taylor and Olivia.

This is madness, Sofi thought wildly. She wanted to defend herself. Get his badge number. Report him to his supervisor. This was unconstitutional, a violation of her civil rights! Illegal? Who was he to call her illegal? But her words came out all jumbled. The officer gave her an annoyed look.

Sofi took a deep breath. "You must be mistaken. I've been living in San Inocente for fourteen years. I am a lawful resident."

"Do you have any paperwork to prove this? A Mexican passport? Maybe an advance parole form that gives you permission to leave the United States? Visa? Anything?"

Sofi stared at him in horror.

"Is this where you live? Maybe your parents can straighten this out. That's if they're *really* legal residents as you claim?" Sofi's breath caught.

"Where did you get this card?"

"I didn't."

"Who did?"

"I don't know. I don't know. My dad . . ." Sofi held her tongue. If her dad had broken the law, she didn't want him to get in trouble. He didn't even know she was here. The guy waited for her to continue. No one breathed. The sound of the AC dominated the room. After a minute, the officer shook his head. Sofi couldn't tell if he was deeply saddened by what he was about to say or tired of having to break things down to a total idiot.

"Your friends are free to return to the United States, but you are not. Unless you can bring me some proper identification or forms, you'll have to return to Mexico."

Sofi shook her head in disbelief.

Officer Cohn exhaled deeply. "Well, I don't have all day for this. If what you're saying is true and you are a legal resident, then call your parents and get them to come down and straighten everything out."

"No!" Olivia said, jumping out of her chair. "We won't leave her behind."

For a brief moment the officer's eyes showed genuine concern, but the harsh words coming out of his mouth did not. "You girls need to be happy that I'm letting you off with just a warning. Contraband is a very serious offense. If I ever see any of you here again, I'm writing you up without a second thought."

That shut them all up. Sofi couldn't believe it. This was *not* happening! Panic seized her heart like a hostage. She took several shallow breaths to stop her hands from shaking uncontrollably. This had to be a mistake. Her entire life flashed before her eyes: playing at the beach as a child, sitting at her desk in grade school, cheering for Nick from the sidelines. *Was her entire life a lie?* She turned to her friends. Olivia muffled her sobs with her closed fist. Taylor stared blankly at Sofi. What was she supposed to do?

Taylor put her hands on Sofi's shoulders and said in a steady voice, "You know that this is a mistake." Olivia nodded, her face flushed from crying. It felt like they were a million miles away from the icy cold room.

Sofi focused on Taylor's eyes as if her life depended on it. "Don't worry. Your parents will know what to do," Taylor said steadily. Sofi flinched. Her parents were going to kill her. She sighed. It was out of her control. There was nothing she could do. Sofi nodded. "We'll go right over and explain everything."

"Okay." Sofi sniffed, trying to sound confident.

"You can't be serious!" Olivia exploded, throwing her arms into the air. "We're not leaving her!"

Officer Cohn was watching from his desk. He grabbed something from inside his desk and approached Sofi. "You got anyone to stay with?" he asked.

Sofi looked away from his penetrating gaze. "My aunt lives nearby, I think."

"Well, there's this organization in Tijuana," he said, handing her a business card. "They help people like you who have immigration problems. If you got no place to go or nothing to eat, call them and maybe they can help you out."

"Is there a public phone around here?"

"Out there." He pointed toward Mexico.

"Oh," Sofi said. Her voice sounded dead to her own ears. She felt hollow, gutted like a fish. She was only going through the motions of a normal human being. *Breathe*, she told herself. Sofi stared at her cute strappy sandals, unable to look Olivia or Taylor in the eye. Were they disgusted with her? Horrified? Angry? All her ugly dark feelings began to surface like bubbles.

"Take this," Taylor said, emptying her wallet of Mexican and American bills. Sofi bit her lower lip. She didn't want to take the money, but she also didn't want to admit that she was scared she might really need it. "I'm sure it's just some mistake, a computer glitch. You'll be back in no time."

"Yeah, sure." Sofi tried to force a laugh. *Act cool*, she told herself. *Act like it's no big deal.*

"We could stay with you," Olivia said, looking down.

"No, don't worry," Sofi said. "I'll be fine. Trust me." Olivia started to cry again. People in the waiting room turned to see what all the commotion was about. A couple of officers looked at her with nasty frowns. Sofi didn't want to create a scene and told Taylor to please take Olivia home. Taylor nodded. Sofi watched them go. There were no words to say. Her two best friends in the whole entire world walked to the end of the hallway. Sofi felt her heart being pulled apart and snapping like a rubber band. Taylor looked over her shoulder, a pained look of disbelief in her eyes, before leading Olivia out the glass doors to the United States. Sofi turned mechanically toward the opposite end of the room. She was hardly breathing, and the anxiety in her belly was about to erupt. Dusty, cracked glass doors led back to Mexico. Sofi wondered if they didn't bother to clean them on purpose.

Sofi slung her backpack over her shoulder and gripped her duffel bag in her hand. She pushed the door forward with her hip. The heat-congested air smacked her in the face, and panic gripped her. Everything around her was cloudy gray. The incessant honking of hundreds of cars in line made her double back in shock. But the glass door was closed behind her and there was nothing she could do.

Sofi stared at the graffitied pay phone at the end of the crumbling sidewalk, as if the instructions were written in hieroglyphics. She pressed a button for the operator. Thank God the operator spoke English. Soon she would be home, she told herself as her home phone began to ring. "Please, someone be home."

"Hello?" her mother answered.

"Collect call from Sofia Mendoza," the operator said in a thick Spanish accent. "Do you accept the charges?"

"Collect call? Sofi? Of course I accept."

"Mom," Sofi cried, beside herself. "You got to help me!" She swallowed. "I'm in trouble. I'm in Mexico. . . ."

"You're where?" her mother screamed, and for a moment Sofi didn't know what to say. She'd forgotten about the little lie she'd hoped they wouldn't find out about.

"Mom, don't be mad."

"Don't tell me how to be! You lied! I can't believe how you stood in front of our faces and lied. *Chamaca desgraciada. Sinvergüenza. Vas a ver cuando te agarro—*"

"Mom!" Sofi tried to scream over her mother's voice as she ranted on and on in Spanish. Sofi was shocked. She had never heard her mother curse like this. After what seemed like forever, her mother took a breath long enough for Sofi to tell her the worst part of her news. "Mom, they won't let me back into the country." Sofi heard the phone drop—or was it her mother who fainted to the floor?

After a moment, her father picked up the line. "Sofia?" he asked, as if he didn't know how the phone worked.

Sofi couldn't hold back her tears and broke down. "Daddy, I'm so so so so sorry." She tried to use the back of her hand to wipe away the tears, but they were coming too fast. "I don't know what to do. They won't let me back in. They said I'm illegal. Daddy? Are you there? I'm scared."

After a long pause, her dad came back on the line. "Yes, I'm here. Sofia, listen, everything is going to be all right. Don't worry." Hearing his soothing voice comforted Sofi.

"I'm really sorry, Dad. I swear I'll never do anything like this again."

"Tell me exactly what happened."

Her heart began to pound as she recounted her conversation with Officer Cohn. She told him that he'd taken her green card and called her an illegal. Sofi paused, waiting for him to laugh, get mad, or say one of his funny quotes. Nada. The unnerving silence said volumes.

"Why in God's name did you go down there?"

Sofi flinched, thinking about Operation *Papi Chulo*, her plan to snag Nick right before the prom, and their future marriage. It all seemed so incredibly stupid now.

"Are you okay?" he asked softly.

"Sort of."

"They didn't hurt you, right?"

"No, I was with Olivia and T the whole time."

He sighed with relief. "I want you to go stay with my sister, Luisa, until we get everything figured out, okay?" Sofi felt something inside rumble. "She and your uncle Victor live outside of Rosarito in Rancho Escondido. Write that down."

Sofi unzipped her navy blue JanSport backpack and pulled out her pink date book and pen. "Um, how do you spell that?"

Her dad slowly spelled out the neighborhood name and described the house. "I don't know if they had a phone installed. I don't think they did, so I'll call Luisa at work. She works at the Miramar Hotel, but she gets off pretty late." His voice sounded far away for a second and then he came back. "Take a taxi back to Rosarito. You got money?"

"Yes," she said, grateful that Taylor left her some extra cash.

Then, after a pause, he asked, "You sure you're all right?"

"I'm really really sorry about all of this."

"So am I," he said.

His words tugged at the thin threads that were holding her together. Ashamed, Sofi hesitated. "I love you, Dad," she said.

"I love you too, Sofi," her father said. And then Sofi hung up the phone. She looked down at her duffel bag and the backpack on the sidewalk. Tears rushed down without restraint and Sofi wondered, *What now?* She was on her own for the first time in her life.

A swarm of voices caught Sofi's attention. "Taxi! Taxi!" a group of men in ragged clothing yelled out, arms swaying in the air, competing to be her personal valet on the busy downtown Tijuana street corner. There was so much noise, Sofi wanted to cover her ears and scream, "Quiet!" She couldn't think with all the cars honking, buses fuming, vendors shouting, meat sizzling at the sidewalk stands, and people arguing. The racket rattled her already-fragile nerves.

She focused on the edge of the block and walked south. Noisy trucks speeding past her left her coughing in clouds of dust. Peddlers with water bottles and plastic squeegees ran up to cars stopped at red lights. School-age boys walked between those same motorists, holding small paper bags in the air and yelling, "*Churros!*" Sofi looked up as she passed two- and three-story buildings squished together like Legos. Some were old and dilapidated and others were unfinished cement constructions that had been started and abandoned long ago. She stumbled on a broken piece of concrete and was then pushed aside by a hefty woman with tight dyed-blond curls.

"Excuse me." She racked her brain for the right Spanish words. "*Con permiso.*" The angry-looking woman ignored her, hurrying on to catch a bus. Three little boys with spiky hair ran up to her. Their pants and shirts looked like they'd never, ever been washed. Their hands were out, waiting for change. Sofi noticed a woman three feet away shaded behind the beam of a building. She held a baby suckling at her exposed breast with one hand and with the other hand she extended a paper McDonald's cup, shaking it at passersby. The pedestrians walked right by, as if they didn't even see her. Sofi wondered if she was the mother of the boys and if she, too, had been turned away at the border. If Sofi didn't find her dad's family, would she have to resort to begging too? Her heart started to pound, and she looked to the right and left. She had to find her aunt right away.

"Taxi, miss?" asked a dark man in jeans and a gray shirt.

"¿Hablas inglés?"

The guy held up his hand, his first finger and thumb an inch apart. "A little."

"Oh my God. This is great!" She wanted to give him a hug but quickly decided against it. "I need to go to Rosarito."

"I take you to Rosarito," he said in a thick accent. "Come." He motioned with his dark, meaty fingers. Should she go with this stranger? Her dad had told her to take a cab. But what if he was a rapist or a kidnapper? Chills swept up and down her back. They did that sort of thing around here, didn't they? When he opened the front door of his yellow jalopy Buick station wagon, she was confused. Wasn't she supposed to sit in the back? Why did he want her to sit next to him? Was he a pervert? She ignored him and opened the back door. Despite all the late-night child-abduction TV reports and milk carton photos screaming, "No!" in her head, she got in.

Sofi placed her duffel bag next to her. She peered over the seat that separated her from this stranger. What did she know about this guy anyway? She sneezed. The inside of the car was covered in a thin film of dust, just like the street outside. The brown vinyl seats were ripped in places, with white stuffing spilling out. His license hung from the glove compartment. It said that his name was Rudolfo Silva Suarez. At least he was a real taxi driver, she thought, connecting the mug shot to the man driving. He smiled, pleased at himself, and turned on the knobless radio with a set of rusty pliers. Madonna's "Borderline" was playing. Sofi crossed her arms in front of her and stared out the window. She wondered what Taylor and Olivia were talking about on the drive home. What would they tell everyone back at school? Her eyes grew moist. This had to be the most horribly embarrassing thing in the entire world.

"First time in Tía Juana?" he asked.

"Tía Juana?"

"*Sí.*" He nodded. "All that you can see"—he motioned to the busy intersection—"and part of San Diego used to belong to one woman. Tía Juana."

"Really?"

"Yeah, but that was before the border, when all this was Mexico."

Driving in TJ was part NASCAR racing and part Monster Truck Madness. Faded lane markers must have been used solely as decoration for tourists, because none of the locals seemed to notice them at all. Drivers used any space and sometimes created their own lanes, driving on the unpaved sidewalks. Rudolfo Silva Suarez expertly whizzed through traffic, barely missing a head-on collision with a bus. Sofi chewed on her manicured nails. Everything around her was so strange and confusing that she forgot for a moment that she'd been turned away from the border. All she wanted was to be somewhere safe, away from the craziness of this unnerving city. She held on tight to the handrail as he wove in and out of traffic at high speed. Pedestrians ran across the middle of the street, dodging the taxi like matadors in a bullring.

Tijuana was huge and seemed to go on forever. The deeper into it they traveled, the thicker the congestion became. Traffic was at its worst when they reached the statue of a tall bronzed Aztec warrior holding a spear. Sofi wondered who he was but didn't get a chance to ask, because suddenly, her door opened. A woman with short brown hair and a cute toddler with pigtails almost sat on Sofi's lap. Shocked, Sofi jerked to the side. The nerve of this woman, getting in *her* cab! But Sofi had no time to protest, because cars started to honk behind them. Sofi lugged her heavy backpack and duffel bag onto her lap and the woman squeezed in beside her. Anxiety coiled around her lungs. Her heart pounded in her head. She didn't like not knowing what was going on. Were taxis in Mexico a community affair? Just then, the trunk door opened and three men hopped into the rear cargo area without saying a word. This was crazy, she thought, looking over her shoulder. Sofi wanted to complain. She was cramped and the woman's perfume was giving her a headache. But her mouth stayed shut. She wasn't about to announce to the entire car that she was a tourist, confused and a little scared. Someone might try to kidnap her, then kill her when they found out she was worth nothing.

Three traffic lights later, the woman got out and paid the driver. Sofi was about to put her bags beside her when an old man holding a live chicken beat her to it. Didn't they have laws against riding with uncaged farm animals? And furthermore, this did not look like the road to Rosarito she had taken that same morning!

Sofi soon learned that there were two routes to Rosarito. One was the scenic toll route she'd taken with Taylor. It was recommended to tourists because it went along the Pacific coast and had killer views of the mountain cliffs and the ocean shore. The other, narrower route was the more heavily traveled Mexican National road. From the looks of the license plates, the second one was the one the locals took. It wasn't as pretty, but it was free of charge, though not of potholes. Big rigs clogged up the two-lane highway, going bumper-to-bumper with pickup trucks loaded with workers, while numerous old VW bugs dodged in and out of the two lanes.

Sofi's eyes again filled with tears, but she refused to start crying. Who would she cry to anyway? She was in a car full of strangers, yet she was all alone. The backstreets of the residential areas zoomed by. She could see arid mountaintops, thirsty for vegetation, and cardboard-constructed shanty houses with tin roofs hanging dangerously close to the cliff's edge. Barbed-wire fences separated them from million-dollar mega-mansions. Sofi took a breath and inhaled the air; it was filled with the smell of meat from the taco carts on the side of the road and the scent of burning gas from outdoor auto repair shops. Everything was kind of mismatched, as if things just happened without a master plan. It was a free-for-all for rich and poor; everyone was an entrepreneur. This was a city of whatever it takes.

The farther out they went, the more her heart sank. Sofi was traveling in the wrong direction. She was going away from everything she'd ever known and loved. To the left was a row of ten tract-style duplexes in the middle of acres of barren land. A large billboard advertised Gated American Dream Homes. Sofi wondered why people would have to come to Mexico to get the American dream. Then she noticed a small green sign to the right that said, BIENVENIDOS A PLAYAS DE ROSARITO.

Was this the same place she'd left just a couple of hours ago? This town looked all wrong. It looked sort of like Tijuana, with regular Mexican-looking people in regular-looking clothes walking down the busy commercial street. Where were all the Americans in shorts and sandals? The old man with the poultry smell got off in front of a chicken place, saying something to the driver but not paying. Sofi was relieved when he got out. She hoped it wouldn't be the chicken's last stop. In place of the FOR SALE signs, there were advertisements for small specialty shops selling mirrors, wooden furniture, facials, videos, tacos, chicken, paper, and lobster. It wasn't until Sofi saw the familiar McDonald's and a Staples mega-store that she sighed with relief. She'd made it back in one piece.

"Here we are." The driver parked alongside the red-tile-roofed Rosarito Beach Hotel.

"Oh," Sofi said, looking around, confused. "Can't you take me to Rancho Escondido?"

The guy shook his head adamantly. "I only go to the hotel and back to the border. I don't know this area."

"But how am I supposed to get there?" she asked helplessly.

The taxi driver shrugged. "Try one of those green taxis over there."

He gestured with his chin to a line of green Toyota Camrys in front of a café.

"How much do I owe you?" She pressed her lips together, hoping that she had enough to pay him.

"Thirty pesos," he said. Sofi's eyes widened. That was it? Thirty pesos was like three dollars. It wasn't bad for a twenty-mile ride.

Sofi handed him three crumpled bills. Then she looked around the busy street corner; the smell of hot dogs was making her tummy rumble. She hadn't eaten a thing all morning. But the hot dogs being offered by the young man with a friendly smile looked nothing like those sold at Anaheim Stadium. Skimpy little weenies wrapped in bacon and topped with shredded cabbage, diced tomatoes, cheese, and hot sauce! A Mexican hot dog? Sofi ate four.

A long high-pitched whistle made her turn as she chewed the last bit of the delicious treat. A very handsome guy with a brown ponytail and a beefcake physique was motioning to her. He was trying to woo her into the Macho Taco shop. Sofi was familiar with this custom. It must have been some unspoken rule that these clubs on Boulevard Benito Juarez hired only hot eye candy to work the front door. Their job was to get customers inside by any means necessary, which meant that the guys flirted like hell. Mr. Ponytail Man had an incredible body, but Sofi couldn't take his advances seriously. Maybe yesterday she would have been more willing to play. Heck, if Olivia were here, she'd be licking the table he served their drinks on. Today was a different story.

Sofi extended her hand nervously in the air. She had to get to Rancho Escondido. That was where her parents were expecting to find her. A green four-door Toyota with the word Taxi painted on the door sped past her. Another green car passed in the opposite direction. Sofi felt like a dork with her hand in the air. Should she shout? Her throat was dry and her limbs felt heavy. All she wanted was a long hot shower and a fluffy bed to rest on until her parents arrived.

There were lots of people on the street. Old couples walked hand in hand like young lovers; little girls with colorful beads hanging off their braids strolled along with their parents. Leftover party boys walked off hangovers with stringy girls hanging on tightly to their late-night conquests. Sofi stared as a group of Mexican girls in matching plaid uniforms passed by her, talking really fast in Spanish.

They reminded her of what she'd be missing. Tomorrow was the senior trip to Knott's Berry Farm! Everyone was going—everyone but Sofi. Her parents better hurry up, she thought. The prom was this coming Saturday and she had tons of finals to study for before graduation. This was absolutely the worst time to get stuck away from home. She just had to get back. But then what? Just thinking about the disappointment in her father's voice made her cringe. Who was she kidding? Her parents were so mad, they'd probably ground her until she was sixty!

Sofi scratched at her arm nervously. *Oh no,* she thought. *I can't start breaking out now. I need to stay focused. Calm.* She had to find her aunt Luisa. Sofi started to shiver. The sky was darkening and the breeze picked up as if a storm were brewing just for her. Sofi removed her gray Mat Maids sweatshirt from her duffel bag. She watched a green taxi park across the street. Her father's directions were in her organizer. Sofi dived into her backpack and searched through her date book for the right page.

Rancho Escondido. Take Boulevard Benito
Juarez and make a left at Hotel Festival.
Go under bridge and follow the road until you
pass a soccer field. The road will twist
and turn; three blocks past the second Oxxo
Convenience Store, take a right. It's the
third house on the right. Big yard with a
horse corral on the side.

She tucked the book under her arm and picked up her bag to cross the street.

But getting to Rancho Escondido was not as simple as it seemed. They were lost for over an hour. The driver swore he knew where it was, but stopped twice to ask for directions at different corner taco stands. It was getting dark and Sofi's arms started to itch. What was she doing? This was crazy! She could be lost for hours and then what? What if her family no longer lived there? Why didn't they have a phone? Why couldn't they just have picked her up at the border? She watched the man talking to the sleepy-eyed vendor. The guy was pointing in the opposite direction and talking way too low for her to hear. Sofi was fed up. She was going to call her dad.

"*¡Oye!*" the man screamed as she pulled her bag out of the cab. He hurried over to her on his short legs.

"*No, gracias,*" Sofi said, trying to do a hand gesture to let him know she didn't want to continue this hopeless ride. The driver started yelling real loud in her face. He pointed to the meter. Sofi noticed that the meter wasn't even on. He was trying to rip her off. He grabbed her arm. "Let me go!" Sofi shouted.

But he continued to demand his fare. "*Tú no puedes dejarme así. Me tienes que pagar la tarifa.*"

"No." Sofi pulled her arm free. She couldn't understand all that he said, but she knew that he was lost. People on the street watched from a safe distance. Sofi looked around for a cop or someone who could help her. This part of town was nothing like downtown Rosarito. The neighborhood was far from deserted, but there were no tourists walking anywhere, just teenagers congregated on the corners, laughing children chasing one another, roaming packs of dogs, and regular people going about their business. It was all so foreign to Sofi. Her heart started to race. What was she going to do? Then she saw someone she recognized. Or at least, he looked kind of familiar. He was walking down the street with a pretty girl. Without a second thought she cried out, "Hey, hey you!"

The young guy with messy brown hair and a Rosarito Beach Hotel shirt looked over his shoulder. They locked eyes for a second. "You're

talking to me?" he said in unaccented English. It took Sofi two seconds
to realize where she knew this guy from. It was Cabana Boy!

"Oh my God!" she cried when he came over. "You gotta help me."

"You're the girl who threw the chair at me." He smirked and said
something low to the girl. She took one look at Sofi and started to laugh.
Maybe this was a mistake.

"Do you know this girl?" the taxi driver asked in Spanish, his nostrils
flaring. Cabana Boy gave her an annoyed glance. "This brat is trying
to gyp me out of my fare." He turned to Sofi. "You want me to call the
police?" he said, looking around.

Sofi pleaded with her eyes to Cabana Boy to help her. He was her
only hope.

Cabana Boy sighed. "I'm sorry, sir. Yes, I know this girl," he said
in Spanish. Sofi's eyes lit up excitedly. "She's my cousin Chencha. I
thought I lost her." The driver gave him a confused look. "She's kind of
slow and not allowed to leave the house." The driver looked at Sofi and
scratched his head. This was ludicrous. There was no way that he was
going to get away with it. "Let me give you this for your trouble." Cabana
Boy handed the guy ten dollars. The driver looked from the boy to Sofi
and back again. He looked at the money in his hand, shrugged his
shoulders, and got back in his cab.

When the cab took off, Cabana Boy leaned in to Sofi and said, "You
owe me."

"Yeah, totally." She pulled out ten bucks. She noticed that she had
three twenties, a ten, three ones, and five hundred pesos. It seemed like
a lot. Her mind calculated the exchange rate. She had a total of $123.

He looked at the ten-dollar bill and turned it over as if checking for
its authenticity. "You still owe me." The girl he was with had wavy brown
hair and lots of makeup. She whispered something into his ear and then
took off, giving him a kiss on the cheek.

Sofi felt herself blush. She hadn't meant to ruin his date. "I'm
sorry if I—"

He stared at her flatly. "It's a little late for that."

A flood of emotions swept over her, bringing tears to her eyes. She could no longer bottle up her distress. "I already said I was sorry. What more do you want? Okay, I know I behaved like a brat at the beach. I'm sorry, okay? But this is serious. I'm lost. They won't let me back into the United States. I have to find my aunt, but I'm freaking out because I don't know what's going on or when I'll be able to go back! You happy now?" Her voice cracked. She knew she sounded crazy.

Cabana Boy's eyes softened. He looked down at his worn-out cross-trainers. People were staring at her, but she didn't care. "It'll be all right," he said in a soothing voice. "I'll help you find your family."

Apparently there were three Rancho Escondidos. Each one was far from the other two. Her dad's directions were outdated. Cabana Boy pulled out his Nextel phone and walkie-talkied a friend who drove a taxi. He asked his friend to come right over. Sofi was totally floored! He was going all out of his way to help her, and she didn't even know his name. "I'm really sorry about that whole beach thing the other day."

He smiled. "Don't think I've forgotten. You still owe me."

"What do you mean?"

"I just saved your butt from that taxi shark. The least you can do is help me with some housekeeping."

"Housekeeping?"

"You're a girl." He shrugged. "You should know that kind of stuff."

"I don't know how they do things in this country. But in the United States, there's a thing called equal rights."

"So does that mean I have the right to kick a chair at you?"

Sofi blushed. "Okay, fine. I'll clean your house." She held out her hand. "My name's Sofi."

"Nice to finally meet you, Sofi. Mine's Andres." He shook her hand firmly. Sofi noticed that there were tiny wrinkles at the edge of his light brown eyes when he smiled.

They stood there quietly on the corner, waiting for Andres's friend.

"Hey, you don't have to go with me. I don't want to get you in trouble with your girlfriend."

He smiled. "It's all right. I'm cool. Plus, I, like, make it a rule to help out one damsel in distress every week."

"Ha! Yeah, right." Sofi smiled to herself and before she realized it she was checking him out. He didn't have much of a butt and she wondered if he always wore that faded uniform. His face wasn't that bad, but he was neither dreamy nor slapalicious.

His friend, Huero, arrived in a white VW bug with a map of Rosarito. He seemed nice, asking Andres shyly if Sofi spoke Spanish. His football jersey was two sizes too big, making his arms look childlike. He had a lot of pimple pockmarks on his cheeks. Andres opened the door for her to get in the back. Together they went looking for her family's house.

"Rancho Escondido was once one big *ejido*," Andres explained as the VW crept over the bumpy dirt road toward the group of small houses in the middle of the large stretch of farmland. "But it's now broken into three sections." Sofi gave him a confused look. "*Ejidos* are communal lands that people can farm at no cost."

"That's strange. I never heard of people sharing land."

He laughed. "It's actually an old Aztec custom that was brought back by the Mexican government to try to get the people to help themselves."

Sofi did a double take. "How do you know so much?" Andres blushed. He was actually kind of cute when he was nervous. Although not in the dreamy *papi chulo* kind of way. Her heart started to ache for Nick. She couldn't believe all the money she had wasted listening to that fake fortune lady. When she got back, she was going to give that lady a fat lip to go with that phony third eye.

"I studied agricultural engineering at the University of Tijuana for a bit. I might go back after I save some money."

"That's cool. I'm going to UCLA in the fall, but I have no idea what I'm going to study." Sofi turned to Huero and said, "*Colegio*," pointing at her chest.

Andres started to laugh. "You're going to high school?"

"I meant college."

"Well, that's *universidad*, not *colegio*. Where did you learn Spanish anyway? Aren't you Mexican?"

"Well, yes, and no." Sofi started to grind her teeth. She didn't really know what she was. Back home, she'd thought she was like everyone else, but that was before she was turned away at the border. Sofi frowned and grew quiet. She looked out the window at the rolling countryside. "I don't know. I don't know anything anymore." She felt Andres's eyes studying her. The fields were vast, lush, and vibrant. Sofi was about to ask him more about his studies, but Huero interrupted.

"*Aquí estamos*," he said, bringing the car to a halt. Sofi sighed with relief. The image of the poor native woman on the side of the street still haunted her. At least Sofi had a place to sleep for the night. However, the minute she looked at the house her jaw dropped. The place was a dump.

Sofi gazed out over the rolling green fields with wonder. The crunch of dried, cracked weeds on the dried, cracked earth under her feet filled her ears. Chickens scrambled over to greet her, pecking at her open-toed sandals. Two skinny shirtless boys howled as they chased each other around a half-finished two-story home; metal frames protruded like antennas from the cinder blocks. Slouching from the side of the house was a dilapidated corral, where a brown horse stopped chewing straw and turned to take a look at her with his one good eye. A goat tied to a pole in the front yard bleated loudly, announcing her arrival like the family watchdog.

Sofi stood there, mesmerized by the sight before her. She didn't know what to do. Everything about the place felt wrong. This couldn't be her family's house. People didn't really live like this anymore . . . did they?

"Sofia," Andres said again, louder. "Are you all right?"

Sofi looked at him with shocked disbelief. He couldn't leave her here. This place was unsanitary and full of who knew what! Her friends would die if they knew she was staying here and that this was her family. This was not happening!

A heavyset man with salt-and-pepper hair and a bushy mustache appeared from the darkened doorframe.

"Uncle Victor?" she said, too softly for anyone but Andres to hear. She hoped that this was all a mistake and that her real family lived somewhere else, far, far away.

Andres cleared his throat and asked for the house of Victor and Luisa in Spanish. He leaned in to Sofi. "What's their last name?" She shrugged her shoulders. "You don't know your family's last name?"

"Well, I never met them before," she whispered back.

"*¿Quién habla?*" the man asked in a loud gruff voice. He was leaning firmly on a wooden cane as if he was in a lot of pain.

Andres gave Sofi a hard stare. She closed her eyes and took a deep breath. "*Mi nombre es Sofia Mendoza. Soy hija de Edmundo and Evangelina Mendoza.*"

Before she could say another word, the lumberjack-built man had her in a big bear hug. He was quite swift for a burly man and smelled of wet earth and Irish Spring soap. It was a comforting smell. The two little boys stood shyly together. They had chocolate-colored skin, baggy shorts that hung loose under their bellies, and matching bowl haircuts. Looking at them made Sofi feel like she was seeing double.

"*Miren, chamacos, es tu prima Sofia del Otro Lado.*" Uncle Victor let out a whoop and slapped his thigh in excitement. The fresh tears in his eyes moved her. She smiled shyly. She hoped that they would like her. Her uncle spoke quickly. It was hard to follow, but his voice sounded happy to see her. The boys stared through her. "*Salúdala.*" Her uncle pushed one of them forward.

Awkwardly, each boy came up to her and gave her a stiff hug. These had to be her cousins. They looked just like the kids selling candy and plastic roses on Boulevard Benito Juarez. The realization hit her like a ton of bricks. Her chest constricted, making it difficult to breathe. If Sofi's parents had stayed in Mexico, this could have been her life! Her uncle introduced one boy as Mando and the one in her arms as Mundo. She couldn't tell them apart except that one scratched his head a lot.

"*Éste es Andres,*" she said, trying to keep her voice from cracking. Andres looked uncomfortable standing there. He had his hands shoved into his jean pockets. "*El ayudar a mí.*" The words didn't sound right. She hoped he could make sense of her broken Spanish. Her uncle thanked Andres for bringing her to the house. "Y . . ." She gestured to the waiting taxi bug but couldn't find the right words. Sofi's mind went blank and her tongue wouldn't work. Her uncle stood there, his callused hands on his big belt buckle. The buckle had what looked like a real scorpion in it. He was waiting for her to continue.

Andres interrupted to introduce Huero, who waved from the driver's seat. "Well, I think you can take it from here." Andres shook her uncle's hand again and then patted the boys on the head. Mando or Mundo jumped in front of Andres.

"Hi-ya!" the boy cried, making kung fu moves.

Andres chuckled softly. Then he started making wide, swinging gestures as if preparing to fight the kid. "Roar!" The boy yelped and ran behind his dad. Her uncle laughed heartily. Then Andres turned to Sofi and shook her hand awkwardly.

"Thanks." Sofi wanted to say more, but she didn't know what.

"Now remember, you owe me."

"Yes, yes, I know." Sofi nodded.

"I plan to collect." Andres smiled, then headed for the car. "Oh yeah," he said, stopping by the gate. "The cab ride downtown is thirty pesos— three dollars. Don't let them cheat you."

"Thanks," Sofi said, waving good-bye. Huero beamed from behind the wheel. He gunned the engine loudly before taking off toward the west in a cloud of dust. Sofi watched them for a second. She shook her head slowly. Cabana Boy was pretty cool after all.

Sofi turned back to her family's house. She breathed deeply to quell the anxiety knotting in her chest. Maybe she wouldn't actually have to spend a night in this place. Movement from inside the dark-ened house caught her attention. A teenage girl walked out from the shadows. She was small and petite like Sofi, with dyed blond streaks in her frizzy brown hair that she wore in a side ponytail. Her long bangs framed glittery brown eyes caked with layers of green eye shadow. The foundation she used was a couple of shades too light, and she was dressed oddly, in a white T-shirt, black skirt, striped tie, and boots.

"I'm Yesenia, your cousin," she said with a bored tone. Yesenia checked out Sofi's oversized pullover and faded jean shorts, not bothering to hide her disappointment.

"You speak English. Great. I'm Sofi."

"*Papá*," Yesenia whined in an annoying high voice. "*¿Puedo ir con Britannica?*" Uncle Victor made an angry face. He told Yesenia that she couldn't go anywhere. Her cousin was here. Yesenia crossed her arms and pouted, stomping around the dirt in her knee-high black boots. "*Papá!*"

"*¡Mando! ¡Mundo! ¡Agarren las maletas!*" Her uncle pointed at her bags. Sofi jumped at the sound of his thundering voice. She hoped that he wasn't as mean as he sounded. The boys screamed in excitement, though, and grabbed Sofi's bags, dragging them through the dirt and into the house, creating a stream of dust. *Not my brand-new UCLA bag!* she wanted to scream as she hurried after them. Inside, the boys tore through her bags like airport security officers. Her gel, makeup bag, and even her tampons were scattered on the speckled beige linoleum floor.

"Hey, hey, hey," Sofi said, picking up her bottle of Ralph Lauren perfume. This stuff was expensive, even with her mother's discount.

"*¿Dónde están los regalos?*" Mando or Mundo, she wasn't sure which, asked. They stared expectantly, holding her bikini tops and sunscreen. Sofi turned to Yesenia for translation.

"Don't you speak Spanish?" Yesenia asked, sliding into one of the metal folding chairs around the table.

"A little," Sofi said, "but they talk so fast."

Yesenia sighed deeply and pushed herself out of the chair. She walked over and smacked one of the boys lightly on the head. "They think you brought gifts," she said, studying Sofi's reaction. Sofi turned red. They thought she was *visiting* from the United States, and she hadn't brought a single gift.

"I'm sorry, I didn't know . . . ," Sofi began. Her ears burned with embarrassment. The boys caught the gist of her response and mumbled something that she knew wasn't good. Then they took off through the kitchen and slammed the back door. Sofi wanted to say something to make it up to them, but she had no words. The situation was making her head pound, and she wanted to scream. This wasn't her fault. She didn't want to be here, either. If it were up to her, she'd be on a one-way trip home. Yesenia sucked in her cheeks, making a loud pop.

Her uncle walked into the living room, heading straight for the black fridge in the adjacent kitchen. He offered Sofi something to drink.

"*No, gracias,*" she said politely as her eyes took in her surroundings. Sofi thought of her parents. They were probably worried sick, wondering if she had survived the trip. But Uncle Victor wanted to show her around the house he had built himself. As the three of them crowded into the narrow, unlit hallway, Yesenia hunched her shoulders and eyed the floor. She wasn't happy to be the translator.

"This is a beautiful house," Sofi said, touching the warm, scratchy white walls. "*Muy bonita.*" Yesenia looked up suspiciously. Her uncle smiled brightly. He had a good set of big teeth. With his fist he pounded the walls to show her how strong they were. Sofi liked her uncle. He looked all bulky and frightening because of his size, but he was actually very sweet, and he had built his own house.

Yesenia led them into a small room with a single window overlooking the backyard. Red sunlight streaked in through the sheer rose-colored fabric that hung loosely over the window frame. "This is where you will be sleeping. It's ugly, I know," Yesenia apologized, looking down at her scuffed pointy heels.

"No, it'll do," Sofi said, reaching out to touch the metal bunk bed against the side of the wall. She didn't plan to actually sleep there. Sofi kept listening for her parents. They were sure to arrive at any moment. Plastered on the walls were torn-out magazine pictures of Britney Spears,

Power Rangers, Shakira, and a handsome, boyish-looking man with a thin mustache in a pearl white mariachi outfit. *This isn't so bad*, she thought, before almost tripping over a Godzilla action figure. The floor was covered with pieces of off-white carpet, brightly colored Legos, and toy cars. Sofi then realized that she would be sharing the room with Yesenia and the terrible duo.

The rest of the tour was very short. The only other bedroom belonged to her aunt and uncle. It had a huge gaudy-looking king-size bed with wooden acorn posts, a velvet painting of the Last Supper over the headboard, and an antique-style oak glass cabinet stuffed with candles, rosary beads, framed black-and-white photographs, and an army of tiny saints. *Freaky*, Sofi thought as she walked over to look at the different types of saints. There were women dressed in colorful robes, baby saints, and old men with pointy beards. The statutes were arranged as if in the middle of a dramatic scene. Sofi kept glancing at the door. Her parents had to come, and quick. The stale, foreboding air of the room was suffocating her.

"This," Yesenia said, opening the cabinet, "is Our Lady of Sorrows, and this one is Nuestra Virgen de Zapopan. This is Nuestra Virgen Rocío de Talpa, and, of course, La Virgen de Dolores."

"You sure do have a lot of virgins," Sofi joked.

"Yeah." Yesenia crossed her eyes in a familiar way that made Sofi smile. "My *mamá* collects them." Yesenia tried to hide the smile that crept onto her lips. "I get confused. They say that if you put a candle upside down in front of Saint Anthony, the boy you will marry will come to you in your dreams."

"Does it work?"

"I'll let you know," Yesenia said, and turned quickly so Sofi couldn't read her face.

"Have you tried it?"

Yesenia walked out of the room. Uncle Victor blocked the bedroom doorway. Sofi smiled awkwardly at him. Although he was her uncle, he was still a stranger. Yesenia explained how her dad was planning to build two additional bedrooms and an indoor bathroom.

"What do you mean indoor? What do you have now?"

"It's not a hole in the ground." Yesenia began to laugh. "We're not that poor. The bathroom was added onto the house. You just have to go outside to use it. Make sure you put on your shoes. There're lots of bugs, snakes, and scorpions out there." An icy shiver ran up Sofi's back. "You'll get used to it. This is the kitchen. . . ." Yesenia twirled slowly. "It's not much." A green-tiled counter divided the kitchen and living room areas. There was a two-burner gas stove but no oven. Yesenia walked over to the faucet and turned it on and off. "We use this for washing dishes and cleaning. We use that"—she pointed to a freestanding water dispenser in the corner—"for cooking and drinking." The drinking-water container was draped with a canary-yellow crocheted cover.

"You mean that you don't drink the water, either? I thought that was just for Americans," Sofi said. Uncle Victor watched their lips, trying to follow the conversation.

Yesenia rolled her eyes. "Anyone can get sick from the water. Not just Americans."

Sofi flinched, feeling like she'd somehow insulted Yesenia without meaning to. Yesenia crossed her arms in front of her chest. Sofi looked at the walls. They were covered with violent scribbled drawings (courtesy of the boys no doubt), an antique-looking clock, and a calendar advertising a bakery. The dishes were stacked up in a neat pile, and there was a line of ants marching across the counter.

The tour ended back in the living/dining room, where Sofi sat down on the plush purple sofa. *Now what?* she thought nervously, looking around. On top of the black entertainment center, housing a TV and stereo system, were a series of family portraits. High up above was a black-and-white photograph of a handsome man with dreamy eyes and a thin mustache like her dad's. There was a small shelf underneath with a dozen unlit candles and some yellow satin roses.

"Is that my grandfather?" Sofi asked.

"Ha!" Yesenia said bitterly. Sofi gave her a sideways glance. Why was she being so rude?

"That's Pedro Infante," Uncle Victor explained. "A famous Mexican singer and movie actor."

"He's my dad's idol," Yesenia said, giggling to herself. "He has all his records and movies."

Yesenia reached out and grabbed a black-framed eight-by-twelve black-and-white photograph of a sexy woman with a flower in her hair and wearing a Tropicana dancer–style dress. "That's your grandmother." She made a pinched expression. "Abuela Benita."

"She's beautiful," Sofi said, taking the photograph from her. The woman's haunting eyes looked familiar.

"*Es una loca vieja.*"

Sofi looked at Yesenia in shock.

"She's real mean. Nobody likes her. She lives over by the cemetery, but we don't visit her."

Sofi wondered about the woman as she glanced at the other photographs of distressed-looking relatives. She reached out and picked up a faded framed photograph. Her parents! It felt odd to see their faces in this strange house. But it was also so comforting. Her hands trembled silently as she touched her father's bright smile. A sheer veil was draped over her mother's small heart-shaped face. Sofi felt light-headed. Her heart ached. What was she doing here? She regretted coming to Mexico, Operation *Papi Chulo*, and lying to her parents. They both looked so young and happy in the picture. Beside them stood Uncle Victor, grinning in a dark suit, and a woman with dark curly locks. The woman had a limp smile on her face, as if she'd been standing in the sun for too long. Was that her Aunt Luisa?

All at once a flood of memories flashed before her, making her step back. She remembered the shoe box of bent photos tucked in the hallway closet. Her mother had scolded her for putting her fingerprints all over them, but Sofi liked to look at pictures of relatives she'd never met. She made up stories about who they were and what they did. But this was not what she'd imagined, she thought, looking around her uncle's cramped living room.

Uncle Victor nodded happily and opened a beer, reclining back in his black La-Z-Boy. He kicked off his dusty slippers and scratched his potbelly. Sofi glanced at the remote control that was on a glass coffee table beside the fake floral centerpiece. At least they had a TV. She sighed.

"Do you guys have Internet?" Sofi asked, rummaging inside her backpack for her organizer. She wanted to contact her parents right away. They had to clear up her immigration situation. Sofi had things to do: tests to study for, last-minute shopping for the prom, and what about graduation? She couldn't stay here another minute.

Yesenia shook her head.

Okay, don't freak out, Sofi told herself. *It's no big deal.* She took a deep breath. *Mom and Dad will know what to do. All I need to do is relax and I'll be on a bus back home in no time.* She looked at the TV and remembered that she'd missed the finale of *America's Next Top Model.* "How about TiVo?"

Yesenia gave her a confused look. Sofi figured that that meant no.

"You do get American TV?" Yesenia shook her head. The house was dark. *Wait a minute—do they even have electricity?* Sofi thought.

"Sometimes the lights go out," Yesenia explained, seeing Sofi look up at the ceiling fan that wasn't spinning.

"Does it happen a lot?" Sofi asked, trying to hide her discomfort. *No TiVo! No Internet! No electricity!*

"I guess," Yesenia said, sounding unsure. Her cousin looked at her dad. He was staring at both of them, smiling.

Sofi remembered how her dad had called Luisa's job because he wasn't sure if they had a telephone installed in the house yet. "How about a phone?"

Yesenia exhaled a long breath as if Sofi were asking her for her left lung. "We don't have one. If you want, we can go to my friend's house, but we have to make an appointment first. Britannica doesn't like people who just drop by."

"You can't be serious!" Sofi cried. "What if there's an emergency or something?" *This is not happening,* she screamed in her head. Yesenia and Uncle Victor stared at her. *Oh my God,* she thought, panic gripping her heart. She stepped back and bumped into the entertainment center. *I'm trapped in Mexico!* "Thank you for everything, but I don't think I can stay here," she said to no one in particular. *Go!* A voice screamed in her head. *Go now. Quickly.*

Sofi kneeled on the cold floor and shoved a pair of socks and her cute sparkly tank top into her duffel bag. *I'll figure something out. I have to get home.* Her purple mini was stuck under the leg of the couch. It must have happened when the boys were tearing through her stuff. She pulled hard, trying to jerk it free, and she heard a long, high-pitched ripping sound. It felt like someone had torn out her heart. Sofi crumbled, and a deep wail escaped from her lips. Was she illegal, as the immigration officer had said? And what did that mean? What about her dreams? The prom? Her warm fluffy bed? Graduation? And UCLA? No. This was not fair. It wasn't happening? Sofi had slaved away for so many years, trying to meet her parents' and teachers' expectations. Where were her parents and what was taking them so long? Sofi choked on her tears; all she wanted was to cry herself away.

Big warm hands rubbed her back slowly. "*Ay ay ay, mija,*" Uncle Victor said softly in her ear. "*Todo va estar bien. Vas a ver. Todo va estar bien.*" Sofi looked up and into his soulful brown eyes. He crushed her in his embrace, taking her breath away for a moment. "*No te preocupes,*" he consoled, rubbing her back as her father used to do when she was very small and hurt herself. "*Ya estás con familia.*"

Sofi pulled back, her eyes blurry from crying so damn much. "Family." He nodded. She wiped her face with the fleshy part of her palm. He was right. This was her family. She needed to blow her nose. Yesenia stared with a confused look on her face.

"Here," Yesenia said, handing her a paper towel from the roll on the table.

"Thanks." Sofi blew her nose noisily. She noticed that the boys were watching quietly from the kitchen door. Sofi wasn't used to breaking down in front of complete strangers. Sure, they were family, but they knew nothing about one another and lived totally different lives. Sofi didn't want to be rude, but she also didn't want to spend another minute stranded here in the middle of nowhere, with no way of contacting the outside world.

"*Ándele*, Sofia." Uncle Victor punched her playfully, grinning and nodding. "*No te pongas triste.*" Sofi forced a smile to appease him. "*Tenemos que celebrar!*"

The boys ran into the house yelling, "Woo! Woo! Fiesta!"

Her uncle waved them over to the kitchen. He put his finger to his lips, winked, and reached behind the refrigerator. Then he pulled out a velvet coin purse. Yesenia took the crumpled-up colored bills from him and headed to the store.

Sofi followed her uncle out back. The sky was yellow and orange, with white clouds streaked over a vast hilly area. She took a deep breath, encouraging the beauty around her to lift up her soul. But her heart flopped. This had to be the worst day of her entire life. Sofi kicked at the dust. She couldn't believe that Officer Cohn had called her an illegal. How could she be? She was infinitely more American than she was Mexican. She barely understood anything about this strange, backward place. She sighed, lugging her heavy heart after her uncle. Her eyes took in the countryside around her.

The plot of land to her right was dried to the core. It seemed deserted except for the sounds that came from the TV in the small house. To her left were rows of green vegetable-looking things. A fresh cilantro scent wafted on the breeze. There were ten cottage-sized houses and a couple of shacks on the block. Some were in a similar state of disrepair and held together with different types of materials. Others were gaudy Greek-pillared dwellings with high metal fences and barbed wire. Her uncle stood by a pigpen. He motioned for her to come over.

The boys ran over to the pen, shouting wildly. Three older men in jeans and cowboy boots walked behind the boys toward the backyard. They were neighbors coming over to help with the fiesta preparations. One of the men, who looked a lot like her dad but with a mane of wool-like hair, started building a fire pit with pieces of wood stacked on the back porch. Sofi was a little confused and wondered if her uncle was going to give her a tour of the farm with his friends. Uncle Victor pointed to the pigs. Maybe he wanted to give her one? What would her mother say?

"Which?" Mando or Mundo asked in a thick accent.

Surprised, Sofi did a double take. "Hey, I didn't know you spoke English."

"A little," the boy answered, squinting his eyes. Sofi leaned over to look at the pigs. The three lounging by the fence were old, ugly, and hairy. *I want something cute*, Sofi thought, *like Wilbur. Taylor will be so jealous.* There was a little runt by the tub, sniffing at leftover beans and rice.

"I want that one," Sofi pointed to the runt. The men argued amongst themselves. Sofi chewed on a hangnail, wondering what was going on. Then, without warning, the two neighbors jumped into the pen and pinned one of the bigger male pigs to the ground. The animal screeched wildly and Sofi closed her eyes. She heard the sound of a blade being pulled from its case and jumped with a start. Uncle Victor held a long knife and slashed the pig's neck open. Sofi's mouth opened with shock! The remaining pigs squealed with grief, while Mando and Mundo jumped up and down in glee. *These guys are demented*, she thought, taking a step away from the scene. Her pulse raced wildly. *Don't they have supermarkets?*

Uncle Victor climbed out of the pen with blood all over his shirt and cowboy boots. The men carried the now-limp pig to the back porch. Both fascinated and appalled, Sofi grabbed a wobbly stool to watch the men at work. The man with graying hair slit open the animal's stomach and dropped the insides into a pail. Sofi winced every time the knife touched the pink flesh, but she also couldn't take her eyes away from the scene. Mando picked out the heart from the bucket and offered it to Sofi.

"No!" She jumped up and raced behind the chipped porch beam. Uncle Victor snapped loudly and Mando dropped the warm organ back into the bucket. The men talked loudly and laughed as they cleaved the animal into pieces. *What would Taylor think?* she thought, keeping her distance from the boys and the pig. Taylor was always trying to convince her to stop eating meat.

"*Oye, Sofia,*" Uncle Victor called out to her. "*Ven aquí.*" He motioned to the bench space next to him. Slowly, she sat beside him. "*Ándele.*" He passed her the knife. She tried to refuse, shaking her head. It was one thing to eat pork chops, quite another to hack them out yourself. She preferred to get her meat already sliced and packaged in white foam and plastic wrap. "No be scared," he said, switching to broken English. "You understand? This pig is good. We loved him. Feed him. Now he feed us good, understand?"

It was strange, but it made sense in a way. Besides, the pig was full-grown. *Wait!* she cried to herself. *Am I rationalizing the death of Wilbur?* Her uncle shrugged and continued to cut up the pig. The guy who was working the fire turned on a handheld radio and found a station that played accordion-based Norteña music. Uncle Victor let out a high piercing cry: "*Ajua!*" Another guy started dancing around the dirt floor by himself. Sofi smiled. Despite her dismal state, it was comforting to be around happy people. She watched and wondered if she'd ever feel that carefree again.

"You careful here, you understand?" He gestured with his sharp knife all around them. "Cops bad." He nodded to the guy next to him and continued in Spanish. "Bernardo got picked up the other day for no reason than he was ugly." The men chuckled at her uncle's joke. His smile disappeared. "I joke, but it's because that's all we can do. The cops took his money and left him thirty miles from his house. He was lucky. Nothing bad happened to him. Others not so lucky. You understand?" Sofi nodded, feeling annoyed by all his clarifications. Yes, she understood! "This place is not what it appears. These are hard times. An honest man can't support his family. Young people have few options. If they don't go to the Other Side, they get into drugs or steal from *gringos'* homes. Be smart. Watch your back. Understand?" Sofi peered around the rancho, wondering exactly whom she could trust in this foreign land.

Yesenia arrived with one bag of chips and a two-liter bottle of Coke. The boys were jumping around, threatening to douse each other with the blood from the pig's intestines. Sofi wondered why Yesenia had taken so long and why she had this peculiar grin on her face. She was about to ask her when the smell of roasted pork made her salivate. She couldn't believe how she was reacting. Maybe she was going crazy from all the traumatic events.

It was dark when her aunt Luisa arrived home. Sofi was finishing up a second helping of her uncle's *carnitas*. She knew that Taylor would say it was wrong, but it tasted so good. They were all sitting in the backyard, warming by the fire pit, listening to music, and watching the starry sky. A dark silhouette of a big woman in a starched dress and a tight bun stood in the doorframe. A chill breezed in behind Luisa and carried the scent of ammonia and bleach on its apron strings.

"*¿Qué pasa aquí?*" Luisa hollered, throwing her arms in the air. Yesenia and Uncle Victor jumped up as if lashed by an invisible whip. Luisa stood over Sofi, sizing her up. "*¿Y tú debes ser la hija de mi hermano malcriado?*"

Sofi trembled under her aunt's stare. She swallowed a huge lump of nervousness that had caught in her throat. Obviously, her aunt wasn't crazy to see her. "*Soy Sofia,*" she said, taking very short breaths. "Um . . ."

"I know who you are." Her aunt switched to English. "I was there when you were born. What's the matter?" Sofi couldn't help but quiver at the sound of her voice. "You can't talk?"

"I didn't know that," Sofi said, feeling as small as a pea.

"There's a lot you don't know." Her aunt sighed and looked up at the night sky. "This is all I needed, another mouth to feed. *Ayúdame, San Judas.*"

"My dad—"

Luisa raised her hand, signifying the end of their conversation. "I don't want to talk about him right now," she said, and stormed back into the house.

Sofi was forced to share the bottom bunk with her cousin Yesenia. She couldn't remember the last time she'd slept with another person besides her parents. Yesenia stole all the covers, leaving Sofi to fend for herself in the cold room. The house creaked and sighed as if it were ready to collapse on her head. Sofi cringed and turned over when her cousin started to snore. She never knew a girl could breathe so loud. It was driving her insane! With each inhale the sound grew louder and louder. Sofi sat up to make sure Yesenia wasn't choking. The boys slept on the top bunk.

"Sofi, this one's for you," Mando said before letting a big fart rip.

Sofi held her breath and tried to ignore him.

"No, no, mine better," Mundo interrupted, making a series of short farts and one real long one. "Hee, hee."

It went back and forth, with each twin trying to outdo the other. It was a competition of gastro gusto. Sofi twisted in the lumpy bed, frustrated. She had to get some rest and rolled on her side. She'd tried to remind herself that this was only temporary. Her parents were going to get her home. Then she could forget all about the rancho and her annoying cousins. Sofi thought about the big econ final that week. She had to get at least a B+ to keep her GPA up. But how was she supposed to take the test if she was stuck here in Mexico? The farting and giggling continued well into the night. Sofi held her breath, hoping no one would notice that she was awake.

Sofi didn't think things could get any worse, but she was wrong. In the early hours of the morning, she shuffled noisily through the darkened house and out back to the bathroom. She reached for the switch. The bathroom adjacent to the house resembled a big Pepto-Bismol–pink tiled box. It had a toilet and shower area, and there was no curtain or door separating the spaces, either. Sofi suffered from a ghastly case of explosive diarrhea and stabbing cramps. The Virgin Mary stared down at her from the wall with pity in her eyes but offered no relief from the pain in her bowels and the fermenting around her heart. She hated this place. Tears welled up in her eyes. Life wasn't fair! While all her friends were preparing to go on the senior trip to Knott's Berry Farm today, Sofi was trapped in Mexico on the toilet!

All morning, her family had checked in on her. Uncle Victor had made her a special tea made from some herbs growing in the yard. But it didn't help. Every few minutes, Sofi had to run back to the bathroom. Her aunt's disapproving glare told her that she didn't believe that she was really sick. Why would she lie about something like this?

"Sofi, are you all right?" Andres called out from the other side of the bathroom door.

"Andres?" Her head popped up, cheeks burning hot. "What are you doing here?" Sunlight streamed in from the window.

"I'm sorry, I, um, didn't mean to bother you. Your uncle told me you weren't feeling . . . I, um, wanted to see . . . I brought you an Egg

McMuffin." He paused. "I thought . . . I don't know. I'm sorry to bother you. I'll leave."

"I think I need a doctor," Sofi called through the door as she wiped her nose. The stabbing pain made her body quake and her forehead sweat.

"What are your symptoms?"

"I've got horrible stomach cramps and . . ."

"I'll be right back," Andres said. Sofi closed her eyes as tears ran down her cheeks. This was horribly embarrassing.

Ten minutes later, Andres slipped a packet of white pills under the door crack. Sofi reached out and looked at the label. She didn't recognize the name. But she had to take something quick or else her stomach might split open.

"I'll leave the McMuffin here in case you get hungry," he said softly through the door. "I hope you feel better."

"Thank you."

The pills had an almost immediate effect. It was less than an hour later, but Sofi felt remarkably better. Although her face was still sickly pale, her stomach was finally at ease. *It was really nice of him to bring the sandwich and the medicine,* Sofi thought, holding on to the brown McDonald's bag.

"*Queremos huevos!* Eggs!" Mando and Mundo chanted, banging their forks on the table. Sofi turned, hoping that maybe Luisa, Yesenia, or Uncle Victor were around. But then she remembered Yesenia telling her the night before that she was filling in for her father at the horse-riding beach tours while he nursed a hurt back, and her aunt was at work. The boys couldn't be talking to her. Sofi didn't cook. Then the memory of her aunt's parting words that morning rang in her head like a gong. Luisa had spun around so fast, Sofi thought she'd get whiplash.

"You live here." Luisa pointed at the linoleum floor. Her brown eyes dared Sofi to talk back. "You help. No lazy bums." She raised her finger in the air. "Boys to school at one. Don't forget to give them break-fast. They need clean uniforms. The chickens need to eat too and house swept. . . ."

Whoa, whoa, whoa, Sofi had thought. It had been only a little while since her nightmare in the bathroom and her aunt was already listing chores. What was this woman thinking? Sofi was *not* the hired help. Besides, she was planning to go home today. There was no time to clean.

The boys' continued chanting made her ill. "How about some cereal?" Sofi said, smiling hopefully.

"No!" Mando cried.

She pulled out the McMuffin sandwich that Andres had brought her. "How about this?" Mando smiled and took it from her hand.

"Where's mine?" Mundo asked defensively.

"I only have one. We can share it."

Mando gave her an angry look as he unwrapped it.

"I don't want to share. I want my own." Mundo crossed his scrawny arms in front of his chest.

Sofi huffed in annoyance. Why did he have to make this difficult? "Fine, where is the McDonald's?"

"You got a car?" Mando asked, with his mouth full. "It's on the other side of town." Sofi sighed. If she had a car, she'd be a hundred miles away from here.

"Maybe we can make one." Sofi rummaged through the refrigerator. The sooner she got this over with, she thought, the sooner she could call her parents. Sofi couldn't wait to get out of this crazy place. There was a frying pan filled with orange-colored rice, a pot of beans, leftover pork, withered-looking vegetables, apple juice, and three cans of Tecate beer, but no eggs. "Sorry, Mundo. No eggs." He stared at his brother, who was finishing the last bite of Sofi's McMuffin sandwich. How could Mando be so greedy? Then a chicken clucked from the back porch.

"That's not fair!" Mundo cried, fresh tears welling up in his eyes. "He ate it all!"

Mundo wouldn't stop crying until Sofi promised to get him eggs. He gave her no other option. His yowls were driving her crazy. Sofi stomped out of the kitchen, letting the screen door slam behind her. She grabbed an empty bucket that had been tossed onto the dirt. The chicken coop was a wooden cage with torn pieces of barbed wire fitted together hastily. A shuffling sound behind her told her that her cousins were following. Someone in the neighborhood was playing a Spanish romantic song. The wails of the singer filled the crisp cool air. The coop was dark and smelled moist. *I can't believe I'm doing this*, she thought as she entered. Her feet crushed the scattered pieces of loose hay, making a crackling noise.

Three brown chickens were hanging out in the yard, pecking the dirt for food. Sofi made out the silhouette of three hens resting on straw nests. *The eggs must be there*, she thought. She raised her right arm and hesitated. Did chickens attack? The sound of the boys breathing behind her made her nervous. Sofi quickly shoved her hand under the first fowl's soft feathers. The hen let out a squall and Sofi jumped back. The animal pecked her hand. Sofi pulled back and saw blood. Then a flutter of black and yellow feathers blinded her. The red-faced rooster pounced on her, flapping its wings in her face. Its claws felt like knives tearing at her chest. Sofi raised her arm to cover her face and leaped back through the door. She tripped on the pail, shot back up, and ran for the house.

The sound of the boys laughing made her grit her teeth with anger. Did they enjoy taunting her? Mando and Mundo hurried in after her holding several eggs tucked into their arms. They tossed them into a basket on the table. Sofi held her tongue.

"*Quiero una torta de huevo con chorizo*," Mando demanded, as if he were king of the house.

"What's that?" Sofi felt her shoulders tense up with frustration. She did not enjoy being their personal slave. However, she also didn't want them complaining to Luisa. Her aunt scared her.

"It's a sandwich with eggs and *chorizo*."

"What's *chodizo?*"

Both boys started cracking up. Sofi squirmed.

"Not *chodizo. Chor-r-izo.*" Mando rolled his tongue effortlessly to show her. He pulled out a long sausage from the refrigerator. "This," he said, waving it in the air like a flag.

"You can't talk right," Mundo said.

"I can talk fine. I just have trouble with my *r*'s."

"Say *carro.* No, no, say *Parangaricutirimícuaro.*"

"*Para-* what?"

"*Parangaricutirimícuaro.* It's easy."

Sofi's head hurt just hearing it. "Para-guar-rimi-cuado?"

The boys laughed. They fell out of their chairs and rolled on the floor. Sofi felt her stomach tighten.

"Say it again?" Mando begged, holding his stomach between chuckles. "Say it again."

"I think we should eat," she said, turning to the electric stove. Their drowning laughter filled her ears. She hated her cousins, hated Spanish, hated everything about Mexico. All she wanted was to go home and forget all about this horrible place. Back home nobody cared whether or not she could roll her *r*'s. Sofi spoke English. That was the language of the world, of big business, and success. Mexicans in Mexico even studied English. *In the real world, English is all that matters,* she told herself.

The boys raced ahead of her on the dirt road toward school. It was a quarter to one, and Sofi was afraid of getting them to school late. She hurried down the dirt road with the boys' Power Rangers backpacks strapped over her shoulder. She studied the map Uncle Victor had drawn for her. The sun was high overhead, beaming like a ball of hot fire and warming her scalp. They passed a few houses, the general store, and a tortilla shop. The air danced with the warm, comforting smell of freshly ground corn. Sofi's mom bought tortillas from the store sealed in a plastic bag, but Sofi's nose told her that these had to be a whole lot better. She noticed an old lady with beautiful brown skin and white hair working a machine behind the counter of the shop.

"*Apúrate*," Mando hollered, waving his scrawny arm in the air, motioning for her to hurry.

"Coming," Sofi said. The old woman looked up at the sound of her voice and smiled. According to the map, they had to pass through onion and radish fields. Sofi continued walking west. The route was busy. Water trucks passed her, spitting water onto the dirt road. A small pick-up truck with loudspeakers attached to the cabin passed them slowly, carrying brooms, bags of dirt, and brushes. The booming voice with a catchy tune announced the products for sale. There were other people walking, women trying to get a cab along the route, or children in uniforms on their way to school. Sofi raised her hand to wipe the beads of sweat from her forehead. How much farther would they have to travel?

They reached the edge of the rolling green fields and came to a paved road that led them through another neighborhood. Colonia Mazatlán was more modern because they had paved roads, more stores, and food stands. She followed the boys down the heavily trafficked avenue, onto a crumbling bridge that went over the freeway. The houses on the other side of the bridge were newer and constructed with better materials. She passed an Acura with California license plates parked in front of a cute cottage with a huge concrete fountain. The air was sweet with the fragrance of beautiful, well-manicured flower gardens. She wondered if Americans owned these homes. Up ahead she caught a glimpse of a blue strip on the horizon. It was the ocean. Sofi hurried to catch up with the boys at the end of the block. Her eyes lit up with recognition. This was Boulevard Benito Juarez.

Abraham Lincoln Elementary was located on the main boulevard. It was pretty far from Rancho Escondido. Mando and Mundo had been kicked out of two other schools, so they had no other option. The gray building looked more like an office. It was too quiet for a school. Sofi read the plaque by the front gate. There were a lot of words she didn't know but she learned that the school was named after the U.S. president because he freed the slaves. It was comforting to see a familiar name in this foreign country.

"All right, boys," Sofi said, smiling. "Here we are." She reached out to pull open the gate, but it was locked. A thick, heavy chain coiled around the wire gate. Her watch said it was 1:10 p.m. "Oh, c'mon." She shook the gate. "This is ridiculous." But there was no one there to complain to. Sofi turned to her cousins, who were watching her with amused looks on their faces. The idea of trekking back to Rancho Escondido to clean and care for these brats like a nursemaid was not appealing. She had to call her folks.

"Can you take me to Yesenia's friend? The one who has a phone?"

Yesenia's friend Britannica lived across from the cemetery. Her parents worked on the Other Side and visited on the weekends. She lived in a newly completed brick house with a wrought-iron fence. There was a huge satellite dish on the roof and, best of all, a working phone, which Britannica made extra money charging her neighbors to use.

"Does she speak any English?" Sofi huffed, already out of breath. It was rough walking back with nothing but the hot sun baking her back.

"*No sé.*" Mundo shrugged.

Sofi's stomach twisted.

"Don't worry," Mando said, squinting behind his long black bangs. "Say *te-lé-fo-no por fa-vor.*" That didn't sound hard, Sofi thought, pressing down on the chimed doorbell.

A tall lanky girl with a sour expression and limp dark hair that she'd combed over her left eye opened the heavy wooden door. She regarded Sofi with sleepy gray eyes, like a cat welcoming a stray to her milk bowl.

"*Hola.*" Sofi smiled nervously. Yesenia had mentioned needing to make an appointment first. Hopefully the girl would be nice enough to let it pass.

"*¿Qué tu quieres?*" she barked, crossing her arms.

Sofi's heart started to pound. She looked at her cousins for help.

Britannica looked at the boys and asked, "*¿Qué onda con ésta? ¿Es muda?*"

Sofi didn't know that last word, but she could tell it wasn't good. "*Te-lé-fo-no por fa-vor. Es emergencia,*" she blurted. Britannica took a moment to think, then waved them into the dark house reluctantly.

The cool dark living room looked like it had been decorated by a team of tiny old ladies. There was plastic everywhere: on the firm gray couch, on the ruffled yellow lampshades, on the brown recliner, and covering the kitchen table. The room was small, and damp, and had a decaying smell. Britannica led her to a phone at the end of the hallway.

She told Sofi that it would be five dollars for the first minute. Appalled, Sofi looked at Mando, who was standing next to her. He shrugged. Sofi rolled her eyes. She reached into her pocket. Britannica held the cream-colored cordless phone that was just like Sofi's back at home. Her heart ached, remembering her warm and cozy bed in San Inocente. Britannica asked for her mother's cell number as if she didn't trust Sofi to dial by herself. She dialed and handed Sofi the phone.

"Mom," Sofi said, relieved when her mother picked up on the first ring.

"*Mija*, is that you?" Evie's voice cracked, and she started to sob quietly on the other end. The sound of her mother's voice brought tears to Sofi's eyes. "Why did you take so long to call? I was up all night waiting for you. Are you okay?"

"Mom, I'm at Rancho Escondido."

"How are your arms? Are you eating okay? Now, I know the food is a bit different, but you must remember your manners. I don't want you make faces while eating. Just grin and bear it, okay?"

"Mom." Sofi rolled her eyes. Proper etiquette was the least of her worries. "There's no phone on the ranch. There's nothing." She looked over her shoulder and saw Britannica holding a stopwatch. "This call is costing me a lot."

"Do you have enough money?"

"When are you getting me out of here?" Sofi said in a desperate tone. "I don't want to be here. You know I missed the senior trip."

Silence.

"Mom, are you there?" She heard her mother breathing on the other line. "What aren't you telling me?"

"It's nothing," her mother said quickly. "It's just a little misunderstanding that we will clear up in no time. I don't want you to worry."

"Mom, how long?" Sofi tried hard not to grind her teeth. "Finals are next week. I need to be at school."

"Can I call you at this number?"

"I don't think so."

"Check your e-mail, then. Your dad went to see a lawyer. He's very expensive, but your friend Taylor's parents recommended him highly. I'll have more information for you by the end of the day. Okay?"

"A lawyer? But why, Mom? Why can't you just come and get me?" Silence. "What's the big deal?" Sofi's heart started to race. What was going on? And why was her mother acting so weird? Didn't her mother realize all the things she had to do? "I have finals, Mom! I'm supposed to be graduating next week."

"*Mija* . . ."

Her mother's tone was making Sofi crazy. Why was she acting so calm? "Do you know where I am? I'm living in the middle of nowhere. The electricity goes out every day. They have no phone or Internet. This morning I got attacked by a rooster!"

Her mother chuckled softly. Sofi felt her anger boiling. This was not a joke!

"Don't worry, *mija*. Your dad and I have this under control. We'll have you home in no time. Just be patient."

Her mother's comforting words had the opposite effect. Sofi stared angrily at the rough white wall in front of her. The phone was jabbing her chin. She was pressing it hard, as if trying to force her mother's voice inside her. This was not just some misunderstanding, Sofi thought. If it were, they'd be there at the border right this minute, not talking to a lawyer! "Mom." Sofi struggled with the boiling fury inside her head and the pounding in her chest. "I'm not a child! Will you just tell me what's the holdup?"

"I know, *mija*. I love you."

"Mom!"

"I need you to trust us. Your father knows what's he doing."

"Oh, c'mon," Sofi whined. They were punishing her, she thought. Her parents were going to make her pay for going to Mexico. This was worse than getting grounded, much worse. "Mom, this is so not fair. Why are you guys doing this to me?" Her anger erupted, making the hairs on her arms stand on end.

"*Mija*, please . . ."

"*Mija* nothing! This sucks. It totally sucks big-time. I don't want to be here. I hate it. I hate Mexico. Luisa and her whole family are crazy. And I refuse to stay with them another minute. You hear me! Not another minute. I'd rather live on the street, beg, whatever!" Britannica grabbed her wrist and tore the phone from her hand. Sofi hadn't realized that she was making a scene. Her heart squeezed like a wet sponge. Tears welled up in her eyes. Sofi blinked them back in; everyone in the hallway was staring at her. "What are you looking at?"

Mando and Mundo blinked with blank expressions on their faces.

Britannica scrunched up her nose. "*Oye, tú no me puedes hablar así. Ésta es mi casa. Vete.*" She pointed at the door.

A wave of frustration flowed through Sofi. She imagined grabbing Britannica by her shoulders and shaking her real hard. She wanted to hit something. But Britannica looked solid for a skinny girl and would probably hit her back. "Fine," Sofi spat, marching toward the front door. She didn't want any of this crap. Mando and Mundo followed quietly behind her. The sound of their breath pestered her like a blister on her toe. They said nothing. A noisy truck passed in front of her, blowing dry dust into her eyes. "Damn it!" Sofi pounded the ground with her feet. This was an insane joke! The boys stood a safe distance away, watching her curiously. "What are you looking at?"

"¿Estás bien?" Mando asked.

"Do I look all right to you? Look where I'm at!" She waved her arms in the air as if she were swatting invisible flies. Sofi looked up. There were brushstrokes of thin, wispy cirrus clouds in the blue sky. All of her friends were at Knott's Berry Farm having the time of their lives. They were celebrating the end of an era without her. This was not happening! Sofi clenched her teeth and balled her hands into tight fists and screamed. Mando and Mundo continued to stare. Their pathetic eyes clawed at her skin. "Go away." They didn't move. "I said get away from me. I want to be alone. Sola!" She took a couple of steps as if to chase them. The boys took off, disappearing down the block. People stopped and stared as she passed, wondering who she was. Sofi rubbed her dusty palms over her dry face. Her mind was bogged down with questions she had no answers to. She walked down the street, consumed in her border nightmare.

"Con permiso," a thin man with dusty pants and an old baseball cap said. Sofi stared at him, wondering what he wanted. The guy took out a piece of paper and asked her for directions.

"Do I look like I'm from here?" she yelled in English. The guy gave her a confused look. Sofi shook her head in disbelief. This was ridiculous!

Her mother's words were still ringing in her head when she got back to Rancho Escondido. Uncle Victor snored loudly on the front porch. Three empty Tecate cans were by his bare feet. He was still wearing the ragged orange bathrobe from that morning. What was he thinking?

Sofi let the screen door slam shut behind her as she walked into the living room. Luisa was standing in the kitchen with her hands on her hips and a big frown on her face. Her hair was tied back so tight, it made her eyes look like they were going to pop out of her head. The sound of her aunt's heavy breaths sent shivers up Sofi's back. She knew she was in trouble. Sofi wanted to hide in a dark closet the way she had when she was small. But she couldn't run, not while her aunt blocked her exit. "Why didn't the boys go to school?"

"Um, well . . ." Sofi huffed loudly to herself. This was all that she needed. "I tried to get them there. But the gate was locked."

Luisa dropped a cast-iron pan onto the stove. "I ask you to do one little thing." Her aunt moved around the kitchen in a hurried manner, trying to prepare dinner. "And you can't even do that right. What is wrong with you?"

Sofi looked away from her aunt, pressing her lips tightly together. Her pulse was racing. She didn't know what to say. She hardly knew this woman. Why was Luisa expecting her to work around the house, when Sofi wasn't even supposed to be there? It wasn't fair.

"Look at the boys," Luisa spat. Mando and Mundo were half-naked, playing on the living-room floor with their action figures. Their navy blue pants and bare feet were caked in dirt. "Can't you stop and think of anyone but yourself?"

Sofi had no words. A part of her wanted to complain about the long walk to school, the chicken fiasco, and her mother. Sofi hadn't asked to be stuck with this family in Mexico. She wanted to be home, in her bed. But her aunt's viperlike tongue gave her cold feet.

"And look at the house," Luisa continued to complain. Sofi noticed that dirt had blown through the house, coating everything. The dishes from lunch were still in the sink, and the goat had escaped through the broken fence, looking for food. "Can you tell me what you *did* do?"

Under Luisa's callous stare Sofi crumbled like a child. Fat tears welled up in her eyes and rolled down her cheeks. "I tried," Sofi stammered, choking on her rising anxiety. "My mom's going to get me any minute. I swear. She'll pay you for your trouble."

"*Chamaca idiota!* This isn't about money. That's the problem with you American kids. You have no sense." Her aunt shook her head in disapproval and filled a pot with pinto beans to boil. Sofi wanted to cry, "No!" She wanted to tell her about how she had to do chores and had a job. (Okay, so she was paid under the table, but it was a job.) But instead she ran to her bedroom and cried in the dark. Through the paper-thin walls she could hear Luisa yelling at Uncle Victor for sitting around all day doing nothing (which he did very well). She couldn't understand why her aunt was being so mean to her. She hated this place more than anything in the world. She hated Rancho Escondido. Why couldn't her parents just pick her up? Sofi didn't belong here. She belonged in San Inocente with all her friends.

The lights burst on and Sofi tried to hide her teary face behind a stuffed SpongeBob toy. Yesenia came in with concerned eyes.

"You miss your boyfriend?" Yesenia asked.

Sofi shot right up. What was she talking about? Who could think of guys at a time like this? Yesenia was holding Sofi's binder that had been left in the living room. One day during English class she'd covered a whole page with hearts. Inside the hearts she'd written *Nick + Sofi*. Seeing it brought back a wave of misery and homesickness. All she wanted was to go back in time and return to her old life. "Leave me alone." Tears streamed down her cheeks. Sofi muffled her sobs into the pillow. Yesenia turned off the light and closed the door, leaving Sofi alone in the blackness.

The next morning the big metal bathroom door rattled loudly, startling Sofi. Was some pervert trying to break in while she showered? Sofi looked over her shoulder as hot water trickled in spurts over her body. A small window was centered high above the shower area, to provide the steam with an escape route. Sofi felt exposed, even though she had made sure that the door was locked tight behind her. The laminated picture of the Virgin Mary hung high up on the wall. Her sorrowful eyes watched Sofi. The door continued to shake loudly. Would it come off its hinges? Her eyes darted quickly to the white towel that was on top of the toilet seat, too far away to reach. It was already soaked from the wild splashes of the busted showerhead.

"*Un momento,*" Sofi said, trying to hurry and wash the shampoo out of her hair. A moment ago she'd been relishing the privacy. She'd never imagined how uncomfortable she'd feel with her cousins or how much she took personal space for granted. As a kid, Sofi wished for a brother or sister to play with. She fantasized about teaching them how to play hide-and-seek or staying up all night waiting for Santa Claus together on Christmas Eve. However, her *real* relatives were nothing like her imaginary playmates.

The clatter continued outside the bathroom door. Sofi's skin broke out in goose bumps. Who could it be? "*Hola,*" her voice wavered. "I'm in here." She squinted her eyes, watching the door as suds dribbled down her face, blurring her view. Hopefully, whoever was on the other side would understand and leave her alone. Then a horrible thought passed through her, as the bar of Ivory soap slipped from her hands and onto the floor. Maybe they *had* no boundaries? Maybe they were used to coming and going while people showered? Scrambling for the soap, she wished for some sort of Mexican manual or rulebook to understand this family.

The shrill sound of a wolf whistle made her look up just in time to see Mando or Mundo's shiny black helmet of hair outside the bathroom window. Sofi screamed, "Perverts!" as she tried to cover herself with the wet towel.

There was a thump outside, as if the boys had jumped off something, and more giggling. Suddenly the water turned ice cold. "Yikes!" she cried and jumped out of the shower, suds still clinging to her hair. She ran out of the room, her wet towel wrapped around her, and screamed: "Mando! Mundo!" Sofi stopped. Then she looked down at her dirtied feet. She'd forgotten to put on her sandals before stepping out onto the hard-packed earthen yard. *Damn it! Damn it! Damn it!* She tried to clean off her feet but she just muddied them further.

Yesenia and Uncle Victor ran outside.

"*¿Qué pasó?*" her uncle asked.

"Those boys turned off the hot water! *Apagaron el agua,*" she repeated angrily.

Mando and Mundo stood a polite distance away, looking as innocent as the ceramic angels in Luisa's glass cabinet. Uncle Victor quickly turned on them, shouting angry threats and taking off his black leather belt. The boys leaped under the banister, screaming at the top of their lungs around the house.

"Serves them right," Sofi said. She sniffed loudly and marched back into the bathroom to wash her feet again.

A couple of minutes later, Yesenia walked in on Sofi while she was changing in the bedroom. Sofi grabbed her shirt off the bed to cover her chest. *Doesn't anyone knock around here?* Yesenia plopped down on the bottom bunk.

"The hot water ran out," Yesenia announced. She was wearing a pair of faded blue jeans with pink hearts sewn on the front pockets, a Hooters baby tee, and house slippers.

"What? No hot water?" Sofi asked. *Oh no.* She was getting the hell out of this crazy place as soon as she finished getting dressed. Yesenia watched Sofi lace her white K-Swiss sneakers. It made Sofi uneasy. Yesenia had a strange look of awe in her eyes. Sofi wasn't wearing anything fancy, just a pair of green shorts that tied in the front and a white tank top.

"The hot water runs on gas. We have to buy it by the tank. These big trucks come by and exchange them. They honk. You'll hear it." Yesenia was acting friendly for once. The gesture touched Sofi, and she wondered if they could be friends.

"A tank? That's so weird." Then it suddenly hit her. "Oh my God! Those poor boys . . ." Sofi rushed to the window to look outside. Why had she gone flying off the handle like that? She hoped that the boys hadn't been severely punished.

"Don't worry about Papá." Yesenia smiled and started to straighten the Mickey Mouse comforter on the bottom bunk. "He's never raised a hand to any of us. He's like the *mayates*, the big flying beetles, all scary looking but perfectly harmless."

"I'm sorry." Sofi rubbed her hands over her face briskly. Yesenia was trying to be nice. "I'm sorry about last night, too. This whole situation with my papers has me jittery about everything. I've got all these things back home to do and I feel helpless out here." She looked around the room. Her stomach quivered. How long would she have to put up with this strange place? "I guess I didn't sleep well last night." She showed Yesenia her arms, which were covered in bug bites.

"*Chinches.*" Yesenia nodded. "You'll get used to that." Sofi tried not to roll her eyes. It was really hard. She couldn't believe how weird her family was! Sofi's mom would have called the exterminator and rushed her to the emergency room.

Sofi continued, "That rooster wouldn't let me sleep either. Does he always cry at three o'clock in the morning?"

"Only when he wants . . . um . . . how do you say? Sex." Yesenia smirked.

Sofi couldn't help but laugh. "Are you serious?"

Yesenia nodded. "Yeah, you should see him when he gets crazy. Once he climbed on the goat and—"

"Stop! I've heard enough," Sofi said, squeezing her eyes shut as she raised her arm in front of her face. The image was too much to bear. Yesenia laughed even louder. She had a nice bright smile that lit up her face.

"Sofia!" The tone in her aunt's voice made them both freeze. Aunt Luisa had a rich deep voice that reverberated throughout the house, giving one the sense that she was everywhere at the same time. The woman commanded reverence by her sheer size and rigid pose. Luisa was the spitting image of Sofi's father but about five times wider around the hips. They even had the same mustache. However, unlike Sofi's dad, there wasn't an ounce of sweetness in Aunt Luisa. She stood in the kitchen dressed in her maid uniform, her hair pulled back in a tight bun. Luisa was holding a coat hanger in one hand and a plastic bucket in the other.

What could she be mad at now? Sofi wondered. *All I did was take a shower!*

"*Vente,*" her aunt commanded, motioning to her with the flick of her head. Luisa led Sofi to the bathroom, where she found, to her dismay, a flood. The toilet was overflowing, spewing out pieces of toilet paper. Gross. "*Ay ay ay.*" Luisa shook her head. Her slippers splashed in the murky water. Sofi cringed at the thought of tiny little feces germs swimming about. Her white shoes were going to be filthy. Luisa handed Sofi the hanger. "Doesn't your dad teach you anything?"

Sofi's eyes grew big. *What was she talking about?*

"We do not put paper in the toilet. That's what this bag here is for." She picked up a plastic bag full of paper wads. *Gross!* Sofi thought as she tiptoed around trying not to ruin her shoes. "I want you to unclog the toilet with this." She handed her the hanger. "And don't put paper in there again." Luisa turned and noticed Yesenia watching from the door. "Let's go, let's go," her aunt said in a heavy accent. She clapped her hands together.

Sofi heard the back screen door slam shut. The sound of running water filled the air. With the coat hanger in hand, Sofi broke down quietly by herself. What had she done to deserve this?

Uncle Victor was on the porch, making cutesy sounds to his goat. He was wearing his ratty orange bathrobe and Hush Puppies slippers, and his hair was sticking out in different directions. The brown dairy goat circled around him in complete adoration. Sofi dumped the plastic bag full of wet wads of paper into an old oil drum by the side of the house that was used for trash. She would never again complain to her mother about scrubbing the toilet, she swore.

"Excuse me," Sofi said in a low voice. She asked Uncle Victor about Internet cafés. He didn't know anything about them but offered to get her a phone card. Sofi was desperate to call her mom. She had to know what was going on. Uncle Victor got up and put on his cowboy hat. He changed into a jean jacket. They were going to the store.

"*Buenos días*, Don Victor!" a young man with big ears and a nice smile called out on his bike. He was expertly maneuvering through the street with a large basket of freshly baked bread on top of his head. Her uncle waved back, telling Sofi that the boy's name was Miguel and that his family owned the best bakery in town. As they continued down the road, Uncle Victor pointed out the different neighbors' houses.

"That is where your grandmother Benita lives," he said in Spanish, pointing to a peeling pink shack with yellow roses and white bougainvilleas crawling up the side. The metal fence had big rips and the yard looked neglected. An angry mutt barked at them wildly as they passed. Sofi wondered about her grandmother and why Yesenia hated her so much.

It was a beautiful bright day, with white puffy clouds accenting the bluish sky. Despite the warm day Sofi felt sick to her stomach. She didn't want to be here. The familiar cries of happy children playing pierced the air. There were knots of people walking about. Uncle Victor greeted everybody with a *"Buenos días!"* Sofi thought about how friendly her uncle was. She herself was usually always in a hurry and never stopped to say hi to any of her neighbors.

They stopped in front of a small storefront, next to the tortilla shop. Cheerful mariachi music played from inside. The air was filled with the scent of fresh tortillas. It made Sofi's stomach growl. Sipping from a mug of hot chocolate was the old woman Sofi had seen the day before. She was very cute, sitting on a milk crate with her long white braid running down her back. Uncle Victor introduced her as Doña Clementina. She was the oldest woman in the neighborhood. Sofi instantly liked this old woman. She had a fiery no-nonsense spirit and a childlike, mischievous smile.

"¿Habla español?" she asked Sofi's uncle. Victor nodded a little and Doña Clementina turned to her and shouted in a high voice: "Welcome to Rancho Escondido. So you're Edmundo's daughter."

Sofi flinched. She wasn't deaf. "You know my father?"

The old woman started to laugh. Her dark eyes disappeared under her wrinkly eyelids. Uncle Victor explained that Doña Clementina knew everybody and had a habit of always finding out the juiciest gossip first. The old woman laughed even harder. "Your father used to work right here." She went into the shop and brought out two fresh tortillas for Sofi and Uncle Victor to munch on. "I think he had three other jobs, too. Your dad"—she paused, smiling—"was such a good boy. Very hardworking and serious. I was so sad when he went north. I knew he wouldn't come back. He always told me that he was going to be a big man one day." She took a sip from her chocolate. "Well, is he?"

Sofi nodded, smiling shyly with pride. She wondered what her father was doing right now. Had he contacted the lawyer? Were they on their way?

"Good." She slapped her thigh. "Now what about you? I hear you got yourself into trouble at the border."

Sofi's heart tightened. This woman knew everything. She searched her brain for the right words in Spanish. "Yeah, I don't know what's wrong," she said hesitantly, looking at her uncle's face for some reaction. "My parents said they have it under control."

"Do they now," Doña Clementina said as she stared out at the road ahead. Sofi and Uncle Victor waited. "The border is a strange thing. It's brought lots of joy and sorrow to my life. I remember the time I crossed into the United States through a dirt tunnel in Texas. The cavernous path was so dark, I could hardly make out my own hands. The worst part was the smell." She made a disgusted face. "It smelled of piss and rotten flesh. That must have been over thirty years ago. I ended up here in Rosarito after my fifth deportation. It's hard living like a scared *pollito*— you know, baby chick. That's what the coyotes, the smugglers, call us people who want to cross. I like Rosarito, though. It wasn't my American dream, but I think I gained much more. I have a nice shop that's close to the beach. There're lots of friends who stop by. Life is good. I don't stress about being deported or about managers trying to cheat me because of papers. Here, I'm in charge of my life. I like that."

Uncle Victor interrupted to apologize, saying that Sofi had to buy a Ladatel phone card to call her parents. Apparently, Doña Clementina had a way of making people lose track of time. Sofi said good-bye and promised to stop by again to *charlar* (as Doña Clementina called it). Her uncle told her that there were many public phones along Boulevard Benito Juarez. She could call her parents after dropping off the boys at school.

That afternoon Sofi called out to the boys from the front gate. "*Vámonos.* Let's go!" Her uncle had hailed a cab. He explained to the driver where they were going and told Sofi to pay up front. They arrived at Abraham Elementary School *before* the bell. Their teacher, a large woman with short bangs framing her long face, seemed pleased.

"Ha!" Sofi cheered as she watched the boys begrudgingly march into their classroom. She smiled, feeling a deep sense of triumph. Sofi wanted to call Taylor or Olivia. They wouldn't believe the hell she'd been through. But she decided to try her parents first. She would explain everything to her friends in full detail right afterward. With her teeth she ripped open the phone card wrapper. She was about to toss the wrapper on the floor, as she'd seen Mando and Mundo do with just about everything, but she thought better of it and stuffed the plastic into her back pocket. Taylor would kill her; plus the streets were already crawling with enough trash.

Sofi walked to the corner and picked up the receiver of the blue public phone with the word TELEMEX written across it. No tone. *Weird*, she thought, and pressed a couple of buttons. *Nada*. Dead. She looked at her phone card. The word LADATEL was written across it in neat red letters. Down the block there was a red booth with the name Ladatel. *Maybe*, she thought, *the cards only work for certain phones?* She stomped her foot on the ground. Why hadn't she asked her uncle about the phones? She hated feeling so dependent on others, like she was a baby!

She continued down the palm-tree-lined sidewalk, enjoying the warm sun caressing her face. A white station wagon taxi with people stuffed inside like a pack of Oscar Mayer wieners honked at her. Sofi tried to imagine her mother as a teenager, sitting in the back of one of the taxis. She couldn't see it. Her mother hated public transportation. She wouldn't even take the bus. Noisy trucks blared Spanish tunes and scattered the dust in all directions. Sofi fanned herself as they passed. Although she was close to the beach, the air was dry and made her thirsty. She watched schoolkids in plaid uniforms fool around with their friends. A boy was messing with one of the girls, pulling on her hair. Her mother had said that her family was too poor to pay for uniforms. In the United States, there was free public schooling, in nice buildings, and all kinds of materials.

She looked both ways as she crossed the busy street, recognizing some of the residential side streets from the day before. The single-story houses had nice gardens filled with bright pink bougainvilleas. Some of the walls were littered with gangster tags she couldn't make out and political announcements, or advertised products like Nestlé chocolate or potato chips. In the opposite direction, not three blocks away, was a thin blue line: the ocean. She approached the Ladatel booth and stepped back in shock. The entire phone was missing. Someone had stolen it, leaving behind a hole with wires hanging out.

Sofi refused to give up and stomped down the block. It wasn't until her fourth attempt that she found a phone that seemed to work. However, Sofi quickly realized that nothing in Mexico was ever *that* easy. Every time she tried to dial her home number, the operator told her that she'd dialed wrong. There had to be a special international code to dial. She looked at the phone, under it, and around it. *Don't give up. Ask someone*, she scolded herself. Sofi looked around at the people hurrying about their business. There were three blond teenagers in bright summer outfits speaking English obnoxiously loud as if desperate to announce to the world that they were Americans. They wouldn't do, she thought, watching several kids follow their mother, who was selling the beaded necklaces that were hanging off her forearm. Anxious, Sofi reached out to a heavyset young man wearing faded jeans and eating an ear of corn on the cob dashed with a creamy substance and cheese.

"Con permiso," Sofi said, holding up the phone card and pointing with her other hand at the phone. "¿Me ayuda?"

"¿Eres americana?" the guy asked, smiling warmly. Sofi said yes and told him that she wanted to call her parents in the United States. The guy nodded, handed her his corn, and took her card. The cob smelled delicious and made her stomach rumble. She hoped the guy didn't hear it. He showed her how to dip the card into the reader. Then he pointed out the U.S. prefix in tiny markings along the side of the phone.

"Muchísimas gracias," she thanked him, passing him back the corn. The moment he was ten feet away, she picked up the receiver and repeated his directions in her head. Then she heard the familiar odd ring. *I did it*, she thought excitedly, pressing the receiver to her face as if it were an expensive bottle of her favorite perfume.

"Hello?" Her mother's voice went through the phone directly into Sofi's heart, rekindling her homesickness.

"Mom!" Sofi shouted. Two businesswomen in suits jumped at the sound of her voice.

"Sofi, you all right?" her mother cried.

"Yes, I'm here." There was a break in the call. A recorded operator informed her in Spanish that she had thirty seconds left on her card.

"Baby, I'm sorry I didn't get—," her mother began.

"Mom," Sofi interrupted. She had to explain how horrible it was for her here. Her mother had to understand and get her back home. "This phone is going to cut me off. You have to get me out of here! It's awful. Luisa hates me and is making me do all kinds of work. I have to take care of my cousins. Yesterday a rooster attacked me. I got real sick from the food. I can't believe all the stuff I'm missing at school. How am I supposed to graduate? You said not to worry, but it's taking too long and I don't know what'll happen if—"

The line went dead. Damn card.

Thursday was *mercado* day. The main street in Rancho Escondido transformed overnight from a dusty, rain-rutted, unpaved road into a lively street fair. Tents were set up side by side for several blocks, selling locally grown produce, clothes from the Other Side, and all sorts of trinkets. Uncle Victor called it the market on wheels, because each day it moved to a different neighborhood. This was where the people in the community shopped if they didn't go to the U.S.-priced mega food chains downtown. The vendors sold everything and anything a person could need.

Sofi crumpled the list had Luisa handed her that morning and tossed her loose, just-washed hair over her shoulder. The air was cold and dry. Dust clouds swirled around her whenever a car drove by. Noisy birds chirped overhead, dancing back and forth as if playing tag in the trees that lined the road. The electricity poles sizzled and crackled as if ready to explode. Sofi hated being here. She couldn't imagine being stuck anyplace worse. *At least I still look cute*, she thought, strutting down the street in her denim mini, pink tank top, and gem-studded shades. Mando and Mundo ran ahead. Sofi stumbled forward. Her high heels kept getting stuck in the cobblestones. Luisa made her take the twins wherever she went. Why did she have to buy the groceries anyway? Wasn't that her aunt's job? Luisa was totally dumping all her motherly duties on her, as if Sofi didn't have anything better to do, like calling her parents and getting the hell out of here.

She approached the first produce stand. The blue tarp shaded the produce from the sun but did nothing to stop the wild swarms of flies. Sofi lifted her shades to the top of her forehead and cringed at the sight of the food. The fruits and veggies were covered in dirt, as though they'd just been picked. Egg-shaped tomatoes, twisted green chili peppers, and yellow squashes were stacked hastily in box crates. Feeling the ripeness of an avocado, she wondered if it was sanitary. There were other people shopping too. A large woman with a messy bun was gabbing at the counter with the shop clerk. Toward the back, there was an old man with a little girl pouring pinto beans from a bin into a plastic bag. Sofi glanced back. Mando and Mundo were sneaking grapes into their mouths. Why was her aunt punishing her like this? They couldn't be taken anywhere. A girl with thick dark curls standing at the edge of the aisle handed Sofi a plastic bucket.

"*Gracias,*" Sofi mumbled under the girl's scrutiny. She knew that the girl was checking her out. Could she tell that Sofi wasn't from around here? Maybe by her name-brand clothes or the way she carried herself? Then again, maybe she couldn't. Maybe she thought Sofi was someone from school? Her stomach quivered. Back home Sofi was known for her pretty year-round tan and long black hair. Although there were other Latinas in her school, she never hung out with them. All her friends were white. Sofi didn't like always being the different-looking one. A small smile played on her lips. It was odd, but she liked blending in.

She grabbed a couple of things from the list and hurried to the cash register. She didn't want to be here and didn't like the way the girl with the dark curls kept looking at her.

"Huh?" Sofi asked the cashier. She'd said something Sofi didn't catch. The girl rolled her eyes, huffed loudly, and said something to the woman standing next to her. Sofi felt her cheeks burn. She wondered if she could get away with just keeping her mouth shut for the remainder of her time in Mexico. Every time she opened it, she inadvertently made a fool of herself. Mando tugged on her shirt. "Don't forget to say thank you when you're done. You know how to say it, right?"

"Of course," Sofi said, holding back a chuckle. "*Gracias.*"

"You *could* say that," Mundo said, crossing his arms in front of his pint-sized chest. "But you want to talk like a Mexican or a *gringa*?"

"Well, I can't talk like a *gringa*; I'm not white," Sofi said.

"Anyone who thinks they're American"—he flicked his nose with his index finger—"is a *gringa*. But if you want, we can teach you some slang so that you sound more like a Mexican."

Sofi sucked in her cheeks, thinking. Maybe if she passed as a Mexican, she wouldn't get ripped off. Besides, she already looked Mexican. "Sure."

Mando smiled and cleared his throat. "Here in Rosarito we say, "*Comételo, buey*," when we are thanking someone. It's like, 'Thank you, my friend,'" Mundo said, plucking a grape from the bag and sticking it into his mouth.

At the counter, the cashier rattled off a list of numbers that made Sofi's head spin. After Sofi paid, she waved good-bye to the shop clerk and said, "*Comételo, buey!*" Everyone in the entire area stopped to stare at her. Sofi looked around wondering if maybe she had pronounced the words wrong. The girl started cursing under her breath. Mando and Mundo dragged Sofi away as the girl's voice started to get louder. "What's wrong with her?" Sofi asked, bewildered and confused. Mundo took a plastic bag from her. Mando shrugged, laughing quietly behind her back.

Sofi checked her list. "I still need something called *piloncillo*."

"Oh." Mundo nodded. "We call that *panocha*."

"*Panocha?*"

"Yeah." He grew serious. "I know where we can get it, too." The boys took off and ran into a store at the corner. They hugged the man behind the counter. A soccer game was on a black-and-white mini TV. The man had light blue eyes, a square jaw with a cleft chin, and was at least six feet tall. He had to hunch his shoulders over because the ceiling was low. Behind him was a framed photograph of a young man with sad eyes, thin lips, and hair parted on the side. There were a vase of daisies, some candles, and a Corona beer in front of the photo. Sofi wondered who it was. The store felt cramped, with no windows. It felt like a wooden box. Every inch of space was stacked with rows of potato chips, candy, warm soda and juices, and some household items like paper plates, sponges, and laundry detergent.

Mando introduced the store owner, Lalo Jiménez. He was Mando's *padrino*, or godfather. Lalo gave the boys free candy from a bowl on the counter. "*¿Hablas español?*" he asked warmly. Sofi squirmed and shook her head. Why bother trying? Lalo smiled and offered her a cup of coffee. She hesitated, feeling out of place. Everyone in this town wanted to talk and hang out. She was divided between the desire to call her friends and her duty to be courteous. Sofi accepted the drink. The coffee was instant but warmed her body.

"Do you have a *panocha*?" she asked.

Lalo gave the boys a quick look and then started laughing until tears squeezed from his eyes. He pulled down a dried sugary-coned thing from a shelf. "*Panocha* has two meanings. You watch what those boys teach you."

"Thank you." Sofi felt her anger rising.

"Don't worry about them. They're just having a little fun with you. I heard you got into some trouble at the border," Lalo said in Spanish. Good gossip travels fast. Sofi nodded her head. His eyes were sad like those of the guy in the picture. Sofi noticed a black ribbon tacked to his door. Was it a Mexican holiday?

"What's the ribbon for?"

"We have this tradition on the border," he said, sighing deeply and taking a sip from his cup, "when a family member dies trying to cross." Lalo motioned to the framed photograph. "My brother's body was just sent to our village in Sonora." Sofi's eyes grew wide. "He was riddled with bullets. Those damn Minute Men," Lalo said heatedly. He was quiet for a long moment. "The Minute Men is a U.S. vigilante group that patrols the border. A bunch of trigger-happy racists who feel that the country is being invaded by Mexicans." There was pain in his words. "What those fools don't understand is that it is we Mexicans who make it possible for them to have big cars, big houses, and even bigger guns. It's these hands," Lalo said, lifting up his wide, callused palms, "working in the fields, washing dishes, and cleaning their houses. You can't have a superpower nation without stepping on someone's back to get there."

"I'm sorry for your loss," Sofi said. She'd never heard about the Minute Men, but what they were doing was horrific!

Lalo smiled and patted her shoulder. "Okay, no more talk about killings. Let's talk about something happy. Tell me, how do you like Rosarito?"

Sofi smiled awkwardly. Her body felt stiff. Should she tell him that she hated it? That she wanted to get the hell out of there? "It's nice. But I really miss my parents and need to call them."

Lalo sold her a calling card and asked her to come back soon. Sofi hurried back to the house. On the walk, she noticed lots of houses with black ribbons on the front doors. Had all these people also lost loved ones at the border? Sofi couldn't think about that now; she had to hurry because it was almost time to take the boys to school.

The sound of a low, deep growl made her freeze. Slowly she turned and saw three stray mutts following her. Mando and Mundo were nowhere in sight. She tried to ignore the animals, but her heart was pounding wildly and she was already covered in sweat. As Sofi continued walking, she could hear the sound of paws pattering behind her. She looked at the cottages to her left and right. There was no one about. A sudden panic gripped her heart. A dog barked angrily behind her. *He must be the leader, telling them to get me*, she thought. Sofi screamed and took off running around the corner, waving one arm wildly in the air. The dogs chased her as if they were on a foxhunt. She was the worst runner in her entire class. She tripped, twisting her ankle. Was this how her life was going to end?

Luckily, the dogs stopped at the edge of the block. Sofi watched them from behind a cement fence covered with violet bougainvilleas growing up the side like veins. She'd lost her cute heels! But there was no way she was going back to fetch them. The three mangy mutts growled softly, sniffing the air, then returned to sunbathing in the middle of the dirt road. The dogs were horrible. They roamed the streets like thugs. But what about the boys? Her breath caught. Had the dogs gotten to them first?

A boy's shriek rose above the now familiar country animal sounds of her family's ranch. It was coming from behind the house. She knew it was Mando. He had that high-pitched voice. She found him tied to a pole. Mundo was throwing grapes at him. *"¡Chamacos!"* she shouted. But she didn't have time to be mad. She had to get them ready for school.

A short while later, Sofi dragged the boys from the taxi just as the principal, in a brown suit, was closing the school gate. The woman looked annoyed but allowed the scowling boys to come in. Sofi smiled at the busy boulevard before her. Cars were jammed at the intersection as some motorists refused to wait their turn to pass. So much disorganization! Sofi wondered where the traffic cops were. But just then a sign on the opposite side of the street caught her eye: EL GORDO'S INTERNET CAFÉ. It had a cartoon picture of a fat kid at a computer.

"Yes!" she cheered, and raced into the air-conditioned little room furnished with fifteen decade-old desktop computers. Okay, so the machines were out of date, but they had high-speed Internet and a Web cam, so what did she care? Behind the counter sat a girl with dyed blond hair tied in a ponytail with lots of cute star-shaped hair clips. She had on thick eyeliner and was yapping away on the phone while downloading music onto her computer.

"Computadora, por favor," Sofi requested. The clerk assigned her cubicle number twelve, all the way in the back. Three schoolboys looked excitedly at a WWE Web page at station number three. A girl was intensely IMing someone while checking her Yahoo! account at station five. Next to her, there was an older man in a tie typing a document with

his index fingers. Sofi hurried to her seat. The mouse didn't work too well and all the text was in Spanish. It didn't bother Sofi, because she could log in with her eyes closed. Her heart jumped as she typed in her login "sofilicious1," and password, "*********". It felt like ages since she'd seen her screen name.

Her home page opened up and with one click she was back in a virtual version of America. There were tons of messages. Tears welled up in her eyes. Her heart was racing so fast and she wanted to shout at the top of her lungs. She hadn't been forgotten! People loved her. Sofi couldn't make her hands move fast enough as she excitedly opened the first e-mail.

> To: sofilicious1@yahoo.com
> From: livygrl@gmail.com
> Subject: Where da hell r u?
>
> sofi!!!!
> what da hell! where r u? i miss u crazy.
> every1 is talking bout u. ur like hecka popular now.
> even jerk-off nick came up to me to ask about u.
> crazy crazy. im sooo jealous. will u b back 4 prom?
> call me!!!!! im dying to no what's goin on!!!!!
> ;o

Sofi hit reply and started to type.

> Olivia,
> You'll never believe what's happened to me. It feels
> like I've woken up in a total nightmare. I'm living in
> the country with pigs, horses, roosters, and even a
> goat. I swear to God, no joke. I hate it here! It's hell.
> There are these creepy-crawlers in the bed called

chinches that bite me every night and the friggin'
rooster cries in the middle of the night. There's no hot
water and the lights go out all the time!! There's no
cable, no Internet, and no phone!!! Can you believe it?
And I have a horrible aunt who bosses me around
like I'm her slave. I hate it all. I don't know how long I'll
be here. My parents say that I'll be home soon. The
sooner the better! I'll write more later. Love you.
Miss you. Tell everyone I'm all right. Make up
something cool.

Later,
Sof

Taylor had written a three-page account (single-spaced) of what had happened when they got home. In summary, both Taylor and Olivia were grounded. Neither one had gone on the senior trip. Steve got back from Rosarito with a bad allergic reaction to the shrimp. He'd swollen up so much that he had to go to the emergency room. Nick was going to the prom with Sarah Baker. Sofi looked away from the screen. She didn't want to read another word about Nick. In her mind he was dead, gone forever, and buried six feet under. Sofi scrolled past a couple of lewd e-cards from Olivia and a bunch of e-mails from other people she sort of knew. *Wait a second*, she thought, looking at all the e-mails. There were at least a dozen messages. It looked like the whole school knew about her situation. Sofi saw an urgent message from her dad and clicked it open.

To: sofilicious1@yahoo.com
From: edmundomend@yahoo.com
Subject: How are you?

Sofia,

How are you? Your mother and I are very worried. I
hope you are well and getting along with your aunt
and uncle. They are good people and will look after
you until we settle this matter. I'm sorry that it is
taking so long. Don't worry. We will get this taken care
of. Just stay at the rancho. I love you very much.☺

Dad

We can let circumstances rule us, or we can take
charge and rule our lives from within.
—Earl Nightingale

Sofi's pulse began to race. This was not the news she'd expected.
That's it? Sofi cried to herself, scanning all her mail entries for a part two
or another message from her dad. Something was *not* right. Although
her parents had told her not to worry and sit tight, her instincts told her
that they were keeping something from her. Her eyes glazed over as his
words sank in. He wanted her to stay in Rancho Escondido. But for how
long? A day? A week? This was taking too long. What about the prom,
finals, and graduation? Sofi sadly thought of the baby blue prom dress
that she'd picked out with her mother, which now hung in her closet
back home collecting dust. Would she ever get to wear it?

Sofi pulled out her wad of cash. There were three twenties, one ten,
and two hundred pesos. She handed the clerk ten dollars and got fifty
pesos back in change. Ouch. Her money was going quickly. She took a
deep breath to calm her nerves. Her parents were going to get her home
soon. There were two hours left before the budding Einsteins were
released. In Mexico the kids went to school for only three hours in the
morning or late afternoon. It was a beautiful summer day. She decided
to take a walk.

Boulevard Benito Juarez always had something new to show her. She'd walked the drag countless times, but she was only now seeing that this town was like a wedding cake: built on layers and layers of different perceptions. There were the American tourists who came down on the weekends for cheesy knickknacks, cheap pharmaceutical drugs, and free watered-down shots of tequila. Then there were the people who lived off the tourism, like the handsome older man with the silver hair holding up a thick silver necklace as she walked by. Did he see every American as a fountain of wealth? she wondered as she shook her head at him. There were the American expatriates, older folks who spoke Spanish and lived off their pensions in well-lit, gated communities. She remembered seeing the secured condos outside of town. Thick high walls were dotted with broken pieces of glass to keep the natives at bay. Sofi lowered her eyes quickly when they locked with those of a mean-looking thug with a thin goatee and lots of tattoos. Rosarito was a strange place. She jumped down the two-foot curb and waited for a bus to pass before running across the street.

On the next corner was Club Zone. The place had a taco grill on one side and tables for lounging and people-watching on the other. There was bumping music pouring out of the large speakers and a huge flat-screen TV above the entrance showing music videos.

"*Debe ser día festivo en el cielo porque todos los ángeles están aquí,*" someone said behind her.

"Huh?"

"Are you lost?"

"No," Sofi turned, flustered. The man smiled. Sofi jerked back, surprised. He was gorgeous! She thought he must be a model or something with his chiseled profile, thick kissable lips, rich olive skin, and dark curly locks that fell over his dreamy eyes. The man oozed sexiness. Olivia and Taylor would give him a perfect ten.

"'Cause you're a long way from heaven," he said with a sexy Enrique Iglesias lisp. Then he clutched his chest and pretended to fall over.

Sofi giggled. She never giggled. It was the corniest thing she'd ever heard. But coming from him, it was magical. "You okay?" Sofi asked. Her body was starting to shake. She tried to take short, shallow breaths, but her flushed cheeks gave her away. This guy was so hot, totally out of her league, but he was totally flirting with her. With her! Sofi offered the sexy stranger her hand.

"I am now," he said, pulling himself up and closer to her, within licking distance. Every word out of his mouth made her stomach tickle and her arm hairs stand on end. He was wearing Hugo cologne. She nervously backed away from him.

"C'mon, you can't leave," he said, leading her to one of the round tables inside Club Zone. It was still early and the place was empty except for a couple of tourists in loud Hawaiian shirts. "You just got here." He gestured to a metal chair with a palm tree design for a backrest. Everything about him was smooth and confident. The way he pushed her seat in, the way he ordered the waiter over with a flick of his wrist. She felt like she was in some elegant Puff Daddy video—maybe it had something to do with the background music.

"Can I offer you something to drink?" the sexy stranger asked.

"I'll have a Coke."

He gave her a curious look. "You sure?" Sofi nodded with a goofy smile. His proximity thrilled the hairs on her neck and her arms broke out in goose bumps, in a good way. She felt her heart flutter. Maybe this was fate's way of making it all up to her, she thought.

"People call me Rico," he said. Sofi wiped her sweating palms on her skirt and looked down at her now-brown slippers. Why hadn't she changed her shoes before going out? Maybe she should carry an extra pair in her purse. The dust was like a virus infecting everything it came into contact with. Sofi glanced back at Rico and hoped he wouldn't notice. He was looking at her expectantly, but she couldn't think of anything clever to say. This guy was so slick and cool. Sofi started to panic. What if he found out that she was a total dork with zero experience?

"You're not from around here, are you?" He played with his beer coaster and glanced at her coyly.

Thankfully, the Coke arrived. She took a big gulp. It wasn't very ladylike but she had to wet her dry throat and stall for time. "I'm from San Inocente."

"Orange County," he said, leaning back in his chair in a relaxed manner. "They got the best beaches."

"Totally."

Rico flexed his bulging biceps behind his head, studying her like she was a rare jewel. "I've been around there a couple of times," he said, reaching out to grab the back of her chair. Rico had this air of sensuality that made Sofi's skin burn. Watching him sip on his iced drink, she reviewed her boyfriend-material checklist in her head.

Romantic: He had to be. He'd bought her a drink. ✓

Not gay: He didn't pluck his eyebrows, always a good sign. ✓

Stylish: He had good taste; she admired his dark slacks, shiny black shoes, and expensive-looking dress shirt. ✓

And unlike Nick, Rico was trying to *woo her*. He was definitely interested in her. ✓✓✓

This guy was not a boy. He was a total, 100 percent, grade-A, top-choice man. *Now*, she thought, sitting up real straight, *I have to say something really cool and not act like a total goofball.* She leaned back in her chair and tried to sound relaxed.

"You here on vacation?" she asked, trying to imitate the way Olivia's voice got husky when she was flirting with a guy. She tilted her chair a tad too far back and suddenly felt it falling backward. Rico caught hold of the chair and steadied it. They both laughed.

"Thank you."

"All in a day's work for Prince Charming," he joked. "Now what was your question again? Oh yeah, you could say that I'm on vacation. And you?"

"Well, I . . . I'm kinda staying with family. It's complicated." She shrugged, feeling her cheeks get hot. *Real smooth, dorko.* She looked down at her chipped nails and balled her hands into tight fists.

"This is your first time in Rosarito," he stated, as if reading her mind. Boy, was this guy good, Sofi thought. "It sure must be different for you. Rosarito isn't like you imagined, huh?"

Sofi instantly liked Rico. It felt like ages since she'd been able to just be herself and hang out. There wasn't anyone she could really talk to about her situation, she realized. At the ranch, her family was too caught up in their own dramas. E-mails were okay, but she really didn't have anyone to just rant to.

"I did something real stupid. My friends and I drove down to this party. My parents didn't know." Rico listened carefully, nodding his head. "It was a horrible weekend, but whatever. When we were going back there was some problem with my green card. I don't really understand, because my parents are total model Americans and would never break the law. But the border agent took my card. He said it was fake. I know it's a mistake. My parents are going to fix it."

"Wow." Rico breathed out slowly. "That's crazy. Did your parents tell you when you'd be going back?"

Sofi looked at the ice cubes in her tall glass and shook her head.

"I'm really sorry about all that," Rico said, his eyes creased with concern. *Rico is different*, she thought as he slicked back his hair with manly hands. He sincerely cared about her. Sofi wanted to tell him everything: about her mean aunt, the boys from hell, and the dogs that chased her in the neighborhood. But before she could begin, Rico continued, "It's always so hard to be lied to. But you must know that your parents are just trying to protect you, right?"

"Protect me from what?"

"The truth."

Her heart started to race and she felt a bit woozy. She didn't want to know. Nor did she want to hear it. She refused even to think about it. "The truth?"

"That the card is fake."

"No, it can't be. My parents wouldn't lie to me like that. They're not like that. I can't be an . . . an . . ."

"Illegal?"

She nodded.

Rico shook his head slowly. She could see how painful this was for him, too. "It's not hard to get a fake green card. You can get IDs, passports, driver's licenses, just about anything."

"But how? Where?"

He shrugged his shoulders. "There're places in downtown L.A., San Diego, in San Fran, where people will just come up to you and offer, like regular salesmen." Sofi stared in shock, imagining her dad in a seedy part of town, cutting deals in back alleys. Why had he done that? Did he know it was against the law? "It's really easy now, too, with digital cameras. You can have a card in like an hour for a hundred bucks."

"That's it?" It was surreal. Sofi looked around the busy street corner. The refreshing breeze shook the branches of the palm trees. Hip-hop jams bumped from car stereos. Girls were flirting with guys. Vendors sold their products. But Sofi was a million miles away. She couldn't feel her body. She was not a legal anything of America. Sofi was a criminal, a border bandit. Visions of high school, her friends, her house, and her warm fuzzy bed danced before her like a dream. Damn it! She'd been living a lie.

"Don't be sad. I'm sorry. I didn't mean to upset you," Rico said, putting his hand on her shoulder.

"No." Sofi looked past him at the busy street, grinding her teeth. She hated her parents. This was their fault. They'd done this to her. "It's just that I don't want to be here. I want to go home. I have things to do."

Rico sighed deeply, relaxing back into his chair. "I don't know how desperate you are, but if you want to cross on the under, I've got some friends."

"Oh, no," Sofi gasped. She couldn't. The image of Doña

Clementina traveling illegally through a disgusting tunnel flashed before her eyes. "My parents will figure something out, but thank you."

Rico motioned to a jewelry vendor (who looked like a Mexican Pillsbury Doughboy). The round-faced man with tattooed teardrops under his left eye and matching designs on his neck and knuckles opened a briefcase filled with silver necklaces, bracelets, and earrings. Rico picked out a curvy bracelet and fit it onto her slender wrist.

"I can't take this."

"C'mon," he said softly. "I'm sorry. It's not my place to say those things." He paused. "It's just, you seem like such a tough girl. I thought you should know the truth."

Sofi sniffed, taking a couple of breaths. The truth. Whose truth? Sofi had more questions than answers. Her chest constricted. She had to talk to her dad. A sparkle from the pretty bracelet caught her eye. It shone nicely against her caramel skin. She'd never received a gift from a boy before. She used to pray that Nick would buy her something special for Valentine's. But it had never happened and now it wouldn't ever.

"It's yours," Rico said, waving the man away without paying. The guy didn't flinch. He went right back to his corner as if nothing out of the ordinary had happened.

"But I can't."

"Consider it a welcome-home gift."

"Well, it really is quite lovely," she said, holding it up to the light.

All of a sudden there was a commotion at the corner. A group of police officers was huddled in a circle.

"¡No! Déjame en paz," cried a child's voice. Sofi recognized the voice begging for help before she understood the situation. It was the same pestering voice that had tried to teach her Mexican slang that very morning.

"Mando! Mundo!" Sofi cried, jumping out of her seat. Luisa would definitely skin her alive and smother her with black widows if anything happened to her precious babies. Rico ran up right behind her.

Three big husky police officers in dark blue uniforms were scrambling for the arms and legs of the boys, who were trying to fight them off. Sofi jumped right into the middle and tried to tug the officers' arms off Mundo. Then she felt bony fingers digging into her shoulders. Rico was shouting, trying to calm everyone down.

A short stocky guy with a sour expression explained that the boys had been caught pestering tourists for money. Sofi gave Mando and Mundo a heated look. She wanted to poke out their eyeballs for acting so stupid. They were supposed to be in school! The officers wanted to lock up the boys until their mother came in order to teach them a lesson.

"No." She tugged on Rico's shirt. "I'll get in big trouble," she mumbled low enough for the cops not to hear. Luisa would totally blame her for everything. Scorpions. Her aunt would use a bag full of scorpions for punishment. Then Sofi had an idea. She dug into her bra. Pulled out *all* her money. Olivia had said that Mexican cops took bribes. With the crumpled bills in her hand, she tried to slip the officer the money. She hoped that it would be enough. The officer was quick for a fat guy. He grabbed her by the wrist and pinned her arm behind her back. He started yelling at her real loud in Spanish, but she couldn't understand the angry words coming out of his mouth. This had been a big mistake! She felt cold metal handcuffs clicking around her wrists. A huge mistake!

What had she done? The sound of her heart beating wildly flooded her head. Prison! Even if her parents did find a way to get her back home, she was going to be locked up in jail. Could things get any worse? She felt dizzy. Sofi knew she was in way over her head. She didn't understand anything about this country, this culture, or these people.

"*Un momento,*" Rico said, sternly putting up his hand. "*Señores, por favor.*" He explained that Sofi was an American.

"*Americana,*" she agreed, nodding her head hard. Sofi couldn't help but stare in shock as the officers stopped. *Rico is so brave,* she thought. *He would make a perfect boyfriend.* The look on the policemen's faces told her that they were actually listening. She sighed, relieved at this sliver of hope. The officer glanced at Sofi and then at the boys, who were huffing and puffing, trying to wiggle free. But what if the officers asked for proof of her citizenship? A cold shiver ran up her back. Her green card had been taken away. Her school ID was back at the ranch. She didn't even have her birth certificate. Sofi had nothing, just her word and a bag full of American dreams that were blowing up in her face like a border nightmare.

Without U.S. or Mexican papers, she was borderless. Sofi was caught in a web of two cultures, two languages, and one scary border. What would the authorities do with her? How would her parents get her out of Mexico now? Her head hurt. It was so not fair. Why was she in this horrible situation? None of her friends had had to go through this. Why her? Rico was still talking to the officer. The porky cop grunted loudly.

"A mistake," the officer barked in Spanish, looking Sofi sternly in the eye. Then he turned to Rico and told him to take his friend home as he removed the handcuffs. Sofi wanted to cry in gratitude. The officer was letting them off with a warning. This was great! Rico was a total dream. He'd just walked out of the dust clouds and saved her from two of the worst things she could think of: a Mexican prison and her aunt's wrath.

The house that Uncle Victor built was a magnet for creepy-crawlers. After an especially rainy night all the creatures dashed into the house for cover. Centipedes, spiders, moths, and mosquitoes showed up behind bookshelves, under chairs, or between the bedsheets. And no matter how often Uncle Victor sprayed that foul-smelling bug repellent, the critters found a way back. Night after night the *chinches* devoured Sofi's skin. Before she got into bed, she was forced to cover herself from neck to toe. The thought of them in bed with her, waiting for her to fall asleep, kept her up at night. They were at the top of her scary-creatures list, right up there with wild dogs.

The pain of what Rico had said enveloped her in a blanket of fear. How could her parents lie to her about something so important? Sofi couldn't stop thinking about all the things she'd never have, never get to accomplish: graduation, college, marriage, the cute condo, and the cute Mini Cooper. Was her life over? She sat up in her bed and looked around her prison with red-rimmed eyes. She was dying for a glass of ice-cold water, but they had run out yesterday. The walls of her cell closed in on her.

A huge ugly spider was chilling on her bedspread. The horrible sight made her forget all about her worries. It wasn't the sweet garden-variety *Charlotte's Web* type, either. It was ten times bigger, with hairy legs and white speckles on its forehead. Sofi was sure that it had to be some mutant venomous critter yet to be discovered. It probably jumped and killed with one bite. She froze. She remembered screaming her head off as a little girl when a spider wove a web right above her headboard. Her dad had come in and swept the things away with one fierce swoop. But Sofi's daddy wasn't here to protect her. The spider followed her with its six eyes. She thought about the new bright pink mark on her stomach. Was this her late-night attacker?

Like the stupid border, the bugs were cold, indiscriminate, and uncaring. Sofi could feel her anger rising. Her heart started drumming loudly in her ears and her face became hard as stone. She glanced sideways for something to grab. Mando's black high-top was within arm's reach. Carefully, she picked it up and sneaked up on the spider. It stayed still, trying to camouflage itself against the Mickey Mouse spread. Before either of them could take another breath she smashed the sucker into a gooey stain. Sofi smiled triumphantly, wiping the carcass onto a wad of toilet paper. A rush of energy surged through her veins. Facing her fears was kind of exhilarating, she thought, hurrying down the hallway for the orange fly-swatter she'd seen in the kitchen cupboard.

Swat!

"What are you doing?" Andres asked from the doorway. His hair was a bit disheveled and he was carrying a white laundry bag over his shoulder.

"Andres!" Sofi flinched, trying to hide herself. She was wearing a pink thermal long-sleeve shirt her cousin had lent her and her pink fleece sweats. Her hair was wild and she had gook in her eyes. Not cute at all. Andres chuckled at the sight of her. "What are you laughing at?" She swatted him playfully on the shoulder.

He dropped the bag at his feet. "No, don't let me stop you. Carry on with your bug slaughter." Mando and Mundo poked their heads through the doorway, impressed.

He came over to the squashed insect. Thick red blood oozed from its body. "Hey, that was a spider. Spiders are our friends."

"Maybe they're your friends, but look what they did to me." She raised her sleeve to reveal tiny red bite marks.

"Spiders are cool. They prey on those insects that are really getting you. What's got into you?" he asked.

Sofi shook her head; tears welled up in her eyes. She wasn't really angry at the spiders. The insects were actually the least of her worries. What she really wanted to do was squish Officer Cohn and the INS. Sofi huffed, feeling powerless. She couldn't do anything right. "I don't know. This place is driving me crazy. I can't stand being trapped."

Andres took a step toward her. "I thought your parents were going to fix your problem."

Hot tears burst from her eyes and ran down her cheeks. Sofi didn't care. Nothing mattered anymore. "Lies. My parents are liars. They lied to me. I can't go across. I'm illegal. I'll never go home again." She collapsed onto the bunk and buried her face in the lumpy pillow.

She felt his hand pat her back. "You can't give up."

"There's no point," she cried. "No point at all. It was all a lie. My parents told me that I could be anything. They promised that if I worked real hard, I could make all my dreams come true. I planned to go to college, live in a condo by the beach, and drive a cute Mini Cooper." She threw her arms in the air. "All those years of slaving away at home—it was all for nothing." Sofi sobbed.

Andres was quiet for a long time. "You can't think like that," he finally said. "Everything happens for a reason."

"Andres." Sofi looked up into his concerned eyes. "I'm not in the mood."

"Maybe that's your problem," he said, turning away from her.

Sofi didn't like the sound of his voice. *What are you doing here anyway? Who invited you here?* "What do you want?"

"I told you that you owed me," he said, pointing to the bag. "I brought you my clothes."

"Aghh! Do I look like a maid to you? Why does everyone treat me like a damn servant around here? Just go away! Leave me alone. I don't need you. I don't need anyone."

Andres started to say something but then stopped. He stiffened up. "Okay," he said quietly, and got up to leave. A wave of fresh tears overcame her. Her body shook as she cried loudly. Andres came back and sat down next to her. "Sofi, please stop crying. You'll be all right."

"No, I won't," she sobbed, salty tears seeping into her mouth. "You don't know how horrible it is for me here. My aunt hates me and gives me all these chores to do. I can't do anything right." She looked at the lump of clothes on the floor. "I don't even know if they have a washing machine."

"Ha," Andres said, smiling brightly. "That's not a problem. We can wash them by hand." She looked at him sideways. Sofi sniffed, wiping her face with the back of her hand. "Come on." He nudged her lightly.

"I don't know." Sofi turned around, looking over her room. Mando's and Mundo's dirty clothes were piled in a corner like a mountain.

"Come on, it'll be fun."

"Fun. How is washing supposed to be fun?"

Andres got up and grabbed his laundry bag. "Just come on."

Sofi grabbed the boys' clothes and some of her dirty tops and followed him out the back door. Outside the sky was blue and the sun warmed her face. The rooster was sitting on top of a wheelbarrow. His red chest puffed out like that of an opera singer as he pierced the air with his cry. Sofi took a deep breath. *Another day trapped in Mexico,* she thought. The air felt crisp and clean and refreshed her lungs— which was surprising, what with all the farm animals milling about.

Andres scanned the backyard and then headed over to a crumbling shack with two sinks. He turned on each faucet to make sure they worked. Sofi watched him nervously from the back porch.

"What are you doing?" Mando asked, wearing nothing but his moon-and-star-print pajama bottoms.

"What does it look like I'm doing? I'm going to do the wash."

His eyes bugged in disbelief. "You know how to do the wash?"

Sofi huffed and lugged her pile of clothes over to where Andres was standing. He smiled when she approached.

"It's not that bad," he said, pulling out a faded SAVE THE WHALES shirt from his bundle. By the sink was a plastic container filled with powdered detergent. She watched him soak the garment with cold water with one hand and grab some detergent with the other. "Sprinkle a little and use your palm to scrub." He showed her how to knead the wet shirt like he was making bread. "Come on. You try."

Sofi grabbed one of the boys' tops and followed his instructions. "How do you know it's clean?" she asked hesitantly. Andres started to rinse and squeeze his shirt. She noticed his muscles flex. He shook the shirt roughly, splashing her with drops of water.

"Smell it. If it smells clean and there are no stains, it should be clean," he said, walking over to the clothesline to hang up the shirt.

"Where did you learn how to wash?" Sofi asked, surprised.

"I grew up in a house full of women. I have three older sisters. I had to learn how."

Sofi smiled as she sniffed at the worn garment in her hand. It smelled like sweat. She turned on the faucet long enough to get the shirt wet. Then she pinched some detergent onto it and scrubbed like he showed her. The scrubbing motion felt good. She clenched her jaw and used all her strength to wash it clean.

"Not bad," he nodded, as she squeezed all the water from the shirt. Holding the shirt by the top, she shook it, splashing Andres with the spray. He squinted and then started to laugh. Sofi giggled too.

Sofi hung up the last pair of pants to dry on the clothesline. She looked at the rows of sort-of-white shirts, dark pants, and underwear swaying in the cool breeze. Her fingers and her arms ached, but she felt good. She smiled at Andres standing next to her. She'd accomplished something; it was small, but still something.

Andres looked at his watch. "Damn, I'm late. I'll come by tomorrow to pick up my things," he said, preparing to leave. Sofi walked him to the front gate. The boys were running around playing cowboys and Indians in the front yard. Mando was wearing a store-bought feathered headdress and tying Mundo to the goat's pole. The animal was bleating angrily.

"Thanks," Sofi said.

Andres turned and smiled brightly. It made her heart palpitate. He really was sweet. "I told you it was no big deal once you get the hang of it."

"No, I mean about this morning. Thank you for listening."

Andres understood and nodded his head. He climbed into an old rusty green pickup that was parked next to the fence. It had a huge crack across the windshield and a dented door. He started the ignition. The truck growled loudly and died. Had it ever worked? Nobody at her school would be caught dead in that. There was a chow mein smell in the air. On his second attempt the engine started. Andres waved before disappearing in a cloud of dust. Sofi waved back. Andres drove a junky old car, but she was still glad he was her friend.

While Sofi was still standing outside, a woman approached. "*Buenos días,*" the woman said in a sweet voice. "*¿Se encuentran tus padres?*" The woman wore a red wool jacket that was a size too small, a dark flowery skirt, overstretched knee-high stockings, and suede clogs. She was tall enough to change a lightbulb and had the air of a door-to-door salesman.

"No speakie Spanish," Sofi said in a total *gringa* accent, shaking her head. She didn't want to deal with any more people.

"I speak English," she said, surprising Sofi. "Is your father home?" The woman walked right past her into the house.

"Everyone is sleeping. You should come back—"

"I see," she said, sitting down on Uncle Victor's chair as if she'd been invited. "I guess you will do. My name is María Rita and I am with the Colectivo de Juan Soldado." She waited for Sofi to react to the name; when she didn't, she continued. "We're a group of concerned believers who're bringing awareness of the miraculous powers of the border saint Juan Soldado. You have heard of Juan Soldado?" Sofi shook her head. The woman's jaw fell open. "He is only the most important patron saint of Tijuana, despite whatever you've read in the papers or what the pope says. I'm living proof of his benevolence."

Sofi nodded, hoping that she would get to her point and leave.

"You see, I used to be a lover of the flesh." Sofi's eyes widened in shock. Shouldn't she be talking to a priest? "I left my small town with a man who promised to make me a dancer on the border. I've always had great legs." She glanced at her stockings. "I wanted to help my family."

"You're serious?"

"Very," the woman answered in a businesslike fashion. "Then I figured that I could make even more money in Las Vegas. Greed is not always a bad thing." She winked. "But I fell into a ditch while I was crossing through the Yuma desert. I was foolish and went at night. I thought that I was going to die there. Then, all of a sudden, a young man with a boyish face, wearing a tight-fitting soldier's uniform, came out of the darkness. I screamed, thinking that maybe he would try to rape me, but he was so sweet. He carried me to the road. There, a truck appeared with a family, who agreed to take me to a hospital in Mexico. I turned to thank the boy, but he was gone. I thought I was crazy, until I told the family what had happened. The man driving the truck pointed to a small statue on his dashboard. It was my savior, Santo Juan Soldado."

"Wow. That sounds amazing." Sofi rolled her eyes.

"Sound nothing. It was a miracle, I tell you. Santo Juan Soldado saved me. He is on the side of the poor, like me, who're failed by life. He was a real person, who was wrongly accused of murdering a little girl and was killed by a mob. The Catholic Church in Rome won't recognize him, but what do they know about life on the border?" Maria Rita stopped and put her hand on Sofi's shoulder. "And he can help you, too, if you let him. He led me here to you."

"He did?" Sofi pulled back. Was this woman crazy? Maybe she'd hit her head when she fell into that ditch? Sofi's uncle had told her not to trust anyone, and here she was listening to the first person who walked up to the house.

"Of course he did." She smiled, prying into Sofi's soul with her eyes. "There's no such thing as coincidence." From a brown knitted purse resting on her lap she pulled out several leather-braided necklaces with pictures of the boyish-looking soldier, San Juan Soldado. "You see, your aura called me."

Sofi looked around her head, expecting to see a halo or something crazy pop out.

"It's right there." María Rita pointed around Sofi's temples. "All brown and smoky gray."

"You see things?"

"No," the woman said, chuckling softly. "But there's some fogginess here." She touched Sofi's forehead. "And here," she said, touching her heart. "There's a bad energy that's affected by your surroundings. The border can do that."

Sofi felt herself becoming ill. If she were karmically sick, would that explain her bad luck?

"You need this," she said, holding up the Juan Soldado necklace. The catch. *This woman is a pro*, Sofi thought. But Sofi needed all the help she could get.

"Thousands of people cross illegally to the Other Side each year. Some make it, but most don't. Four hundred people have died just this year trying to cross. I bet you not one of them wore one of these," she said sadly.

"I don't have much money," Sofi let out.

"Well, how much do you have?"

Sofi stuffed her hand into her pocket and pulled out a five-dollar bill. María Rita's eyes opened wide and she snatched it out of her hand. "That's just fine," she said, sticking the money into her purse. She motioned Sofi to stand up. María Rita smiled warmly as she placed the necklace over Sofi's head. "Now you have the protection of Juan Soldado, patron saint of the U.S.–Mexican border, to guide you on your path." Then she pinched her cheek.

"Did he bring you good luck?" Sofi asked as the woman turned to leave.

María Rita shrugged her shoulders. "I guess. I never got to Las Vegas but I'm working at a gentlemen's club in Puerto Nuevo now. The tips are good."

"Wait a second. I thought Juan Soldado saved your life and that you changed your ways and you're a good Catholic woman of high morals now."

"I'm a great Catholic," María Rita smirked, lifting her purse strap over her shoulder. "I confess all my sins every Sunday." Sofi gave her an incredulous look. "This I do," she explained, "because of a promise I made to my Santo Juan." María Rita walked to the front gate.

"Isn't that hypocritical?" Sofi called out after her.

"You're definitely not from La Frontera," María Rita said in an amused tone, and took off down the road. Sofi stood in the front yard, watching her swagger away.

12

"Sofia! Are you listening to me?" Tía Luisa said, impatiently fumbling with her heavy overcoat.

"Huh?" Sofi shook herself from her dismal spell. The idea of staying in Mexico was like a lump stuck in her throat. She'd tossed and turned all night long with frightful dreams. INS officers with dark faces had disrupted her final exam to take her away in handcuffs. Sofi was dying to talk to her parents. She wanted to speak to their lawyer. Wasn't there anything she could do?

"I said," Luisa repeated, as if she were talking to an old lady who'd lost her hearing aid, "you need to go with Yesenia."

Fridays were Luisa's day off. Yesenia joked that it was the day that Luisa washed and cared for her *santitos*. Sofi had watched her aunt dust the miniature statues with a tenderness she'd never seen before. Her aunt showed more affection to them (humming and talking in a conspiratorial whisper) than to her own children! Six days a week Luisa arrived at work at 7 a.m. wearing the same dark blue cotton dress and white apron (which she washed every night in the sink). And this was supposed to be her day off, but that morning, Britannica had charged in announcing that Luisa's boss had called her in for an emergency.

"But what about the boys and school?"

Her aunt's head turned so quickly, Sofi swore she'd get whiplash. "Don't you worry about them." She lifted a large trash bag filled with the boys' unused toys onto the table. "You do as I say. They'll be here any minute."

Today, Yesenia and Luisa were supposed to distribute used clothes and stuffed animals to a migrant camp outside of San Quintin. Luisa's church visited this community once a month. Sofi didn't want to go in her place. The prom was tomorrow night at Anaheim Grove. The Mat Maids had pitched in for their own limo and a suite at the Crowne Plaza for the after party. Sofi was dying to contact Taylor and Olivia. She had to know what was going on. The idea of not attending the prom was unbearable. Her arms itched badly and she was out of hydrocortisone cream.

"Hurry up," Luisa growled, grabbing her handbag off the table. Sofi could see her grumbling to her saints as she walked down the street, pulling the plastic pink rollers from her hair and shoving them into her brown handbag.

Uncle Victor stood next to her, watching Luisa disappear around the corner. He looked at Sofi's arms. They were covered in ugly red welts and scabs from scratching all night. "*Mira*," he said gesturing to a prickly plant growing on the side of the house. Carefully, he whispered to the plant, then ripped a section from the tip. Sofi was curious. What was he going to do? "*La saliva te va a aliviar.*"

Sofi scrunched up her nose. The plant was dirty and full of cobwebs. Was it sanitary? She watched silently, too surprised to object, as he peeled the skin of the plant back to expose the clear mushy insides. Uncle Victor instructed her to spread the goop over her bites. Sofi sighed. Her family was really backward. Didn't they believe in modern medicine? But when she applied the gel, it was cool and refreshing to her skin. Aloe.

Twenty minutes later, a burgundy van with white graffiti honked in front of the house. The roof was piled with black trash bags that looked exactly like the ones Sofi and Yesenia had lugged outside. Sofi grumbled. Why did she have to go on this stupid trip? She wanted nothing to do with her aunt's church group. This was so not fair. She never got to do what she wanted.

Yesenia introduced her to the five old ladies squished into the car and to the bald, cockeyed priest with multicolored braces.

"*¿Habla español?*" the priest asked hesitantly. When Yesenia said yes, he began talking so fast, it made Sofi dizzy. She couldn't understand a word he said. It didn't even sound like Spanish. Yesenia told her that he was from Mexicali and that the people from there talked real fast.

"*Más despacio,*" Sofi said shyly. The priest nodded and began to speak much slower, as if she were two years old. Sofi cringed. She wasn't dumb! He started the engine. Hallelujah music boomed out of the scratchy speakers as if angels had descended from heaven and were blowing trumpets inside the van. The women in the back screamed in delight, bouncing and clapping their hands. They ignored the jarring potholes and speed bumps that bounced them back and forth. Sofi had no idea where they were going; the windows were clouded with a thick storm of dust, but she could smell green onions.

Sofi could feel her heart breaking. She wondered what Taylor and Olivia were up to. Had they taken the day off from school for last-minute shopping? Sofi thought about the magazine clipping she'd ripped out, with different prom hairstyles and advice on preparing for prom night. This was so not fair.

Yesenia tugged on her sleeve. "I hate coming here," she griped under her breath. "My *mamá* thinks I need religion. It's stupid." Sofi steadied her palm on the car roof to keep her head from hitting it. "She's a . . ." Yesenia snapped her fingers trying to find the right word. "*Mandona.* She never lets me do what I want."

"That's where we're related." Sofi smiled. "My parents don't let me do anything, either." Sofi sat up and imitated her dad's voice. "'School is your job.'"

"Really?" Yesenia whispered. Her eyes brightened with disbelief. "I thought your *mamá y papá*, being American, would be modern." Sofi laughed as she remembered the time she'd stayed late at school to go to one of the school dances. Her dad showed up just as the lights went out and dragged her home. It was so embarrassing.

"Can you keep a secret?"

"Of course," Sofi said in a hushed whisper.

"I've been seeing this boy, Javier. My parents don't know." Yesenia smiled. "The other day, I went to the park with him during my break time. It was so nice. He held my hand."

"And . . . ?" Sofi said excitedly. She couldn't believe her cousin's nerve. If Luisa found out, she was liable to break a dish over Yesenia's head. Yesenia must really like him. Sofi thought about Rico. Maybe staying in Mexico didn't have to be so bad. The bracelet felt cold against her skin. Sofi thought about telling Yesenia her own secret.

"Today he invited me out for ice cream—the good kind, too. Dreyer's." This obviously meant something big because Dreyer's was an American brand and thus more expensive than the shaved ices and fruit Popsicles sold on every corner.

"Well, what are you doing here? You should be out there with him."

"I know, I know." Yesenia nodded, fidgeting with the ties on her thin purple blouse. "But I don't know. Britannica came to where I was working yesterday and she was all over Javier. She's supposed to be my friend." Yesenia bit her thumbnail.

Sofi noticed the distressed look on Yesenia's face. It tore at her. "You need to talk to her right away. You don't want to ruin your friendship over some guy."

"What do I tell her?"

"Tell her what you told me. That he's been hanging out with you."

"You think?"

Sofi nodded.

Yesenia slouched back and looked straight ahead. "You don't know Britannica. She always gets what she wants. She might do something real mean."

"Like what?"

Yesenia shrugged. "I don't know. But she's always trying to copy me. When I wanted to dye my hair, she went to San Diego and had it done professionally."

"This is your friend?" Sofi couldn't believe it. Olivia and Taylor would never do anything like that. Yesenia looked down at her hands and didn't respond. "You've got to tell her about him right now." Sofi thought a minute. "This is actually a perfect opportunity. Luisa's at work and she won't be home until late. You can go talk to Britannica, then hang out with Javier. It's perfect."

Yesenia looked at the priest in front and then turned to the ladies behind them. She gave Sofi a thoughtful look. "You don't mind?"

Mind? Her aunt never asked her if she minded. No one asked her how she felt about anything. Actually, she hated the entire situation. Sofi wanted to be on the next bus home. She wanted to get back there and go to the prom. But Yesenia was being so nice to her. A part of her wanted to show Yesenia how much she appreciated her friendship. Sofi patted her leg. "Don't worry about me. I got this covered."

"Are you sure?" Yesenia hesitated, looking at the church ladies singing in the back.

"How hard can it be? I just got to pass out clothes, right?"

Yesenia jumped into her arms, tumbling Sofi over. "Thank you." Sofi relaxed and hugged her back, smiling. At least someone was happy she was there.

When they arrived at the camp Yesenia explained to the priest that she had an emergency and that Sofi would stay to help. Then she flagged down the first cab she could find. The priest ushered Sofi and the other churchwomen to a narrow opening in the center of an open field, where a long line of people was waiting.

Sofi stared at the makeshift box houses; they looked like they'd been constructed overnight with the resources found around them: portions of cardboard, loose bricks, old wood, anything flat to keep the sun and rain away.

"It always breaks my heart when I come out here," the priest said in Spanish. "There's no running water or electricity. The people of these migrant camps are the invisible members of our society." Sofi nodded, overcome with sadness. "They come from small villages in Oaxaca and Chiapas. They speak little Spanish and many have never been to school." Sofi caught a glimpse of a Coca-Cola billboard sign that was being used as a wall. She wondered where that sign had been and how it got to this house.

Dirt was the foundation of everything here. It was on the roads, on the toys the kids played with, in the gardens, and especially on the floors in the families' houses. The dirt was different from the dirt back home. In her mother's house, dirt was an invader; something to be cleaned out, exterminated, gotten rid of. But here in this satellite community, dirt was just dirt. What would happen if someone tried to get rid of the dirt here? She smiled at the absurd image of her mother in this place on hands and knees, scrubbing until the floors sparkled.

Sofi realized that this was another world, one she never knew existed. Was this how the rest of the world lived? Sofi thought about her family's town house and the immaculately kept yard, her state-of-the art school, and her comfortable bedroom. *Why do I live there and have everything and more? Why do some children go hungry while others pick and choose what they want on a whim?* Sofi thought about the Taco Supreme she'd thrown out the other night because she was full.

A group of kids who were playing a game on the dirt road with sticks and rocks stopped and watched them pass. It was cold outside, yet they were not wearing shoes. Sofi wondered what they were thinking as they looked at her group. Were they wondering about what kind of life she lived or if they'd ever leave this poverty? The more she watched, the more questions she had. What about the Mexican government, how could they let this happen? And where were the kids' parents?

"It's a shame," the priest said.

A line of people waited for them. Copper-toned women with harsh lines framing their eyes, their long skirts sweeping the dirt as they walked. Sofi smiled at the faces of small children and old wizened grandfathers who said nothing in a respectful hesitation she didn't understand. Sofi knew that although she wasn't rich, she had more in one closet than one of these whole familes had. How did these kids perceive the difference? Did they resent her for bringing them used clothes? Did they think she was just one of those selfish outsiders?

Sofi took the bag of toys to hand out to the children. She handed a football to a cute boy with dimples. He lowered his dark eyes in reverence. It shook Sofi, making her step back. It was just a toy! The kids wouldn't look her in the eye. Many wore hole-riddled clothes. The poverty around her was too real. It was like nothing she'd ever seen before. She overheard a couple of kids chattering in an indigenous language. The sounds were so unfamiliar. They were like her, she realized, foreigners in their own land. A little girl's sad eyes brightened when Sofi placed a doll with blond ringlets in her small brown arms. Sofi choked back her emotions. These kids had nothing. No toys. No new clothes. Sofi remembered how her mother went on about how poor they used to be. She was now looking at the face of what it meant to be poor.

Eventually, all the toys ran out and it broke her heart to turn the last couple of kids away. A little brother was consoling a girl her age. He tried to give the girl his football. The girl shook her head. Sofi noticed that the dark-skinned girl had long black hair just like her. Then something stung Sofi right in the middle of her chest. If her parents hadn't come to the United States, she could've been that girl. Her heart swelled as a full-sized smile leaped to her lips. Her parents really must love her very much. Sofi was struck by the girl's disappointment at not getting anything. She wondered if the girl had ever had a Barbie to play with.

Sofi glanced to the side. A woman lowered her eyes as she accepted folded clothes from one of the church ladies. She recognized her mother's strong nose. Behind her stood a man who looked just like her uncle. Everywhere she turned she saw familiar-looking faces. Sofi felt their eyes in different ways, too: from some she felt warmth, acceptance, and appreciation of an honest attempt to make someone's life better. From others she felt the cold stare of judgment or maybe resentment for being an uninvited guest and rubbing their noses in their neediness. But Sofi dismissed those negative thoughts. A new feeling was spilling into her heart. It was a crystal-clear awareness that she was related to all these people. *They are Mexican like me*, she thought.

Sofi saw the teenaged girl begin to turn, shoulders hunched over. All the bags were empty. She couldn't let her go home with nothing. Without thinking, she took off her jean jacket, the cute one she'd bought at American Eagle for the trip. Sofi ran up to her.

"Here," she said in Spanish. The girl looked surprised by Sofi's gesture and shook her head no. But Sofi was not going to take no for an answer. Besides, she had tons of jackets back home. The girl finally relented and tried on the jacket. It fit perfectly and looked cute on her, too. Sofi walked back to the van, feeling satisfied. She couldn't help but wonder if this was what her aunt had wanted them to experience.

Then all of a sudden, Sofi noticed someone she thought she knew, a guy with a portly build carrying two pails of water down the road. *No way, it can't be*, she thought. Sofi followed him at a discreet distance. The guy walked with heavy steps around the block, stopping in front of an old shack that looked like it would crumble if you sneezed too hard. Was this his house? An old balding man sat hunched over in a metal chair, looking out at a small cornfield in the front yard. The guy whispered into the old man's ear before disappearing into the darkened house. *It's him! That's Andres.* Sofi knew she'd recognize that cocky strut anywhere.

The glare from the sun, high overhead, reminded Sofi that she should get back to the van. As the dust picked up around her steps, she realized that all the streets looked the same. An ugly mutt began to bark ferociously at her, making her walk another block over. She must have walked in circles until she finally found the spot where the van had been. But there was no van. It was too late! The van and all the church folks were gone.

"Damn it!" Sofi said, kicking up dirt with her sneaker. Her socks had turned brown. She wanted to hit herself for being so nosy. Now how was she supposed to get home? She hadn't brought any money with her. Maybe she could go find Andres and ask him for a ride? But she was embarrassed about what she'd seen, his house. Sofi realized that she didn't know anything about him, his life, or life in general for people in Mexico.

Her feet guided her back to Andres. She took a deep breath by the gate. The old man was still out in the sun. His eyes were closed.

"Hello?"

"Sofi?" Andres poked his head through the front door. "What are you doing here?"

She looked down at her once-white K-Swisses. "You'd never believe it if I told you."

He walked out with a big smile on his face. He was wearing a tight-fitting navy shirt and jean shorts. "Try me." He folded his arms in front of his chest. The old man continued to sleep undisturbed.

"My aunt asked me to do this favor with her church group and I kind of got lost. The van left me."

He started to laugh. "Only you."

A small smile danced on her lips. Yeah, only she would have been dumb enough to wander off.

"Want a lift back?"

"If it's not too much trouble."

He made a face. "It's no trouble at all." Sofi breathed out, relieved. "Let me just check out the rainwater-catchment system and I'll be set." *What's rainwater catchment?* she thought as she watched him climb up onto the roof of the rickety house. He was standing dangerously close to the edge. Was he going to fall? Andres climbed back down and smiled. "All done."

"What were you doing?"

He gestured to the roof. "My grandfather filters the rain to provide water for washing dishes and use around the house. There's no water system around here. Even if there were, the old man swears that this is the best method for getting water. I put in some pipes last summer."

"That's pretty cool."

Andres smiled proudly. "Yeah, I do that for old people. Our grandparents were so smart. They knew how to live harmoniously with the land." His cheeks grew hot. "But you don't want to hear about this."

"I do."

"Really?"

"Sure. I was wondering how people were able to survive out here without electricity and sewage. I thought it was so sad."

Andres raised his hand, cutting her off. "Let me get the old man inside. I don't want him to burn." He went over to his grandfather and gently woke him up. The old man with chocolate brown skin smiled widely at Sofi. He handed Andres something before going into the house. Sofi wished she could meet her grandmother and have that family connection.

She climbed into the truck. There were no seat belts, and the radio was missing. There was sand on the mats, and the dashboard needed polishing. Andres didn't seem to mind, though. A strange chow mein smell surrounded her. Hanging from the rearview mirror was a tan leather pouch.

"So where'd you get this contraption?" she asked, raising her eyebrows at the busted leather seats. "At the dump?"

His eyes grew big. "Yeah, totally. How did you know?"

"Seriously?"

He nodded his head excitedly. Andres rubbed the dashboard as if it were made of gold. "This truck is the car of the future." He tried to turn on the engine. Nothing happened.

"You must be joking."

"Naw, it's cool. All my friends laugh at me, but we'll see who's laughing when peak oil prices reach ten dollars a liter. This baby here"—he slammed his hand on the wheel—"runs on used cooking oil. The Chinese restaurant downtown gives me all the oil I need."

"That's crazy," she said. He turned the ignition on again and the truck coughed into life.

"The future is full of endless possibilities when we learn to see outside the box." They traveled down the road. Sofi looked at the houses they passed, wondering if they also used rainwater. Andres was a real smart guy. She liked that. Most of the guys at school were just into sports, parties, and hanging out. He was like no one she'd ever met before.

"Any word from your parents?"

Sofi frowned. She remembered how happy she'd been to leave them Saturday morning. Her mother had given her a big hug, squeezing the air out of her lungs. Sofi missed those suffocating hugs. "No news. They hired some fancy lawyer, but I don't know. Being here makes me think it's hopeless. There're tons of people trying to get across."

"Why don't you do like my friend Huero? He doesn't speak any English, but he's so light he can pass for a white boy." Sofi smiled. "He just went up to the border and told them he was an American and crossed."

Sofi's eyes grew big. "Really?"

"Yeah, but they caught him two days later on the bus. Times are crazy right now. You know, the INS pulls over trains and buses at random to check people's paperwork. It's ridiculous. The United States is so scared of dishwashers and cleaning ladies taking over that it's becoming a police state."

Sofi laughed at the image of Luisa in her maid uniform bringing INS officers to their knees with her heated stare. "I should just sic my *tía* on them. Ha!"

"So what did you think of San Quintin?" Andres asked, pulling her out of her thoughts.

"Oh my God. It was great. I loved it. You should have seen the look on those kids' faces when we handed out gifts. They were so happy. I'd love to get all my friends at school to do something like that. It kind of made me think about my own life and how much I take for granted."

"Do my ears deceive me?" Andres looked at her, impressed. "You! Miss I-Want-a-Bucket-of-Beer-Now. Wow." Sofi squirmed on the worn-out black leather seat. "I'm just kidding." He gave her a playful punch on the shoulder. "A lot of people around here wouldn't do a thing for those families. They're too worried about making it. You know, having flashy American clothes or going to the Other Side."

"Yeah, I didn't know my aunt cared so much. She always seems so mad all the time. I guess she does have a heart."

"I'm sure you could learn a lot from her," he said.

"She doesn't much like me." She shrugged her shoulders and watched the coastline view outside. "She thinks I'm this spoiled American brat who's so helpless."

"And what do you think?"

Sofi turned to him and thought hard. "I don't know who I am anymore. I used to think I was just normal. You know—going to school, hanging out with my friends, and looking forward to college. But since I've been here, my whole world has turned upside down." Sofi grew quiet. Her heart squeezed. The border had taken away all the things she loved and valued, her parents and friends. Her entire life had fluttered away from her grasp. Sofi was left holding nothing but air.

"No, no, no." Andres groaned and the car stalled. He put his head on the steering wheel and said a prayer as he tried to turn the ignition on. Nothing.

"What's the matter?"

Andres looked up at her and smirked. "I think I'm out of fuel."

Sofi learned an important lesson that day: A girl in shorts should not sit by herself on the side of the road, even if her male friend is only five feet away. Her exposed legs were like a flashing neon advertisement to perverts behind the wheel. Cars slowed down as they passed, and guys leaned out the window making kissing sounds, or honked wildly. But none of them offered rides. Sofi couldn't believe all the unwanted attention she was getting. She huffed, sitting in the back of the truck while Andres tried to contact Huero on his phone. She looked out at the sea and the dry mountainous areas where housing developments were being built. The sky was a brilliant shade of blue. A flock of seagulls was flying north toward America. She wished she had wings to fly away with them.

A big banana-colored Hummer with bright seventeen-inch chrome wheels cruised by. Gangster rap music played on the stereo. The car stopped five feet away and pulled into reverse. Sofi's eyes got big. Maybe they could hitch a ride in that cool car? The tinted windows rolled down electronically. Rico smiled from behind a pair of dark shades.

"Problem?"

"Oh, Rico!" Sofi shouted, jumping out of the pickup's rear cargo area. "It's you." Rico looked sharp in his light blue oxford shirt and dark khaki chinos. He parked right in front of the truck and got out of the car. He was so gorgeous.

"Now, what kind of trouble has my little brown angel gotten into this time?"

Sofi turned red. She wished she'd put on some makeup or could fix her hair. "We ran out of gas." Andres got out of the truck quietly. He looked a bit uneasy. "Rico, this is Andres." The two guys locked eyes and shook hands.

"Gas. That's it? I got an extra couple of liters I always drive around with."

"That won't do," Andres said rather forcefully. Sofi gave him a mean look. Why was he being so rude? "My car runs on used cooking oil."

"Ha!" Rico laughed. "Well, let me offer you two a ride into town then." He was so nice and generous.

Andres cleared his throat nervously. "Actually, my friend is on his way."

Rico turned to Sofi. "Are you two together?"

"Oh no. Andres was just giving me a ride."

"You go ahead if you want to," Andres said to Sofi. "My friend won't be here for a while."

"Are you sure?" Rico asked. Sofi's eyes brightened with the idea of riding in Rico's hot car.

"Yeah," Andres said sourly.

Sofi ran up to Andres. "You sure it's cool?"

"Yeah, I'm sure. I'll be fine," he said.

"You're the best." She gave him a quick hug and ran back to Rico.

"This is the second time I've saved you," Rico said, starting up his car effortlessly and taking off down the road. Rico had the best car, with heated black leather seats, a DVD navigation system, and a state-of-the-art stereo system.

"I know—you're like my Prince Charming."

Rico laughed easily. It made Sofi relax into the comfy seat. He thought she was funny.

"I hope I wasn't intruding?"

"Oh no, not at all. Andres is just my friend. He's cool."

"I'm glad to hear that." He smiled. "I was starting to get jealous."

Him, jealous? The thought tickled her stomach. Sofi forgot all about her problems, the border, home. Rico was so easy to be with. This was a total dream. No, it was better. Rico was total boyfriend material. Olivia and Taylor were going to die when she told them. Sofi nodded her head in time with the music, enjoying the ride with a hot babe.

13

"Dad!"

"*Corazón*, how are you?"

Sofi looked away, unsure of how to answer. She'd been in Mexico a week but it felt like a lifetime. She wanted to be home so bad; she bounced up and down nervously by the public phone. The prom was in a couple of hours. Maybe by some crazy miracle they'd found a way to get her across.

Then a poor indigenous woman selling beaded jewelry walked by. She reminded Sofi of the people at the migrant camp in San Quintin and the girl she'd given her jacket to. That girl would probably never go to a prom. Sofi felt ashamed. All she could think about was getting home for a big party while others were just trying to survive the day with enough food to eat.

"I'm okay. I have a roof over my head and food to eat. It could be worse."

"You don't know how much we miss you. Your mom is at the mall. She wanted to send you some stuff so that you won't be homesick."

"I'm beyond homesick, Dad. I'm lifesick. My whole world has been torn from under me. What did the lawyer say?"

"Don't get upset, *corazón*. I know this is a stressful situation. But you're a Mendoza. You need to rise above this. It'll just take a little time."

"What?"

"I don't want you to worry—"

"Dad," Sofi cut in, "I already know what you did. I'm not stupid. I know we're illegal."

He sniffed loudly. "We do not say that word! No person is illegal!"

Sofi cowered under her father's voice, embarrassed by her outburst. Her cheeks turned hot. She looked over her shoulder to see if her cousin had heard her. Yesenia was busy talking to a woman at a store five feet away. "I'm sorry, Dad."

"I know things are rough. But there's nothing we can do right now. Mr. Wilcox is a smart guy. We trust him. He's trying to find a way to get you home as soon as possible."

"But why didn't you tell me? I would never have—"

Her dad said nothing for a long time. "Your mother and I love you very much."

Tears streamed down her cheeks. "I know. I love you too."

"We didn't want to worry you. We wanted you to have a normal life. You don't know the fear we live with every day. We worry all the time about this. You have to know that we did all this for you. . . ."

His candidness tore at her wounded heart. It was strange, because he wasn't talking to her like he was her daddy. It was like they were both adults. Her heart swelled. They loved her. "Dad, I know you and Mom are doing your best. I appreciate all that you've done, everything you've ever given me." She sniffed. "I don't care about the prom, about school, or any of that stuff. I just want to see you both and to hug you so tight." Sofi paused. "What will happen to me?"

"I don't know, *corazón*. This is our worst nightmare come true. You should talk to Mr. Wilcox. He needs you to write an explanation of what happened. Take down his number."

Sofi hung up the phone with a bittersweet lump in her chest. Her truth was open and exposed like a raw wound.

"Sofi." Yesenia came over. Sofi sniffed loudly and tried to wipe her face quickly. "You okay?"

"No." She shook her head. "My dad doesn't know when or if I'll ever be able to come back."

Yesenia gave her a hug. Sofi stiffened at first but then relaxed. "I know you don't like it here," said Yesenia, "but it doesn't have to be that bad."

"I'm sorry, Yesenia, but try to imagine what I'm going through. How would you feel if someone came and snatched you away from your home, your friends, Javier?"

Yesenia looked down the street, thinking. "I guess I wouldn't like that either. Okay, but tell me something. Back home, did you have many boyfriends?"

"Many boyfriends? I wish. Back home I had no boys. Nada. I had a major crush on this one guy, Nick. But it was a silly girl crush. He didn't really like me." The thought of Nick made Sofi's stomach flip. He was going to the prom with Sarah Baker as if nothing had happened. Sofi thought about Rico. He was a total babe. But she had doubts. Was she even in his league? Did he want her for a girlfriend? He was so hot and totally smooth. "I'm afraid I may be jinxed."

"Now you're talking like a *loca*. What about that boy who brought you home?" Yesenia asked, giving her a playful nudge.

"The guy with the Hummer? His name is Rico. Isn't he gorgeous?"

"No, no, I meant the other one. The guy who brought you to our house the first night?"

Sofi laughed. Andres? Her cousin needed glasses. "Oh no, he's just a friend." Yesenia gave her a smile that told her she didn't believe her. "C'mon," Sofi said in disbelief, "he's so not my type." Sofi could feel her cheeks growing hot. "Have you noticed how close together his eyes are? He's got the tiniest lips. And he's not that in shape. And . . ." Yesenia rolled her eyes. "Don't do that!"

"Do what?" Yesenia asked innocently.

"You know what. Roll your eyes like that. I'm totally serious. I have this boyfriend checklist, you see. And Andres doesn't measure up. He's a good friend. And that's cool." Sofi huffed. "But I can't think of my love life right now anyway. I have to talk to this lawyer and try to see if there's anything I can do."

"Sofi, don't be so hard on yourself." Yesenia's eyes lit up. "I know what you need." She grabbed Sofi's hand. "Come with me." She pulled her down the street. "My *tía* knows all about that stuff. She's Kumeyaay."

"What's that?"

"Native, but she's also a *curandera*. She's the one who told me about Saint Anthony." Sofi gave her an uncertain look.

"A nun?"

Yesenia shook her head adamantly. "She's like a fortune-teller/healer. You'll love her." Yesenia didn't give Sofi a choice and pulled her into a small shop tucked between a record store and a real estate agency selling oceanfront condos with no down payment. The place was dark, hidden away from prying eyes. A small placard over the doorway said, LILIANA'S BOTANICA.

Sofi followed Yesenia into the small dimly lit rectangular room. There were no windows for ventilation. The air spun with a strange earthy smell. A large L-shaped glass counter took up most of the room, forcing the two girls to huddle at the entrance. Sofi's eyes widened at the sight of the religious icons. She kneeled down and touched the cool display case. The glass case was filled with miniature saints like the ones Luisa had at home, candles of all different colors, photos of dragons fighting angels, animals and nature scenes, stone Aztec sculptures of gods and goddesses, spiky quartz and amethyst crystals, charms, and silver talismans.

A row of clear jars lined the shelf above. The names on the jars were foreign to Sofi: Sinicuichi, Argemore Chicalote. They sounded strange as she whispered them to herself. Inside were pastel-colored powders, weeds, and dried flowers. The whole place felt strange, as if she'd walked into a hazy dream: a place of magic and mystery. Sofi was a little excited but also a little wary. She'd already been burned once by the cosmic work of spells and incantations. In the corner was a three-foot-high marble statue of a boy on a throne. A picture of an older woman with caramel-colored wrinkled skin and her hair tied in a bun was at the statue's feet. Had this woman also died at the border? Candles, flowers, sand dollar seashells, and smoky incense adorned the statue's feet. The place felt holy, but Sofi wasn't sure what kind of religion it was.

"Look at this." Sofi pointed to a candle on the shelf. It was a picture of Juan Soldado standing at attention in his army uniform. "It's like my necklace." She pulled out the leather strap with the dangling picture.

Yesenia picked up the candle as if she owned the place and read a passage from the back. "It's a prayer for crossing the border illegally."

"Wow." Sofi couldn't believe it. "They have saints for everything, don't they? I bet they have one for partying too much at Papas and Beer."

Yesenia's eyes lit up. "They do! Saint Nepomucene." Sofi laughed. Yesenia turned the candle over and read the prayer aloud in Spanish, then in English: "'I recognize that I have defied human laws. They arrested me for crossing a line that men have drawn as a frontier. I ask that you give me serenity to accept these conflicts of life and the necessary strength to overcome it.'"

"Taking a trip?" a cheery woman with rosy cheeks said in Spanish, appearing from behind a velvet curtain. The woman's smile was contagious and lit up the room like a bright ray of sunshine breaking through a storm. Yesenia rushed into her thick arms and buried her face in the woman's embrace. The woman had a small round face, wide hips, and big bones, but she moved with the agility of a deer. She wore her long black hair loose. There were hints of gray at her temples. Dark, intelligent eyes studied Sofi from behind wire-rimmed glasses.

"Tía Lili, I want you to meet my *prima*," Yesenia said, introducing Sofi as her cousin. Lili drifted over to Sofi. The cascading earth-tone robes and scarves made her appear to be floating over the green tiled floors.

"Is this Luisa's brother's daughter?" she asked. Yesenia nodded. "Does she speak Spanish?" Sofi couldn't help but roll her eyes. Why did everyone ask that same question? And why didn't they just ask her? Sofi stood there, unsure whether she should hug Lili or shake her hand. The woman read her thoughts and opened up her arms. Her long nails were painted pink and decorated with little sparkles and crescent moons that matched her dangling silver earrings. "Welcome, *mija*. It is a pleasure to meet you. I met your father and mother a long time ago." She gestured with her jeweled fingers. "You have his eyes."

"*Gracias*," Sofi said, feeling her heart swell with pride.

"Sofi needs a *limpia*. She had her heart broken by this pig and now she thinks she's cursed," Yesenia announced as if she were talking about her split ends. Sofi felt her cheeks grow hot. She'd never said she was cursed. It was one thing to be open and honest with your cousin but quite another when you were with a stranger.

"I'm *embarazada*," Sofi admitted, looking down at the tile floor.

"Pregnant!" Yesenia screamed in shock.

"No!" Sofi felt her heart leap. "I mean I'm embarrassed." Now Sofi's face was bright red like a big fat tomato. "Embarrassed, not pregnant."

Liliana started to laugh. "You mean *me da vergüenza*." She reached up and cupped Sofi's chin in her warm palms. The intensity of her eyes made Sofi nervous. She felt like the woman was looking into her soul and uncovering her darkest secrets. Liliana smiled, crinkling her nose like Yesenia did when she was being funny. It made Sofi relax. "*Ay, el amor.* I wish I had a spell to take the hurt away." Yesenia nodded in agreement. The woman glided behind her counter and leaned down. Yesenia gave Sofi's hand a hopeful squeeze as Liliana mumbled to herself. With a clank, she placed a jar of clear liquid, a bundle of sweet-smelling weeds, and a book of matches on the countertop. Then she popped up, holding a clay bowl in one hand and some pebble things in the other. Liliana looked like a royal priestess, with the sleeves of her long robe flowing down from her arms.

Yesenia's aunt lit a round coal that sizzled and sparked as it caught. "Sometimes the Creator brings us lessons." She dropped the coal into the bowl. Dark tendrils of smoke swirled up, filling the air with a harsh aroma. "Shows us what we don't want or need in our lives. The trick is not to take things so personally and learn the lessons." She walked around the counter and stood in front of Sofi, gazing at her with unassuming warmth. "Now, think about the boy or boys who broke your heart."

Sofi glanced at Yesenia. Her cousin nodded. Sofi closed her eyes and thought about Nick. She imagined his messy blond hair, cute smile, and athletic body walking down the school hallway. This was the guy she'd wasted her entire high-school career lusting after.

"What did you learn from him?" Liliana's voice startled Sofi.

Sofi thought about when they were at the beach. She thought he cared about her. But he was just trying to get laid. He was nothing like she imagined. "I don't think I even knew him," she admitted. "I think I was in love with my idea of him." The realization stung her. Nick was a made-up fantasy she'd created. It was just like the *Latina caliente* image Nick had created of her. They'd both been caught up in false ideas of the other. Sofi didn't understand this love stuff at all. It was so confusing.

"That's good." Liliana waved the dark-colored incense in Sofi's face and used the loosely tied bundle of herbs to fan the smoke. "I'm giving you what we call a *limpia*, a cleansing. It's to take away the bad energy, feelings, and memories that hold you back from living a full life." She reached back and grabbed a bottle of clear liquid and dabbed her fingers with it. Her touch felt cold on Sofi's forehead.

Sofi asked, "What was that?"

"Holy water." She noticed the question in Sofi's eyes. "We Mexicans are truly a mestizo. We're a mixture of Native, Spanish, and African, a blending of different bloods, traditions, and knowledge." Sofi smiled. She liked the idea that she was part of an ever-changing culture. It was alive, evolving like her. She thought about what it meant to be a Mexican who'd lived most of her life as an American. Maybe she was just another link in this evolutionary cycle? "You'll be fine." Liliana patted her head. "We've all been heartbroken. It's a part of being alive. You have to be willing to risk loss for true happiness." Liliana sighed deeply, resting her hand on the counter. "I remember that English-speaking bad actor who stole my heart. He said his name was Erik Estrada, but who knows? I cursed that boy so bad, he had diarrhea for a month." They all started to laugh. "But I learned my lesson: Never trust an actor. It's hard. My heart still flutters when I drive by Fox Studios."

"Isn't she great?" Yesenia said, putting her arm around Sofi.

"Thanks so much," Sofi said to Yesenia as they walked away from the botánica. Sofi clutched a paper bag that contained a miniature statue of Juan Soldado that Liliana had given her free of charge. She'd reached for her cousin's hand and held it while they walked, as she'd seen other teenaged girls do with their friends. Yesenia was the sister she'd always wanted.

"Oh no, thank *you*," Yesenia said. "Britannica is very . . . selfish. I did what you said. I told her that I liked him and she still went looking for him at the park. But it was too late. Javier asked me to be his girl." Sofi couldn't help but laugh.

"That's more like it," Yesenia said, nudging her in the ribs. "Now you're not sad about missing the big dance?"

Sofi's face fell. She knew Yesenia hadn't meant to hurt her. Here she was, taking her out and trying to save her with her aunt's *limpia* from a cursed life of spinster hell. However, at the mere mention of the prom, Sofi's heart sank. A Gwen Stefani song was playing loudly out of someone's speakers. It reminded her of Olivia lip-synching in the girls' bathroom mirror with her iPod. Sofi looked at her wristwatch and wondered if they were at the Aveda store in Newport Beach, getting their hair and makeup done. This was so unfair. Sofi moped, kicking a plastic wrapper on the sidewalk. The wind picked up the wrapper and twirled it in the air before dropping it next to the redbrick wall of a café. A part of Sofi wanted to be lifted and hide under the brick and cry forever.

They walked a few blocks without talking. Sofi stopped to watch the yellow, orange, and brown layers of the sunset melt into one another.

She wanted to wallow in her well of self-pity and be alone with her thoughts. They were in front of her grandmother Benita's house. Sofi touched the metal gate, wondering about her father's mother.

"Don't get too close," Yesenia warned. Just then the angry mutt started barking. Sofi noticed movement from inside the dwelling. Her heart leaped. Was that her? A small pebble hit Sofi on the arm. She cursed under her breath. Another pebble came flying wildly between her and Yesenia. Yesenia grabbed her hand. "Let's go."

"Was that our grandmother throwing rocks?"

"I told you she was crazy."

They continued walking down the block. At the edge of the corner there was a huge warehouse that sold new and used furniture during the day. A crowd of young people was standing to the right of the door, smoking and joking around. Loud mariachi music, flashing disco lights, and smoke escaped out of the open doorway. Yesenia turned quickly to Sofi and gave her a mischievous look before poking her head through the door.

"Yesenia," Sofi whispered, "what are you doing?"

"Sofi, it's a *quinceañera!*"

"A what?"

"A sweet fifteen. You'll love it," she said, heading for the door. Sofi pulled Yesenia back. What was her cousin thinking, going to a stranger's party uninvited?

"You can't just go in there."

"Why not?" By the bewildered look on Yesenia's face, Sofi guessed that this was just another Mexican thing.

"Let me guess, everyone knows everyone."

"Uh-huh; and if not, we can always say we're friends of José's. There's bound to be at least one José there."

Sofi rolled her eyes.

"Oh, come on," Yesenia pleaded. "There'll be tons of food and cute guys to dance with. Didn't you say you wanted to go to a party tonight?"

"This is not the prom."

"No, it's not." She jabbed Sofi's ribs. "It's better." Yesenia grabbed her by the wrist.

There were so many people packed into the place that it was easy for them to blend in with the crowd. Yesenia was right. It was an incredible party with a huge disco ball bouncing twinkling lights all over the dance floor. There were all kinds of people, from babies sleeping in strollers to old ladies dancing with their walkers. Everyone was laughing and having fun. A heavy woman who was probably about fifty was whisking around a diaperless toddler in her arms. Along the wall stood a line of cute, anxious-looking boys with messy gelled hair. They were watching a row of girls in party dresses who were closely guarded by potbellied fathers and tight-lipped older brothers. Sofi thought of all the times she'd lounged around her bedroom while her friends went to house parties. Tonight was her night.

A conga line emerged from the crowd and a short guy with a nice smile pulled her in. Sofi laughed as they danced along. The line went faster and faster. Sofi reached out and held tightly to the dark jacket in front of her. She lost her grip and almost tripped over an old lady sitting in a metal folding chair. It was Doña Clementina, from the tortilla shop. They hugged quickly.

Sofi pushed her way through the crowd looking for her cousin. She smiled at an older couple dancing. The woman's loose straps hung off her shoulders and the man's fancy shirt was unbuttoned low to reveal too much hair and gold chains. They reminded her of her parents, except for the attire. A little girl in pink-ribboned braids pushed past her chasing a little boy between and around couples.

Yesenia was in the middle of a big circle strutting her stuff to a Ricky Martin song. Her cousin looked so self-confident and relaxed, shaking her hips. Sofi beamed with pride and clapped with the audience. Someone pushed Sofi into the middle and for a second she stood there frozen like a statue. What was she supposed to do? She couldn't dance. Sure, she pretended and tried to shake like J.Lo in the privacy of her own room. But this was totally different. Sofi thought about making a run for it. The crowd was shoulder to shoulder. *Maybe if I dive between the legs of that lady in the purple dress?* Sofi was about to bail when she heard Yesenia shout her name.

"So-fi! So-fi!" The crowd quickly caught on and started chanting her name like she was a rock star. On the spot, Sofi closed her eyes and gave in. She moved awkwardly at first and then slowly found her groove. When she opened her eyes she noticed that people were smiling back. Nobody cared how she danced, or if her hips shook to the beat of the song. People were just having a good time. No one expected Sofi to be funny or entertain the crowd. They just wanted her to be herself and have fun. Sofi shouted and shook her butt as if she were alone in her bedroom with no one home. The crowd encouraged her with whistles and cheers.

As the next person took center stage, Sofi danced over to her cousin. Everything seemed beautiful as they moved with the happy guests. No one was reprimanding her, making her feel bad or out of place. For the first time, Sofi felt like she belonged. The lights flickered in different hazy colors and Sofi thought about how no one here cared about where she was born or if she spoke *correct* Spanish. They were all the same. Sweat poured down both of their faces, and Sofi and Yesenia went to find a couple of empty chairs so they could sit down.

"Water!" Sofi cried over the deafening music. She walked over to a table where there was a huge pitcher.

"Having fun?" A sexy voice tickled her from behind. Sofi turned toward Rico's gorgeous face. The man was wearing a loose-fitting white dress shirt and black slacks. His dark curls were gelled back, making him look like an Italian runway model. "Rico!" She gave him a big hug. Sofi quickly turned to her cousin, who was sitting at a table, to point him out. Yesenia stared at him in shock.

"Let's dance." Rico pulled her onto the dance floor before she could introduce them. The lights had dimmed and a slow song came on. She followed his natural sway and tossed her head back thinking this had to be ten times better than the prom. *Just wait till I tell Olivia!* Rico pulled her close. "Your party dress at the cleaners?" Sofi jerked back, feeling her cheeks burn with embarrassment. She looked down at her jeans and long-sleeved cotton top. It was obvious she'd crashed the party. "It's cool. It's cool. It's too late for anyone to care. It's always a pleasure to see you, though."

Sofi smiled brightly into his soulful eyes. Her heart was racing, but she was too excited to be nervous. Was the *limpia* working its magic already? Maybe Rico was the one? Sofi glanced at the flowery cursive lettering pricked into the side of his neck as if drawn by a fine ink pen. Funny, she hadn't noticed the tattoo before. It said something like *Churro* or *Chorro*, or something like that. His friend? Mother? Girlfriend??!!! She'd heard about how people put names on their bodies as a sign of their undying love. Sofi knew that she shouldn't ask, but jealousy stoked her fire.

"Who's that?" she pointed at the tattoo with her index finger.

"That's my homeboy Chato. He committed suicide last year." Sofi gulped, realizing how little she actually knew about Rico. All of a sudden the cell phone on his hip started vibrating intensely. He held up a finger and took the call. Sofi looked around and smiled at the many happy couples dancing around her. After a minute, Rico covered the mouthpiece with his hand and apologized. "I'm sorry. I really need to take this call. Let's finish this dance over dinner." Sofi nodded. Rico kissed her cheek sweetly before taking off into the crowd. She sighed, wishing she could be a piece of lint on his shoulder and follow him outside.

"Now why aren't you dancing?" Andres asked, sneaking up behind her. Sofi jumped, surprised. He was all dressed up in creased slacks, a white button-down shirt, and shiny shoes.

"Where did you pop out from?" she asked, curious. Was he spying on her?

"Who, me?" He tried to look innocent and pointed at his chest. Sofi couldn't help but laugh. "C'mon, don't leave me hanging. People are watching." Sofi looked around, wondering who he was talking about. "This is a party," he continued. "Everyone, even Miss I-Want-a-Bucket-of-Beer-Now must dance. It's the rule."

Sofi started to laugh. "You are such a fool."

"Hey," he said, pretending to be upset. "Don't get mad at me because your boyfriend can't dance." Sofi scrunched up her nose and pinched him on the arm. He cringed. "Ouch! You're feisty. I like that."

"You are too much," Sofi cried, holding herself back from hitting him. What was it about Andres that always made her want to hit, punch, or pinch him? she wondered. "And Rico is not my boyfriend, if you must know, nosy."

"Mr. Rico Suave is not your boyfriend? Come on," he insisted in disbelief. "He was all over you and you had this dumb goo-goo look all over your face." He put a goofy grin on and batted his eyelashes.

"I'm going to—"

"Dance?" Andres completed her sentence. He took her in his arms, not giving her a chance to protest. As if on cue, a totally fast song came on and couples hopped onto the dance floor with relish. He pulled her into a quick polka step. Sofi had never danced like this before and held on tight to his neck. He twirled her around several times really fast, making her dizzy. She couldn't stop herself from laughing uncontrollably. This was crazy fun.

"Do you trust me?" Andres asked, after he'd spun her like a hundred times.

Sofi needed a moment. Her head was still dizzy from all the twirls. Despite the fact that he was a total dork, she did trust him. Andres smiled as he took her by the hips and threw her in the air as if she were a cheerleader. Sofi couldn't believe how strong he was. He spun her several times before picking her up and swinging her legs to the left and right of him. A crowd formed around them and egged them on. Andres was happy to oblige and threw her up again to their delighted cheers. All of a sudden he rocked her down so low to the floor, Sofi was sure she'd bump her head. The music stopped just as the tips of their noses met. It took her breath away, and Sofi couldn't help but wonder if he'd planned it that way.

14

As the claps and whistles died down, the main fluorescent lights came on, illuminating the entire room. Older men in ill-fitting suits and women in bright church dresses squinted and rubbed their eyes. Sofi knew that it was time to go when several young guys in wrinkled tuxes began sweeping the confetti-littered floor. Yesenia sneaked up from behind.

"Yesenia, you scared the hell out of me," Sofi said, trying to sound mad, but the big smile on her face gave her away.

"You two looked so good. You should compete," she said, introducing herself to Andres. "Didn't you go to school with Felicia Ortiz?"

Andres put his hands on his hips and grinned widely. "She's my sister."

"I knew I'd seen you before." Yesenia looked from Sofi to Andres. "Could you do me a big favor and take Sofi home?" Andres nodded without reservation.

Sofi grabbed her cousin by the wrist and pulled her aside. "What are you doing?" Yesenia was out of control. Andres glanced at his watch, waiting for her. *I hope he doesn't think that we planned this*, Sofi thought. Yesenia gave Sofi a mischievous grin as if that explained everything. Then she motioned with her scrunched-up nose at a burly guy with green eyes and skintight jeans. Javier.

Sofi and Andres walked silently down the dark street toward his truck, which was parked by his house in the Colonia Mazatlán neighborhood. Rosarito was a totally different world at night. On Boulevard Benito Juarez, all the restaurants and clubs were alive with bright disco lights and rump-shaking music. But once you crossed the freeway, it was like entering a small Mexican town. Sofi wondered how her parents had met and if they had ever walked down this very same street. There was so much of her parents' lives she didn't know about.

They passed darkened houses with bright lights from the TVs shining through the windows. Dogs howled behind them as if serenading the moon. A whistle from the rent-a-cop sirens pierced the air. The streetlights that worked were few. One could walk entire blocks in the dark. Despite the menacing shadows, she felt safe here. (Maybe having Andres along helped a little.) People were out laughing joyfully in the street. Kids screamed wildly as they played in the poorly lit road. They dashed to the curb when a car drove by. Spanish rap music played on car radios and swarms of people stood around steaming, late-night taco carts. It was nothing like her quiet suburban street back home.

An old brownish-yellow mutt approached them from the opposite direction. He was sniffing a trail on the sidewalk. Instinctively, Sofi flinched, getting out of his way. She bumped right into Andres.

"What's the matter? You scared of dogs?"

"Deathly afraid." She cringed as the dog sniffed her leg. Unimpressed, he carried on. "I was bitten as a little girl. See that?" She pointed to the tiny scar by her mouth.

"Yeah, okay, so what? Get over it."

Sofi didn't like his tone. "It's not that easy."

Andres smiled. "Sure it is. Dogs smell fear. So just don't be afraid."

Sofi shook her head. How could she not be afraid of some animal mauling her to death? What about all those ten o'clock news specials about kids getting attacked by the family dog? "Thanks for walking me. My cousin has a way of ditching me whenever Javier is around." Sofi smiled awkwardly. Andres dug deeper into his pockets as if he were looking for something. He was trying to keep his teeth from chattering. Sofi held his Windbreaker tightly over her shoulders. She felt bad about accepting his jacket three blocks ago.

"It's cool." He shrugged.

In the darkness a face emerged, a face the size of her house. It was a man. He had a familiar bushy mustache and deep, penetrating eyes.

"Who's that?" Sofi asked, pointing. Andres stopped to study the mural.

"That's Emiliano Zapata."

Sofi walked up behind him and noticed that there was an eagle eating a serpent on a cactus. The mural looked violent in a strong, proud way. She could tell that it was important. "It's the *Tierra y Libertad* mural. It's kind of famous. Some fancy artist from Mexico City did it."

"What's it about?" Sofi asked. Andres's features were hard to see in the dull light. But she could tell by his expression that he thought she must be kidding him.

"It's the history of Mexico."

"Oh."

"Are you for real?" he asked. The dark shadows made his face look disapproving.

"What do you mean?" Sofi asked. She could hear the defensive tone in her voice. She crossed her arms. Why did everyone expect her to know everything about Mexico? Was there some Mexican gene she didn't know about that explained this stuff?

Andres's body relaxed. "I'm sorry. I didn't mean to upset you." His voice sounded sincere.

"No." She shook her head. "It's not you. It's me. I guess. I'm just a little hypersensitive. Everyone always assumes that I speak Spanish and know everything about Mexico, and I don't."

"But Sofi, don't get mad," he said with the biggest grin on his face. Sofi couldn't help but smile. "You should be proud that people assume you're Mexican. It's like a badge of pride here. Dark skin, dark eyes, dark hair—that's what sets us apart from the rest of the world."

"Lots of people have dark eyes and dark hair."

"Okay then." He took a deep breath. "Let me show you what I mean. Let me be your guide. I would be honored."

"Well, when you put it like *that*," Sofi said, smiling, "how can I say no?"

"Somebody's got a hot date," Yesenia announced the next morning at breakfast.

"And somebody's got a big mouth," Sofi said, kicking her cousin under the table. She'd told Yesenia about Andres in the strictest of confidences. She hadn't expected her to go blabbing to the whole world. It *wasn't* a date. Uncle Victor looked up from his oatmeal and Yesenia told him all about the *quinceañera* and how everyone was talking about that pretty *pocha* who was dancing with Andres all night.

Uncle Victor told Sofi that he liked Andres. He gave Sofi a thumbs-up. She smiled meekly, feeling totally uncomfortable with the conversation. Wasn't Uncle Victor the one who told her not to trust anyone in Rosarito? Sofi would never dream of talking about boys with her parents. They would freak out! Her heart was thumping loudly and her ears were hot. Mando and Mundo started to make sloppy kissing sounds across the table.

"It's not like that." Sofi tried to make her uncle understand in Spanish. "Explain it to him," she told her cousin. Yesenia ignored her, scraping her bowl clean with her spoon. "He's just a friend."

Everyone started to laugh. This was a hundred times more embarrassing than the time she'd accidentally waxed off her left eyebrow the day before picture day. But something in the way her uncle kept winking and nodding his head told Sofi that his teasing was all in good fun. In some crazy way, she understood that this was how her family showed affection.

Uncle Victor winked again. Yesenia was totally blowing the whole thing out of proportion. Andres was just going to drive her around;

maybe they'd have a taco or something. It wasn't like she was going out with Rico or anything. Now, dinner with Rico would be a *total* date. Andres was someone she could talk to and have fun with, who just so happened to be of the opposite sex. They were just *friends*! Mando and Mundo continued to tease her. They were acting out a love scene using their spoons as lips. She was going to kick them, but Luisa walked into the room.

"What's so funny?" Luisa asked. Her shoulders were hunched over like she was a fuming bull. She was hurrying to get to work and quickly poured the remaining oatmeal into a mug. Her *tía* had yet to thank Sofi for getting the boys to school three days in a row last week. She seemed to notice Sofi only when she did something wrong, like when the toilet overflowed or when she forgot to put away the food. Uncle Victor explained in Spanish that Sofi had a date. Sofi gave him a heated look that he laughed off. It was not a date! But her *tía* was not in a kidding mood. Luisa's disapproving stare made Sofi squirm. She felt like the snake in the *Tierra y Libertad* mural caught in the eagle's beak.

Her aunt sniffed loudly. "You don't seem to have enough work to do. You think I work all day so that you can go off and mess around with boys? You have no sense. None at all." Uncle Victor interrupted, saying that she was not being fair. "Fair? You think it's fair that I work while you all stay home to laugh and do nothing. What if I decided to put my feet up and have a beer? Who would put food on the table? Who would pay for the boys' school, huh?" No one said anything until she left. There was no pleasing the woman, Sofi thought. Uncle Victor told Sofi not to worry about Luisa. She didn't mean what she said.

Andres picked her up in his beat-up green Ford pickup. He looked all dressed up in his ironed black slacks and white polo. He'd even gotten a haircut! Her cheeks burned as she looked down at her jeans and red top. Did he think this was a date? She jumped into the car and sniffed the chow mein smell. It was starting to grow on her.

"You ever been to a *tardeada*?" he asked.

"Tartar what?"

Andres leaned back and laughed. He grabbed his ribs. "No, a *tardeada*. It's a traditional afternoon fiesta." Sofi's face felt hot. She wasn't trying to be funny. Andres noticed her discomfort. "You'll love it." Sofi tried to smile back. It was hard for her to deal with the fact that she didn't feel Mexican enough. Taco Bell, margaritas, and Cinco de Mayo celebrations seemed so superficial and bland in comparison to all that she'd experienced in Rosarito. Was it her parents' fault? They'd pressed American culture on her growing up. Or was it her fault? Sofi had never really cared about Mexico before. Maybe she was partly responsible for her awkwardness.

She noticed the pouch dangling from the rearview mirror. "So what's with the bag?"

Andres winked. "That's my pet project. I call it Operation *Semilla*. Go ahead, take a look."

Sofi had a strong feeling that it was nothing like Operation *Papi Chulo*. Andres was such a strange guy. He was like no one she'd ever met. She unhooked the pouch and opened it. "Seeds?"

"Those aren't just any seeds. They're our history, our future. Have you heard of terminator seeds?" Sofi shook her head. "Check this out. They're these genetically engineered sterile seeds that U.S. corporations are pushing on Mexico. You see, farmers save seeds to replant for the next year's harvest. They've been doing it for over five hundred years. But now there're these terminator seeds that are sterile and force farmers to buy new seeds every season. It's ruining poor farmers all over the world." Andres looked at Sofi's face.

"You think I'm crazy, don't you?"

"No, no, I'm just not sure what to think. I've never heard about this stuff before. Tell me more."

"Really? I'm not boring you to death?"

"Just tell me." She slapped her hand on her thigh for emphasis.

"Well, you met my grandfather the other day. He's been growing his own vegetables all his life. All his seeds are organic. But new farmers use the genetically modified seeds that promise bigger crops."

"So you collect seeds because you believe that these terminator seeds will ruin the agricultural economy."

"Exactly," he said, smiling brightly.

"That's how you plan to get rich?"

Plaza Hacienda was a quaint shopping area with restaurants and shops styled like an old Spanish village off of Boulevard Benito Juarez. The cobblestone floor made Sofi's footsteps sound loud to her ears. Sofi was impressed; there was no dust. They walked down a small corridor that led to a huge garden patio with a refreshing waterfall on one side and surrounded by lush palms, ferns, and a wall of bright yellow, violet, and white bougainvillea. It was summertime and everything was bright and in full bloom. The poignant aroma reminded Sofi of her mom's porch with its brilliant color schemes: red and pink hollyhocks, white and yellow daisies. *She would love this place*, Sofi thought. There were some tourists, mostly retirees in sun visors and flower-covered shorts, sitting around a main stage. Young, pretty girls in peasant blouses and long flowing skirts were floating from table to table.

They sat at a round table in front of the stage and ordered finger food called *botanas*. Sofi kept straining her neck to look around. It felt like a hidden oasis tucked deep within the busy commercial street.

"Stay away from the salsa. It's hot," Andres warned.

"What do you mean, hot?"

He shrugged. "I'm just saying. You might not be used to it."

"What are you trying to say? You think I can't handle it?"

Andres stared at her with an amused look in his eyes. "Well, they do say that only real Mexicans can eat chilies."

"Real Mexicans?" Sofi thought for a minute, looking at the red sauce in the ceramic bowl. She waved over a waitress and ordered the hottest chili peppers they had. "For your information, I suck down packets of Taco Bell hot sauce, and I'm not taking about the mild kind, either. I always choose Fire Hot." Andres started to laugh. "You think I'm lying, right?"

"I'll believe it when I see it."

The waitress brought over an assortment of chilies. There was a dish of green jalapeños, red skinny chilies, and yellow buttonlike chilies she'd never seen before.

Sofi challenged Andres from across the table. "Let's see just who is more Mexican," she said, picking up a green jalapeño.

On the count of three, they each bit into a chili. Tears tried to come out of her eyes, but she held them at bay. She refused to let Andres think she was weak. His face had turned bright pink. He was sucking in his teeth and making hissing sounds that made her laugh. They both looked at their glasses of water, but neither wanted to be the first to give in.

Sofi sniffed loudly. "Okay, how about the next one?" She reached for a yellow button. How bad could it be? It was yellow.

"No, wait," Andres protested.

Sofi smiled. "What's the matter, Andres? Chicken?" She started clucking loudly.

"All right. All right," he said, picking up a habanero.

Sofi looked him straight in the eye, "Now we'll see who's more Mexican." She took a big bite from the fleshy skin. Her ears started to ring like an ambulance siren. Sofi screamed out as tears streamed down her cheeks. She couldn't think and waved her hands wildly.

"Here, here," Andres said, pouring salt into her hand. "Put this on your tongue."

Sofi chugged down her glass of water and coated her tongue with salt. Her mouth was on fire and her lips were numb. Everything hurt. Just then, a group of singing mariachis in matching white outfits came out from behind the stage.

The musicians were joking with one another and the audience in a jovial manner. They made Sofi loosen up and want to participate, hollering and clapping along to a song. Andres sang along with the mariachis. He knew every ballad. He taught her the chorus of "Cielito Lindo." Sofi couldn't remember ever laughing so hard. Everything in Mexico was over the top, she decided, and celebrated in a community. She'd never realized how nice it felt to be part of a community. It made her heart swell with joy.

A slew of painted ladies in white lace dresses danced onto the wooden stage. The sound of their heels hitting the boards in complicated rhythmic patterns mesmerized the entire audience. Handsome men in white partnered up with the girls for the second number. It was breathtaking. It reminded Sofi of when she was small and her parents took her to the Cinco de Mayo celebrations in downtown San Inocente. She used to beg her mom to take her up front so that she could see the pretty ladies. Sofi was just a little kid then. She'd forgotten about that, and that made her sad.

The next dance involved a guy dressed as a cowboy, in brown leather pants with a real-looking gun belt strapped to his waist. He whirled a big lasso high over his head. The audience gasped as the cowboy expertly jumped through the hoop. Sofi looked at Andres, who was smiling back at her. This was such a treat, she thought. After the show a frail old man carrying a vintage camera asked to take their picture.

"Oh yes," Sofi said. "I want a memento." She leaned over and put her arm around Andres. Andres straightened up, looking a bit nervous. Sofi laughed. It so was not a date. She was relaxed, for one thing, and Andres, although nice, was not the type of guy she could show off to her friends. She thought about Nick. The ache was still there, but it didn't burn anymore. She'd always imagined him taking her to a fancy place like this. But whenever she got around him, she felt so awkward and nervous and made a total dork of herself. She wished her real dates could be half as nice as this day had been. Minutes later, they sat in the truck in front of her house, watching the dust settle.

"If you want, we can go check out a museum in Tijuana," he said shyly. Why was Andres acting weird? On the drive home he'd hardly joked around at all. Sofi held her picture and looked past him, awash in the glow of the festive afternoon. Her eyes drifted to the old horse in the corral, staring blankly with its one good eye.

"Know what I'd really like to do?" she said, more to herself than to him. "I'd like to go horseback riding on the beach."

"Let's do it," he said excitedly. "It wasn't part of the tour but—"

"Really?"

"I'm off on Thursday."

"Sounds good to me," Sofi said, slamming the door of the truck behind her. He was so cool, she thought. She waved as his truck made a U-turn and disappeared in a cloud of dust.

When Luisa heard about the second date, she scolded Sofi for being too forward. "*Resbalona!* Mexican girls never act so eager," she said. Yesenia rolled her eyes and motioned for Sofi to follow her to their room.

"How was it?" Yesenia pulled her onto the bed.

"It was really fun. I didn't know what to expect, but Andres took me to this cool place with mariachis and dancers and great food."

"Did you kiss?"

"Hello? Andres is just a friend," Sofi insisted.

"Okay, so that means no, which is a good thing," Yesenia said, sounding like a talk-show expert. "Mexican boys are nothing like American boys."

"Why are we talking about this?" Sofi sprang up to do something. She didn't know what, but she didn't like where her cousin was going with this.

Yesenia pulled her back down. "I know you don't want to hear this, but I'm doing it for your own good. My *mamá* is right about some things. There are certain . . ." She paused to choose her words carefully. ". . . codes that we follow. For example, most Mexican guys are old-fashioned. They walk on the right side by the street. They'll lend you their jacket if you're cold, and they *always* pay."

"Oh really?" Sofi sat straight up. Why didn't anyone tell me before? Sofi thought about Rico. He seemed so gallant and chivalrous. She had to take notes in case she did go out with him.

"They're very formal and respectful." Yesenia crinkled her nose like when she had to shovel horse manure. "Sure, it's romantic, but they also want a woman to cook and clean for them. Make tortillas . . ." She rolled her eyes. "That's why I like Javier. He's modern. Modern guys are like Americans. They think a woman should go to college, work, and pay for her own drinks. And that's only because they spend all their money on hair gel and clothes." Yesenia laughed at her joke. "Unless they're modern old-school . . . " She tapped her finger against her bottom lip, considering.

Sofi remembered Andres lending her his coat on the walk home. But he'd also seemed excited when she told him she was going to UCLA. "Do you think Andres is modern?" Sofi asked in a timid voice. Although she liked the part about walking on the edge of the street, she didn't want Andres to think she was expecting to marry him and stay home with the babies. She knew she had to talk to him, make sure they were on the same page. They weren't dating. Sofi stared at her cousin, who was still thinking. She liked talking to Yesenia about guys. Sofi felt relaxed and open. Yesenia didn't act supercool and experienced, like Olivia and Taylor did.

"Maybe." Yesenia thought for a second. "He was born on the Other Side."

"He was?" This was news to Sofi.

"Yeah, he and Felicia were born, I think, in San Isidro, right by the border. She came to Rosarito in the seventh grade. I was in her class. She spoke hardly any Spanish and they wanted to put her in the fifth grade." Yesenia laughed. Sofi couldn't help but empathize with Felicia. Their experiences weren't very different. A lot of people came to Rosarito from the Other Side and vice versa. Sofi turned and noticed Yesenia watching her curiously. "So where is he taking you next?"

"Horseback riding."

"Okay." Yesenia put her hands on Sofi's shoulders. "This is the test. When you two are walking down the street, position yourself on the street side of the sidewalk. If he's traditional, he'll switch places with you. If he doesn't, that means you two are going dutch."

Impressed, Sofi asked, "Where did you learn all this?"

"We have a Latina Dr. Phil. She's called Laura." Yesenia eyed her mischievously. "You better watch out. Mexican boys have a way of sneaking up on you and stealing your heart."

"Ha! You don't have to worry about that. Like I said, Andres and I are just friends."

15 ↗

The next morning Uncle Victor stood in the doorway talking to a very pregnant young woman who was standing next to a cute little girl in pigtails. The woman noticed Sofi and smiled sweetly.

"Sofia, I want you to meet Aurora." Her uncle gestured for her to come outside. Sofi shook the woman's hand and smiled at the cute girl, who was hiding behind her mother's faded brown skirt. The woman thanked Uncle Victor, patted the heavy bag in her hand, and went on her way. He explained that Aurora's husband had returned to the United States six months ago. She was waiting for him to send for her. Uncle Victor let Aurora cut down as many nopales as she could to make money. Her husband hadn't sent any money for over a month and Aurora was nervous that something had happened to him. "Life here is very rough; we have to depend on one another to survive." Sofi was moved by her uncle's generosity.

"*¿Tienes hambre?*"

Sofi nodded. She was tired of eating eggs and chorizo, even though she'd become quite good at fixing them. He nodded and motioned for her to follow him around the house. Uncle Victor disturbed the dust with his heavy steps. She could tell by the way he walked that his back bothered him, but he didn't complain. He stopped in front of a huge green cactus. Its long green prickly pads reached up into the sky like muscular arms. Sofi took a deep breath of fresh cold air. The day was bright, vibrant, and alive. A pang of guilt hit her. She hadn't talked to Taylor or Olivia in days. What were they doing? What had happened at the prom? She wanted to tell them about Rico, the *quince*, and her *limpia*. So much had happened. She smiled at the little black-headed brown birds chirping melodiously in the evergreens. The turquoise blue sky contrasted with the dark green plants and brown hills. It was a soothing sight and nursed her homesickness.

"Nopales," Uncle Victor said, pointing at a cactus with his callused finger. Sofi looked at the plant and noticed that each limb had five fingerlike branches. Sharp thorns poked out of fan-shaped cactus leaves. Bright red fruit pods adorned the tips like Christmas stars.

"No-pa-les," she whispered, practicing. She liked how the word rolled off her tongue. Uncle Victor pulled out the knife that was always tucked in his back pocket. Then he handed Sofi a black plastic bag and motioned for her to open it up. He severed the eight-inch stems and handed them carefully to her one by one. Sofi thought about Abuela Benita, wondering if she ever cut nopales.

"How come Yesenia hates Abuela Benita?"

Her uncle looked at her sideways, considering. "Your *abuela* is a very hard woman."

"Is she really crazy?"

Uncle Victor chuckled softly. "Your *tía* and dad think so. You see, she was very young when your *abuelo* ran off. She had to make tough decisions. Either she could watch her children starve or try to give them a better life with someone else. Who knows what was going through her head? She left them with an aunt. Your *tía* and dad never understood, nor did they ever forgive her for leaving them. I don't think she's crazy. I feel bad for her."

Sofi thought about how much she missed her parents. She was sure that her grandmother missed her kids too. There were six pads in the bag when Uncle Victor decided they were done and led Sofi back into the house. The kitchen was dark. No electricity?

Mando and Mundo looked up from the living-room rug, where they were coloring with broken crayons. They watched as their father ripped open a brown paper bag to cover the table. Uncle Victor motioned for Sofi to stand next to him. He pulled out a pad and expertly shaved off the thorns and the little black dots that looked like eyes. Then he examined the pad, trimming off the yellowed, discolored area with his big knife, and sliced the cactus pad into long strips. Uncle Victor looked up at Sofi. He offered her his knife.

"Oh no," she protested. The boys crept up behind.

"*Sí, se puede*," he insisted.

The phrase reminded her of her father's plaque on the living-room table. She was a Mendoza, she told herself, and Mendozas were not quitters. Sofi took the cold hard knife from him. It was actually quite heavy and felt huge in her hand. She sat across from Uncle Victor and picked a floppy nopal from the plastic bag. The boys watched her curiously. Sofi looked from them to her uncle. *How difficult can it be?* she thought and began to shave off the needles. The knife was extra sharp, and with her first slice, she sheared off three-quarters of the pad. The boys giggled. She picked up the larger piece and tried to skin it again.

"Ouch." A thin stream of blood oozed from her thumb and she instantly put it in her mouth. Skinning cactus was obviously *not* her thing. Uncle Victor smiled and motioned for her to continue. "What? But I hurt myself." She showed him her thumb.

"*No te agites*," he said, encouraging her with a nod to go on.

"*Ándele*," Mando added as if he were Speedy Gonzalez. "*Tú lo puedes hacer. Tienes la cara de nopal.*"

"Ha ha." Mundo laughed. "That's you. Cactus face with all those spots." They all started to laugh, even Uncle Victor. Sofi's face burned hot. She wanted to die. These people were crazy, insulting her like that. Didn't they have any manners? Besides, she did not have a lot of spots. She had just four, okay, five pimple scars, but they weren't *that* bad! Sofi considered trimming their tongues, but she pressed her lips tightly together instead. She wasn't going to let them get to her. The image of Luisa's disapproving stare flashed before her. *She thinks I'm weak and helpless*, Sofi thought, looking at the pads before her. *Well, I'll show her. I'll show all of them.* "Never give up," she grunted to herself between clenched teeth. She grabbed a new cactus leaf and started again.

"Don't get mad," Uncle Victor said between chuckles. "We *meji-canos* like to joke. We make up funny names for everybody."

That's a crazy tradition, Sofi thought, rolling her eyes.

"Besides, in life you'll see that there are only two types of people who always tell the truth: kids and drunks."

After a delicious breakfast of nopales *con huevos*, Sofi noticed the boys changing clothes. Were they getting ready for school? she half hoped.

"Hey," Mando asked, as he put on a sequined mask. Mundo was tying a black cape around his bare shoulders. "Do you want to play with us?" Sofi looked over her shoulder to see who the boys were talking to. The boys had never invited Sofi to do anything with them, and she was touched. Had they accepted her as part of the family?

"What are you playing?"

"Wrestling, of course." Mando shrugged, as if it were the most normal thing in the world to strip down to his underwear and chase someone with a mask.

"I don't have a mask."

"You don't need one," Mundo said, adjusting his blue mask. "You just need a name."

"A name? Like what?"

"Well, I'm El Santo," he said, flexing his skimpy arms as if he were a professional body builder. "And he's Blue Dragon." He pointed to Mando. "We're famous wrestlers."

"I know! I know!" Mando said, jumping on the couch. "She can be La Diabla Americana." Sofi winced. There was always a catch. Mando and Mundo looked at her expectantly.

"Okay, but only if I can use a pillow," she said, grabbing two throw cushions from the couch and pounding them both on the head. The boys screamed with delight and ran around the room in circles. Now she really felt like part of the family. Sofi wished Andres were here. He'd love to see this. "Ugh!" She moaned, falling back onto the couch. Mando and Mundo grabbed their own pillows and thrashed her wildly. Sofi started to laugh. That's what she got for letting her guard down around these tyrants. "You win! You win!" she cried.

"The world champions!" Mundo jumped on the couch and yelled, raising his fists in the air. Mundo gave him a high five. "*Los campeones de Rancho Escondido!*"

"What happened to you?" Yesenia asked, clunking into the living room in wooden platform heels, skintight hip-hugging shorts, and a half-cut baby tee. Her outfit was more appropriate for dancing on tables than for leading horse-guided tours. Sofi looked at herself in the mirror above the table. She felt a tad self-conscious. Her hair was in total disarray, as if it'd been hit by a tornado.

"Just messing with the boys." Sofi grinned, combing her fingers through her hair.

Yesenia smiled, shaking her head at her brothers. "*Pórtense bien con Sofi*," Yesenia warned as she smoothed out a lock of hair that was hanging over her right eye. "What do you think?" She modeled her outfit.

"I think it's a little much," Sofi said hesitantly, wondering how her cousin would react.

Yesenia huffed. "But I told you, Javier is modern. He hangs out at Papas and Beer."

Sofi stared at her cousin in shock. Did she know what she was saying? "Trust me, you don't want to look like the girls at Papas and Beer," Sofi said, grabbing her cousin by the wrist and leading her to the bedroom.

Yesenia wiggled free. "I have to do something. Britannica is trying to steal him from me. She told me so herself."

Sofi looked at her cousin's desperate face. It reminded her of when she'd been bending over backward and falling off mechanical bulls to get Nick's attention. He'd been everything to her. Sofi had thought she had to have him to make her dreams come true. But the real Nick had fallen way short of her fantasy. Yesenia was going about this wrong. Sofi didn't really know how to snag a guy, but she knew that wearing hoochie outfits and throwing herself at him wasn't going to work.

"You are an amazing girl," Sofi began. "You're smart, funny, and a good friend. If Javier doesn't see that, then forget him. He doesn't deserve you." Sofi remembered hearing a similar speech come out of Olivia's mouth. Her heart swelled, thinking about how much she loved and missed her friends.

Yesenia stared at her in shock. "You want me to forget Javier? *Estás más loca que Abuela Benita.*"

"Okay, okay, maybe not forget him totally, but don't start pretending to be something that you think he wants. You think that dressing like a hoochie will make him choose you over Britannica? Well, you're right. He will want you. He'll want to screw you. But that's all he'll want. Believe me, I know."

Yesenia sat down across from her with furrowed brows and pouting lips, and crossed her legs. "I thought you said you knew nothing about boys."

"Well, I know what not to do."

Yesenia laughed.

"Hey, I got something that'll totally match those cute jeans you had on yesterday. You'll like it. It's classy." Yesenia's face fell. "Don't worry, your mom will hate it." Sofi smiled to herself as she rummaged through her UCLA duffel bag. She pulled out a pretty olive-colored spaghetti-strap top.

"Oh, I like that."

The two girls giggled as they tried on different tops. Yesenia pulled out her bucket of makeup. She showed Sofi how to apply dramatic green shadow and even added sparkly dots to accentuate her eyes. Sofi lost herself in playing dress-up. She forgot all about Nick, the border, and her aunt Luisa. It was the kind of day she'd always dreamed of having with an imaginary sister.

A ringing sound made them both look up.

"You have a doorbell?" Sofi asked. Rancho Escondido never ceased to amaze her.

Mando and Mundo were talking to someone at the door. Sofi wondered if it was another solicitor. A beautiful white smile greeted her. The guy took off his dark shades and raised his hand.

"*Hola*, my little brown angel."

"Rico," Sofi gasped, rushing to the door. Without thinking she gave him a hug. Rico smelled cool and spicy, as if he'd just taken a shower. His chest was strong and comforting. But then Sofi remembered where she was and jumped back. Her cheeks were bright red. She reached up and touched her hair. It looked ridiculous teased out, and she had on a ton of makeup. Worse yet was the dismal state of the ranch. The goat bleated loudly and the chickens were clucking in the background. Sofi wished she were somewhere, anywhere else.

"Wow. I should come by more often," he joked as Sofi pulled back. Her face flushed. Yesenia and the wrestling twins were standing behind her.

"Oh, these are my cousins Yesenia, Mando, and Mundo." She gestured to each with her hand. Her whole body tingled with excitement. She looked at him, impressed by his cool demeanor. He was actually at her house! His olive slacks and black polo made his tanned skin glow. He was so sharp and sophisticated that even the dust bowed down and stayed away from him.

"Nice to meet you guys." He nodded. "I'm sorry for just dropping in like this. . . ."

"Oh no, it's totally fine." Her heart started racing. "You can stop by whenever you like. *Mi rancho es tu rancho*. Isn't that what they say?" Sofi covered her mouth with her hand. She knew she was talking too much. *Relaaax*, she told herself, remembering Taylor.

Rico laughed softly into his fist. "I think you mean, *Mi casa es su casa*."

"Well, yeah, that too."

"Are you a drug dealer?" Mundo asked, coming up to Rico's belt. He was still in his underwear, and his little cape flared out behind him.

Oh my God! Sofi shouted in her head. No, he did not just insult Rico. Sofi grabbed Mundo by the forearm and pulled him away. "I'm so sorry. You have to excuse my cousins." She shooed both boys into the house before they could embarrass her further. "They have no manners. They're beasts. You should see how they eat," she joked.

"Because you look like one!" Mando screamed from inside the house.

"Yeah, I'm telling Mamá!" Mundo added.

"*Cállense el hocico, chamacos!*" Yesenia hollered back.

Rico laughed softly into his fist. "It's all right. I'm used to it. A regular guy like me does well and everyone in the neighborhood assumes he's dealing drugs. That's what I hate about our people. They don't like to see others get ahead."

"You're so right. There's this girl at my school and she is always talking smack about me because . . . " Sofi caught herself. She realized that that wasn't her school anymore. San Inocente High was her past. A heavy weight pushed down on her chest. Rico and Yesenia were staring at her. "Forget it. It's nothing."

"I just wanted to stop by and see if you and maybe your cousin would be interested in a couple of free tickets for the Linkin Park show this Saturday. It's going to be right on the beach. A full stage with lights, and I think MTV will be there to tape it." He pulled two tickets from his back pocket.

"Are you serious?" Yesenia asked. Her eyes were so big, they were about to pop out. Sofi couldn't believe it herself, and her mouth hung open.

"It'll be fun. What do you say?"

"Yes! Yes! Yes!" Sofi cheered. Yesenia started to scream and both girls bounced excitedly together. Sofi ran up to Rico and gave him another tight squeeze. "This is amazing. I love Linkin Park."

"Great, so I'll pick you ladies up at eight. Dress sharp. You might just get on TV."

16 ↗

Uncle Victor sat in a darkened room with his back turned toward Sofi. Power outages were a daily occurrence. They never lasted very long and sometimes they passed without notice. But the power wasn't out; Uncle Victor had the TV on low. He had his favorite bathrobe hastily wrapped around his large waist and a Tecate resting on his knee. Breakfast? A couple of days had passed and all Sofi and Yesenia could talk about was the concert that Friday. Sofi held a printout of e-mails from Taylor and Olivia in her hand. They were her link with her old life.

> To: sofilicious1@yahoo.com
> From: twilson@hotmail.com
> Subject: hi
>
> Sofi,
> How are you? I'm worried sick. Can't you call? I read
> your e-mail. It sounds horrible. I wish I were there
> with you. Life here sucks. At least you got out of Mr.
> Portman's stupid econ prep. It was sooooo boring. I
> wanted to jump into my car and drive to see you. But
> I'm still grounded. I'm not allowed to take the car
> anywhere without a chaperone. And Olivia doesn't
> count. Can you believe it? My parents think I'm out of
> control. They want me to go to counseling. They're

afraid that I'll only get worse in college. I miss you soooo much. When are you coming home? Will you make it for finals? I attached the econ notes just in case. Call me as soon as you can I'm dying to know what's going on.

T

To: sofilicious1@yahoo.com
From: livygrl@gmail.com
Subject: Re: crazy girl

crazy girl
I hope u don't mind, but everyones buggin me with ques bout how u r and all that. i heard emily talking in bonehead math. she said u'd fallen 4 some hot ass mexican mafioso. LOL. and now chilling in cabo sipping margaritas. is it true? dont b holding out on me!!!!! anthonys telling people u were kidnapped by an antigovernment guerrilla militia, and training in the mountains to start a revolution. J he said he'll marry you so u can come back 4 100 bucks! 1 know its dumb, but what do you think? I posted ur e-mail on my blog and guess what? ur famous now. everyone is reading it!!!!!!!! so whats the deal? when u coming home? call me!!!!!
;O

Sofi's eyes hurt as she reread the e-mails over and over again. Her heart ached. The prom was gone forever and Sofi was still stuck in Mexico. Uncle Victor was really engrossed in the Spanish soap opera. She saw a tear trickle down his gray-stubbled cheek. Uncle Victor was the total opposite of her dad. Sofi's dad was always presentable, taking his toothbrush and razor to work. He hated when she forgot to clean her hair out of the sink and was always on Sofi's case for slouching. Her uncle was a professional moper. There was a permanent groove in the couch from where he sat all day long. He liked to cry when he sang along to the romantic songs he listened to on his handheld radio. Something really bad must have happened on TV.

Sofi looked at the images on-screen and noticed a woman facedown in a ditch.

"*Siéntate*," he said, and motioned for her to sit next to him. She never knew what to think about Uncle Victor. Sometimes he seemed so distant and lethargic, listening to his radio with his eyes closed, snoozing in the sun as if on a paid vacation, all the while ignoring how unruly his sons were. But then he would come back with those intelligent eyes that left you wondering if it was all just an act. Sofi leaned back and watched the story of the beautiful girl unfold.

"See her, that's Casandra, understand?" he asked. She had gorgeous wavy red hair and a hot bod. "She was a wealthy woman who was trapped on a deserted island with a handsome pirate." Uncle Victor was a nice guy. But it was ridiculous that he stayed home all day while Luisa slaved away at her job. Her uncle seemed to have lost his way in the world. Sofi had seen the same thing happen to her mother, before she'd started taking Prozac. Depression. She looked across the couch at the sprawling shadow of a man and decided that she had to do something to turn his life around—without the use of legal drugs. She just didn't know what.

That afternoon Andres came for Sofi. This time she felt confused and excited, like a tumbleweed blowing aimlessly in the desert. Their outing was starting to feel like a real date. Sofi took extra time to fix up her hair and, after changing four times, decided on a cute yellow top and capris. Andres looked nice too, in his button-down shirt and jeans. She'd wanted to walk on the street side of the sidewalk, but they were on the beach. Did that mean the ocean side of the beach? She wished that Yesenia were there to explain.

"Are you okay, Sofi?" Andres asked, walking beside her. The sand in her shoes was making it uncomfortable to walk.

"I'm fine," she said quickly. This was all Yesenia's fault. Why had she put all these crazy romantic ideas into Sofi's head? Why was she pushing Andres on her? Had Yesenia not gotten a good look at Rico? He was a hot *papi chulo! This is ridiculous*, Sofi thought, watching several kids screaming as they jumped the waves. Andres gave her a cheesy grin. Sofi smiled back, shaking off her uncomfortable feelings. "Race you?" she said, and took off running.

"No fair," Andres cried behind her. Sofi ran past strolling tourists, hair-braiders, and waiters passing out drinks.

"I won! I won!" Sofi danced with her arms in the air. "And the crowd goes wild. Woo!" Andres came up behind her. Sofi made an L shape with her index finger and thumb and threw it in his face with a grin. "Loser."

"Hey." Andres grabbed her from behind. "Who you calling a loser?" Andres's arms were thick and he was stronger than he looked. His closeness made Sofi nervous. She wiggled away from him and walked over to the horses, hoping that Andres hadn't seen her blush. "Hey, where's Yesenia? She was supposed to meet us here." An older man with a cowboy hat who was watching the pack of skinny horses came up to them.

"Are you Yesenia's cousin?" the guy asked in Spanish. Sofi nodded. "Yesenia told me you might stop by. She's off on her break. If you want, I'll give you and your boyfriend a discount."

"*No es mi novio*," Sofi tried to say, but the cowboy had turned away to gather two horses. Andres just stood there and smiled. He didn't even try to correct the guy! "Whoa," Sofi said, fanning herself as the cowboy brought over the horses. "I will never get used to the smell."

Andres laughed. "This is part of Mexico's charm," he said, and gestured with his hand. "The beautiful beach and the filthy sewage pipes.

The quaint dirt roads with abandoned cars and burned mattresses. Mexico is a country of extremes."

Sofi's was about to crack a joke when a huge brown horse busted in between them. The brown mare huffed and stomped in place as if resentful of the fact that she had to carry annoying tourists on her back. Sofi hesitated, looking up at the horse. Maybe this wasn't a good idea. The animal might throw her off. Plus how was she supposed to get on that thing?

"Don't worry, she looks like a good horse," Andres assured her calmly, slapping the mare's backside. "I won't let anything happen to you." Sofi inhaled deeply, and on the count of three Andres helped her pull herself up by the saddle handle. She sat on top of the horse, feeling light-headed. The beach was thrilling to look at from this angle. The sun was bright and the ocean glistened. Andres handed her the leather reins. "Now pull back if you want it to stop. Loosen the reins if you want it to go. Remember, you're in control."

The brown mare leaned to the right. "Whoa," Sofi said. She looked over her shoulder and saw Andres expertly hopping onto a white horse. He looked comfortable, as if he'd been riding his whole life. He led his horse next to hers with a slight nudge. The wind played with Sofi's hair, tossing it in her face. The relaxing sea sparkled like a jewel on her right. After a while, she didn't even mind the uncomfortable bouncing. Her horse was called Paquita. Before she knew it, their fifteen minutes were up. Andres helped her get down. Sofi smiled brightly, combing her fingers through Paquita's coarse black mane.

"And now for the surprise," Andres said as they walked back toward his truck. His eyes lit up as they passed a fireworks shop called Inferno, with a cartoon image of a huge stick of red dynamite with a happy grin painted on its face.

"Don't tell me that this is part of being Mexican?" Sofi asked, raising her right eyebrow in disbelief.

"Is there anything more Mexican than fireworks?"

"We have fireworks in America," she stated, putting her hands on her hips.

"Yeah, but can you fire them up all year round?"

Andres looked like an excited puppy. Sofi couldn't resist. "Okay." She followed him into the shop, where he ordered the biggest rocket launcher they had. They laughed as they scrambled onto the beach. The sun was beginning to set and the cooling wind picked up locks of her hair. She loved the smell of sea air and took a deep breath. Although the salty scent reminded her of home, the scene before her was totally Mexican. There were families along the shore packing away umbrellas and lawn chairs. A Spanish rock song drifted out from one of the clubs. Andres offered Sofi his Windbreaker.

"*Gracias*," she said.

The rocket launched without a hitch and, just like the shop clerk promised, it exploded into a fury of sparkling colors and fiery sounds. They lay on their backs with their hands behind their heads, enjoying the light show.

"So, I hear you've lived in the States?" Sofi asked. She couldn't help but be curious about Andres's past.

"I was born in San Diego," he said, rolling onto his side to look at her. He had pretty brown eyes. "But when I was twelve, my mom got deported, so I had to come with her."

"Wasn't it tough for you?"

"Sure it was." He shrugged, as if it were a normal childhood experience. "But what choice did I have?"

Sofi sat up. "So if you're American, then how come you're so mean to tourists?"

"You're still pissed about the beach?"

"No, I'm not!" Sofi flushed and hoped he couldn't see her face.

"You totally are," he said, grinning hard.

"All right. All right." She put up her hands in defense. "So I'm still a little pissed."

"A little?"

"Yes, but I have every right to be. You were rude."

Andres sat up and looked at the sunset. A flock of seagulls was flying in a V formation along the horizon. He was very quiet, deep in thought. The sound of crashing waves soothed the awkward moment. A child's excited scream broke his silence. "It's kind of complicated, I guess."

Sofi said nothing, giving him time to find the right words.

"You see," he began, but grew silent again. It seemed like Andres was struggling to understand the situation himself. "It sucks living in Rosarito," he finally said. "Tourists come here for a jolly-ass time. They want to escape their troubles and frustrations back home. This is their vacation, so they do as they please without any real regard for the people who live here." He sniffed, looking toward the ocean. "Yeah, it's pretty, but it's also really tough to make a living. Everyone is competing for jobs. The customers are always right and take full advantage of that. Cops abuse their authority. Nobody cares about the community, because it's a border town. No one expects to stay here. It's just a stop on the road to the American dream," he said, scratching his head as if that would help him make sense of it all. He turned to look Sofi in the eye. "Most girls don't care about us. We're the cabana boys who bring them their drinks."

Sofi jerked as if stung by a jellyfish.

He was quiet for a long time, trying to decide how to continue. "American girls are all the same. They like to tease. I learned that the hard way," he said, biting down on his lower lip.

"What do you mean?" Sofi asked softly. His body expressed a vulnerability that made Sofi want to hug him and take his hurt away.

Andres stared at her a moment. Then he looked back at the sun. "Her name was Jessica. She was a girl who came to the hotel with her family every spring break. I was shocked when she asked me out. I never in a million years thought a girl like her would be interested in me." Sofi flinched. What was that supposed to mean? Andres was great. He was really smart, sweet, and funny. He was a total catch. Andres combed the sand with his fingers, unable to look Sofi in the eye. "She was my first love, you could say." He sighed. "She promised to write. . . . You know the drill." He paused. "I still remember that hot day in June like it was yesterday. Everyone at the hotel was sweating. She hadn't written or called, nothing. But she did come back. I felt like such a fool. She brought some big buff guy with biceps the size of watermelons," Andres joked, motioning with his hand. "Her new boyfriend taunted and ordered me around. He called me *his* cabana boy and Jessica just laughed."

"Not all girls are like that," Sofi said, reaching out for his shoulder.

"No?" he asked, with a pinched look on his face. "Don't tell me you didn't try to bully your way into getting a chair. All you Americans are alike. You think you can come here and do whatever you like without a thought about the country you're entering. We have manners here," he said indignantly. "If you come to someone's house, you don't start demanding things and jumping on their bed."

"Okay, so maybe you're right." Sofi felt ashamed for her behavior at the beach. She'd been so stubborn and selfish. "We were kind of despicable. We didn't mean it." But it wasn't as simple as he made it sound. "You said it yourself, this place is a mess. Look," Sofi said, pointing behind them. "These clubs encourage girls to give lap dances and act stupid. And what about all the horny Mexican men whistling at the old ladies limping down the street?" Andres smiled even though he didn't want to. "Those guys on the corner will say anything to get you into their bars and try to get you ripped with all their tequila shots. All they care about is money. C'mon, this place is not as innocent and helpless as you make it sound."

"True." He nodded, obviously still unwilling to let go of his pain.

"I don't think we're very different. You scratch at the surface and we're all walking contradictions." He was still sulking. "If you're so unhappy, why do you put up with it?"

"Huh?"

"You have papers. Tons of people, including myself, would kill to be in your shoes." She remembered the woman who'd sold her the Juan Soldado necklace. "People die every year trying to cross the desert into the United States. Can you imagine how desperate someone has to be to do something like that? Doña Clementina, my neighbor, crossed five times through a stinky tunnel! Life is rough, I agree. But life is rough everywhere. My parents work their butts off and live with the constant fear of getting deported every day. But like you said, everyone has the right to be happy."

"When did I say that?"

"When you were talking about the mosquitoes."

Andres smiled and nodded his head.

"That's why people make the sacrifice to go to the Other Side. Why my parents left their families and all they knew to start from scratch in a foreign land. They worked two jobs to give me the best education, after-school tutoring, dance lessons. You should have seen my mom's face when I got into UCLA. It was like *she* was going away to college." Sofi looked away from him as tears tried to force themselves into her eyes. She really missed her parents. She'd taken so much for granted, and now it looked like all their hard work was in vain.

Staring at the sunset before her, she thought of the families in San Quintin. Sofi refused to allow herself to wallow in self-pity. Not while others with less made an effort to get up each morning and strive for something better. There were fatherless kids who didn't have food and had to depend on the kindness of strangers for things like toys and shoes. Sofi noticed that Andres's head was cast down. "Is any of this making sense?" she asked.

"Yes, it is," he said reluctantly.

"You have opportunities I will never have," Sofi pressed. "I gave up everything for a stupid boy who cared nothing about me. I thought that if I could make him be my boyfriend, then my life would be complete. I was such a fool." She laughed out loud. "Now I'm not going to graduate or go to college. All my life, all I wanted was to run away from San

Inocente and my parents. All I cared about was my independence, being able to go to parties, and having a cute boyfriend to brag about. I never realized how blessed I already was."

Andres chuckled softly to himself. He looked at her sideways, as if seeing her for the first time. "So what now? Has Mexico ruined you forever?" He elbowed her playfully.

Sofi couldn't help but smile and elbow him back. "No, it hasn't ruined me. It's actually made me whole." Andres looked up. "It's crazy, but I love my Mexican family. Yeah, the house smells, the boys are always in trouble, and my *tía* scolds me for everything. But I've grown stronger out here. I'm not so scared."

"It's all that washing by hand," he joked, making a scrubbing motion. Sofi paused, taking a moment to feel proud of herself for all she'd accomplished. She wasn't the same scared girl who'd cowered at the Tijuana border.

"I'm trying to be serious," she said.

"Okay, I'm sorry, continue." He waved his hand in the air.

"And Yesenia is a fabulous friend. Back home I never felt like I fit in. I never had enough money or was pretty enough to date the cool guys. I felt gawky and unsure about everything. But now I have this big crazy Mexican family that I love with all their contradictions. It's so different from my quiet, well-organized, groomed neighborhood in San Inocente. This is messy and fun and just plain real. The fights are real. The celebrations are real. I've never felt so alive in my entire life."

"Mexico is complicated." Andres nodded with a big grin on his face.

"It sure is." Music was coming from a nearby club. It was a sexy, sweet Shakira lullaby.

"This moment calls for a dance," Andres announced, dusting sand off his jeans. He offered Sofi his hand and pulled her up. They both smiled nervously. She could feel him breathing on her face. It sent a nervous shiver up her spine. *Why am I feeling so weird?* she wondered. This was Andres, her friend. Sofi told herself to relax. Her past had been ripped from her. Her future was unknown. All she had was this beautiful moment. She concentrated on the music and how it made their bodies flow effortlessly with the rhythm. They fit together like puzzle pieces. The strangeness was gone. She stared up and noticed blue and red fireworks lighting up the darkening sky. How cool, she thought, before looking into Andres's brown eyes. He smiled and it tickled her belly. It was nothing like any fantasy she'd ever had. She realized that she wanted to be here, with Andres.

He leaned in to her. Sofi's worries and anxieties disappeared. Her mind totally emptied as his soft, sweet lips covered hers. Time stood still for a moment. They lingered there, holding on to the pause. A yummy tingling sensation washed over her like a warm, soft breeze. She'd never experienced this kind of rush and wanted more! Sofi threw her arms around him and kissed him again. They were lost in the wave of sweet pleasure. Sofi had a sinking feeling that she was falling.

17

"Sofia Mendoza, this is John Wilcox. How are you doing?"

Sofi squirmed as she listened to the lawyer's voice coming through the pay phone. How was she? Looking inward, she felt a gooey knot of emotions. She missed her parents and friends desperately. The prom was over, and next week her entire class was going to walk across the stage without her. Her dreams of college and a fancy house were lost in the tides. But she'd met a great guy who was warm and sweet and more than she'd ever dreamed. Mexico was bearable. She could actually sleep through the rooster's crowing, and the *chinche* bites were fading. "I'm okay."

"Good. I told your parents that, as is, the chance of your coming home any time soon is almost nonexistent, I'm sorry to say." Her heart sank. "There are a lot of people applying with better cases. You see, you don't qualify under the usual routes. You don't have any siblings born in the United States or relatives who can sponsor you. Your dad is talking to his boss to see if he can get sponsorship. If his boss can say that he must have your father there, then we may be able to apply for residency. But I don't want to give you false hope. It may take years to go through." Years! Sofi wanted to scream. Why was he telling her this? "I thought you should know." He paused. She heard him shuffling some papers around. "I haven't given up hope. There are several congressional bills being discussed that may apply to you. If you're just patient, I'm sure in time something may work out." Sofi thanked him for his help. Her heart felt like lead. In her bones she knew there was no hope.

On the way home she passed the familiar pink shack. A woman in her late sixties was outside clipping yellow roses. Sofi noticed that she wore a rose in her flowing white hair. That had to be her grandmother. Abuela Benita was small with a plump, round frame. She wore frumpy brown slacks and a flowered shirt.

"*Permiso*," Sofi asked, standing hesitantly by the metal gate.

The woman looked over her shoulder and gave Sofi a heated stare.

"I'm sorry to bother you," Sofi said in Spanish. She wasn't quite sure of her words, but hoped her grandmother would understand her. "Are you Benita Mendoza?"

"Who wants to know?"

"My name is Sofia Mendoza. I think I'm your granddaughter."

The old woman stiffened. "I have no granddaughters," she replied heatedly, and went into the house. The screen door slammed shut behind her. It sent shivers up Sofi's spine. She noticed that a yellow mutt was tied with a thick rope to a pole by the side of the house. She bit down on her lower lip as she opened the squeaky gate. Her desire to know her grandmother was stronger than her fear of the dog.

Sofi knocked on the door. "I know who you are," Sofi said through the closed door. "I don't want anything from you. I just want to get to know you."

"Go away!"

Sofi flinched. Her heart began to race. "Please."

"Go away!"

Andres picked up Sofi that afternoon. He was taking her to the beach with Mando and Mundo as their chaperones. It was a beautiful summer day. A cool breeze swept her dark hair back as she watched the boys scream wildly in the water. Being with Andres soothed Sofi's nerves.

"So your grandmother didn't want to talk to you?" he asked quietly.

"You don't know how jealous I am of you and your grandfather. I love the way you care for him. He sounds like a cool person." Andres beamed. "I never had that growing up. I always wanted to know my family in Mexico. I always felt that there was something missing in my life. You know, that connection to your past." Andres nodded. He was such a good listener. "Maybe Yesenia's right." She picked up a handful of cold sand and threw it. "Maybe she's just a crazy old lady."

Andres stared out at the crashing waves. "Old people are funny. My grandfather is really grouchy at times. But you can't give up, Sofi. You have to try again." Sofi tried to smile. She knew he was right. "You hungry?"

"I'm starving."

Andres got up and headed to one of the food stands. Sofi watched him walk. He was shirtless, showing off his less-than-muscular body and big belly. Olivia and Taylor would die of laughter if they saw him with her. Andres was not the type of guy she would have gone for back home. But her heart swelled whenever their eyes met. He was so cute.

Andres wasn't just her friend anymore. But Sofi didn't know what they were, either. Were they dating? In a relationship? What about that girl she'd seen him with a couple of weeks ago? Who was she? Sofi had never been so open about her feelings with a guy. A part of her was afraid to lose him. Andres ran back with a strange concoction called Tasty Locos. It was pink and had chips, hot sauce, and pickled onions. The color tainted his mouth and fingertips. "Try it."

She made a sour face. "It looks gross."

He tried to kiss her and smear her with dye.

"Stay away from me," she yelled, getting up and running from him. The cold sand felt good under her toes. She'd borrowed a tangerine one-piece from Yesenia. She was surprised to notice how good it looked, being a one-piece and all. It felt like ages since she'd been to the beach. Steve's Memorial Day had been two weeks ago, but to Sofi it seemed like another lifetime. She looked at the small islands in the distance, enjoying the taste of salty sea air on her lips.

"C'mon," Andres said, grabbing her from behind. Sofi laughed as he tickled her.

"Stop it!" she screamed. He picked her up easily. Sofi squirmed, trying to free herself from his tight grip. He carried her toward the water. Sofi never went in the water, especially since she spent all morning fixing her hair and makeup. Andres laughed as he tossed her into the knee-deep, icy cold water. Sofi yelped as her warm body pierced the frigid ocean. She struggled for a minute, trying to regain her poise. But a wave crashed into her, knocking her off balance. "That's it," she yelled, trying to stand up. "You're in big trouble, mister!"

Andres ran toward the shore in his soggy cargo shorts. She pulled her legs up high to try and catch him, but it was tough running through water. Mando and Mundo grabbed Andres by his arms and held him until Sofi tackled him from behind. They all tumbled down into the water. *This is the most fun I've had in a long time*, she thought, splashing Andres.

Later, as the sun began to set Andres leaned over and said, "What are you doing tomorrow?"

Awash in the glow of the beautiful evening, Sofi smiled and said, "Nothing."

"Great. Let's meet in front of the Rosarito Beach Hotel at nineish."

"Sounds good to me." The wind picked up and played with her hair. Sofi turned to the left. Dark clouds swept over the beach.

"Let's take these little rabble-rousers home before your aunt begins to worry." Ten feet away the boys were building a dam out of sand. "I promised to have you home by three."

The next morning Sofi went back to Abuela Benita's house. She brought some delicious-smelling *pan dulce* from the local bakery.

"*Buenos días.*" Sofi knocked loudly at the door. She heard a shuffling inside, but no one answered. "Abuela Benita, it's me, Sofia. I brought you some *pan dulce.*" No answer. "I'll leave it right here for you," she said in Spanish, feeling more confident in the language. Sofi put down the bag and started walking back toward the gate. When she closed the gate behind her, she heard the door crack open. Sofi kept walking. There was a big smile on her face.

That evening Rico's yellow Hummer waited outside with the engine running. Five women came out of their houses to see what the commotion was about. They were talking quietly among themselves. A dog was sniffing at the spinning back hubcap. Sofi couldn't believe all the excitement as she peeked out the window.

"Yesenia, hurry," she called out. Sofi fluffed her curled hair in the mirror. She was about to add a coat of powder when she noticed how clear and glowing her skin was. *Must be all the nopales I've been eating,* she thought. (Her uncle swore nopales were good for everything, including hangovers, high cholesterol, and diabetes.) Sofi had totally forgotten about Rico's invitation until Yesenia reminded her an hour ago. She'd thought about backing out, but her cousin was so excited. *Maybe I can do both*, she wondered. Her date with Andres wasn't for another couple of hours anyway.

"I like that top," Yesenia said, clunking in with her heavy platforms. She looked fabulous in Sofi's black miniskirt and gold off-the-shoulder shirt. She also had on silver hoop earrings, bright green eye shadow, and a gazillion bracelets that clinked when she moved. She'd tied her hair back in an elegant French twist.

Sofi smiled in Yesenia's flowing white skirt, braided belt, and white halter top. The round wooden earrings Yesenia had lent her dangled beautifully from her ears. It was a totally different look than she was used to back home. It was soft and pretty *a la mejicana*. It fit her mood exactly. "You ready?"

Yesenia smiled and reached for her hand. "I can't believe we're going to a real concert. The tickets must have been real expensive. That Rico is such a cool guy and so cute."

"He is," Sofi agreed, feeling a bit wary. She felt a pang of guilt. What would Andres think?

"Ladies," Rico said from the doorway, looking scrumptious in a black polo and khakis. His thick wavy curls were gelled back and he flashed that incredible smile. Maybe she'd been too quick to kiss Andres. What did they have in common anyway? Rico took her hand and led her gently to his hot ride. Rico was so elegant and suave— everything she'd ever dreamed of. He was the type of boyfriend she would be proud to show off to her friends. "You girls are going to love it. I know the manager, so we'll be in the VIP section. You'll get to mingle with the musicians."

"Really?" Yesenia said, wide-eyed, from the backseat. She was bouncing with excitement. "You have the nicest car."

"Thanks," he said, giving Sofi a wink.

The outdoor concert was off the hook. There were hundreds of people dressed in tight, revealing clothes, and heart-thumping music drifted on the cool night air. The moon glowed high up above. Yesenia and Sofi danced in the front row. The band was totally hot. Sofi felt so glamorous and special by Rico's side. Tons of people came up to him, giving him high fives. Sofi couldn't believe how popular he was. She beamed when Rico introduced her to the lead singer. This had to be the best night of her life.

After the concert, the audience streamed off the beach in knots. Sofi held tightly on to Rico's and Yesenia's hands so that she wouldn't lose either one in the sea of bodies. Outside, people were laughing and talking as they walked back to their rides. A trail of white taxis lined Boulevard Benito Juarez. Sofi was beaming as Yesenia gabbed about all the cute boys at the concert.

"Did you see the guy with the ponytail? He was so hot and he asked me for my number. I can't believe how cool everyone was there." She held up her pink wristband. "I'm going to save this as a *recuerdo*."

"I think you were the prettiest girls there tonight," Rico said, holding Sofi's hand.

Sofi blushed. Rico was such the gentleman. "Oh, Rico, this was the best night in the world. I loved everything. It was perfect."

"The band was pretty good, right?"

"They were so cool. I loved them. Thank you so much." She gave him a peck on the cheek. Rico swept his arm around her back and pulled her into a warm embrace. Her breath caught in her throat. She looked into his deep, soulful eyes and could feel herself melt as he pressed his warm, soft lips over hers. Wow! A jolt sneaked up on her, sending sparks all over her body. Slowly, he released her. Her head spun out of control.

Yesenia stood five feet away from Sofi, staring dumbstruck. Next to Yesenia was a guy who looked familiar. His jaw hung open. It was Andres. Sofi quickly pulled herself out of Rico's embrace. Her heart stopped in terror.

"Andres," Sofi cried, rushing over to him.

He stared back at her with cold, dead eyes. She noticed the pink wristband on his wrist. Had he been at the club? "I waited for you for two hours."

"Huh?"

"We had a date. Don't you remember?"

Yesenia backed away from them and hurried over to Rico. Rico lit a cigarette and watched with an amused look in his eyes.

"A date? Oh yeah . . . I'm so sorry. Rico stopped by the other day with these free tickets and I was planning to see you but I kinda got caught up . . . you know." The minute those last words slipped from her mouth she regretted it. Andres's face fell. "I'm really, really sorry."

"I can't believe you. I thought you were different."

"I am."

"I'm such a fool," Andres said before turning his back toward her. And suddenly, she knew that she loved him.

"Andres," Sofi cried as he walked away. A drunken couple bumped into her. Andres kept walking, his shoulders hunched forward. "Andres, please let me explain." He turned the corner and disappeared. Sofi could feel tears welling up in her eyes. Her heart tore open. "Andres." Her voice cracked and echoed in the lonely night.

19

To: sofilicious1@yahoo.com
From: evangelina_mendoza@yahoo.com
Subject: checking in

Sofia,

I hope everything is well at the ranch. Your father
went to see the lawyer today. I hope they can work
something out. We're selling the Honda. I'm sorry. I
know you wanted it, but I'm sure you'll agree that this
is worth it. Mija, I'm so worried. Are you eating all
right? Please don't eat anything on the street. You
don't know how they prepare it and could get sick. I
miss you so much. Please call me. I miss you.

your mamá

Sofi hit the reply button.

To: evangelina_mendoza@yahoo.com
From: sofilicious1@yahoo.com
Subject: Re: checking in

Hey Mom,

I miss you very, very, very much. I'm so sorry for all
the trouble I caused. I feel horrible. You'll never

215

believe all the stuff Luisa makes me do, like babysitting and WASHING BY HAND! Some of it's been bad, but not everything. I went to this migrant camp with Luisa's church group. At first I hated it because all I wanted to do was call you. We gave clothes and toys to the poor kids there. It felt good to help the less fortunate. I realized how much I love you and Dad! If I ever get to go home again, I promise that I'll be a good girl. I'll listen to everything you say. I'll scrub the toilet until it sparkles!!! ☺ I don't care about the dorms or anything like that. All I want is to be home with you and dad.

Sof

To: sofilicious1@yahoo.com
From: livygrl@gmail.com
Subject: big news!!!!!!!

hey girrrrl,
wazzzz up? i miss u so much!!! i wish u were here. so much has happened. you missed the dopest prom ever. i danced all night with james. member james? from english lit. the angry poet. anyway i think im in luv. im so over wrestlers. its all bout poets now. he wrote me a poem yesterday and its not bout my breasts. ☺ hes so cool. youll totally like him. t and i are going to this café in Newport to hear him do spoken word. i cant wait for u to meet him. when r u coming home?!!!
;O

Sofi Mendoza's Guide to Getting Lost in Mexico

To: sofilicious1@yahoo.com
From: twilson@hotmail.com
Subject: hola

Sofi,
I miss you more as each day passes. I can't believe
you're still in Mexico. It's surreal. We had a bonfire
yesterday and everyone was asking about you. Please
tell me you have a hot stud out there. The image of
you surrounded by farm animals and a mean family is
heartbreaking. It makes me want to jump into my car
and get you. We got our caps and gowns today. I'm
thinking of sticking a big peace-sign sticker onto my
cap. I have your cap and gown. Will you be back in
time???? Let me know.

T

Sofi's fingers froze above the keyboard. A heavy weight pressed down
on her chest, making it hard for her to breathe. Life in the United States
was continuing at a crazy pace, while time stood still in Rosarito. Sofi
thought of her old dreams, her life on the ranch, and Andres's cute face.
Her heart ached. She'd royally screwed up any chance of happiness in
this lifetime. She took a shallow breath before typing. Hot tears ran down
her cheeks.

To: twilson@hotmail.com, livygrl@gmail.com
From: sofilicious1@yahoo.com
Subject: Alive and well in Rosarito!

Hey,
Sorry I haven't written in forever and a day. I've been
so tied up at the ranch. The boys keep me busy, you

know, chasing after them. They like to dress up like
crazy wrestlers. It's cute. They even got me playing
along with them. I finally got them used to the idea
of going to school every day. I think they have more
fun tormenting their schoolteacher than me. Ha!
My uncle's got me totally obsessed with Spanish
soap operas. They're better than American ones,
because they actually end. I'm watching this one
called *Pasión Ilegal*. Olivia, you would love it! The
main girl, Casandra, is always getting herself into all
kinds of crazy trouble. She gave birth to a bouncy
baby boy with curly black hair. FYI: Her husband's a
blond. The whole town is scandalized, trying to figure
out who the real father is. Then her long-lost pirate
lover, who she met while trapped on a deserted
island, kidnapped her. Sounds like my life, no?
The woman's life is so crazy it makes my head hurt
trying to figure out what will happen next. Anyway,
I've met some cool people. Went to see Linkin Park
play a concert on the beach. Tell everyone that
I'm fine.

Luv,
Sof

Sofi wanted to write about Andres and all the drama with Rico. Just
remembering the horrible events of the night before pierced her heart.
Andres was one of the most amazing people she'd ever met. Her stomach tightened as she remembered the look on his face when he saw her
with Rico. But how could Sofi tell her friends that she was in love with
the chubby cabana boy? What would her friends think? Besides, he

hated her guts now. Even if she did tell them, there was no way Andres would be with her now. Sofi hit her forehead with the fleshy part of her palm. She was such an idiot!

Later that day, Sofi returned to Abuela Benita's house with another bag of *pan dulce*. Andres had told her not to give up. Sofi felt compelled to try again. Andres would want her to, she thought.

"*Buenos días.*"

The door opened abruptly, making Sofi jerk back. "You must be my granddaughter," the old woman spat in Spanish. "You just don't give up." Sofi's eyes grew wet and her heart leaped with joy. Abuela Benita motioned for Sofi to enter.

Brilliantly colored fresh roses were arranged in glass vases all over the tidy-looking house. The delicious aroma tickled her nose. There was a small green love seat in front of a wooden coffee table. The peach-colored walls were covered in beautiful hand-painted scenes of Rosarito Beach. Sofi wondered if her grandmother had painted them. The room felt warm and cozy. Nothing like she'd imagined.

"Sit," Abuela ordered, motioning to the sofa. Sofi sat stiffly while the old woman disappeared into another room. Was she going to beat Sofi up? Yesenia swore Abuela was crazy and had thrown rocks at her. A horrible feeling twisted in Sofi's stomach. Maybe she should just flee? Abuela Benita came in carrying the *pan dulce* on a plastic tray with cartoon characters on it. Sofi tried to smile, but her nerves wouldn't let her.

Her grandmother took a seat in a wooden chair across from her. They sat quietly, measuring each other. Sofi noticed that she shared her grandmother's eyes, coloring, and nose. Sofi hated her nose. She thought it was too big for her face and not at all dainty like her friends' noses. But as she stared across at the same nose, she realized that she loved it. Her grandmother wore her straight white hair tied back in a bun. A red rose was tucked behind her ear.

"Thank you for seeing me," Sofi began in Spanish.

Abuela Benita gestured for her to have some bread. "What is it that you want?"

Sofi flinched. "I don't know." She hesitated, choosing her words carefully. "I guess I just wanted to meet you."

The old woman laughed. Hundreds of fine lines sprouted around her eyes and smile. Sofi coiled back, recognizing Luisa's angry mouth and sharp tongue. "So you decided to come? You're braver than I thought. You're Luisa's brat."

"No, I'm Edmundo's daughter, Sofia. I'm sorry. I didn't know you were here. My dad never talks about you."

Abuela Benita huffed. "I haven't seen my son in over twenty-five years. I heard he married some whore from *Mexico City*."

Sofi could feel her anger rising like steam in a boiling kettle. "Hey, you can't talk about my mother like that." Abuela Benita glanced at her, surprised. "She's a good woman. My mother sacrificed a lot to bring me to the United States so that I could have more opportunities."

"What do you know about sacrifices?" her grandmother spat. "Do you know what it's like to give up your kids?"

"Like La Llorona?" Sofi said without thinking, referring to the tale of the wailing woman who'd drowned her babies after a lovers' spat.

"I didn't say kill my kids," Benita corrected angrily.

Sofi mumbled an apology.

"Everyone wants to judge me." Abuela stood up and paced in front of Sofi. "But I did what I had to do to survive. I had no choice. No money. I couldn't let them starve. Maybe I was foolish. I thought that if I could marry again, I might be able to provide for them. You know. But the guy I found didn't want a woman with two kids. I did what I thought was best for everyone. Your father and *tía* can't forgive me." She studied Sofi's face for a reaction. "Who sent you? Do you need money? I have none. . . . "

"No, it's nothing like that," Sofi stammered, turning away. She'd never expected her grandmother to be like this. She took a deep breath and pushed away her judgments. "Like I said, I just want to get to know you."

"Me? Huh." The old lady started chewing on her tongue, thinking. "There was a time when I thought maybe . . . I tried to talk to them, you know. Did your dad ever tell you that?" Sofi shook her head no. "I didn't think so. Years later, I came back. I brought gifts, expensive toys. But by then they were grown. They had no room in their lives for a crazy *vieja* like me. A mother's betrayal is the worst thing to endure." A tear trickled down her grandmother's coffee-colored cheek.

"I'm sorry, Abuela. I don't hate you. I know you loved my dad and *tía* more than anything. I didn't come here to make you sad. I just want us to be friends."

"Friends?" Her grandmother huffed as she walked to the small window overlooking her roses. She was quiet for a long time. "I was born in 1940 in a small town called Lemoore." *That's a strange name for a Mexican town*, Sofi thought. "My daddy, your great-grandfather, worked as a farmworker. In those days the *gringos* wanted our money. He paid three cents to cross the border in El Paso." The old woman smiled softly. "I don't remember much of that time. But there was this huge raid. INS officers swarmed into our barrio and took everybody. They called it Operation Wetback. We were brought here, to the border. My father refused to ever go back. He was so disgusted with the United States, he made me swear never to go back there again."

There was a huge lump settling in Sofi's throat. "Back where?"

"To the Other Side."

"What?" Sofi jumped out of her seat. "Are you telling me you're an American citizen?" The old woman looked away and sat down in the chair. "Abuela, please," Sofi knelt by her. "This is very important. I have to know. My parents have to know. I was turned back at the border because my green card was fake." Tears streamed down her cheeks. "Abuela, please. My whole life is in the United States. I was going to go to college and make my parents proud. It was their dream. They've sacrificed so much, broken the law, done everything for me."

Abuela Benita had tears in her eyes. "I wish I could help you," she whispered.

"You can! You can!" Sofi jumped up excitedly. "Come with me to the border. Tell them what you told me. They have to believe you. They have to let me go home."

"I'm sorry, *mija*." She wiped away one of Sofi's tears gently. "I have nothing to help you. No birth certificate. No papers. Nothing."

"There has to be something! Maybe if my mother checked hospital or school records?"

"I was born at home. A local midwife brought me into the world. She must be long dead by now." Her grandmother became very quiet. "I think you should go now. I am no good to you. I'm no good to anyone."

Sofi hugged her grandmother tightly. "That's not true, Abuela. Maybe you can't help me get back home, but I do need you. Luisa needs you. The whole family needs you. You carry our family's history. Our blood. Will you come back to the rancho with me?"

Abuela Benita was quiet for a long time. "I think it's too late for me. So much time has gone by. There are so many things that I regret."

"Abuela, please come back with me. I'm sure that once Luisa—"

"I said no."

"Won't you—?"

"It's time for you to go. Thank you for the *pan dulce*," she said, getting up.

Sofi wiped her face. This was insane, she thought. Why hadn't anyone told her that her grandmother was a citizen? But there was no proof. Officer Cohn at the border wanted proof. The lawyer needed proof. There was no proof.

20

"What you doing?" Luisa asked on her way to work the next morning. Sofi looked up at her aunt's frigid stare. That morning she'd woken up feeling hollow. Now, all her hopes of returning to San Inocente were flushed down the toilet. Sofi had to do something good to make herself feel better. Looking at her family now, she smiled. She had to admit that they were an unusual sight. Uncle Victor was sweating profusely, pushing his hands down to the floor and sticking his wide butt in the air. Yesenia, a bit more limber, was stretching out each leg in the same downward-dog position.

"Yoga," Sofi said. Luisa frowned. "It's really good. . . ."

"*Ayúdalos, Dios*," her aunt mumbled to the ceiling as she pulled on her heavy overcoat. "When you finish your games, there's real work to do." Sofi's heart sank. She wanted to show her aunt that she could be helpful, that she could do more than just babysit.

Sofi told Uncle Victor and Yesenia to take a rest. She noticed that Mando and Mundo had been spying from behind the dusty window. When Luisa hurried out, Sofi turned to her cousin.

"Hey," Sofi said, lowering her voice so that her uncle couldn't hear. "I wanted to talk to you about Andres."

Yesenia sighed knowingly. "You should ask my *papá*." She motioned with her chin. "He's a guy."

"No." Sofi tried to shush her, but it was too late. Yesenia told Uncle

Victor that Sofi needed relationship advice. Sofi's cheeks turned red. She wanted to hide. Never in a million years would she ever ask her father something like that. Mando and Mundo watched from the couch. Why was everyone so fascinated by her life?

"Well, you see," Sofi looked at Yesenia for help. Her Spanish still wasn't that good. She felt hot and flustered, trying to find the right words. "I kind of screwed up with Andres. He saw me—"

"He saw her kissing someone else," Yesenia finished.

Uncle Victor sighed deeply as he served himself a glass of water and then sat down in his La-Z-Boy recliner. He motioned Sofi to sit on the couch. The smile on his face told Sofi that he enjoyed being up to date on Sofi's love life. His eyes got all misty as he spoke.

"There're a lot of songs that talk about love. But what I've learned is that the greatest thing you can do is be open to love in whatever shape and form it comes to you. Pure love sees with the heart, not with the eyes. The eyes are deceptive. They will play with your mind and show you things that aren't really there. Do you really like this boy?"

"Yes, I do," Sofi said simply.

Uncle Victor smiled and nodded his head. He leaned over and said, "Then you need to go for him. You must be willing to swallow your pride and make a fool of yourself." Obviously, watching all those soap operas was paying off, Sofi thought as she listened. "Most men are simple. We think with our heads, our hearts, and our stomachs." He pointed to his round belly. "Make him something special and he'll be swooning all over the floor."

"But I can't cook," Sofi responded.

"Make one of those *tortas de chorizo* and egg," Mando said. "You make them every day for us." Sofi smiled at her cousin. He was being so helpful. Maybe she had misjudged them both too quickly. "And we almost never get sick," he added.

* * * *

224

That afternoon Sofi stood on the back porch calling out to the boys. It was time for school. No answer. Yesenia had taken Uncle Victor to the chiropractor downtown for treatment. Sofi was desperate to see Andres. She searched inside the pink bathroom, around the horse corral, and under the decrepit wooden shack where Uncle Victor kept his tools. She stopped and listened. Little brown birds were chirping noisily. The wind brushed softly against her cheek and tangled her hair. Rancho Escondido was growing on her like her favorite pair of old fuzzy pink fleece sweats. It was old and falling apart, but it was cozy. Then she heard what she'd been waiting to hear. Hushed little voices were coming from the chicken coop. Tiptoeing quietly around the back, she found Mando and Mundo on the floor, wearing their colorful wrestling masks. The boys were playing with their action figures peacefully, which was a total surprise. But this moment was just too good to be true, she thought. Quietly, she sneaked up behind them.

"*Ayyyy, mis hijos!*" she wailed like an old scary ghost.

"La Llorona!" the boys cried, hugging each other. Looking at the two terrors huddling like scared cubs made Sofi crack up. "La Llorona" was a story from her childhood that she thought she had forgotten, until her visit to Abuela's house had jogged her memory. As a kid she'd made her mother tell her the tale over and over again, about how the ghost of La Llorona, a mother who drowned her children, wanders the streets at night, moaning and stealing children. The night before, Sofi had scared Mando and Mundo with her crazy wails until both of them had started to cry. Luisa didn't like it one bit and yelled at her, but secretly Sofi thought that it was worth it.

"Hey, that's not nice," Mando said, threatening her with his fist. Sofi didn't care and stuck out her tongue to taunt them. She'd gotten them good.

"C'mon, guys," she said, still giggling. "I need to go see Andres."

"No!" Mando looked ridiculous with his green-and-red sequined mask. His cape flapped wildly behind him. He looked like a miniature superhero.

Sofi looked at the time. The warm sandwich was on the kitchen counter. It was to be her peace offering. She wanted to surprise him. He had to let her explain. Sofi didn't care if she looked crazed. Rico meant nothing to her. He was just a pretty face. He had no depth. There had been no connection. Andres was the one she wanted. He was her friend, but more than a friend. Standing around the yard was killing her inside. Sofi had to go before he got off work. "Okay, I'm sorry for scaring you."

"No!" they cried. Mando and Mundo refused to budge. They wrapped themselves around a pole. She reached for Mundo, but he held on even tighter. Sofi checked her watch again. If she was going to do this, she had to go now.

"Come on," she begged, trying to pull Mando away from the metal rod.

"No way, José."

"Please." She put her hands together in prayer. "I'll do anything you want." The boys considered her proposition a moment but declined. Sofi gave up. "Okay, I give up." She threw her arms in the air. "You guys don't want to come, fine! But you better not get into any trouble or make a mess." She wagged her finger like Luisa. The boys promised to be good and not get into any trouble, which was not possible, but Sofi didn't have a choice.

Andres was pissed off at her and she had to do something quick. Her heart throbbed. She yearned to see him. She missed his Chinese-food–smelling truck, all his crazy farming dreams, his easy conversation, his jokes, and the way he made her feel. He was the most amazing person and she couldn't lose him. Sofi was dying to tell him that she loved him, and she wanted to scream it out at the top of her lungs. Excited energy coursed through her veins. She felt strong, fearless, and able to conquer the world. She'd be quick, she told herself as she raised her hand to catch a cab on the road. In and out. Luisa would never notice she'd left.

* * * *

The Rosarito Beach Hotel was a historic landmark built during the era of Prohibition. It had been a popular hangout for Hollywood stars in the 1920s. Now people were attracted to its old-world charm, beautiful Spanish colonial-style structure, tropical grounds, and modern resort-style spa amenities at Mexican low prices. Sofi walked slowly through the parking lot, past tiled fountains and curio shops. It was a beautiful hotel. The main entrance was bustling. Sofi looked all around, taking in the wooden beams, the decorative tiles, the heavy dark furniture, and the historical murals. It felt like she was walking into an old movie where the women wore long silky dresses and furs and the dashing gentlemen always broke out in song.

A petite receptionist with pulled-back black hair, a dark suit, and no makeup was talking on the phone. Sofi waited for her to finish.

"*Hola*," Sofi said, feeling the shiny wood counter. Her heart was pounding in her ears. A shiver of fear sneaked up her spine. Was this a mistake? "I'm looking for Andres. . . ." Sofi hesitated. The woman smiled warmly.

"He's at the pool," she said, before answering the ringing phone. Sofi was so excited, she didn't notice that she was crushing the brown lunch bag to her chest. She was in love. Her heart told her that the minute she confessed how she felt, Andres would have to forgive her. Rico's kiss was meaningless to her. Andres had to know that. She hurried past the elegant restaurant and fancy ballroom floor toward the glassed-in pool deck overlooking the sea. *Here goes nothing*, she thought, pushing open the door.

Andres was in the pool with a pretty brunette. It was the same girl she'd seen him walking with that day on the street. Her chest felt like it was going to burst. There they were. Her arms were around his neck and their foreheads were touching. They looked so in love and oblivious to the rest of the world. She stood there in shock. Tears flowed freely over her cheeks. This was not what she'd imagined. Sofi couldn't hear the happy splashes of kids in the pool or the cheerful chatter of tourists lounging in bathing suits and tanning oil. She couldn't feel the warm sun on her face or the cool sea breeze. A cold dark fog filled her heart. She wanted to flee, to run far away. As she turned to go, Andres called her name.

"You . . ." Sofi choked on her words. "You're despicable!" she cried, throwing the carefully prepared lunch bag at him in the pool and dashing through the door. She had to talk to Taylor and Olivia this very second or else she would die. Nothing mattered anymore. She was such a fool. How could she ever have thought Andres wasn't like all the other guys? The image of him with that girl made her eyes water. What had she been thinking? Andres didn't want her. She wiped her blurry eyes. Nobody wanted her.

"Sofi, wait," Andres called out behind her. She quickened her pace. He was the last person she wanted to talk to. Sofi broke out into a full run. Andres grabbed her wrist and forced her to look at him. "What was that all about?"

Tears streamed down her cheeks. She sniffed. "Forget it. I was stupid. I didn't mean to interrupt your little romantic thingy." Andres stared at her, dripping wet. A pool of water formed at his feet. He didn't have the hottest body or style, but he was so incredibly perfect that it hurt her eyes to look at him.

"I don't understand you at all. I thought. . . . Then I saw you and that coyote with the flashy car kissing, so I thought—"

"You don't understand," Sofi said. *Tell him*, a small voice said inside. *Tell him you love him.* Sofi cleared her throat.

"Andres," the girl from the pool cried. She was running toward them with a towel over her shoulders. Sofi's heart sank. Andres had a pained look on his face.

"*Un momento*," he said to the girl. She huffed, looking very annoyed, and crossed her arms in front of her chest. The girl was very shapely, with big boobs. She made Sofi feel flat. "I can't do this." He sighed painfully. "I can't do this roller coaster of emotions. We're very different. You know this. You're high maintenance and I'm just a cabana boy. I can't give you what you want." *No,* Sofi cried in her head. "You have your dreams, the fancy house, the Mini Cooper. I know you'll find a way back to San Inocente. That's your life. My life is here." He looked back at the girl. Sofi felt the wind knocked from her. Andres reached out and wiped a tear from her cheek.

21

Luisa was smoking a cigarette on the front porch when Sofi arrived. Sofi cringed at the sight of her aunt.

"Where were you?" Luisa asked in a low voice. She was looking off into the distance, past Sofi. Smoke blew out of her nose like a chimney. Sofi stared listlessly at the barren landscape. Her heart was muddied from being dragged in the dirt and stepped on. She felt dead inside. Luisa inhaled deeply, burning the cigarette down to the butt. She carefully stubbed it out in an ashtray that was littered with recently smoked butts. Luisa turned quickly and shouted in Spanish, "How dare you leave those boys alone? What kind of irresponsible, stupid girl are you? You ungrateful brat! After all I've done for you. I feed you and give you a place to stay. I open my house to you and this is how you repay me. The boys could have died, been kicked by the horse, or kidnapped. Don't you think of anyone but yourself?"

All of a sudden the boys burst through the front door. They were just fine. They smelled a little from playing so close to the corral, but they were perfectly safe.

"What the hell is wrong with you?" Luisa yelled, pacing in front of Sofi as if at any moment she would reach out and bash her head into the doorframe.

Mando began to tug on her skirt, crying out, "It wasn't her fault," in Spanish.

"She told us to come, but we wouldn't listen," Mundo yelled from the front pole. Their gesture touched Sofi, but it didn't stop Luisa from making her feel miserable.

"You think you can do whatever you want?" Luisa continued in Spanish. "Run around like a *gringa* without a care in the world? This is not America! Anything could have happened to the boys. But all you care about is yourself. You're so selfish!"

Her words sank into Sofi like Uncle Victor's knife had sunk into that pig on her first night. She felt so ashamed that when Yesenia and Uncle Victor got home, she ran to her room to hide. *This was the worst day of my life*, she thought, throwing herself on the bottom bunk. Sofi had hit a brick wall. This was not happening! She covered her head with the pillow and sobbed loudly.

The idea of being trapped with Luisa in this hellhole forever was unbearable. She opened her eyes and saw the UCLA duffel bag in the corner, taunting her. Everyone back home was preparing for finals, going to graduation rehearsals, signing each other's yearbooks. She'd tried so hard to do right by her aunt and make the best of this horrid situation. Why was she being punished?

Andres is a spineless wimp, she thought, looking up at the cracked white walls. She knew that he was afraid of getting hurt again. Uncle Victor said that love required risk. She wished her uncle would explain this to him. However, Andres had already given up. He was willing to go with someone he didn't love to protect himself. Who was that girl? The idea of her enjoying Andre's caresses and sweet kisses made Sofi burn with jealousy. He didn't love that girl. She could see it in his eyes. The truth felt ice-cold in her chest.

Who was she kidding? She didn't belong here. Hadn't her aunt made that clear, like, a hundred times? These people were crazy, she thought, wiping her face. She'd never be good enough and she hated them all. Hated Mexico. Plus she couldn't wait for the lawyer any longer. He was taking too long and even said himself that there were no guarantees. Sofi wanted to get out of there.

"Are you okay?" Yesenia asked, watching from the doorway.

"Yesenia, I need to use Britannica's phone." Sofi wiped her face.

"What're you going to do?" Yesenia asked, wide-eyed.

"I have to call my parents," she lied, as she combed her hair in the mirror.

Britannica rolled her eyes when she found Yesenia and Sofi at her doorstep like lost orphans. Sofi ignored Britannica's dirty look.

"It's an emergency," she pleaded in Spanish.

"You can use the phone," Britannica said, letting Sofi through. "But you"—she pointed to Yesenia—"have some explaining to do."

"There's nothing to explain," Yesenia said. Sofi headed into the living room. She could tell from Yesenia's tone that she wasn't happy. It wasn't hard to gather that they were fighting over Javier. Sofi heard Britannica yelling that she had been secretly going out with Javier on the side. This made Yesenia mad, and she started cursing at Britannica. Sofi picked her way through the room and down the dimly lit hall to the phone on the wall.

She pulled the Club Zone flyer from her back pocket. Her fingers nervously dialed the numbers. Rico picked up after the first ring. She hesitated as her stomach muscles tightened.

"Rico," she said, hearing only the sound of her heavy breath in her ear. "It's me, Sofi."

"What a delightful surprise," he said in his sexy, toe-curling voice.

"How soon can I be home?"

"Straight to business," he teased. "That's what I like about you, my little brown angel." She could almost hear him smiling on the other end of the line.

"I need to leave as soon as possible." Sofi thought of her big fight with her *tía*. "Something happened at home and I need to get out of here," she hurried, keeping an eye on the entryway. Yesenia and Britannica were now shouting at each other. Sofi knew that she didn't have much time. Any minute now, Yesenia would come storming down the hall, demanding that they go.

"Well, I usually charge fifteen hundred dollars," he said. Sofi gasped. The border was only twenty miles away! His voice never wavered. "But since we're such good friends, I'll give you a discount." Sofi started to feel ill. Her hands were shaking so hard, she thought she'd drop the phone. Rico told her to meet him at 1 a.m. at his place. She hastily wrote down the directions. She remembered María Rita's story and that of Javier's uncle, who died trying to cross. She could be raped, mugged, or even killed. But there was no turning back now.

Yesenia pulled on her hand. "We're going!" she said. Sofi stared at her cousin in shock. Her hair was in disarray, as if she'd gotten into a fight with a blow-dryer.

Sofi hung up the phone without saying good-bye. Britannica was screaming obscenities from the door. Her face was flushed and she was shaking her arms angrily in the air. It was a good thing that she was leaving, Sofi thought. She probably wouldn't get another chance to use that phone again.

Yesenia couldn't sleep that night. She turned over every three minutes. "I really hate that girl," she whispered. "I don't know why I said she was my friend. Javier is going to get it, too. When I see him, I'm going to rearrange his face."

Sofi's heart was beating so loud, she was surprised that no one said anything. She kept eyeing the digital clock on the nightstand, watching the time march closer to one. *Maybe if I ignore her long enough, she'll give up*, Sofi thought, pretending to be asleep.

Finally, Yesenia stopped talking and rolled over. It wasn't until she began snoring that Sofi sighed in relief. She watched her cousin's chest rise and fall for a minute, thinking about how Javier and Andres had both turned out to be jerks. But Andres only became a jerk when he caught her kissing Rico. *I'm such an idiot! I had the perfect guy and he was totally into me and I screwed it up all by myself.* She sighed deeply. It was hopeless, she thought, watching the shadows dance on the scratchy walls. The rooster cried out. No one moved. She had to get out of here. Of course, she'd be breaking a gazillion laws. And then there was the danger involved. The altar for the woman at Liliana's shop and the faded picture of Javier's dead uncle blazed into her head. Would people put flowers on some unmarked grave if she didn't make it? Sofi pushed the thoughts away. *Everything is going to be fine,* she told herself. With any luck, she'd be back in time to surprise Taylor and Olivia at graduation rehearsals.

Sofi held her breath as she peeled off the sheet. The room was dark, but she could make out the bulky furniture and scattered toys on the floor by the hazy glow of the moon. She'd packed her things earlier that night while Yesenia was showering. She'd left a couple of cute tops and skirts for her cousin folded neatly on the desk chair. It was her way of apologizing for bailing in the middle of the night. Sofi put the small statue of San Juan Soldado in her hands. She said a little prayer in her head, wishing for a safe journey, and then tucked it into the front pocket of her jeans. Quietly, she swung her backpack over her shoulder and lifted her duffel bag in her right hand.

She made her way into the kitchen by the beam of the Precious Moments porcelain night-light on the wall. Stashed behind the grumbling refrigerator was her aunt's purple velvet purse. It was Luisa's emergency savings. She didn't trust banks. This money was important, because something was always breaking down, disappearing, or running out.

Well, this is an emergency, Sofi told herself as she opened it up. Sofi counted six twenties, four fifties, and fifteen tens. It was nothing close to what Rico had asked for, but it would have to do for a down payment. She wrote her aunt a quick IOU, telling her that she would pay her back as soon as she was safely home.

Sofi sneaked out under the cover of night. She hesitated a moment by the gate. Nothing moved. It was as if every person and animal were holding their breath. Not even the late-night rooster was clucking about.

Sofi's heart sank as she started walking away from the house. It shouldn't have ended this way. In her mind, she'd thought that the entire family would come to the border to wave a tearful good-bye. She'd grown used to the boys and would miss their mischievous smiles across the breakfast table. And what about Uncle Victor? He was finally getting the hang of touching his toes while doing a forward bend. Who would make sure that he didn't overexert himself? The wind picked up and carried a crumpled newspaper past her. The neighbors' boxlike homes were dark, devoid of life. Sofi thought about Yesenia and Javier. Their love triangle was like a soap opera, and it pained her to know that she was deserting her cousin in her time of need. Luisa would be happy, that was for sure; Sofi winced at the thought of her aunt. She'd probably throw a party and invite the whole town. Sofi glanced over her shoulder when she reached the end of the block. Was this the last time she'd look upon Rancho Escondido?

The sleepy-eyed taxi driver drove her to the tourist side of Rosarito. Boulevard Benito Juarez was still shaking at this hour. But Sofi was not the least bit interested in the scene and directed the driver to her destination. Rico lived in a big two-story house, with white marble cherubs along the high brick fence. An angry dog announced her arrival. Sofi froze, remembering the neighborhood dogs from Rancho Escondido. The mangy canine sensed her unease and growled angrily. Andres's words popped into her head: "Show no fear."

Rico made his presence known by stepping out of the shadows. He was cradling a glass of red wine between his slender fingers. A soft breeze disturbed the awkward silence and ruffled the white silk shirt he wore opened loosely to show off thick gold chains. Thick globs of slobber ran down the Doberman's sharp fangs. Sofi wanted to step back, but she wouldn't let herself give in to her growing fears.

"Don't worry about Lexus." Rico smiled as he tied up the hound. "*Cálmate,*" he said to the dog in a strict tone. "Come on," he said, turning to Sofi and using the same tone. "There's nothing to worry about now." Sofi took a hesitant step forward. The dog growled. She didn't know whether she could move until Rico grabbed her by the hand.

He led her inside his spacious modern living room with track lighting and polished hardwood floors. The room was toasty, with the scent of sandalwood in the air. On the back wall there was a huge plasma TV and a killer micro hi-fi CD/stereo system. A blend of electronica, soul, and Latin rhythms flowed out of the speakers. He noticed and seemed pleased by Sofi's reaction.

"Would you like a tour?" He motioned with his arm. Sofi glanced at the sunken kitchen to the right, the spiral staircase that led to the second floor, and at an unlit hallway. She was curious, but Rico's look was making her nervous. He had these intense, unreadable dark eyes.

"Maybe later." She smiled shyly and sat on the plush red couch. He handed her his glass of red wine. Sofi shook her head, trying to refuse.

"Drink it. You'll need it," he said softly. Sofi sipped from the glass as Rico glided into the kitchen and returned with another glass and the half-empty bottle. He sat next to her and took a long drink from his new glass. The silence was killing her. Far away she heard the splashing of a water fountain.

"This is all I could get." She pushed the wad of dollars at him. Rico accepted the folded bills without counting and slipped them into his back pocket. Then he offered her more wine.

"Tonight is going to be a long night," he said as he refilled her glass. "A friend will be arriving in a bit." He glanced at a Coors beer clock over a glass cabinet. "You'll be traveling by truck." Sofi's heart began to race as she imagined herself sandwiched between numerous sleeping people. "You'll have to be very quiet. It'll be a long trip and you won't be let off until you reach Los Angeles." *What if I have to pee?* Sofi wondered. "That's the best I could do on such short notice. But there should be no problem. Now," he said, as if remembering something inconsequential, "if you get caught, you'll be deported. You don't want to get deported. Once they have you on record, there's no way to immigrate legally for at least ten years. Okay?"

Sofi nodded. "Are you sure it's safe?" she asked, feeling her anxiety rise.

He gave her a sideways glance. "There's always a risk. I'm sure you've heard all kinds of tales about the people who get lost in the canyons and die of dehydration?"

Sofi nodded, thinking about María Rita being abandoned in the middle of nowhere with nothing but her duffel bag for protection in the frigid night.

"Yeah, well, everybody has a sob story. Most of those people don't know what they're doing. They're either cheated by corrupt coyotes or take off on their own."

"And you're not a corrupt coyote, right?" Sofi asked warily. She hoped her voice didn't reveal her growing apprehension.

"'Course not." He grinned, downing his glass. "I'm Prince Charming, remember? Hey, let's have some fun before your pumpkin arrives." Rico got up and called her over with the nod of his head. Sofi wordlessly followed him down the darkened hallway to a door at the very end. Her heart was pumping loud.

"In there," he said, gesturing to the doorknob. Sofi could feel him standing so close he could smell her. His breath was slow and shallow, enveloping her ears. Did he want to kiss her? Sofi wasn't feeling it and turned the knob in a hurry to get away from him.

Her hand reached for the light switch, brightly illuminating the room. But what she found was anything but pleasing. A single twin bed with a flattened pillow and patched quilt was in the center of the bare white room. An eggshell-colored lamp and olive green nightstand stood beside it. A guest room? Rico hadn't mentioned anything about staying the night or changing her clothes. Sofi turned with a bewildered expression. The hungry look on Rico's face told her that he expected something in return for his "discount."

"Whoa." Sofi stumbled back away from him. "What is going on here?" She turned, trying to get out of the room, but Rico blocked the exit. A mischievous grin danced across his sexy lips. He reached out for her, but Sofi was quick and dodged his arm.

"C'mon, Sofi, I just want to have a little fun."

"I didn't come here for fun." Her eyes bounced around the room, looking for something to use as a weapon. Rico followed her eyes, reading her thoughts. He smiled when she realized that there was nothing within arm's reach. All of a sudden, she felt the bulge in her front pocket and pulled out her border saint.

"Stay back!" She waved the miniature soldier in his face as if its image would strike fear into his heart.

He let out a howl. "What's that?"

"Don't worry about it. This is over. I'm leaving."

"What are you going to do?" he joked, taking a small step toward her. "Pray me to death?"

"I want to go home."

"Go ahead. Go back to your *rancho*," he spat, motioning to the door. The words scorched into Sofi's flesh like a brand. Sofi watched him a second, making sure he meant what he said. Then she dashed toward the door. But before she could reach the doorknob, Rico pounced on her. He grabbed her wrists and held them down by her side, pushing her against the door.

"Stop it! What are you doing?" She tried to kick him.

He laughed and wrestled her Juan Soldado statue from her fist. He threw it over his shoulder. The miniature saint tumbled onto the pillow. Rico put his index finger to his thick wavy lips and then placed it over hers to shush her. He leaned in to her ear. She could smell his spicy cologne. "I really didn't want it to be this way." He pulled her over to the bed. "I thought we could go out to dinner, maybe go to a club and have a good time." He used his weight to hold her down. "But you never called me." Was this guy crazy? She tried to fight him off, but he was stronger than her. He gripped her hands and pinned her to the hard mattress. Sofi squirmed; a loose spring was digging into her back.

"Get off me!" Sofi huffed, trying to wriggle out from under him. It was hard for her to breathe with his chest crushing her ribs. Rico watched her with pleasure like she was a plaything trapped in his claws. He seemed to be waiting for Sofi to realize that her actions were futile.

"Relaaax," he whispered into her ear. "We'll have more fun if you just learn to relax." But Sofi would not. She couldn't. He would have to kill her first. She tried to bite him, but he was quick and pulled back smiling, taunting her.

"I said," Sofi raised her voice, "get off me or I'll scream!" Panic seized her muscles, making her stiff all over. There was no one to help her. Her family and Andres would think that she'd disappeared, like countless anonymous travelers whose bones decorated the U.S.–Mexican desert landscape without markers.

Rico cupped her chin with his free hand, forcing her mouth to open. He shoved his tongue in. Sofi squirmed underneath him. It took all her energy. Rico's hand wandered down her torso and he struggled with her belt buckle.

"No! Stop!" she screamed. He slapped her hard across the face.

"I'm sorry, I didn't mean to do that. But I had to make you stop." The stinging sensation made her squint and see black spots. Rico released his grip. Sofi knew that this was her one chance. Quickly, she reached out for Juan Soldado and with one sharp jab stabbed Rico in the eye. He jerked back, giving Sofi enough room to free her right leg from under his weight. Then she planted Mando's favorite *huevos quebrados* wrestling move, kneeing him hard in the balls.

Rico shrieked and doubled over. He sucked his teeth as if unable to breathe properly. She jumped up and ran for her life.

Sofi didn't stop running until she was five blocks away. Her chest was heaving from the exertion and she lowered her head between her legs to catch her breath. She was by the freeway and watched the flickering red and yellow lights loom up the road. Rico's dog barked in the distance. Damn it, her bags! Now she had no clothes or makeup. She started shaking uncontrollably. Her breath caught in her throat. Was she having a heart attack? Sofi had to stop her mind from racing. Would Rico come after her? She dropped to the ground. Her muscles were sore and she felt dead tired. All she heard was her own heavy breathing filling up the air and the thumping from her heart beating loudly in her chest. The miniature border saint was still in her palm. In a crazy only-in-Mexico kind of way, it had saved her. Sofi started to chuckle, her laughter turning into tears of relief. Leaning her head back, she pulled her knees up and hugged herself under the blanket of bright stars. She was safe.

Sofi never thought she'd feel so happy to return to the crumbling house on the dried, cracked earth. She practically ran toward the safety of the rickety fence that measured the property. Sofi was surprised by her reaction. Just a few hours ago, she'd sworn that she never wanted to see this place again. But the ranch was a comforting sight. The sweet scent of wet dirt filled her senses. The house was still falling apart. A piercing rooster cry rang into the night, and the moon engulfed the place with a soft, soothing beam.

A dim light from the kitchen told her that she was home. Home? Then Sofi's face dropped. She would be in major trouble. Who cared that she escaped from a rapist? She'd run away without an explanation, and worse, she'd taken Luisa's money without asking. These tough feelings seeped into her as she hesitated by the shaky fence that had always caused her so many problems with the goat escaping from the hole at the end. Taking a breath of cold air, Sofi opened the gate. Now, with no hope of returning to the United States, she'd have to face the consequences for her stupid actions. There was no going back.

From the doorway Sofi saw her aunt sitting with her back toward her at the kitchen table. The house was still, except for the rooster, who cried over and over again. As Sofi approached her aunt, she noticed that the velvet purse was opened on the table. Sofi held her breath.

Upon seeing Sofi, Luisa broke down in tears. She took Sofi into a big heartfelt hug. Sofi's muscles tensed. Her aunt was never one to show affection. Since Sofi arrived at *el rancho* Luisa had never touched her—not even to welcome her. Tears flowed down Luisa's cheeks as she held Sofi to her chest, squeezing tightly.

"*Ay, gracias, Santa Rita la Abogada, Santa Ceotilde, y San Antonio,*"

Luisa whispered, invoking a list of benevolent saints and releasing all the tension from her face with her breath. "I was so worried about you." Words, long held back, rushed out of her mouth like a healthy stream after a storm. "I didn't know what to think when I saw that you weren't in your bed. Then the money was gone. I knew you'd run away. My words made you run away."

Sofi stood there in shock. "I'm sorry," Sofi finally mumbled behind a steady flow of her own tears. She hadn't realized how much she'd yearned for some affection or kind words from her aunt. The concern in Luisa's eyes washed over Sofi like her mother's soothing hands.

"No. I'm sorry," her *tía* insisted, releasing her long enough to take her hands. Her aunt refused to let her go, as if their touch would bridge the gap between them. "This is my fault. I feel horrible for the way I treated you. The thought of you out there by yourself reminded me of the time I tried to cross the border." Luisa released Sofi's hands and motioned for her to sit down in an empty chair. "I was about your age," she said, looking past Sofi through the kitchen window. "I'd had a huge fight with my *tía* and decided to run away and join your father in Los Angeles. I didn't know anything at the time. I was very young and stubborn." Luisa looked down at her short unpolished fingernails, battered from working with harsh chemicals. Sofi sat very rigid in the chair, dazed by her aunt's candidness.

"There was a coyote," her aunt said in Spanish. Sofi nodded, thinking about Rico. "He promised to help me cross the desert in Tecate. I was so trusting at the time. I thought that all people were inherently good. That bastard." Her voice turned sour. "He abandoned a group of us there without water or food." Luisa's eyes misted over. "There was this woman with this baby who wouldn't stop crying. That's how they found us." She looked at Sofi. "The robbers. I'm sure they were in on it with the coyote from the start, because they knew exactly where to find us. They beat me up bad, broke my ribs, and took all the money. They were going to leave us there to rot like roadkill in the scorching 110-degree heat without water." Sofi reached out timidly and held her aunt's callused hand. "The baby cried and cried and made the robbers nervous until one of the guys made him stop crying with one fatal pop from his gun. You know, I still hear that baby in my dreams." Luisa wiped away a fresh set of tears with the sleeve of her shirt. "Luckily, the border patrol found us." Her eyes sparkled and she started to laugh. It was the first time Sofi had seen dimples in her cheeks. "I never thought I'd be so happy to see them."

Sofi got up and hugged her aunt. They were more alike than different, she realized.

"*Perdóname, mija.* I'm so ashamed," Luisa said, kissing Sofi's hands softly.

"There's nothing to forgive."

"I'm sorry for treating you so bad. I don't know why I did it. I was just mad and scared to have one more mouth to feed. Mad at the world. Mad at my job, at your poor invalid uncle. I didn't mean to blame you for all the bad things in my life. I should have helped you."

"I'll forgive you," Sofi said, tears streaming, "only if you forgive me for leaving the boys alone." Luisa was smiling now. She was actually really pretty, Sofi decided.

"And I'll forgive you for borrowing the emergency savings without asking," Luisa added with a squeeze. *Ouch. That too,* Sofi thought, as she began to tell Luisa about her own horrible experience with Rico and the miraculous intervention of San Juan Soldado.

23

To: sofilicious1@yahoo.com
From: livygrl@gmail.com
Subject: hating!!!

yo sofilicious,
consider yourself lucky. the econ final sucked. i totally
bombed it of course. my moms pissed and is sendin
me to summer school which totally sucks. whatever.
im so in loooove right now that i dont care. ha!
did taylor tell u what shes doing? its so hot. the
whole school cant stop talking bout it. i cant wait for
graduation. to b free!!!! i miss u terribly. when u
coming back?
;O

To: sofilicious1@yahoo.com
From: evangelina_mendoza@yahoo.com
Subject: mom loves you

Sofia,
I hope everything is well at the ranch. Don't worry
about college. If we can fix this, you can do whatever

you want. I just want you home safe. I'm so sorry if
we ever made you feel bad. We just love you so much.
You're our babygirl. Your father went to see the lawyer
again today. He hasn't been sleeping well since you
left. We are both so worried about you. Are you eating
right? If you can't find a gym, start running around the
neighborhood. It'll do you good. Please call me. I
miss you.

your mamá

To: sofilicious1@yahoo.com
From: twilson@hotmail.com
Subject: hola

Sofi,
It feels like years since I last saw you. It's really
tearing me up inside. I told my therapist about you and
she said that I should do something to release my
frustration. I don't know if you'll be coming home for
graduation this Friday, but know that you'll be missed.
I'm making buttons! I know it's corny, but everyone
has agreed to wear them on their gowns in solidarity
with you. They say: No More Borders! Free Sofi! Is it
too much?
T

Sofi's heart swelled. She loved her friends more than life itself. Sure,
they were cheesy, but they were her peeps and they had her back. No
matter what happened or where their lives would take them, they'd
always be friends.

To: twilson@hotmail.com, livygrl@gmail.com
From: sofilicious1@yahoo.com
Subject: News from the border

Hello my beautiful friends,
Your words are so touching. They bring tears to my
eyes. I love you girls more than anything. Thank you
so much. You're the best. Things are pretty much the
same here at the border. My aunt Luisa is trying to
make a real Mexican woman out of me. She's teaching
me how to cook! Can you believe it? Me with a ruffled
apron! Ha! She's showing me how to make flour
tortillas. They're the best. Of course, I really suck at it
and end up with more flour all over my clothes and on
the floor. It's actually really hard to roll the dough out
into a perfect circle. She says not to worry, that I'll
improve with practice. Move over, Rachael Ray!
There's a big joke now that whenever the house
smokes up with burnt fumes, Sofi's cooking. Miss you.
Luv,
Sof

She logged out, feeling her heart clench. She hated the distance that was separating their lives. It felt like a lifetime ago when she laughed with Olivia and Taylor. Sofi paid the cute shop clerk at the Internet café. He had a cocky attitude that reminded her of Andres.

Her breath caught. Not only had she blown it with the most amazing guy, she'd done it for a slick punk who she hated now more than anyone in the world. How could she have been so dumb? Rico was a total loser. He probably drove that fancy car to compensate for his lack of personality. And Sofi had fallen for it like a ton of bricks! Yet despite what had happened, Andres stayed on her mind and close to her heart. She couldn't stop thinking of him and wondering about his *new* girlfriend. How could he have forgotten her so fast? She wanted to see him, but her shame kept her away. Sofi stood at the door of the Internet café and looked out at the clear blue sky.

Sofi checked her watch. It was time to pick up the boys from school. As she passed the entrance of the Rosarito Beach Hotel, she wondered if Andres was working. Sofi hadn't told her family about the pool scene. Everything had happened so quickly, and Sofi really wanted to forget him. Relationships and boys were just too much drama. She decided to just focus on getting herself together. Which was easier said than done. The thought of their shared kiss on the beach still made her knees weak. But he didn't want her, she reminded herself. He'd moved on.

Sofi walked down Boulevard Benito Juarez, getting whistles and cat-calls from the local boys working the taco joints. She smiled, enjoying the heat of the sun on her face and the fresh breeze on her legs. The flowing red skirt Yesenia had lent her looked fabulous with the sandals and her tanned skin.

"Oh my God, do you see what that wettie's wearing? Fashion night-mare. Talk about what not to wear." Sofi turned at the sound of an American voice behind her. She looked around, wondering which poor fool they were talking about. In front of the Rock and Roll Taco Shop stood a group of long-haired blond girls in lacy camis and jean shorts checking *her* out.

"Poor thing doesn't even have a clue. I bet she thinks she looks hot."

"Please, my dog has better clothes," one girl snickered, petting the Yorkie terrier in her dog purse. Sofi couldn't believe her ears. They were making fun of her and her clothes. And they were using her word: wettie. The irony struck her as comical. But then heat rose in her chest. She was no wetback. That word was just plain racist and mean. *They don't even know me!* Sofi had tons of cute outfits back home in San Inocente. But she also loved this graceful skirt, and Yesenia had been so understanding after Sofi had explained how she lost her bags. She'd let Sofi pick out anything from her overstuffed closet. Sofi considered letting the foul comment pass. They were just ignorant *gringas*. Why bother? But then she thought about how good her cousin and everyone had been to her, despite all the crazy things she'd done. Sofi thought of her grandmother, who'd been illegally deported because she looked Mexican. Ignorant people like these girls did that to her family. She had to do something. Sofi spun around real quick.

"I heard that," Sofi yelled out, walking over to them. The girls stared back in shock. Obviously, they didn't expect Sofi to understand English. "Shame on you," she said, sounding just like her mother. "Who do you think you are, judging me because of the way I look? You don't know me." The girls stared at one another, unsure of what to say. Sofi shook her head. They were all talk. A couple of the waiters from the Macho Taco came up behind them. Sure, they were tourists, and Sofi could bet that they had more cash on them than she would see working at the hotel for a month. But she refused to allow anyone to put her country down. Mexico, the country of contradictions and harsh lessons, was her country too, just like the United States. "You need to learn some manners." The girls stared at her with bewildered expressions.

Two officers in beige uniforms turned up the block, and she figured that now was a good time to go. Sofi hurried down Boulevard Benito Juarez, her heart speeding like a racehorse and swelling with pride. Had she just told those girls off? Ha! She jumped excitedly in the air. It felt good to defend herself and her country. *This must be what it feels like to stand up to a bully*, she thought. The eyes of Zapata in the *Tierra y Libertad* mural flashed before her. It stirred within her a strange but comfortable sense of belonging.

After school, the boys raced on ahead of her on the busy downtown street. Boulevard Benito Juarez was not a street you wanted kids running in, especially since Sofi was convinced that all Mexicans drove like maniacs. Nobody stopped at the stop signs, and everyone seemed to think only of themselves, cutting off other drivers and weaving from lane to lane without signaling. It was madness and she feared that some crazy driver would hit the boys as they dashed (without looking) across the street.

"Mando! Mundo!" Sofi yelled as she tried to catch up. It was hard to run in her sandals.

A car screeched to a halt at the end of the block. A heavy man with a bulging belly and thinning hair got out and shouted obscenities. Sofi's heart stopped. He had to be cursing at the boys. She hurried to the edge of the corner. Were they dead? Bloody? Crippled? To her surprise, Mando and Mundo were waiting at the curb, staring into the eyes of the angry man. She'd never been so happy to see those little dwarfs alive, and she rushed over and kissed them, even though they tried to squirm away.

It was cold when Sofi and the boys arrived back at *el rancho*. Strong winds chased after them all the way from the boulevard and threatened to whisk them away. The boys ran into the house, shaking like Chihuahuas. Uncle Victor had prepared an *albóndiga* soup with big fat pieces of meatball. The entire family was sitting at the table. Luisa inhaled the delicious aroma coming out of the hot, steaming bowls. She'd changed her schedule and was now home in time for dinner. Sofi glared at her soup, seeing only Andres in her mind's eye. A part of her just couldn't believe that it was over between them. Could she stand never seeing him again? She missed his warm smile and the way he bit his lower lip when he was nervous. Mando and Mundo were slurping loudly. All of a sudden there was a knock at the back door. Everyone turned.

Luisa went to open the door and screamed: "*Ay, Santo Juan Soldado!*"

Abuela Benita stood there with a white shawl draped over her head and a red rose tucked behind her ear. In the hazy glow of the moon, she looked like La Llorona. "*Ay, mis hijos,*" she said. Mando and Mundo cried and rushed behind their father. Yesenia had admitted to having gone to see her about some money, and when the old lady had kicked her out she'd enlisted the boys to torment their grandmother by destroying her rosebushes. That was when Abuela Benita started throwing rocks at them. Now, as the old woman stood at the doorway of the house, nobody moved.

"Abuela." Sofi rushed up to her, giving her a hug. "You came."

Her grandmother looked at Sofi nervously. "I didn't mean to interrupt. I saw the lights on and I thought—"

"No, no, I'm glad you came. Come in."

Luisa was white as a ghost and she was pressed up against the wall. "*¿Qué haces aquí?*" Yesenia stood just next to mother for support.

"*Lo siento, hija,*" Abuela began.

"I am not your daughter," Luisa stammered. "I have no mother."

"*Ya déjalo,*" Uncle Victor griped. Her aunt sniffed loudly and crossed her arms in front of her chest. "*Bienvenida a nuestra casa.*" Uncle Victor turned to Abuela and gave her a hug. Sofi smiled.

Her grandmother stiffened up. "I didn't mean . . . I just came to give Sofi this." She pulled out a folded paper from underneath her black wool sweater. Sofi looked at the folded yellowed letter, dumbstruck.

"What is it?"

Abuela Benita sniffed. "After you left, I got to thinking." She looked at Luisa and turned quickly away. "There's nothing I can do about the past. But I found this"—she waved the paper—"in my father's old belongings. I thought it might help."

Sofi opened it eagerly. Was it her grandmother's birth certificate? Round cursive lettering was written all over it. Her heart started to pound in her ears. Was this what she'd been looking for? Inside was a carefully written statement in longhand, signed by a woman named Doña Nicolasa Pérez Fuentes. "A letter?"

"It's a birth statement." Her grandmother hesitated, looking back at Luisa. Sofi's aunt's mouth hung open in shock. "Remember how I told you I was born at home? Well, this is the statement written by the midwife. I know it's not the document you need, but maybe it'll help." Sofi ran into her arms and gave her a big hug.

Her grandmother looked into her eyes. "If you can find this woman or find out that she was a real midwife, maybe you could prove that I was born in the United States and you can go home."

Sofi waved the letter excitedly in the air. "This is great." She turned to her *tía*. "You know what this means?"

Luisa sighed, resigning herself to the situation. Her aunt looked at Sofi with love in her eyes. "Yes. It means that you can go home to the United States."

Sofi nodded. "Yes, but, don't you see, now all of us can go home to the United States."

Luisa coughed loudly. She ignored Abuela Benita and walked up to Sofi. "This is our home." Her words filled Sofi with bittersweet clarity. Rancho Escondido was their home. It was her home, too. But now, it wasn't her only home.

"*Tenemos que celebrar*," her uncle said excitedly. He picked Sofi up and twirled her around in the air.

"I should go," her grandmother said, getting nervous under Luisa's chilly stare. Sofi wanted them to make up, but she knew that it would take time.

Sofi and Yesenia accompanied Abuela Benita back to her house. Sofi thought it was strange when Yesenia volunteered to come along. Her cousin said little on the taxi ride, but the sneaky look on her face told Sofi that she was up to something. On the return trip, Yesenia asked the driver to drop them off in front of the Hotel Sin Sun San. The peeling yellow two-story building had a discotheque by the entrance.

"What are we doing?" Sofi asked, following behind her cousin.

"You heard my dad. We're going to celebrate."

Sofi hesistated. Her aunt expected them to come right back.

"C'mon, Sofi, just think—this could be your last night in Rosarito."

"I don't know that. I still have to talk to the lawyer and—"

Her cousin tugged at her hand. "Well, let's pretend that it is."

The club was dark. The DJ was playing a Spanish rock song. Red, blue, and green lights spun around the empty dance floor. A group of guys were sitting at the bar, cracking jokes and drinking. Teenage girls in high heels, tight skirts, and heavy makeup sat sipping tall frosty drinks at the small round tables scattered along the edges. They were whispering to one another and checking out the guys. Yesenia walked onto the dance floor and started dancing by herself.

"I love this song," she cried over the loud music.

Sofi joined her, stepping in beat with the bass. This place was different, nothing like the rowdy American clubs farther up the strip. The patrons were all Mexicans. Back home, Sofi would never have dreamed of dancing with another girl, but here it was normal and no one seemed to care. The large bay windows were open, allowing in the incessant traffic sounds and the cooling sea breeze. Sofi lost herself, shaking her head wildly to the rhythmic beats. Yesenia was right, she thought, this might be her last night in Rosarito.

"Whenever I feel mad or sad I like to dance," her cousin cried.

Sofi nodded, feeling all her stress loosen. She'd been so wound up the last couple of days thinking about Andres, going home, and her family that she'd had hardly any time to enjoy herself. Across the floor the boys were watching her move. One guy in particular sitting on a stool couldn't take his eyes off her. It was Andres. Sofi grabbed her cousin by the wrist and pulled her to an empty table.

"He's here," Sofi said in a hushed tone.

"Who?" Yesenia called out loudly, stretching her neck to look around.

"Andres."

"Oh."

A slow song came on and three guys invited three girls out to dance. The strobe light came on, illuminating the room with white speckles of light. Sofi looked up to see if Andres was dancing. He wasn't. He had turned around toward the bar. It looked like he'd come alone, without that girl. What was he doing here? Of all the clubs, he had to be at this one.

Yesenia nudged her. "So are you going to talk to him?"

Sofi sighed. "What's the point? He hates my guts."

"C'mon, Sofi. I'm sure he doesn't."

"You don't know him like I do. I broke his heart."

"Hearts can be mended. You remember what my dad said. Sometimes, you got to swallow your pride and make a fool of yourself."

The song pulled at Sofi's heart. The wailing lead singer was in agony over losing his love. Sofi wanted to be with Andres. She wanted to be in his arms. She watched the couples for a while, glancing every now and then back at Andres.

"We should go," Sofi said.

"We just got here."

Sofi didn't want to be there. The tension in the room was unbearable. She needed air. "I'm going to the bathroom." Sofi got up and walked around the dance floor, careful not to pass in Andres's direction. Another romantic song came on. She wondered if she should just confront Andres. She'd be leaving soon. This might be her last chance.

The bathroom was small and reeked of hairspray and cheap perfume. A heavyset woman with her hair tied in a bun sat on a small stool by the sinks. An assortment of hair products, makeup, and candies were arranged nearby. Sofi went to the bathroom and noticed that there was no toilet paper.

"*Con permiso*," Sofi said.

The woman held up two tiny squares of rough toilet paper. "*A ti te cobro cinco pesos, para los gringos son diez.*"

Sofi shuffled uncomfortably. She didn't have five pesos. "*Lo siento*," she began.

The woman nodded in understanding and handed her the paper. Sofi smiled, enjoying the perks of being Mexican.

When she came back, she found her cousin sitting with Andres.

What was she doing? Her cheeks burned with embarrassment. It was a good thing that she was leaving. Yesenia was out of control! Sofi went to sit down at their table. A few minutes later, Yesenia got up and crossed the dance floor toward Sofi.

"Yesenia, I could kill you. What did you tell him?"

Her cousin smiled and waved the incident away as if it were nothing. "Oh, I was just saying how we were celebrating your last night in Rosarito."

"You didn't."

Yesenia shrugged. "It was no big deal."

"No big deal?"

Andres got up. He dug his hand into his jeans pocket and threw a couple of bills on the counter. Was he coming over? Sofi thought happily. Maybe they would make up. Andres looked up directly at her. Sofi wanted to say something, run over to him and beg for forgiveness. But he turned and headed out the door. Her heart flopped.

Yesenia leaned across the table. "If you don't go after him now, you'll regret it for the rest of your life."

Sofi bit down on her lower lip and turned toward the doorway. Her cousin was right. It was now or never. She got up and ran after him. "Andres."

He stopped at the edge of the corner.

Sofi stopped a few feet from him. It was dark out, but she could make out the tight muscles in his face by the light of a streetlamp. The night was alive with chatty couples, blaring music, and the scent of sizzling food, but for Sofi only Andres existed. She took a moment to catch her breath. Her mind was racing, but she didn't know what to say.

"Well, I guess this is good-bye," Andres said, breaking the silence.

"Yeah."

He turned to go.

"Andres, please," Sofi pleaded. He stopped. His back was to her.

"I'm sorry, all right? I'm sorry about Rico, about missing our date, and not telling you my true feelings." Andres didn't move. "I know I screwed up with you, and I won't blame you if you never want to speak to me again. But I just want you to know that I . . . that I . . . I can't stop thinking about you. And I know that I may never see you again, and that we're totally different, but I don't care." Andres stared forward. His eyes blinked at the oncoming traffic headlights. "Andres?"

"Sofi, don't," he said, putting up his hand. "Please don't." And then he walked away.

That night, Yesenia patted Sofi's back, trying to console her. "I'm really, really sorry. I thought—"

"It's okay," Sofi said, sitting up. They were in their pj's, getting ready for bed. "I guess it's for the best. I'm going home anyway." She sighed deeply. Her chest burned. "I guess we weren't meant to be."

Yesenia said nothing, but looked at her with sorrow in her eyes.

"Don't worry. I'll be all right. I've had my heart broken before and I'm sure it'll happen a hundred more times."

"But you two were so cute together."

Sofi smiled, thinking about how they'd danced at the *quinceañera*, ridden in his beat-up, Chinese-food–smelling truck, and kissed at the beach. "We were, weren't we?"

"Love sucks," Yesenia said, crossing her arms in front of her chest. She must have been thinking about Javier.

Sofi sighed. "It sure does."

"*Ya duérmete*," Mundo cried, half asleep. It was late.

Her cousin clicked the light off. "Maybe I'll come visit you," she said in the dark.

"That'll be fun," Sofi said, turning over, trying to get comfortable.

"You could take me around and we could meet cute boys."

Sofi laughed. She lay still and listened to the familiar sounds of the night. The angry wind bustled outside, shaking the branches of the trees.

The rooster cried out, serenading the moon, and the goat bleated from its pole. Sofi took a deep breath. She wondered what it would be like to return to her quiet home. Would she be able to sleep? Then the air exploded with the sounds of mariachi singing and music.

"What's that?" Sofi cried, sitting up in the bed.

Yesenia jumped up and left the room. She came back whispering excitedly, "Come, come, it's a *serenata*."

"A sera-what?"

Her cousin pulled her by the arm into the living room. Uncle Victor and Luisa came out in their robes, wondering what was going on. Mando tried to turn on the light switch, but the electricity was out. Mundo came out sucking on his thumb and wrapping himself around his father's leg.

"Come, Sofia," Yesenia insisted, motioning with her hand toward the front window. Sofi could feel the entire family peeking behind her through the curtains. Seven mariachis were getting out of Andres's truck. Two trumpets, several guitars, and a short violin player were assembled in a straight line. Andres was at the end, wearing jeans and a black shirt. He looked handsome. She recognized the mariachis from *la tardeada*. What was going on?

"Will someone tell me what's going on?" Sofi asked her *tía*. She was so happy, she couldn't sit still. Andres loved her.

"In the old days," Luisa said, giving her husband a reproachful look, "a guy would send the woman he loved a *serenata*. If she loved him, she would turn on her bedroom light to let him know. If the light did not come on, then the guy went home sad. I would guess"—she smiled, looking just like Yesenia—"Andres must really like you."

"Totally old-fashioned," Yesenia interjected, but then her face opened into a huge grin. "But totally romantic!"

The mariachi music continued playing outside. He was singing a dreamy ballad called "Volver, Volver." Uncle Victor explained that the song was about a man who'd lost a love and wanted her to return.

"That's so me!" Sofi cried excitedly. The boys snickered, elbowing each other. "I don't believe this." She wanted to rush around the house and turn on all the lights, start a big fire in the living room, and set the house ablaze, but she froze. Hadn't she already been through this before?

"I don't know." She slumped back onto the couch. Everyone gathered around her with confused looks. She had to tell them. They were her family. The people she had to trust and depend on. "We had a big fight. He caught me kissing another boy and now he's with another girl. He doesn't think we have a future, not with the border keeping us apart."

"Do you love him?" her uncle asked, sitting next to her and putting a hand on her shoulder.

"I love him more than anything. But I can't hurt him. Maybe he's right. Maybe we should both just move on and find love in different arms." For once, no one said anything. Sofi exhaled a long breath, listening to the melodious singer outside.

Then Uncle Victor cleared his voice. Sofi sat up straight and smiled, expecting some wise *telenovela* advice. "Life is either a daring adventure or nothing at all."

"Wait a second." Sofi thought back to all her dad's funny quotes. "I know that. It's . . . " Uncle Victor pulled out a book she recognized. It was her father's quote book, but in Spanish. *Oh no*, she thought, and laughed. Sofi realized, though, that he was right. She couldn't protect herself from possible disappointment and heartbreak by giving up. Life was about taking risks and not settling. Sofi reflected on her journey to Mexico. It had been hard, full of frustrating moments and struggles. But she'd gotten through it all. Sofi pulled out her necklace of San Juan Soldado and looked at it. She was a stronger person because of it.

"Well, let's see if this works," Sofi said, counting down. "Three, two . . . " And miraculously, all the lights in the house came on. Sofi rushed to open the front door and greet Andres. She knew that there were no guarantees in love. She was sure that, as with everything in Mexico, love would not be easy. But she was willing to give it another shot. Andres was standing by the pole with the goat sniffing at his leg. He was sweating as she approached, biting his lower lip.

"Hi," Andres said rather shyly. "I heard you were leaving and I thought. . . ."

Sofi smiled. This was no time to be shy. "I love you, Andres," Sofi declared clasping her arms around him. She gave him a sweet kiss. A wolf whistle behind them broke the spell, and Sofi glanced over her shoulder to see her family cheering along with all the mariachi players. Andres wrapped his arms around her waist as the musicians began another song. The whole family started to dance by the light of the moon. The storm had passed. Sofi couldn't imagine a better ending.

24

"I am an American citizen," Abuela Benita said with a thick Spanish accent to Mr. Wilcox two days later. The whole family and Andres were sitting at the kitchen table listening. "I was born in 1940 in the town of Lemoore, California." Mr. Wilcox was a tall white man with thick glasses and an expensive-looking suit. He was looking at the midwife's statement and shaking his head in disbelief.

"This is amazing. Sofi, when you called me, I couldn't believe your story. That's why I had to come down here myself to see for sure. Your parents . . ." Sofi smiled from across the table. Mando and Mundo were attacking her mother's homemade chocolate cookies. They were Sofi's favorite, but she was too excited to eat or even look through the care package he'd brought. Uncle Victor's eyes were dancing with excitement. He hadn't had a drink all day and really enjoyed waking up early to do yoga first thing in the morning. "Your father is beside himself. He's been online and on the phone all day trying to find the midwife, Nicolasa. There's no record of your grandmother's birth at any of the local hospitals, but if we can find Nicolasa or someone who worked with her, we may be able to find previous statements that can legitimize this claim. After that, it's all smooth sailing. I'll take your dad's and your birth certificates to INS and get them approved. Then all you'll need is a passport."

"Then I can go home?"

"Well, actually, all you really need is a court order supporting your grandmother's claim."

"This is surreal."

Mr. Wilcox leaned over and held Sofi's hand. "Believe it."

"It's about time!" she screamed, jumping into his arms. "Thank you. Thank you. Thank you."

Mr. Wilcox froze up, uncomfortable with all the affection. "You really need to thank your grandmother."

Abuela Benita smiled brightly. She had a good set of teeth. "I guess I was wrong. You do need me." The old woman shrugged.

"Abuela." Sofi gave her a big hug. "I love you so much." Luisa and Yesenia stared at her in shock.

"Yes!" Sofi jumped up and down around the kitchen, feeling giddy. "This is wonderful! Woo!" She was about to race into the bedroom that she would no longer be sharing with her three cousins, but Andres's strained smile made her stop in her tracks. Sofi glanced around the room. Luisa stood rigidly stiff next to Uncle Victor. Her tears betrayed her forced smile. Yesenia stood in the doorway, staring at a spot on the linoleum as if it were the most fascinating thing in the world. Mando and Mundo watched wide-eyed from the couch.

Although Sofi was thrilled by the prospect of going home, her heart felt like it was being ripped in two. How could she leave a place she'd grown to love? How could she leave this wonderful family who'd taught her so much about herself? How could she leave her true love? But Sofi had to graduate from high school. She had to go to UCLA. Tears streamed down her face. This was so not fair, she thought angrily. Life was playing another cruel joke on her.

Mr. Wilcox looked curiously at her, confused by her sudden change in mood. He checked his watch and then looked back at her. "I should be going if I'm going to beat traffic at the border. I'll give you a call." He paused, remembering something. "Um, what number can I reach you at?"

"You can use my number," Andres offered, pulling out his Nextel phone.

Sofi's heart crumbled into a billion little pieces, she was so touched by his gesture. This couldn't be easy for him either, she thought. "Thank you," she said, touching his arm gently.

Andres looked up and their eyes locked. Her breath caught as he grabbed her hand and squeezed it.

Later that evening Sofi and Andres sat on the back porch watching the full moon. The backyard was dark. Shadows danced from the reflection of the dull lightbulb hanging from the porch roof. The chickens ruffled noisily in the coop. Spanish rock music came from some neighbor's house down the street. Children yelled as they played in the street and the goat bleated loudly from the pole in front of the house. Sofi took in a deep breath, enjoying the aroma of the *rancho*. Andres hadn't said much all afternoon. The silence between them was killing her.

"You're not mad at me, are you?"

Andres was scratching a stripe of white paint from the peeling wooden floor. "I'm not mad."

"Well, you're not happy, either."

Andres looked up with real hurt in his eyes. "What do you want me to say? Hurray. Yippee. Sofi is finally free of Mexico. Now she can go back to her *real* life, with her *real* friends, and find herself a *real* boyfriend."

Sofi jerked back as if his words cut her. "That's pretty harsh. We don't know if I'm actually going back."

Andres pulled himself up, holding onto the wooden fence. He sighed deeply, running his fingers through his hair. "Oh, you'll go back. I know you'll go back. This was exactly what I didn't want."

Sofi looked at him, surprised. "Why does everything have to be about you?" Sofi jumped up. "What about me? What about my dreams?"

Andres cupped his hands over hers. "That's the problem. Don't you see, my *nopalita*. Despite everything and how we feel about each other, we have different dreams." Sofi felt her eyes get moist. She hated his words, but deep down they rang true. "You, you want to go to UCLA, and you will. You'll fulfill all your dreams." She smiled. "You'll have your fancy condo and the turquoise Mini Cooper. And anything else your heart desires."

"I want you," Sofi said quietly.

Andres pulled her into a hug. His arms were so comforting and warm. She sobbed quietly, listening to the wails of Laura Pausini playing on a radio inside the house. Andres said nothing and rocked her back and forth. Her conflicting emotions tore at her insides. There was still so much she had to do back home. She couldn't turn her back on all her hard work. But she'd grown so much here in Mexico. She'd conquered so many fears, found her grandmother, and allowed the most amazing man into her heart. All Sofi wanted to do was stop time and stay here with Andres forever. "Do you know what I want?"

Sofi wiped her face. "To collect seeds."

Andres laughed. "Yeah, that, and I think I need to go back to school."

"I thought you were going to make tons of money working at the hotel."

Andres pinched her nose playfully. "I'm thinking of going into politics." He winked. "That way I can come back to Rosarito and institute all these little projects I have." Sofi smiled. She loved how his face lit up whenever he talked about his plans. "Imagine Rosarito, the entire city, running on used cooking oil. And we won't stop there. We'll get rid of the national and international chain stores and go local. Go solar. It'll be great. Rosarito will be the first twenty-first-century economically self-sustaining community in Mexico. It'll be a model for the rest of the country." Sofi's face fell. Andres would never leave Mexico. His heart and his passion were here with the land and its people.

"You'll be amazing," Sofi said, feeling her heart break. She loved him so much, but he was right. They had different paths to follow. "So, what are we going to do?"

"You mean about us?" He looked up at the moon. Sofi noticed a single tear fall down his cheek. She couldn't stand it and buried her face in his chest. She didn't want the evening ever to end.

25

When Sofi saw her dad at the door, she swore she was still dreaming. The sky had barely lit up. A crisp cry from the rooster pierced the air. Sofi wiped the crust around her eyes in disbelief. She was still in her cotton pj's and her hair was in disarray.

"Dad?"

"*Corazón,*" Ed said, opening the shredded screen door and taking her into a heartfelt embrace. Her dad had lost weight. His bones felt so fragile, she worried that she would crush him. Ed was wearing his work suit, complete with American tie and shiny shoes. His hair was neatly combed to the left. She inhaled the familiar comforting scent of Ivory soap and his Brut aftershave. It was so surreal. She didn't want to let go for fear that she would wake. He held her quietly, saying nothing. She noticed Mr. Wilcox smiling behind him.

"What are you doing here? When did you arrive?" she asked quickly, and peered over his shoulder. Her heart soared with excitement. Was she really going home? Tears formed. "Where's Mom?"

Her dad brushed back her hair and stared at her face as if he couldn't believe that he was there himself. "Everything happened so fast," he said, leading her to the table. "Your mother wanted to come." He put his hand over hers. "She really did. But there's the border checkpoint near San Clemente and we couldn't risk her getting picked up before she got her paperwork."

"But I don't understand how you are here, now. Mr. Wilcox?" She finally turned and acknowledged him. "I thought you said it could take a while."

"Aha!" Ed raised his finger to interrupt. Sofi smiled. She'd missed all his funny quirks. "We are Mendozas. Mendozas never give up."

Tears streamed down Sofi's face freely. "That right! *Si, se puede.*" They hugged again. He soothed back her hair and rocked her like she was a little girl.

"It took some time, but we found a hospital that confirmed that Doña Nicolasa Pérez Fuentes was a legitimate midwife."

"You did?"

"The woman is dead now, but her daughter works at a medical office in Downey." Sofi laughed. "When I told her what happened, she marched me around to all these doctors who would sign affidavits that said she was a legitimate midwife. The next day, Mr. Wilcox and I literally ran to the Immigration and Naturalization Services Department, where they recognized my mother's American citizenship and then mine as her son." Ed took a deep breath. Sofi's head felt delightfully dizzy, thinking about her father's hunt. Her dad pulled out a formal-looking document from his coat pocket. "With this court order, we can go home." Sofi jumped into his arms.

"Harr!" Mundo yelled, in his wrestler's mask. He started making karate gestures at Sofi's dad. Mando jumped out from behind the couch in a similarly threatening manner. Ed started to laugh cheerfully.

"*Pórtense bien. Éste es mi papá,*" Sofi warned. She looked sideways at her dad to see if he was listening.

"Wow." Her father took off his glasses and wiped them on a thin cloth he'd pulled out from his jacket pocket. "Your Spanish has improved. I see that you've learned a few things in the *rancho.*"

"Dad," Sofi said, nodding, "you have no idea."

The rest of the day was a blur. When Luisa came out of her room to see who was at the door, she immediately burst into tears. All her anger and resentment washed away upon her reunion with Sofi's father. It was obvious that she'd really missed her big brother. But the real shocker was when her dad went to visit his mother after forty years! Sofi was a bit nervous, because her *abuela* still liked to throw rocks. But her dad did the craziest thing. He bent down on one knee before her and asked for forgiveness.

After that, things happened so fast, Sofi didn't even have time to think. The whole family decided to come along to the border. Her heart swelled looking around at all the familiar faces. Uncle Victor and Tía Luisa stood together. They were holding the boys, who were wearing their wrestling outfits and trying to wiggle free, as usual. Doña Clementina tagged along. She wanted to see Sofi stick it to the border patrol. Andres was holding the brown leather bag that Yesenia had given up for Sofi's few belongings. Her heart ached whenever their eyes locked.

"This is my granddaughter," Abuela Benita said to the young INS agent at the Tijuana border. Abuela was dressed all in black, as if in mourning, with her signature red rose tucked behind her ear. "She is an American citizen. She real smart. She go to college in America."

The officer sighed loudly. "Well, that's all good, lady. I just need you to form a single line."

"Dad," Sofi whispered. Her father jumped up and pulled Mr. Wilcox over to the front counter.

Mr. Wilcox cleared his throat. He smiled at the INS officer, who seemed only mildly amused by the scene. "We're actually only here for this girl." He pulled Sofi by the arm.

She smiled and waved. "Hi."

"Okay." He turned to Sofi, making her heart drum wildly in her chest. Could he tell that she was nervous? What if he didn't let her through? What if the documents were fake? Or what if Grandma had been mistaken? She wiped beads of sweat from her upper lip and tried to breathe.

"This is Sofia Mendoza," Mr. Wilcox stated with a smile. He pulled out several documents from his black briefcase. "I have the court order stating that her grandmother, Mrs. Benita Mendoza, is a U.S. citizen, as well as Sofi's school ID and birth certificate. See here"—he pointed to the certificate—"her grandmother's name is right there."

The officer looked at all the people behind them warily. Then he typed Sofi's name into his computer. "I see that Ms. Mendoza has a record. She was excluded from entering the United States before because she had false documents." Her stomach clutched. She'd known something like this would happen. He wasn't going to let her in. He thought she was a criminal.

Mr. Wilcox spoke up in an authoritative voice. "Ms. Mendoza is a minor who believed she had the correct documents. In the end, she's still a citizen, so let's put that incident behind us." Sofi smiled excitedly. Mr. Wilcox sounded so good! The officer gave Sofi a sideways glance. Would he let her through?

"I guess you're right. Welcome home." The officer smiled. The crowd cheered behind her. "I'll need you guys to step to the side—we have a lot of people here trying to get across."

Sofi reached out and hugged her *tía* tightly. There were tears in her aunt's eyes. Luisa handed Sofi a bag of diced nopales, making her promise to share her recipes with her friends. Uncle Victor gave her a mysterious cassette and told her to play it before she went to bed. Mando and Mundo produced a hastily wrapped gift. It was a black wrestling mask with a big cactus plant around the eyeholes. It fit perfectly with her new wrestler name, La Nopalera Feroz (The Ferocious Cactus). Sofi ran to hug Yesenia; tears ran from both of their eyes. "Now, you know, you can get a passport too. You're welcome to come and stay with me whenever."

Yesenia wiped her face and sniffed loudly. "You're the best cousin a girl could ever ask for." They hugged tightly, squeezing the air out of each other's lungs.

Andres handed Sofi her bag. He was very quiet; his broken heart showed on his face. They hadn't said much. What could they say? After everything that had happened, would they ever meet again? They both wondered. They'd exchanged numbers and addresses, but had done it grudgingly.

Abuela Benita cleared her throat loudly. Sofi turned, letting go of Andres, even though it was killing her. Her grandmother removed the red rose from her hair and tucked it behind Sofi's ear. *"Las rosas son mis flores favoritas.* It's like me and you, a wild Mexican rose. Don't forget that," she scolded. "And don't let no one call you illegal ever again. You remember that your people were here before there was that stinky border. You hear me?" Sofi nodded, smiling behind a heavy flow of tears. "Now I want you to hold your head up high when you cross that border, okay? You be proud of who you are and where you come from. *¡Eres Mendoza, caramba!"*

Sofi looked over her shoulder as the U.S.–Mexican border passed behind her. Her dad was driving at sixty-five miles an hour north on Interstate 5 toward San Inocente. Edmundo Mendoza had changed. Sofi noticed that he was grinning widely and sitting up an inch taller. She turned and looked back to make sure that the border patrol hadn't changed their mind at the last minute.

Mr. Wilcox and her dad laughed at Sofi's reaction. The border made no sense to her. All of a sudden, Sofi caught sight of a man in jeans and a black pullover, running. Her breath caught. It looked like he was running across the border illegally. Sofi looked around to see if the border patrol or Minute Men were chasing after him. She lost sight of him between the cars, but she hoped he got away. Everyone deserved a chance to make their dream come true.

The freeway felt foreign as their car smoothly passed other vehicles. Everything around her looked suddenly new, as if she were seeing things with new eyes. Sofi wondered if this was how Mexicans and other immigrants saw this land of opportunity. The freeway was lined with trees that were strong and healthy, with lush green leaves on their branches. Even the sky was clear, blue, and bright. She turned to look for smokestacks shooting pollution into the air, a familiar sight on the Other Side. Sofi couldn't get over the smooth ride. It was like rolling on silk. The road appeared freshly paved, without a bump or pothole in sight. As they passed the city of Chula Vista, she noted how nice and well organized the new the houses looked. She'd taken all this for granted. Right then Sofi knew she was blessed, and she promised herself that she would never waste the opportunities life gave her.

"Thank you, Mr. Wilcox," Sofi said when her dad switched onto the 405. He smiled at her sideways, relieved that everything had turned out so well. Mr. Wilcox was a good man and really wanted to help Sofi. She was thankful that her parents had been lucky enough to connect with him.

"So, *corazón*," her dad asked, looking back over his shoulder at her. "Tell me, how was Rancho Escondido?"

Sofi sighed, looking out the window. How would she ever explain all that she'd been through? Mexico was a country of many contradictions. She'd gone through great highs and horribly awful lows. But she loved it all, because in the end she'd found a piece of her that was missing. She looked at her dad's curious smile. "Well, first, let me tell you about the driving. I swear no one knows how to drive in Mexico." Both men laughed as Sofi described her border escapade. Afterward she asked, "Would you mind if I play this?" Sofi was holding the mysterious cassette her uncle had given her as a going-away gift. Her curiosity was digging at her and she knew that she wouldn't be able to wait until bedtime. Her dad put it into the cassette player. They waited for something to happen. Sofi figured her uncle had taped some of the Spanish ballads that he loved to sing to while drinking. But when she heard nothing, she wondered if maybe her uncle had made a mistake and didn't know how to record properly. Then a piercing cry of the rooster, the same one that sang all night, burst from the car's speakers. Her dad almost lost control of the vehicle from fright, which made Sofi laugh. She held her hand over her heart, overcome by feelings of profound love. Her uncle had recorded the rooster to remind her of home. It was so sweet.

It was already dark when they got onto the Pico turnoff in San Inocente. Sofi asked her dad to pinch her to make sure she wasn't dreaming. She lowered the window and breathed in the familiar salty air in the cool refreshing breeze. They passed the McDonald's; its lights were blazing inside, and all kinds of people were hanging out. The sight of her school building and the gym where she'd spent countless hours fantasizing about Nick made her eyes moist. The senior trip, prom, finals, and graduation had passed, but none of that school stuff mattered to her so much anymore. She was back! Sofi looked around, admiring everything. She saw things she liked: the clean, well-manicured streets, working lampposts at every corner, the outdoor shopping center where you could buy frozen pork cutlets at all hours. But there were other things she saw that she hadn't noticed before, like the Mexican delivery boy sweating profusely on an old bike and a dark-skinned woman with a long black braid pushing a shopping cart full of laundry and two screaming toddlers down the street. The drunk on the corner holding a sign that said, I NEED A BEER, upset her. The man looked healthy and able to work. He had no right to beg, she thought, thinking about all the people in TJ who created jobs for themselves if they didn't have one.

They wove their way into her neighborhood. She recognized the familiar chirping of grasshoppers and the smell of freshly cut grass, and the silence. . . . Closing her eyes, she remembered Andres on the beach. She wondered what he was doing right then. Her stomach fluttered. Would he go back to that girl? Her anxiety started to rise, but the sight of her house pulled her out of those thoughts.

Her house, although identical to every other house on the block, was breathtaking. It was ablaze, with a bunch of cars parked out front. She recognized Taylor's 4Runner and jumped out of the car without her bag. Her dad couldn't resist the urge to honk the horn to announce their arrival. The front door swung open, and Sofi's mom stood there as if a fantasy. Sofi jumped into her mother's arms.

"I love you so much," Sofi repeated over and over again. It felt like ages since she'd said that, ages since she'd felt her mother's arms wrapped around her.

"My darling," her mother cried. She wiped Sofi's tears away with her hand and kissed her all over her face. "I am so proud of you." She sniffed. Sofi couldn't believe how beautiful her mother looked. It had been too long. "I was so worried. I didn't know how you'd react to life there. I swore you would have a nervous breakdown. Just thinking of you there with the goats and the pigs . . ." Her mother started to laugh.

"It was good medicine, Mom." Sofi smirked with tears in her eyes.

Her mother smacked her arm. "*Chamaca sinvergüenza*, that's what you get for disobeying us like that. Taylor told us about the party." Sofi's eyes grew wide. Her mother smirked as she crossed her arms in front of her chest. There was no way she was ever going to pull another fast one on her parents.

"Mom." Sofi chuckled, so happy to see her. "I learned my lesson all right. I'll never leave your side again."

"That'll be pretty difficult from Los Angeles." Her dad grabbed her from behind and gave her a loving squeeze.

"What do you mean?" Sofi looked from her mother to her father. "No," she said, her eyes widening in understanding. "Really?"

"Well, I'm tired of seeing that dirty room of yours," her mother said. A small smile played on her red lips. "We figure you're never going to learn to clean up after yourself if you don't live by yourself."

"UCLA dorms," Sofi screamed, "here I come!"

Finally they released each other and entered the living room. The crowd screamed, "Surprise!" when Sofi passed the threshold. The dining table that they never used was full of chips, Taco Bell nachos, and six-packs of diet soda. There were balloons and a huge WELCOME HOME,

SOFI sign hanging on the wall. The best part was seeing the faces of all her school friends.

Sofi screamed wildly when she saw Taylor and Olivia. The three girls embraced tightly, squeezing all the breath from their lungs. The girls huddled together as if they hadn't seen one another in forty years instead of three weeks.

"Look at you," Olivia said, practically shouting. "I love the rose. It's very Mexicana."

"You're glowing," Taylor added.

"Well, hello? I just crossed the border!"

They all shouted in disbelief.

"I can't believe this." Sofi's face was wet. "How did you guys know? Who did all this?" she asked. Taylor and Olivia motioned to Sofi's mother, who was handing a Diet Coke to Mr. Wilcox.

"Thank you, Mother," Sofi said, and hugged her from behind. "This is the best party in the world."

"Look! Look!" Taylor said, shaking a plastic bag in Sofi's face.

"What is it?" Sofi heard herself screaming.

"Open it!" Olivia cried.

Inside the black plastic bag were a burgundy-and-silver cap and gown. San Inocente High School's colors. Her heart sank.

"So how was graduation?"

Taylor's eyes doubled in size. "It was amazing. Everyone wore their buttons," she said. Taylor pressed the button she had pinned to her green shirt in Sofi's face.

"You really did it!" Sofi grabbed the button that said, NO BORDERS, FREE SOFI. She didn't have the words to express her gratitude. Tears welled up in her eyes and fell down her cheeks.

"We talked to your counselor, Ms. Potts," Taylor said. "They're going to let you take your finals next week."

"Oh my God!" Sofi waved her hand in the air. "I have so much work to do."

After all the initial hellos, Sofi got to tell her tale. Nobody could believe her experience. It sounded straight out of a movie.

"What did you do?" Emily asked. Her eyes were so big, Sofi thought they might pop out and roll onto the floor. Emily was pressing her cell phone close to her chest as if she were afraid someone might try to steal it. Sofi laughed. A couple of weeks ago she would have said that she'd die without cable, Internet, or a phone, but that was before Mexico chewed up her old self and spit out a new and improved Sofi.

"Well." Sofi leaned into the circle of girls formed around her. "I fell in love. . . . " All the girls screamed in delight. Which was the truth. She'd fallen in love with a brutal, hard place and learned to love herself. The best part had been falling for a terrific guy who loved her just as she was.

"*Hola, bonita,*" a familiar voice said behind her. Sofi jumped at the sight of Nick, standing there looking adorable as ever with ruffled hair, sagging, brown slacks, and that incredible smile. Nick hadn't changed one bit. Curses! For some reason, Sofi had hoped that he'd grown deformed and bent out of shape.

"Oh, Nick, you're here." Sofi looked around for her reinforcements, but Olivia and Taylor were busy digging into the nachos.

"I'm sorry. I didn't mean to upset you. I heard about what happened and I just wanted to apologize for that night. I was soooo drunk."

Sofi felt dizzy. "You're apologizing?"

Nick combed his fingers through his shaggy blond hair. Sofi used to love it when he did that. She'd dreamed of doing it herself. But something had changed and it wasn't Nick. He was still beautiful as ever. Her heart fluttered.

"I thought that maybe you and I could hang out sometime, maybe catch a movie."

Was he for real? Sofi thought looking at him. "How's Sarah?"

Nick smiled awkwardly. "Well, um, you see, she and I aren't together anymore, you know?"

Sofi looked across the faces of family and friends who were gathered to celebrate her return. A couple of weeks ago Nick's words would have been music to her ears. They were all that she'd dreamed about. A part of her wondered . . . what if? Maybe this was what the fortune-teller had really predicted. The old lady hadn't actually said *when* she'd fall in love with the man of her dreams. She thought about Andres. Her heart ached for him. He should be here, getting to know her friends, her mother, her hometown. But he'd never come. He had a different path. Sofi looked into Nick's sweet face and kissable lips. She took a deep breath.

"I appreciate you coming all the way out here to apologize, but you better go," she said flatly.

"What?" Nick asked in shock. He wasn't used to being turned down. "You're not still mad about the beach. Cut me some slack. I was drunk."

Sofi marched to the front door and opened it widely. "My uncle Victor says that there are only two people who tell the truth: drunks and children. *Adiós*, XL." Nick tried to chuckle. He looked around and darted for the door. His cheeks burned bright red.

"What was that all about?" Olivia asked, pointing with her boobs at the closed door.

Sofi dismissed it with her hand. "That was nothing."

"Nothing?" Olivia's eyes opened wide. "You're in love with the guy for three years and then he comes to your house and you throw him out in front of all these people. You call that nothing?!"

Sofi smiled at them, looking them straight in the eye. "I'm not the same girl you last saw at the border."

Olivia gasped, putting her hand over her heart. "What did they do to you out there?"

Sofi laughed. "Maybe it was the water?" She looked at her friends, then scanned all the guests in the living room, realizing that while in Mexico, she'd had to push herself to survive. Her friends had no idea. "You guys need to come back with me to Mexico."

"Papas and Beer," Olivia said, nodding.

Sofi shook her head, "No, I want to show you *my* Mexico."

"Will it be safe?" Taylor asked, looking concerned.

"C'mon, girls, I can't promise that you'll be safe." She laughed, remembering the dogs. "But I swear it'll change your life." Taylor and Olivia gave her unsure looks. Sofi grinned to herself. She felt older, experienced, much more confident in her skin. Life had thrown a bunch of barriers in her way. But now she felt capable of handling any crazy situation. She lingered there a minute, observing the crowd. Something nagged at her. She was happy to be home, but while she'd been gone, life in San Inocente had stood still. It made her feel sad for all the people here. She'd been through a remarkable experience, and as much as her friends and family tried, they would never grasp the full meaning of her experience. Sofi felt removed from everyone around her. As if she were inside a bubble, watching all this with her Mexican eyes.

"You all right?" Taylor asked. "You seem different."

Sofi smiled. She sucked her teeth and raised her index finger, asking for a moment. She wasn't all right. Her bewildered friends stared back at her. Making her way to her room, she knew what she was missing. Sofi stood at the entrance of her room. It was just as she'd left it, a mess. Her mother hadn't touched it. *It must have taken all her strength*, Sofi thought as she entered. The price tag of her UCLA duffel bag was still on the carpet. Everything was in its exact place as if she'd never left. She leaped onto her bed and reached for the cordless phone by her nightstand. She dialed the cell phone number crumbled on a piece of Yesenia's notebook paper.

The phone must have rung ten times. Sofi hoped that there wasn't some complicated prefix code that she'd forgotten to dial. Then she heard his familiar sexy voice in her ear. Her breath caught. Sofi was so happy, she jumped up and down on her bed. His voice overwhelmed her like a wave transporting her back to Mexico.

"Andres."

"Sofi. Are you there already?"

She was deliriously happy, holding the phone so tight, it hurt her cheek. "Yes, we just got in. I miss you," she blurted out. The sound of his laughter filled her heart like a helium balloon.

"I miss you, too," he said.

"I need to ask you something really important." Sofi took a moment and touched the cool, smooth walls. She thought about how she'd spent a lifetime wishing for the right man to sweep her off her feet. The right man was supposed to make all her dreams come true. But she'd learned that she was the only person who could make her dreams come true. Living in Mexico had taught her about having courage to live dangerously. She knew that she couldn't spend another minute worrying about Andres.

"Okay." She took a deep breath. Sofi had accepted the fact that there were no certainties in life. The only moment that counted was the one she was living in right now. She thought about the soap episode where Casandra told Juanito the gardener that she loved him and wanted to be with him forever, even though she was having another man's baby. "*Andres, te quiero,*" she said, repeating her favorite soap stars lines. "*Te quiero mucho. ¿Quieres ser mi novio?*" The phone line went quiet. Sofi wondered if maybe he'd hung up or if she'd said the words wrong.

"I'd love to be your *novio*," he said, "but . . ."

"But what?" Sofi cried, her heart choking her throat. This was not the answer she'd expected. Not how Juanito reacted to Casandra's declaration of love. *No!* she cried in her head. Not after she'd finally gotten the courage to ask him. She knew that they lived in two different countries, but Sofi was a Mendoza. She wasn't going to let a little international border get between her and the man she loved!

"Only if you'll do me a favor," he said.

"I'm not going to wash your clothes!"

He laughed. She imagined him on the other end of the line, grinning widely. "Well, I thought about it and . . ." He paused. "I was wondering if UCLA had an agricultural engineering program. Maybe you could show me around the campus this weekend?"

"What?"

"I figured I couldn't let you be the only one who took risks."

"Aghhh!!!!!"

Sofi sat down on the bed, pulled up her knees, and hugged herself tightly. *It's all finally coming together*, she thought. Her muddied K-Swiss sneakers were spreading dust all over her comforter. *Mexican dirt*, she thought, as her heart swelled. Sofi started thinking about the graduation party she'd throw herself after finals. She'd invite all her peeps from America—Taylor, Olivia, and even Mr. Wilcox—to celebrate with her family at Rancho Escondido. Uncle Victor would want to kill a pig. It would be awesome.

Her heart was elated, because she finally knew who she was.

Sofi was a border girl. Not fully American or Mexican. She was both, a bridge between cultures, the best of both worlds. Her head hurt thinking about the emotional roller coaster she'd been on. First she thought she was legal, then illegal, and now legal again. Crazy! More than anything, Sofi knew she was lucky. Her story could've ended much differently. She thought about Rico and the black ribbons that represented death on the border. Her life was now tied to the imaginary line that separated two nations. But she couldn't help but smile. Despite all the craziness of the border, Sofi felt strong with the knowledge that she'd always belong to both sides of the fence. Her life was now tied to the imaginary line that separated two nations.

A thumping bass line downstairs pulled her out of her thoughts. Her friends would be wondering what had happened to her. She picked up the UCLA tag off the floor and tossed it into the trash can by her desk. She would clean the room tomorrow. Right now, she had a party to attend.

Glossary of Spanish Terms

AKA SOFI'S SPANISH SURVIVAL GUIDE

(Don't go to the border without it!)

p. 3 **papi chulo:** (cute daddy) a term used to refer to a hot-looking boy or sexy man

p. 5 **gringa:** a word commonly used to refer to a white American girl, but it can also refer to any girl or woman from the United States

mija: A contraction of *mi hija*, which means "my daughter," it is also used as a term of affection, descriptive of a familiar relationship even when there is no blood tie between adult and child.

p. 10 **Gracias a Dios:** thank God

p. 12 **Pa' que se le quite:** That'll show her.

p. 21 **Playas de Tijuana:** Beaches of Tijuana, a subsection of the city of Tijuana that is along the Pacific coast. It is on the toll road on the way to Rosarito, Mexico.

p. 23 **papasito:** (daddy) an affectionate diminutive term used to refer to a hot guy. A *papasote* is an even hotter guy.

p. 25 **Buenos días:** good morning

p. 29 **vato loco:** (crazy dude) a term used to refer to a gangster/Latino who does crazy things. Could be used as a term of praise or warning, depending on the person's character.

p. 33 **señor:** sir

p. 40 **¿Qué te puedo ofrecer?:** What can I get you?

por favor: please

¿Cómo?: What? Huh?

¿Eres mejicana?: Are you Mexican?

p. 48 **hola:** hi

p. 55 **Latina caliente:** (hot Latina) The term is used to refer to a sexy woman. It has a vulgar connotation to it.

p. 68 **Chamaca desgraciada. Sinvergüenza. Vas a ver cuando te agarro.:** Bad, ungrateful child. You're gonna get it when I get my hands on you.

p. 70 **churros:** a pastry-based fried-dough treat

Con permiso: Excuse me.

p. 71 **¿Hablas inglés?:** Do you speak English?

p. 72 **tía:** aunt

sí: yes

p. 77 **Oye:** "hey" or "listen"

no, gracias: no, thank you

Tú no puedes dejarme así. Me tienes que pagar la tarifa.: You can't just leave. You have to pay your fare.

p. 80 **ejido:** (common land) a system in which the government takes private lands and makes them into communal lands shared by the people of the community. The intent is to provide communities with resources to produce their own food and local economics.

colegio: high school

p. 81 **Aquí estamos:** We're here.

p. 83 **¿Quién habla?:** Who wants to know?

Mi nombre es Sofia Mendoza. Soy hija de Edmundo. . . .: My name is Sofia Mendoza. I'm the daughter of Edmundo. . . .

Miren, chamacos, es tu prima Sofia del Otro Lado.: Look, kids, it's your cousin Sofia from the Other Side.

Salúdala: Greet her.

Éste es Andres: This is Andres.

El ayudar a mí: He helped me.

p. 85 **papá:** (dad) literally, father

¿Puedo ir con Britannica?: Can I go with Britannica?

Agarren las maletas.: Get the bags.

¿Dónde están los regalos?: Where are the gifts?

p. 86 **muy bonita:** very pretty

p. 87 **Nuestra Virgen de Zapopan, Nuestra Virgen Rocío de Talpa, La Virgen de Dolores:** Our Lady of Zapopan, Our Lady Rocio of Talpa, Our Lady of Sorrows

p. 89 **Ella es una loca vieja:** She's a crazy old lady.

p. 91 **ay, ay, ay, mija:** oh, daughter. (A better translation would
be "oh, honey.")

Todo va estar bien. Vas a ver. Todo va estar bien: Everything
is going to be all right. You'll see. Everything is going to be
all right.

No te preocupes: Don't worry.

Ya estás con familia: You're with family now.

p. 92 **Ándele, Sofia:** "Go ahead, Sofia" or "Hurry up, Sofia."

No te pongas triste: Don't be sad.

Tenemos que celebrar: We have to celebrate.

p. 94 **Ven aquí:** Come here.

Ándele: Hurry up

ajua: woo!

p. 95 **carnitas:** (little meats) a type of roasted pork

¿Qué pasa aquí?: What's going on here?

Y tu debes ser la hija de mi hermano malcriado.: And you must
be the daughter of my good-for-nothing brother.

p. 96 **Ayúdame, San Judas:** Help me, Saint Jude.

p. 99 **Queremos huevos:** We want eggs.

p. 101 **Quiero una torta de huevo con chorizo:** I want a sausage-and-
egg sandwich.

p. 102 **carro:** car

> **Parangaricutirimícuaro:** a variation of Nuevo San Juan Parangaricutiro, a small village in the state of Michoacán. It's the longest place-name word in Mexico. The word itself is a tongue-twister.

p. 103 **Apúrate:** Hurry up.

> **Colonia Mazatlán:** (neighborhood Mazatlán) a Rosarito community located on the opposite (nontourist) side of the highway

p. 104 **No sé:** I don't know.

> **¿Qué tu quieres?:** What do you want?

p. 105 **¿Qué onda con ésta?:** What's the matter with this girl?

> **¿Es muda?:** Is she mute?

p. 107 **Oye, tú no me puedes hablar así. Ésta es mi casa. Vete:** Hey! You can't talk to me like that. This is my house. Get out of here.

p. 108 **sola:** alone

p. 109 **chamaca idiota:** stupid girl

p. 111 **un momento:** one moment

p. 112 **¿Qué pasó?:** What happened?

> **Apagaron el agua:** They turned off the water.

p. 113 **chinches:** bedbugs

p. 114 **vente:** come

p. 116 **doña:** lady, a title attached to a person's given name. A mark of high esteem and distinction.

p. 117 **pollito:** (chick) a term used to refer to people who cross into the United States with a coyote illegally

charlar: to talk or gab

Vámonos: Let's go.

p. 119 **¿Me ayuda?:** Can you help me?

¿Eres americana?: Are you American?

Muchísimas gracias: Thank you very much.

p. 121 **mercado:** market

p. 123 **Cómetelo, buey:** Eat it, sucka. (vulgar phrase.)

piloncillo: Mexican unrefined brown sugar

panocha: Unrefined brown sugar. Also a vulgar term used to refer to a woman's vagina.

p. 126 **computadora:** computer

p. 130 **Debe ser día festivo en el cielo porque todos los ángeles están aquí.:** It must be a holiday in heaven because all the angels are here. (lame pickup line)

p. 135 **No! Déjame en paz:** No! Let me go.

p. 143 **¿Se encuentran tus padres?:** Are your parents home?

Colectivo de Juan Soldado: the Juan Soldado Collective

p. 147 **santitos:** (little saints) an affectionate way to refer to
Catholic saints

p. 148 **Mira:** look

La saliva te va a aliviar: The aloe will heal you.

p. 149 **más despacio:** slower

mandona: bossy lady

p. 161 **corazón:** (heart) a pet name used to refer to someone special

p. 163 **loca:** crazy

p. 164 **curandera:** (healer) a traditional folk healer. *Curanderas* are
respected members of the community who use herbs and other
natural remedies to cure illness. Modern doctors dismiss
curanderas or *curanderos* as superstitious and worthless. As
a result, *curanderas* have experienced discrimination and
been called witches.

p. 165 **prima:** cousin

p. 166 **limpia:** (ceremonial cleansing) a ritual performed by a
curandera to cure the patient of bad energy or other infectious
ailments

me da vergüenza: I'm embarrassed.

ay, el amor: Oh, love

p. 167 **mestizo:** someone of mixed blood, usually in reference to
someone of Indian and Spanish blood

p. 169 **quinceañera:** (sweet fifteen) a traditional celebration that marks a girl's transition into womanhood. In Mexico the Catholic ceremony commonly begins with a thanksgiving Mass at a church. The girl usually wears a weddinglike dress and is accompanied by her *padrinos* (godparents), *damas* (maids of honor), and *chambelanes* (chamberlains). The Mass is followed by a party.

p. 177 **Tierra y Libertad:** (Land and Liberty) a slogan used during the Mexican Revolution. The phrase was popularized by the Mexican revolutionary hero Emiliano Zapata.

p. 178 **pocha:** an Americanized Mexican girl who does not speak Spanish

p. 180 **tardeada:** afternoon fiesta, a family-style celebration complete with food, music, and dancing

Cinco de Mayo: The fifth of May is a national holiday in Mexico and celebrated widely in the United States. It honors the victory of Mexican forces over French occupation forces in the battle of Puebla. It is a common misconception that 5 de Mayo is Mexican Independence Day (which is September 16), but actually it is the date of a legendary battle.

p. 181 **botanas:** snacks

p. 182 **mariachi:** type of musician from Mexico

p. 183 **"Cielito Lindo":** ("Beautiful Sky") a popular mariachi song

p. 184 **resbalona:** (someone who slips) a term used to refer to someone who flirts shamelessly, and gets into trouble

p. 187 **nopales:** a vegetable made from young stems of cactus leaves. They are usually sold fresh or canned and are commonly used in Mexican cuisine in dishes such as nopales *con huevos* (eggs with nopal) or *tacos de* nopales. They are rich in vitamins A, C, K, B^6, and in riboflavin, magnesium, iron, potassium, and calcium.

¿**Tienes hambre?:** Are you hungry?

p. 188 **quince:** (fifteen) a shortened form of *quinceañera*

Abuela Benita: Grandmother Benita

p. 189 **Sí, se puede:** (Yes, it's possible.) It is a motto of the United Farm Workers and more recently a rallying cry for pro-immigration activists.

No te agites: (Don't give up.) common motivational phrase

Tú lo puedes hacer. Tienes la cara de nopal: (You can do it. You have a cactus face.) *Cara de nopal* refers to someone who "looks" Mexican. The nopal has a long historical reference to the Mexican people. The Aztec legend of Huitzilopotchli (the god of war and the sun) says that the god told the nomadic Aztecs that they would find the location of their future homeland when they found an island where a snake was eating a serpent on top of a prickly pear or nopal.

p. 190 **mejicanos:** Mexicans

nopales con huevos: (cactus with eggs) a popular dish in Mexican cuisine

p. 191 **la diabla americana:** the American devil

Los campeones de Rancho Escondido: the champions of
Rancho Escondido

Pórtense bien con Sofi: Behave yourselves with Sofi.

p. 192 **Estás más loca que Abuela Benita:** You're crazier than
Grandma Benita.

p. 194 **Mi rancho es tu rancho:** (My ranch is your ranch.) Sofi's vari-
ant of the common Mexican saying *Mi casa es su casa* (my
house is your house).

Cállense el hocico chamacos!: Shut your traps, brats.

p. 199 **No es mi novio:** He's not my boyfriend.

p. 200 **Paquita:** name

p. 211 **pan dulce:** sweet bread

p. 212 **a la mejicana:** The term usually follows a word and refers to
tweaking something into a Mexican style. For example, *amor
a la mejicana* can mean love in a spicy Mexican flavor or style;
bistec a la mejicana is a Mexican dish where meat is sautéed
with tomatoes, chili peppers, onions, and secret Mexican spices.

p. 213 **recuerdo:** (remember) In this context it means a keepsake,
memento, souvenir.

p. 220 **La Llorona:** (the crying woman) According to folklore, she's the
ghost of a woman crying for her dead children. There are many
variations of the tale throughout Mexico, Latin America, and
the United States.

p. 221 **vieja:** old lady

gringos: a term used to refer to foreigners, especially those from the United States. Although its original meaning may have been derogative, its common usage is not, though it may be considered offensive by English-speakers. Informally, it's used to refer to someone from the United States, since the term *americana* can refer to anyone from the North, Central, or South America.

p. 223 **Ayúdalos, Dios:** Help them, God.

p. 224 **tortas de chorizo:** (pork sausage sandwich) a Mexican sandwich, more traditional than the burrito, served on a white bread roll and usually garnished with avocado, sour cream, lettuce, jalapeño, tomato, and cheese

p .236 **Cálmate:** Calm down.

p. 238 **coyote:** a term typically used in Mexico to refer to a person who's involved in the illegal smuggling of people into the United States

p. 240 **huevos quebrados:** (broken eggs) a wrestling move, named by Mando or Mundo, that involves kicking or hitting your opponent in the groin area

p. 241 **Ay, gracias, Santa Rita la Abogada, Santa Ceotilde, y San Antonio:** Oh, thank you, Saint Rita the lawyer, Saint Ceotilde, and Saint Anthony.

p. 243 **Perdóname, mija:** Forgive me, honey.

p. 249 **ay, Santo Juan Soldado:** oh, Saint Juan the soldier

ay, **mis hijos:** (oh, my children) La Llorona lament

p. 250 **¿Qué haces aquí?:** What are you doing here?

Lo siento, hija: I'm sorry, honey.

Ya déjalo: Leave it (or him) alone.

Bienvenida a nuestra casa: Welcome to our home.

p. 253 **A ti te cobro cinco pesos, para los gringos son diez:** For you it's five pesos. I charge the gringos ten.

p. 255 **Ya duérmete:** Go to sleep

p. 256 **serenata:** (serenade) a musical composition performed for a lover, friend, or other person of honor, typically in the evening and below a window

"Volver, Volver": ("Come Back, Come Back") a traditional *ranchera* song about a lost love

p. 257 **telenovela:** TV soap opera

p. 264 **Pórtense bien. Éste es mi papá:** Behave yourselves. This is my father.

p. 267 **Las rosas son mis flores favoritas:** Roses are my favorite.

Eres Mendoza, caramba: You're a Mendoza, damn it.

p. 270 **Chamaca sinvergüenza:** Loosely translated, it means "girl without shame."

p. 272 **Hola, bonita:** Hi, pretty girl.

p. 273 **adiós:** bye

p. 275 **Andres, te quiero:** Andres, I love you.

    Te quiero mucho. ¿Quieres ser mi novio?: I love you a lot. Do you want to be my boyfriend?

ABOUT THE AUTHOR

Malín Alegría is an accomplished educator, dancer, and actress who has cowritten and performed in several stage plays. She also writes poetry and short stories.

Sofi Mendoza's Guide to Getting Lost in Mexico was praised by *SLJ* for its "emotional and engaging" writing. Malín's first novel, *Estrella's Quinceañera*, has also received rave reviews: *Booklist* noted its "poignant, sharp-sighted humor and authentic dialogue," and Entertainmentweekly.com gave it an A- rating.

Malín lives in San Francisco. Visit her on the Web at www.malinalegria.com

LOOKING FOR THE PERFECT BEACH READ?